CELESTIAL SHIFTERS BOOK 2

FLAMES OF MARS

TJALARA DRAPER

To the whirlwind un-tameable,
the firecracker un-smotherable,
the booty-shaker un-stoppable,
the singer un-silenceable,
the joy un-destroyable,
My daughter Annabelle,
the most magnificent of all Opals.
xxx

FLAMES OF MARS

CELESTIAL SHIFTERS BOOK 2

PROLOGUE

Sagan Branstone shone the flashlight into the cave's gaping entrance, then checked the glowing numbers on his watch face. He was ten minutes early, but that didn't necessarily mean he was the first to arrive.

As much as he tried to ignore it, the nostalgia of this place unsettled him. He swiped his white-blond bangs out of his eyes and glanced at the outcrop of boulders to the left of the dark entryway. His little sister, Lyla-Rose, and his cousin Nika used to climb those rocks and pretend they were the princesses of the mountain, while Sagan and Nika's older brothers would pretend to be knights come to defeat the princesses' pet dragon.

Get yourself together. Sagan shook his head. *You're not a child anymore.*

Shoving aside the memories, he stepped into the cave. Even without a flashlight, he would have had no trouble finding his way, weaving through the familiar passages until the narrow tunnel opened up into a large cavern with an underground pond at its center.

Gravel crunched behind him and he swiveled, only to

find the tunnel empty. His eyes narrowed as his mind raced back to another childhood game. He swung the flashlight's beam to the rocky ledge above the tunnel's opening—just as a young woman clad in black jumped down from it.

Sagan didn't have time to dodge. He *ooph*ed as she collided into him, but in a split second, his training kicked in. Rolling with the force of the fall, he attempted to pin his attacker, but the woman simply kept their momentum going until she was on top.

Before she could lock Sagan down against the rocky floor, he bucked her off. He was about to gain the upper hand when a fist connected with his jaw. His head snapped to the side, and he ground his teeth.

"Fine. You wanna fight dirty?" he growled. He yanked the woman's elbow up and dug his fingers into her ribs.

A giggle escaped his victim and echoed around the cavern. "Stop it!" She wiggled under his tickles. "Stop!"

"Not unless you yield."

"Never!"

"Have it your way, Nika."

She screeched and squirmed as he continued to tickle her sides.

"Okay! I yield."

Sagan smirked. He released her and stood up, but before he could take a step, Nika kicked his feet out from under him, and he slammed back into the ground.

"Hah!" Nika's victory cry echoed around the cavern. She stood and dusted off her clothes.

Sagan grumbled and reached for his flashlight before he got to his feet. As soon as he was up, Nika yanked him in for a hug.

"It's good to see you again, Saggy-Aggy."

Sagan groaned. "Must you keep calling me that?"

She grinned and nodded vigorously, making her light brown curls bounce. "Indeed I must. And by the way, I win."

"Yeah right, only because you cheated."

"Only because you never learn."

"What do you mean? Learn what?"

"You always believe it when someone says they yield." She placed a hand on her hip, the pious stance eerily similar to what Lyla used to do during their sibling fights.

Sagan pushed away the familiar pang of grief. "I do not."

"Yep, you did it even when we were kids."

He frowned.

"Don't worry, cuz. Maybe one day you'll learn." Nika patted him on the shoulder, then shrugged. "Or you won't, and one day you'll play Mr. Nice Guy to the wrong creature and get yourself killed."

He opened his mouth to respond but couldn't form any words.

After a few heartbeats, Nika reached for a camping light he and his cousins had hung up many years ago. Sagan's eyes snapped shut when the bright blaze shattered the darkness. He peered through squinted eyelids, but the brightness only intensified as Nika turned on a second light.

"Can you believe these things still work?" Nika asked.

Sagan blinked, letting his eyes adjust. "Of course they still work. They're powered with Luxium energy cores."

The extra light showcased the abandoned trinkets of their past: some blankets, teddy bears, action figures. Dusty playing cards were still strewn everywhere from the time Nika's oldest brother had lost a game of Scumbags and Warlords and angrily flung them on the ground. Sagan realized with a twinge of sadness that the card game had occurred during the last time he, his sister, and his cousins had visited their childhood hideout. Their annual family camping trips had stopped about eight—or was it ten?—

years ago, thanks to Sagan's grandfather, who expected more and more from them in the family hunting business.

Sagan heaved a heavy sigh to release the building tension in his chest, then raised his eyes to the jagged ceiling. Water drops collected on several of the stalactites and fell to the pond's surface with a melodious *dink-dink-dink*. He breathed in the rich, earthy air laced with the calming scent of mineralized water.

Nostalgia washed over him again, but this time it brought a sense of peace. "Would you look at this place? So many great memories, huh?"

"Yeah," agreed Nika.

Sagan followed a path of stepping stones through the cave pond. The wall on the other side had several natural recesses he and his cousins had used as a pantry, where they'd stashed their candy bars, snacks, and assorted cans of food. A number of items still remained—a lot more than he remembered from last time—although all of it had likely gone rancid.

He picked up a can of peaches and frowned. There was barely any dust on it, and it was well within its expiration date.

Nika snatched the can off him. "So, Saggy-Aggy, what's the deal? It's been what, almost a year? And I've heard nothing from you. No texts, no calls, not even a smoke signal." She punched his arm, hard. "I thought you were dead."

"Close, but not quite," he said with half a smirk.

"It's not funny, Saggy."

"Believe me, I wasn't laughing." He rubbed his thigh, remembering all too clearly the agony of Axel's barbed crossbow bolt.

"Yeah, well, you could have died, you idiot. And for what?

To help a Veniri vermin escape the bunker?" She shook her head in disbelief. "What the hell possessed you?"

"Yeah, about that . . ." Sagan scratched the back of his neck, and his lips pressed into a grimace. "That was one of the reasons I got in touch. I . . ." He glanced around the cave. "Did you tell anyone you were coming?"

"No." Nika scoffed. "You told me not to."

"What about your brothers? Are you sure neither of them followed you?"

She crossed her arms. "I can sneak away from my brothers when I need to."

Sagan sighed and put his hands in his pockets. "How are your egghead brothers anyway?"

"Fine. But to be honest, it's your dad who's gone off the rails." Nika's face scrunched up in disgust. "And I'm not the only one who thinks that. An exchange went down a few months ago, and a hunter came back without a head."

"So?"

"So, it wasn't a shifter that killed him. Apparently, Uncle Matthias was the one who chopped it off."

"*What?*"

"I'm serious, Sagan. More than one hunter who was there saw the same thing."

Sagan shook his head. "Look, I know better than anyone that my father's a royal ass, but he doesn't ki—"

"What? 'Kill our own?' Don't be so naive. The hunter code has become a joke," she practically spat.

Her words were like a slap to the face. Sagan's hand shot compulsively back to his thigh, kneading the silvery scar hidden beneath his black jeans. What was wrong with him? He of all people should know what his dad was capable of. After all, what kind of father sends a hunter after his own son?

Nika's eyes glistened with—was that tears? When had Nika developed the ability to cry? "Ever since Uncle Matthias started making deals with our prey and taking on human bounty orders, things have gone way off the rails. Hunters aren't just losing their heads. Some are going *missing*."

"Hunters go missing all the time."

"Yeah, but only if they're out in the field. And that's not all. His obsession with the winged shifters has exploded to the next level."

Sagan rolled his eyes. "He's been obsessed with those fairytales since forever. Winged shifters, cities in the clouds, interdimensional portals, immortality." He counted them off on his fingers. "He's the only hunter who hasn't grown out of believing those myths."

Nika shook her head in sharp jerks. "Myths or not, things are out of control, Sagan. Your dad is out of control."

"Yeah, well"—Sagan raked his fingers through his hair—"tell me something I don't know."

"Don't you think it's time you returned? To maybe . . ."

"What?" He scowled. "Talk some sense into him?"

Nika chewed on her lip, staring into space for a few seconds. "I was thinking maybe you could call Grandpa."

"No."

"Just hear me out. I think . . ."

Sagan shook his head aggressively, shutting out the rest.

"Come on, Sagan. You're the only grandkid he'll listen to."

"Get your dad to do it."

"My dad's a coward. You know that. It's got to be you."

"I said no! Not after what Grandpa did. Not after what he put my mother through."

Nika threw her head back and groaned. "Don't tell me you're still whining about that? Your mom was the one who left, remember? She abandoned you."

"Don't say that," Sagan growled through his teeth. "You're

using *their* words. My mother never would have left like that." He tore his gaze from Nika. "You'll see. One of these days I'll find out what happened to her."

"Yeah, yeah." Nika waved an indifferent hand and turned her back on him. "Whatever helps you sleep at night, Saggy."

Sagan gritted his teeth, ready to unleash a barrage of verbal abuse on her, but he knew Nika wasn't the one who deserved it. For a few moments, the only sound in the cavern was the subtle drip of water falling into the pond.

At last, Sagan turned away and scratched the back of his neck, his fingers catching the black chain that held the hunter amulet tucked under his shirt. Every hunter amulet held ten tiny glass vials, each to be filled with a sample of luminescent blood from the hunter's first kills of each shifter race. Sagan's particular amulet was in the shape of his family crest.

He glanced back at Nika. For once, her amulet wasn't center-stage on her chest. Sagan frowned—it wasn't like his cousin to keep it hidden. Usually she kept her amulet on display for all the world to see.

Out of habit, he rolled his own chain between his fingers as he scanned their surroundings. A stretcher with a sleeping bag and pillow had been pushed up against one wall. A canvas camp chair sat beside it, along with a small pile of books.

The dust-free can of peaches and extra food supplies suddenly made sense. "You've been staying here?"

Nika's lips pinched together in answer.

"How long?"

She shrugged with practiced nonchalance. "I dunno. Maybe a week or two."

"Why?"

"I told you." She leaned against the cavern wall, planted

her foot behind her, and crossed her arms. "Things are out of control back home."

"Who knows you're here?"

"So far"—she gave him a pointed look—"only you."

"But what about your brothers?"

"Either my brothers are too stupid to figure out I've left, or they just don't care. You're the only other person to step foot in this cave since I arrived."

None of this made any sense. A minute ago she was criticizing his mother for leaving. What had happened to make Nika leave her family and the other hunters she'd fiercely defended her whole life?

He dragged his hands down his face. "Gee, Nika. I, um . . . are you okay?"

"So, what about you? Last I heard, Axel was trying to impale you with his trident. Where have you been this whole time?"

Sagan's lip twitched. Trust Nika to change the subject when she was the one under the emotional microscope. "Yep, good ol' Dad getting Axel to do his dirty work again."

"Yeah, yeah. Enough hedging. Where have you been?"

"Ah, you know." He gave her a sidelong look. "Here and there."

"Hmm . . ." Nika studied him through narrowed eyes.

Sagan tried not to squirm under her scrutiny. He'd always trusted his cousin and never hesitated to confide in her, especially after Lyla-Rose died. But telling Nika he'd spent the last ten months in Maple Shire with Violet could rain down terrible consequences on the small community who'd opened their homes to them. Not to mention, there could still be a bounty order out with Violet's picture on it; Nika could very well jump at the chance for the generous reward.

As the youngest of his family, Nika had earned a cutesy reputation as a child due to her small stature, Shirley Temple blue eyes, and bouncy curls—a reputation she'd despised and fought hard to erase. She definitely didn't lack the ability to rain down serious chaos on a small town like Maple Shire, all by herself.

Sagan cleared his throat and did his best to appear casual. "Anyway, the reason I contacted you. I was wondering if you happened to remember that bounty order for a particular Veniri called Nathan Delano."

Nika snorted. "You mean the one you stupidly helped escape?"

Sagan shifted his weight to the other foot. "Right, him. I was hoping he hadn't been tracked down yet."

"Ha! Fat chance of cashing in on that one, cuz. That stupid slith went back to his house and was picked up the same day you went missing."

Sagan cursed under his breath. "So, he's already been harvested then." His head fell into his hands as a fiery rage boiled inside him. Of course Nathan's house had been the first place his father looked. What was Violet going to say? Should he even tell her? Why couldn't he do anything right?

"No." Nika cut through the onslaught of Sagan's thoughts. "That one wasn't harvested. He was taken to Tempecrest Island instead."

"What?" Sagan's jaw dropped. "To the fight pits? Since when do Veniri get thrown in with the werewolf gladiators? Their Diamantium is way more valuable undamaged."

Nika shrugged. "Like I said, your dad's gone off the rails. He sent *three* Veniri to Tempecrest."

"Three!" Sagan ground the heel of his palm against his forehead. The Diamantium shards of one Veniri alone could pay for the full Ivy League tuition of three students.

"Yeah, and from what I hear, that Veniri you're crushing on is building quite a reputation. Him and that other slith, hmm . . . what's his name? Zane?" Nika frowned. "No, that's not right."

Sagan's heart began to thump faster in his chest. "Thane?"

"That's it! Wait, how did you know that?"

"And you're sure this other one, Thane, he's definitely Veniri?"

Nika cocked an eyebrow. "Yes."

He gripped his skull with both hands. What were the chances of there being two Thanes? Violet had never mentioned Thane being Veniri. Did she know? But if Violet's Thane was Veniri, that would mean her baby . . .

Sagan's eyes bugged. He took hold of Nika's shoulders and shook her sharply. "I need you to do something for me." Nika grimaced as he continued. "I need you to go to Tempecrest Island and break both Nathan and Thane out."

1

PIÑA COLADAS AND INTERNAL HYSTERIA

A SCREAM SHREDDED VIOLET CHAMBER'S VOCAL CORDS, BUT that pain paled in comparison to the excruciating torment of the contraction that clamped around her entire torso. *There aren't enough painkillers in the world! This baby needs to get out. Now!*

As the contraction eased, Violet's shriek reduced to a small whimper. She moaned and gritted her teeth until the ache in her belly mercifully subsided.

"You're doing great." Autumn's voice held a pained edge, either from stress or from Violet squeezing her hand in a death grip—Violet didn't care. Her friend could endure a crushed hand if Violet had to endure the torture of passing something the size of a watermelon out her lady parts.

The waves of agony had increased with each contraction since she'd been induced a few hours ago. That last was the worst by far. The only saving grace through this whole delivery business was the small gaps of relief between contractions, but these suckers were starting to come faster, and the pain-free respites were getting shorter.

"I'll, um . . . go get you some more ice chips." Autumn

pried Violet's fingers from her hand and shook it out with a small whimper, then rushed out of the delivery room.

Violet lay back against the pillows and tried to get comfortable, but it was next to impossible with a belly the size of a beach ball and the next excruciating contraction looming in her very near future.

"Hey." The midwife patted Violet's forehead with a damp cloth. "How are you holding up, love?"

Violet gave her an overenthusiastic thumbs-up. "I'm doing great. Don't know why everyone makes a big deal of this labor stuff. It's just like sitting on the beach drinking piña coladas."

The midwife gave her a kind smile

"Where's Dawn?" Violet asked. "She's been gone a long time."

"She'll be here when she's needed," the woman said calmly, but Violet didn't miss the concerned glance she shot at the door.

Autumn's aunt, Dawn Farrow, was Maple Shire's doctor. She used to be a famous big-city physician, but when she became pregnant with Autumn's cousin, Gus, she left that life to join her sister at the humble community compound. Apparently, Maple Shire's medical care and accessibility had been abysmal when she arrived, but by calling in favors from her big-city doctor friends, Dawn had ensured she had the best medical equipment and supplies to look after the residents of not only Maple Shire but also the surrounding communities. If Violet had been able to think about anything besides the baby trying to tear through her lower abdomen, she probably would've been thankful she wasn't giving birth in conditions equivalent to medieval times—Dawn's words, not hers.

Violet struggled to sit up, and the midwife—*Macie*, she finally remembered—dutifully wedged some cushions behind her back for support. Macie was a relatively new addition to Maple Shire. Apart from the last few prenatal appointments, Violet hadn't spoken with her much, but she'd noted the midwife's guarded demeaner and occasionally haunted gaze. Violet recognized when someone was dealing with a past trauma; she could respect the woman's wanting to keep to herself.

The midwife glanced at the monitor by the bed, where the tubes and cables strapped to Violet's stomach connected. Violet didn't know what the squiggly lines on the screen meant or even what the numbers referred to, only that the machine was reading her heart rate as well as her baby's.

Tightness began to enclose Violet's abdomen once more. "Oh nooooo." She winced and breathed out a low moan, her legs squirming.

In her periphery, Dawn and Gus rushed through the door. Macie began conversing with them, but Violet could only hear snippets over her rising wails.

". . . baby's heart rate drops with each contraction . . ."

". . . window to deliver is closing . . ."

". . . the others are ready . . ."

". . . get her to the theater."

Violet became faintly aware that her bed was moving, but her tormented groans and the severity of the contraction drowned out the rest of the world.

"What's going on?" she managed to say through gritted teeth, but her question was lost beneath Dawn's barked orders to Gus and Macie. Violet tried to ask again, but the torturous ache in her stomach stretched on and on until her screams pitched up to a new level of intensity.

The next thing she knew, Gus was looking down at her, a surgeon's mask partially hiding his face and a cap covering his dark brown hair. He was speaking to her, explaining . . . something, but she couldn't comprehend any of the words.

He and the midwife pulled her into a seated position as the contraction released her at last.

"Violet." Dawn's calm voice came from behind her. "I'm going to give you an epidural so you don't feel anything, okay? I need you to curl up into the fetal position as tight as you can."

"What?" Violet screeched. "How on earth do you suggest I curl up with this wretched beach ball I have for a belly?" Her words morphed into a cry of pain as another contraction clamped down on her abdomen.

Dawn's instructions cut over Violet's whimpers. "I need you to hold still. It's very important that you don't move."

A barrage of insults flew to Violet's tongue, but her howl of agony cut them off. How could she possibly be expected to keep still? She needed to get out of here. She needed some super-strong painkillers. She needed to get this baby out. She wanted to go home, back to Brookhaven, where high school was the hardest thing she ever had to deal with.

Her room at Nathan's place had become a haven after he'd taken her in. How she longed to snuggle up in her bed and wait until her agonizing contractions were over.

But she couldn't go back. Not after Nathan had betrayed her. Not after she'd come home to find both Nathan and that treacherous liar Thane in the kitchen of that house.

While Violet's trauma had hidden her memories of the kidnappers who'd snatched her and her best friend, Lyla-Rose Branstone, Nathan had known all along Thane was complicit in Lyla's murder. And he'd never told her. Never tried to protect her. Instead he'd brought Thane into her home—into her sanctuary—as if he were an old friend and not a manipulative criminal who'd torn her heart to pieces in ways that could never be mended.

It was Thane's fault she was in the Maple Shire infirmary.

His fault she was screaming her lungs out while her body was tearing itself apart from the inside. She hadn't seen Thane since the day she'd discovered his true identity. How she wanted to fasten her hands around his throat, to dig her nails into his stupid neck with his stupid crystal scorpion tattoo.

And yet . . .

Her contraction ramped up into another level of pain, and she couldn't snuff out the sliver of longing to have Nathan, and even Thane, by her side. Nathan for his solid parental support, and Thane for his—

No! Thane's the bad guy. He's the BAD GUY! Her jaw clamped down with tooth-breaking force. She couldn't allow herself to ever forget that.

A sharp prick stabbed Violet's back. Within seconds, numbness flooded her body, and the wails died on her lips. With the help of Gus, Macie, and another doctor Violet had seen around Maple Shire, she was transferred to another bed and laid down flat.

Dawn's face, also covered in a surgical mask, came into Violet's view.

"Wha . . . what's going on?" Violet asked again, her words almost strangled by hiccupping sobs.

"I'm so sorry, Violet." The mask muffled Dawn's voice. "With your baby's dipping heart rate, we couldn't wait for you to dilate to ten centimeters. We needed to perform an emergency C-section. Everything is under control, but if we don't do this, we could lose you both."

Violet's breath heaved. Each inhalation was more constricted than the last, this time because of fear rather than pain. "Is my baby okay?"

"It's all okay, Violet." Gus's voice was low and soothing. "We have a good window of time to get your baby out safely." He'd pulled over a chair and was sitting by her head.

Violet nodded and squeezed her eyes shut. Tears spilled over her temples and into her hair.

"Don't worry." Gus wiped the tears away with a gloved hand. "I'm going to be here with you the whole time."

When Violet first met Gus, he'd had an affinity for ripped jeans and copper-and-turquoise jewelry and was taking Greek poetry and textile classes at college. But it turned out he had a real talent for medicine—which he'd been avoiding for reasons Violet didn't know. However, when she'd passed out and cut her feet on some broken glass months ago, Gus had decided to start helping his mother in the infirmary again. His knowledge and talent were astounding. If he ever went back to school as a med student, he'd give his mother a run for her money. They were a phenomenal team, and Dawn was a proud and enthusiastic mentor.

But as much as Violet trusted his skills, nothing he said could ease her panic, her torment, or her endless inventory of questions. Internal hysteria shot up from her gut as she realized her body was numb below her armpits and the only things she could move were her arms and head.

Never in her life had she felt so trapped.

My baby. What's wrong with my baby? Is my baby okay? What if they can't get my baby out in time?

Her eyes darted around the ceiling. The terror and uncertainty would have been enough to paralyze her if she hadn't already been frozen by the needle numbing her body. If only the epidural had numbed her thoughts as well.

The next few minutes were a haze, a flurried commotion of Dawn, Gus, Macie, the other doctor, and a number of nurses weaving in and out of Violet's sight. A blue sheet was suspended from the ceiling, blocking her view from the chest down.

Gus kept up a gentle stream of encouragement, explanations, and sometimes just trivial things to distract her. Every now and then Violet nodded in response—the only control she still had over her body—as tears flowed down her face. For an eternity, she breathed and cried as silently as possible.

Her panic had zoned in on a single worry that echoed over and over in her mind.

My baby. My baby. My baby . . .

Then Gus's chatter paused as a tiny cry sliced through the theater.

In an instant, all of Violet's anxiety disintegrated into nothing. She glanced at Gus; his whole face was beaming.

Dawn's voice came from beyond the blue sheet. "Well done, Violet! Congratulations! You have a beautiful baby girl!"

Gus hooted his own excitement as Violet grinned, her flood of tears now joyful. Her baby was okay. A crying baby was good, right? "Can I see her?" Violet asked. "Where is she?"

"In a few moments," said Dawn. "Macie just needs to weigh and check over your baby. We're just going to close the incision now."

Gus patted her shoulder. "It won't be long until you can hold her."

Just as Violet was about to nod, Macie's voice cut through the room. "Dawn! I need you. Now!"

Every coherent thought and feeling fled Violet.

A few silent moments passed after Dawn disappeared from her view. Not daring to breathe, Violet waited. Waited.

Then Dawn yelled, "Everybody out!"

2

DOG SHREDDER

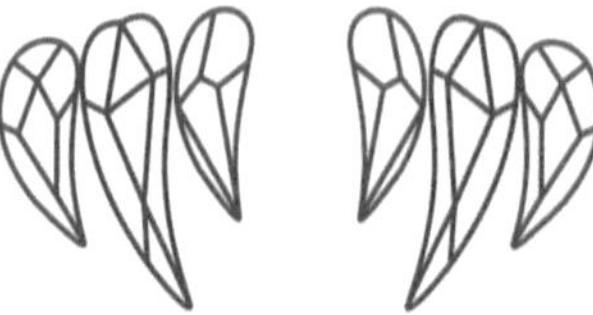

The muted roar of the crowd in the outer arena fueled Nathan Delano's adrenaline. He rested his head against the wall, its cool surface leeching the warmth from his bare back.

On either side of his head, the Metallikite cuffs at his wrists rattled as he yanked. Despite knowing he would never break free, it had become his prefight ritual. To wrestle with his shackles. To suppress his nerves and the impending surge of adrenaline. To keep his inner beast contained a little longer. Or maybe he consistently fought his restraints because he still held out hope that the human hunters would forget to lock them properly, and he could escape from this rotten gladiator hellhole.

Even in the shifter world, humans—or rather, Erathi— had claimed their natural role. As far as Nathan was concerned, that role was to be a blight upon the world. Though they lacked the powers of their prey, they still managed to enforce their dominance over virtually every kind of shifter they hunted down.

And yet, as much as Nathan hated every Erathi hunter on Tempecrest Island, there were still some humans who had surprised him—who cared for the well-being of others, who fought against the darkness of this world. Those like his work partner Jude and his other colleagues back at the Brookhaven police station. He'd also known Erathi who deserved to be looked after and protected, such as Violet and . . . Levana.

His neck and shoulders tensed. It had been a long time since he'd allowed himself to think that name. It brought back too many memories, too much grief, and . . . the image of her. Her eyes, nose, lips, cheeks, hair. The curve of her shoulders. The sway of her hips . . . Every feature was still crisp in his mind's eye, as if he'd seen her five minutes ago.

Another wave of cheering and applause rumbled up through the stone floor, reverberating through the circular metal panel beneath his feet. The hanging fluorescent light overhead shook a little, causing a slight strobing effect throughout the room.

Nathan squeezed his eyes shut and tried to block out the noise: the other gladiators' prefight routines, their mumblings, their whimpers, and the scuffle of feet on their own metal panels.

"Oi, slith," said a guttural voice.

Nathan opened his eyes and scanned the circular room. It was roughly thirty feet in diameter, and at regular intervals the other shifter gladiators—eight in all—also had their wrists cuffed to the curved wall. His eyes met the intense gaze of a dark-haired Lycan across the room.

"This time, you're mine." In human form, the werewolf had severe scarring over his face and bare torso. He'd clearly been through more than his fair share of times in the arena. It was a wonder he had any unmarred flesh left.

Nathan didn't bother replying.

"You hear me, slith? I'm gonna gut you, and I'm gonna tear out your lungs while you're still breathing."

An amused scoff came from Nathan's left. Tio, the young Jiovis shifter, was shaking with quiet laughter.

"What are you laughing at, clanger?" The Lycan's lip rolled up in a sneer.

Tio shrugged. "Nothing. It's just an odd way to threaten someone." He put on a deep mocking voice. "'I'm gonna tear your lungs out while you're still breathing.'" Another loud snicker escaped him. "It's like saying, 'I'm gonna rip your ears off while you're still hearing.'"

The Lycan snarled. "Keep talking, boy, and I'll decide to hunt you down first."

"Is that a promise?" Tio wriggled his fingers. His hand began to glow a brilliant orange, and amber electricity ignited in his palm, crackling and dancing around his fingertips. "Because I'm dying to see what one thousand kilovolts will do to your puppy-dog skull."

Staring pointedly at Tio's electricity, the werewolf bared his teeth but wisely decided to keep silent. Instead, after a final glare at Nathan, he turned his focus to the ground.

"Don't worry, Nathan, I've got your back." Tio smirked and extinguished his power.

"Uh . . . thanks, kid."

Tio winked. "Anytime."

"The Lycan's right," said a new voice.

Nathan turned to the captive on his right.

Thane Alvarez's vintage-gold hair hung in a tangle over his brown eyes, and his scruffy goatee desperately needed a trim. Like the rest of the captives in the holding chamber, he was bare chested. The gladiator lifestyle had forced him to maintain a somewhat toned physique, but his ribs were becoming more defined with each passing week.

Thane lifted his head and shot a pointed look at Tio. "You need to learn to watch your mouth. Just because you're Jiovis doesn't mean you're immortal."

Tio rolled his eyes. "Yes, mom."

Nathan bit back his own scoff. Tio was barely sixteen years old and just as hotheaded and haughty as his kindred shifters who drew their power from Jupiter's energy. But regardless of age, when push came to shove, he was just as tough and bloodthirsty as the rest of them.

After almost a year, Nathan and Thane were well aware that this gladiator prison exclusively held Lycan inmates—until Nathan, Thane, and one other Veniri had been thrown into the mix. Nathan had lost track of Kronan. Hopefully that filth had been disemboweled in the arena and tossed out with the rest of the putrid garbage.

Not long after Nathan and Thane's capture, Tio was thrown into a cell nearby.

As a rule, shifter races didn't intermingle, but of all the imprisoned shifters in Tempecrest, Tio, the out-of-place Jiovis, had chosen to join forces with Nathan and Thane. Nathan could understand the youth seeking to form an alliance, but he hadn't quite figured out why Tio chose to associate with two Veniri instead of any of the hundreds of werewolves.

Tio pulled a face as Thane continued his lecture, once again reminding Nathan of the Jiovis's adolescent age. He still couldn't believe the gall of these Erathi hunters using such a young shifter for their blood sports—but being a Jiovis did give Tio many advantages. In human form, his skin was almost as dark as obsidian. His Jiovis genes already had him bulking up more than most teenage boys, and in height, he was nearly at Nathan's eye level.

The roar of the crowd reached a crescendo; presumably another gladiator had reached their dismal end. A few seconds later, the deafening wail of a siren announced the conclusion of the current round.

Another Lycan on the other side of the room raised his head and released a mournful howl.

"Shut up, mongrel!" Tio barked. "There's no full moon in here!"

But Tio's objections were drowned out as all five werewolves yowled their canine song. When their piercing vocalization came to an end, several silent seconds passed. The tension in the holding room became tangible. Constricting even. Nathan couldn't help shuffling his own feet in anticipation.

Almost as one, the prisoners turned their heads toward the heavy *thunk* and rattle of chains that announced the door to the holding chamber was about to open.

Thane met Nathan's glance. "This can't be good."

Nathan's eyes narrowed as he nodded in agreement.

The door opened, and light beamed into the circular room. Nathan's lip curled into a sneer when he recognized the man who entered. His familiar arrogance was unmistakable in the way he walked, in the metallic gunmetal gray suit, and as always, in the wide shark grin stretched across his face.

Matthias Branstone's polished black leather balmoral shoes tapped with each step along the concrete floor until he finally came to a stop directly in front of Nathan.

Nathan smoothed his sneer into nonchalance, and Matthias's grin grew even wider.

"Well, well, well. So here's the 'Dog Shredder' himself." Matthias hummed out a chuckle. "At least, that's what my men are calling you now." He wagged a finger at Nathan. "You know, the moment I saw you, I had a feeling you'd be one to put on a hell of a show at our little arena. And your little boy-crush here"—he gestured to Thane—"the way he fought when we picked you two up, well, that's when I figured, what the hell? Let's see what these two make of themselves in the fighting pits." He spread his arms wide and slowly spun, making a full rotation back to face Nathan. "And now, here we are.

"You know, everyone said I was a fool to put you sliths into the arena. That it was a waste of profitable Diamantium and that I should harvest your crystal bones before they became completely worthless. They said you'd be lucky to last a week. Perhaps a month, tops. But then a second month rolled by. Then a third. And a fourth. And still you came out of those pits alive. Even the bookies are shouting your praises, claiming the bets are at an all-time high all because of my star fighters." He reached out and pinched Nathan's cheek like a doting granny.

Nathan tossed his head to the side to break the man's grip.

Matthias's chortle dripped condescension. "Who would have guessed? I bet you never would have guessed, huh, Kronan?"

Nathan's blood turned to ice.

Once again, all heads, except for Matthias's, spun back to the holding chamber's doorway. Kronan—the Veniri queen's cousin, as well as a wretched coward who was worth a thousand times less than the crud on one's shoe—swaggered into the holding chamber and stood beside Matthias.

Nathan dragged his fierce gaze over Kronan. He was undamaged—clean, also in a suit, and unshackled.

"Hello, Nathan. You're looking a little more . . ." Kronan looked Nathan up and down. ". . . *unkempt* since the last time I saw you."

Nathan's own shallow breathing thundered in his ears. The rage in his veins tore through every inch of his being.

Thane began hurling insults, cursing Kronan with every foul and depraved word in both the Erathi and Veniri tongue. But for Nathan, there were no words. No utterances were explicit enough.

Though he no longer felt the burning sensation that used to warn him before his Diamantium blades sliced out of his flesh, there was no question his crystal elbow blades were unsheathed. He'd managed to keep them holstered during Matthias's drivel, but now he held only the ferocious desire to strike. To maim. To slaughter.

"Hmm, I don't think they're happy to see you." Matthias tutted and placed a companionable arm over Kronan's shoulders.

Nathan yanked and yanked on the Metallikite wrist cuffs; if he were human, his flesh would have been in shreds. Blood boiled with a berserker's frenzy through his extremities until he exploded into a lunge.

The cuffs jerked him to a stop an inch from Kronan's face.

For an instant, Kronan's eyes widened with shock. But when he realized Nathan couldn't harm him, the corner of his mouth twitched up into a twisted grin. Matthias cackled, his eyes practically sparkling with wicked mirth.

Then, without warning, the cuffs on Nathan's wrists snapped open at the exact moment the floor beneath him disappeared. He threw an arm out, desperate to clutch the traitorous Kronan, but his hand only snatched air.

He gasped, and his stomach flew into his throat. For one or two heartbeats, he flailed in a free fall as gravity yanked him to the ground several stories below. A few of the other shifters screamed during their descent—likely newcomers— but Nathan, Thane, Tio, and the other seasoned gladiators were silent during their fall.

The first time this happened, Nathan had landed ungracefully, severely winded. But over time he'd mastered his landing, bending his knees on impact and bracing his hands on the ground to avoid a face-plant.

The roar of the crowd became deafening; a commentator on the loudspeaker announced the arrival of each gladiator by his fighter name and shifter race. Nathan's gut lurched with sudden nausea as he looked around at the human spectators—Erathi hunters who profited from shifter corpses, and rowdy rich kids wasting their trust-fund money to bet on their favorite gladiator.

Standing up, Nathan blocked out the cacophony and forced himself to assess his surroundings. The arena was the size of a football stadium. Its design changed with every event, giving the gladiators a different scenario to endure and the spectators a whole new show. The previous arena design had clearly been devised by an Indiana Jones fan, complete with a massive rolling boulder. Another had involved flooding the arena, with several islands as the only safe zones to avoid enormous mechanical sharks. Whatever the layout, the main objective was always the same: rip the heart out of another fighter, and you get to live to see another round.

Bile burned the back of Nathan's throat. He didn't want to know how many hearts had become his tickets to survival.

But now was not the time to mourn past actions.

This new arena was hot. Skin-melting hot.

Nathan had landed on a small sandy pillar, about three feet in diameter, towering several stories over a lake of lava. A web of suspended rope-and-timber bridges weaved in a labyrinthine pattern between other pillars and platforms of varying sizes.

All the other gladiators had landed on similar-sized pillars. One unfortunate Lycan on Thane's other side had lost his footing on the sandy surface and tumbled, screaming, into the molten liquid below.

Nathan cringed. A Lycan's leather hide was almost as tough as a Veniri's, but even so, within an agonizing minute, the lava would certainly sear through the werewolf's flesh and kill him.

That left only four Lycans—plus Tio, Thane, and Nathan.

The other gladiators had already started running across the bridges connected to their pillars. Nathan allowed himself a few seconds to clue in to the locations of the other Lycans. Upon a quick glance, it seemed the majority of the fighters were aiming for the largest platform at the other end of the arena.

Joining the others in the race, Nathan weaved over platforms and bridges in the direction he hoped would lead to Thane and Tio. At one stage, his path ran parallel to a Lycan bounding across a rope bridge about two yards away. Without warning, a tower of fire erupted from the lava below, consuming the wolf shifter and his bridge.

Nathan flinched, shielding his face with his hands as the intense heat became unbearable. Then the fire tower receded back into the lava.

That was two hearts gone. Two fewer opportunities to survive another round.

The voice over the loudspeaker announced the death of the werewolf, and the crowd erupted with their taunts or cheers. Nathan's heartbeat bashed at his eardrums. They'd fallen from the holding chamber less than a minute ago, and already it felt as if he'd been in this hellish arena for a lifetime.

As Nathan ran, he kept Thane and Tio in his sights, doing his best to keep a mental map of the bridges and his companions' positions. When he reached a larger platform, he swerved left, his bare feet *thunk-thunk-thunking* over the timber bridge.

Several platforms contained weapons, but he ignored

them. Most were useless anyway. How would a sword or crossbow be of any benefit to a shifter fighter? If anything, it was all part of the aesthetics of Erathi entertainment. But Nathan had noticed with each new event, more and more of the weapons were made of Diamantium. Most likely, the gamblers who kept betting against Thane and Nathan were beginning to demand an advantage for the non-Veniri shifters.

Movement in Nathan's periphery caught his attention, and he turned just in time to see a Lycan lunge at Thane. They swiped and lashed at each other's bare torsos—Thane with his crystal elbow blades and the werewolf with his inch-long silver claws—but appeared about matched in skill and speed. Thane blocked another of the Lycan's swipes and countered with a slice of his own at the shifter's unprotected ribs. A thin, dark line appeared on the werewolf's torso, which quickly began spilling silver blood.

The Lycan paused to inspect the wound, then shot a furious glare at Thane. In a split second, the gladiator hazed, his entire body transfigured into a giant dark gray humanoid wolf.

Nathan's heart pounded against his ribs, and he growled in frustration. Thane needed to haze too, but Nathan knew he wouldn't. Not once since stepping foot on Tempecrest had Thane hazed into his Veniri form. To an extent, Nathan could understand why, but refusing to haze wouldn't make Thane any more human.

He forced his gaze away. Whether in Veniri or human form, Thane was competent enough to take on any of the other gladiators. There wasn't any doubt about that.

Darting across another bridge, Nathan cursed as he realized he'd run in a full circle. He turned around, but before he could reach the next platform, searing heat singed his back. It wasn't until the bridge began to give way that he realized another fire tower had flared up behind him. With a burst of adrenaline, Nathan lunged from his disintegrating bridge and caught the edge of the platform, his legs dangling and kicking against the vertical face.

He grimaced. The surface of the platform was slippery with silver liquid—remnants of the previous round's gladiators—and his hands couldn't find purchase. Ignoring the severed, silver-clawed finger by his elbow, Nathan tried to edge his way up, but his efforts only made him slide farther off the edge.

Panic slammed into his chest. *No, no, no! It can't end like this.*

He couldn't die here, not in this cesspool of degenerate humans and werewolves. He needed to escape. He needed to find Violet, to apologize and explain it all to her. To do everything in his power to make her forgive him.

"Come on," he gritted out through clenched teeth. His bare feet scrabbled against the stone wall, searching frantically for a foothold. "Come on!"

With every desperate cell in his body, inch by inch, he heaved himself onto the platform. Standing up was a laborious job. Grimy sand and Lycan blood streaked his bare arms and torso, but he was alive.

The flood of relief evaporated when he found himself face-to-face with the heavily scarred Lycan.

A low growl rumbled in the wolf shifter's chest. "Your heart is mine."

In a flash, Nathan's whip-like tongue lashed out. No surprise that the most pungent flavor in the Lycan's emotional cocktail was cinnamon—the flavor that represented one's bone-deep intention to murder. Nathan hadn't needed his Veniri tongue to decipher that.

Besides cinnamon, he also detected hints of vodka and saffron. Nathan could understand the presence of vodka; he would be vengeful too if someone had killed several members of his pack—if Thane and Tio could be considered his "pack" in this situation. But as for saffron, why would this Lycan have any reason to be envious?

Before he could think about it further, the Lycan snarled, and Nathan barely managed to dodge the clawed hand that whistled past his face. His attacker didn't let up, didn't allow Nathan to switch to the offensive. All Nathan could do was swivel and weave to avoid blow after bone-crushing blow and keep from tumbling off the edge of the platform.

His foot slipped in the pool of old Lycan blood, and he stumbled to one knee just as a burning sensation sliced over his abdomen. Four new claw marks were carved into his torso, seeping teal liquid. The gashes were several inches below an old scar he'd acquired a lifetime ago, when he was a cop and had rescued a battered and broken Violet.

Nathan frowned. Lycan claws weren't sharp enough to pierce Veniri hide with one swipe. He looked up at the Lycan, who grinned and wiggled his fingers. Instead of silver, shards of diamond glittered off his elongated nails.

"Since when do Lycans have claws tipped with Diamantium? Who gave it to you?" Was there any point even asking that last question? Tempecrest was infested with hunters who used the crystal bones of Veniri as weapons to strike down their prey. Any of the Erathi gamblers who opposed him and Thane could have embedded the crystal shards into the claws of a worthy opponent.

"What does it matter?" the Lycan replied with a throaty chuckle. "I'll have your heart in my hand before you can worry about it too long."

Then the Lycan hazed. His human form morphed into a ferocious oversized wolf-man with a red-and-black-streaked coat.

The mongrel leaped high into the air, but this time,

Nathan took advantage of the platform's slippery surface. Pushing forward with one leg, he coasted on his knees through the silver fluid, swiping at the wolf-man's torso with his elbow blade when he glided beneath the airborne Lycan. Silver rain drenched his face and shoulders before the Lycan landed with an echoing *boom* behind him.

Nathan threw his arms to the ground, gouging his elbow blades into the timber to stop himself before he sailed over the edge. Then he pivoted to face the werewolf. The Lycan was still crouched on the ground, facing away from him.

Elbow blades raised, Nathan charged, but before he could land the death strike, the werewolf swiveled onto his back and kicked Nathan in the chest with his powerful legs. Breath gushed from Nathan's lungs as he hurtled backward, momentarily airborne. Then his back slammed against the platform, his head ricocheting off the wooden surface with a loud *crack*. He slid through the slick silver blood, coming to a stop with his head and shoulders hanging over the inferno below. Waves of dizziness rolled through his skull.

A heavy weight landed on Nathan's chest; the air he dragged in with each shallow gasp became steamy and rancid as growling canine jaws loomed inches from his face. The Lycan's massive hands pressed down on his rib cage, and Nathan cried out as the crystal bones in his chest threatened to crack.

Warm silver liquid dripped onto Nathan's torso. His earlier swipe at the Lycan's belly was deep but not lethal.

With a groan, Nathan struggled to off-load the oversized wolf shifter, but the Lycan had him pinned. Then, like a dog digging for a bone, the werewolf hacked at Nathan's chest, right over his heart.

A Veniri's hide was almost impenetrable, but ironically, Diamantium—the tissue that made up their crystal skeleton and spikes—was one of the only things that could slice through Veniri scales like a hot knife through butter.

Nathan roared. Teal blood spewed from his chest with every searing gouge. After several excruciating seconds, the Lycan raised his fists and pounded, again and again, trying to crack Nathan's rib cage open like an oyster. Nathan began to worry the Lycan's blows might actually rupture one of the venom sacs that encased his heart and cause him to die from his own poison.

Soon all Nathan knew was panic and desperation. Every ounce of coherent thought fled.

This Lycan was larger and more powerful than any other he'd encountered. This wasn't a gladiator fight; this was an assassination.

But by the tiny breaths still gurgling through his lungs, Nathan wanted to live!

Something small brushed against his hand, and he clutched it, feeling the sharpened point at one end. With a swing of his arm, he aimed for the wolf-man's head.

The Lycan howled as the severed, clawed finger impaled his eye.

Using every fragment of energy he possessed, Nathan hazed. His human flesh rippled into scales, and crystal spikes erupted from his body. He slammed his knee up and skewered the werewolf's stomach with the protruding spike, and the Lycan collapsed on top of him.

With an immense effort, Nathan rolled out from under the werewolf's enormous bulk.

He wanted to rest. To go to sleep and never wake up.

But this wasn't over.

Summoning an impossible rush of energy, he punched. His Diamantium-tipped knucklebones easily punctured the Lycan's chest cavity, and with a final burst of power, Nathan yanked out the still-beating heart.

3

BOOPING BUTTON NOSES

THE INFANT'S LITTLE HAND CLAMPED ON TO VIOLET'S THUMB. Everything about the child was tiny, fragile, and absolutely precious. Violet watched, fascinated and delighted, as her baby fussed and cooed, gently wriggled, and opened her eyes —sometimes one at a time before closing them again. It was as if the newborn was testing every feature of her body in this new world beyond the womb.

Voices murmured in conversation outside Violet's infirmary room—likely Dawn and Gus discussing whatever had happened to make Dawn kick everyone out of surgery. Nothing had been said to Violet, despite her desperate pleas to know what was going on. But Gus *had* eventually brought the baby over to her for the remainder of the surgery— maybe because he realized it was the only thing that would calm her down. The moment Violet laid eyes on her infant, she'd experienced instant peace.

Frustrated to be shut out of the conversation, Violet blocked out the low chattering and focused again on her child. Besides, her baby was just falling asleep, and she didn't want to wake her by shouting to the people beyond the door.

The infant's tiny face moved and twitched as she slept, her little hand still tightly gripping Violet's thumb.

"You're a tough one, aren't you?" Violet whispered.

As if in answer, the baby cooed.

Violet's heart melted, or maybe it ignited. She'd felt such a profound connection to this infant from the moment she'd heard her cry. How was it possible to love something so small so much?

She stroked the little eyebrows, the tiny nose and cheeks. "Don't worry, little one. I promise I'll keep you safe. I'll never leave you, and I won't let anyone hurt you." A dark emotion fluttered through her chest. "Ever. I'll always protect my daughter."

Daughter.

The very concept felt alien. Violet had never really been a daughter herself—not after her mother had abandoned her at the hospital soon after she was born. And bouncing around in the foster system hadn't given her much opportunity to find a worthy parental figure.

Except for Nathan—

Violet shook her head. She didn't want to ruin this magical moment by thinking about him.

The voices grew louder as Autumn barged into the room, then faded when the door closed behind her.

"Hey, Vi. How are you both doing?" Without waiting for an answer, she swooped in to get a better look at the baby, chattering away in baby talk and gently tickling the infant's adorable feet. "Guess what I brought? Tah-dah!" A white box appeared from behind her back. "Fresh from Mom's kitchen."

Violet clamped a hand over her nose and mouth the moment the aroma hit her. At the same time, her baby let out a shrill cry and began to kick her legs.

"Get it away! Get it away!" Violet's muffled voice demanded.

Autumn fumbled the container closed and tossed it to the other side of the room, but Violet still waited a few heartbeats before daring to remove the hand from her nose.

"I'm so sorry, Vi. I just thought since you're not pregnant anymore . . ."

"It's okay." Violet gave her friend a reassuring smile, then cast a wistful glance at the box. Cinnamon doughnuts were her all-time favorite, especially Skye's homemade ones, but throughout her whole pregnancy, she hadn't been able to handle the taste. And regrettably the smell of cinnamon had made her want to barf—not just barf, more like run screaming in the other direction. "Unfortunately, I think it might take a little time before my raging pregnancy hormones begin to die down."

Autumn slumped into the chair close to Violet's bed. Her dark brown eyes flicked to the discarded doughnuts in the corner, then to the gradually calming infant. "That's weird. The poor little thing freaked out the same time you did. Maybe she isn't a fan of doughnuts either."

"Hmm, maybe." Violet studied her daughter, whose features had smoothed back into a serene, untroubled expression. "Or it could be gas."

Autumn cracked a grin, relaxing back in the chair. She flicked her waist-length chestnut dreadlocks over her shoulder and began playing with the frayed ends of her red-orange paisley headscarf. The deep purple tones of the indie rock band tee she had on complemented her sun-kissed golden skin.

Violet inclined her head toward the door. "So, what's going on out there?"

Autumn shrugged a shoulder. "I'm not sure. There's a lot of medical lingo being thrown around. I swear, Gus and Aunt Dawn need a subtitle function sometimes." She began cooing at the baby and booping her little button nose. "Have you given her a name yet?"

Violet pursed her lips and shook her head. "No, not yet. Do you want to hold her?"

Autumn's wide eyes practically twinkled. "Ooh! Could I?"

"Sure."

Once Autumn was settled with the baby, Violet nestled farther into her pillows. After a moment, the door cracked open, and Sagan's head poked into the room.

"Hey, stranger. You're back," said Violet.

"Hey. I've been speaking with Dawn and Gus, and they told me you were in here."

"Come on in." Violet gestured to the empty chair on the other side of her bed, but Sagan stayed where he was.

"You sure?"

Violet nodded. "Of course."

Sagan glided in and sat down, shoving his hands in his jacket pockets. His ice-blue eyes stayed fixed on the baby. "So, apparently I missed a lot."

"I suppose you could say that." Violet gave him the abridged version of what she could remember of the C-section. "I'm okay now," she added. "My pain meds have been topped up, so I'm feeling fine. Although . . ." She reached out to retrieve her baby from Autumn. "The little one might be getting hungry. Apparently, the midwife should be coming in to teach me to breastfeed, but I haven't seen her since the surgery."

Sagan's angelic face paled, almost matching his white-blond hair.

Autumn giggled. "What's the matter, Sagan? You don't want to be here when the milk bar opens?"

"No, it's not that . . . I mean, I . . ." His body tensed, as if he were about to spring from his seat.

Before Autumn could tease him any further, Dawn

entered the room with Gus close on her tail, both now mask and surgeon cap free. Dawn's dead-straight fair hair was cropped neatly beneath her ears and bobbed a little as she strode over. The tiny wrinkles that lined her face seemed to have deepened in concern.

Violet searched the doctor's expression for answers, clutching her baby a little tighter. "What's wrong?"

"Nothing's wrong," said Dawn. "At least, it depends on your perspective."

Violet shot a glance at Gus. "What do you mean 'on my perspective'?"

Dawn hesitated. "Well, I'm sure you're aware that . . . now, I'm not saying there's something wrong with your baby—she seems perfectly healthy so far—but . . ." She sucked in a deep breath. "Violet, how well do you know the baby's father?"

"Thane?" Violet winced. "To be honest, not all that well. Why?"

Dawn's mouth twitched from side to side, as if she was trying to find her next words. "It's just—"

"Is Thane Veniri?" Sagan blurted.

Violet's eyebrows shot up. "What?"

"Geez," Gus murmured under his breath, "way to rip off the Band-Aid."

Violet froze as an image of a scaled monster with crystal spikes flashed in her mind. Just days before arriving at Maple Shire, she'd rescued a battered Sagan after he'd been attacked by a reptilian shape-shifter called a Veniri. Violet's world had already been turned upside down, but it almost shattered when she learned that shape-shifters were very, *very* real.

She shook her head. "No, Thane's not . . . at least, I don't think . . ." She thought about all the time she'd spent with him since they'd met at the café: their date at the city's carnival, the night she'd stayed at his place after her college friend

Bessie was killed, the next morning when she'd seen his crystal scorpion neck tattoo and fled his apartment.

For years, that neck tattoo had been her only memory from when she and her best friend, Lyla, were kidnapped. When she saw it again, those memories came rushing back like a hurricane. There had been at least two guys involved in the kidnapping, Thane and another man in a hoodie. The one in the hoodie had eventually turned into a scaly Veniri beast who'd attacked and killed Lyla. But Thane hadn't changed. He'd been human the whole time. But if it could be assumed all the kidnappers were Veniri . . . ?

A violent chill shuddered over Violet's skin, and blood roared in her ears. She looked down at the sleeping infant in her arms—the perfect image of a little human baby.

Heart pounding, Violet slowly nodded. "Yes, it's possible Thane's Veniri. But then, are you saying she's . . . ?" She bit her lip, her thoughts churning. During the delivery, Macie had screamed. Dawn had kicked everyone out.

"Yes," confirmed Dawn. "Your daughter is Veniri."

Several seconds passed as Violet processed that fact. "What does this mean for my baby?" She glanced between Dawn, Sagan, Gus, and even Autumn. "How do you . . . I mean, how do I raise a Veniri child?"

"Does this mean you're planning on keeping her?" Dawn asked.

"Of course!" Violet stared at her, taken aback. "Why wouldn't I? She's mine. I'm not going to give her up." There was no way Violet could abandon this child the way her mother had abandoned her. She could never put her daughter through the damage and pain she'd endured, Veniri or not.

Sagan's eyebrows drew together slightly.

Dawn let out a long breath, and her face relaxed into a smile. "Great. In that case, I'll bring you a formula made especially for Veniri infants. Then I'll do my best to explain their feeding habits, what to do when her fang nubs become sharper, and what happens when—"

Violet, Sagan, Autumn, and Gus all erupted at the same time.

"This has happened before?"

"Hold up!"

"Where did you get Veniri baby formula?"

"*Fangs?*"

Dawn smiled and patiently waited for the hysteria to die down. "Actually, yes, I have seen this before." She held up her hands as everyone's questions started up again, then focused on the baby in Violet's arms. "This is not the first time a shifter baby has been delivered in this infirmary."

Violet's jaw dropped. Gus and Autumn immediately exchanged a loaded glance. Sagan's wide eyes were the only clue as to what he could be thinking.

"But what about Macie, the midwife?" Gus asked.

Dawn inclined her head low. "She's new. Unfortunately, I never considered that Violet could be pregnant with a shifter baby, so it didn't even cross my mind to brief those who would be assisting with the birth on the shifter side of things." Her lips pinched into a thin line. "I certainly won't be making that mistake again, considering the consequences of what happened in the theater room and the lengths we'll now have to go to in counseling Macie and ensuring she doesn't spread this to others."

Violet slowly nodded, trying to let the new information sink in. A ragged whine escaped the squirming baby in her arms.

Dawn looked down at the wriggling bundle. "Hmm, I think she's hungry."

"How do you know?"

"Trust me." Dawn gave her a knowing smile. "When

you've had a baby like Gus who was able to drink his weight in milk from day one, you learn to read the signs. For Veniri babies, breastfeeding is still vital, but the Veniri infant formula will compensate for all the extra vitamins and minerals she'll need that your human body doesn't provide. Plus, with Veniri babies, there's also the challenge of—"

Before Dawn could finish, flickers of iridescent blue began to ripple over the baby's skin. The whining cries grew louder, and in a matter seconds, the infant's form had completely changed. Except for the face, throat, hands, and feet, teal fur about an inch long covered her flesh. Her little face—which showed only a faint impression of the scales to come—had turned a pastel shade of aquamarine, with a distinct pattern of white and darker blues around her cheeks and forehead. Small bumps had risen along her eyebrows and across her cheek bones, and peeking out from her top lip were two rounded glittery teeth, which Violet suspected would one day become part of a triple set of fangs.

During the transformation, everyone had leaned in for a closer look.

"Wow," whispered Sagan.

"Yeah," added Gus. "That was . . . she's—"

"So cute!" cooed Autumn.

"Well . . . yeah," said Gus.

Violet glanced up. "Have you guys ever seen . . . ?"

Everyone shook their heads except Dawn.

Violet turned to Sagan. "But surely you—"

"No," he said with a sharp shake of his head. "I've never seen a shifter baby before, but I have seen some Veniri with fur. They shed it by adolescence. At least, that's the theory hunters have come up with." He reached out and stroked the soft teal fur that now coated the majority of the baby's body. "It's so soft."

Before the baby could get too grouchy, Dawn retrieved a bottle of formula, and the infant began to suckle away.

Violet ran a hand along her baby's velvet-soft fur, which soon faded back into pink human skin once the bottle was empty. Then she lay back in the pillows and chewed her lip. Not only was she a new mother—a concept she could still barely get her head around—but she was a new mother to a *Veniri infant*. Doubt began to cloud the edges of her elation, but she forced it away, swallowing hard to relieve the tension in her throat.

Autumn stroked her arm. "It's okay, Violet. We're here for you."

"Yeah," agreed Gus, "you don't have to do this alone. But"—he raised a finger—"when it comes to changing diapers, I volunteer Autumn as tribute."

Autumn rolled her eyes, and Violet managed a smile.

"Thanks, guys. It means a lot to have friends like you. It's like I'm . . ."

"Like you're part of our family." Autumn squeezed her arm. "You're an honorary Novak."

"Or an honorary Farrow," piped up Gus.

Tears welled up in Violet's eyes, and she nodded. A few minutes passed as she struggled against the lump in her throat. "Yeah. You have no idea how grateful I am. With all that happened at college and with what happened with Nath—I mean, if it weren't for all of you, I would never have found my solace." She hugged her daughter tight. "You know what? I know what I want to call her."

* * *

The next few weeks were an adjustment not only for Violet but also for Gus, Autumn, and their families. The messy routine of diapers, feeding, crying, and sleep deprivation was exhausting, not to mention how much Violet's boobs hurt! Who knew being a full-time milk machine had its downsides?

Staying with the Novaks made everything so much easier. Autumn's parents, Skye and Cruz, were godsends. They'd set up a room for Solace's nursery and were practically live-in nannies. Cruz was a sucker for cuddles and endless games of peek-a-boo, and Skye was an angel in the kitchen, ensuring everyone was fed and happy—and shamelessly enabling Violet's chai latte addiction, minus the cinnamon.

The Maple Shire residents were just as welcoming with Solace's arrival. They showered Violet and her daughter with gifts, a lot of them handmade baby clothes and cuddly toys, and constantly spoiled Solace with visits. Skye and Cruz strictly regulated the visiting hours to ensure the other Maple Shire residents didn't arrive during Solace's feeding times or, worse, when she was in her Veniri form. Apart from Dawn; her husband, Lazareth; Skye; Cruz; the Maple Shire leader, and only a handful of other residents who helped out in the infirmary were in the know about Solace's blue, fuzzy side. As far as the rest of the community was concerned, shifters didn't exist.

Since Dawn's shocking revelation about other shifter babies being born in the compound infirmary, Violet, Gus, Autumn, and even Sagan had all bombarded her with questions. Though Dawn declined to reveal everything to Violet and the others, she did tell them that Maple Shire was a neutral safe haven for all kinds of shifters, a kind of medical halfway house, especially for desperate human mothers who arrived at Maple Shire after discovering their lovers were shifters. Not only were these women terrified of the prospect of having a shifter child, but they weren't sure where they could safely receive obstetric care. Dawn said she had never been able to determine the outcomes for the mothers who chose to deliver their shifter babies in a regular hospital.

Once Dawn had helped the mothers give birth, Skye would find a new home for the mothers who needed it, as well as assist those who couldn't raise the children themselves, helping to find new families for their infants.

This part of the story made Violet sick to her stomach. How could someone abandon their own child? How could her own mother have done that to her?

Dawn tried to explain that a lot of these women were in complicated situations where bringing home a shifter baby wasn't an option. Some had come out of abusive relationships and were trying to escape their shifter partners. One woman claimed to have fled some kind of Veniri enslavement, where she'd been forced to bear a Veniri child. Though Violet wasn't a Veniri expert, this story seemed really far-fetched.

No matter what excuses Dawn gave for these women, Violet just shook her head and blinked back tears of lifelong heartbreak, resentment boiling in her core.

* * *

"Come on, time for a checkup." Gus gently took hold of Violet's arm and steered her toward the infirmary.

She glanced back at her daughter's bedroom door. "But what if—"

"Don't worry," said Skye.

"We'll be right here the whole time," Cruz said from the kitchen sink, where he was rinsing off some fresh produce from the vegetable garden. "We'll hear her if she wakes up."

"See?" said Gus. "Aunt Skye and Uncle Cruz have it covered. Besides, you've had this cold for weeks now. We need to figure out what's wrong with you. We don't want Solace getting sick too."

"But I don't need to—" Right on cue, Violet broke into a coughing fit. A glass was pressed into her hand, and she managed to take a few sips, the cool water soothing her itchy throat. "Okay," she wheezed, withering under Gus's condescending smirk. "I'll go see your mom." She shot Skye and Cruz a look. "You'll come and get me the moment she's awake?"

"You have my word." Skye's dreadlocks, a little longer than Autumn's, danced with her firm nod.

Before Violet could say anything more, Gus whisked her out the door and through the gardens to the infirmary. They found Dawn beside one of the exam beds, putting a bandage on her husband, Lazareth.

"Have the roses been attacking you again, Dad?" Gus asked.

"It was the barbed-wire fence this time." Autumn was lounging on one of the free beds with her laptop. "The goat twins escaped again, and Uncle Laz got tangled in the fence trying to catch them. Lucky I was walking by. Otherwise he probably would have severed his arm trying to get free."

"Damn goats," said Lazareth. "It's the third time this week. If their milk didn't make such amazing cheese, I would have allowed Skye to serve them up for dinner ages ago."

Violet hid a smirk. She'd never known someone so obsessed with cheese, although she supposed Lazareth's multiple awards justified the obsession. Not to mention his famous fig-and-lychee cheesecake.

Dawn pecked Lazareth on the cheek before sending him on his way, then had Violet sit on the edge of a nearby examination bed. "How's your hand?" she asked, pulling out a digital thermometer.

"It's fine." Violet gently caressed the fabric bandage over

the webbing between her thumb and pointer finger. "You weren't kidding when you said Solace's fangs would sharpen up fast."

"Hmm . . ." Dawn frowned. "I'll need to examine the bite mark again. It's a little concerning that it's taking this long to heal. How long has it been again?"

"Maybe three weeks."

Dawn *hmm*ed again as she checked the reading on the digital thermometer. "Your temperature is still a little high, which suggests your immune system is fighting something. I initially thought it might have been due to the vaccination I gave you after the delivery. It isn't uncommon for people do get cold-like symptoms as they become immune to the injected viruses, but that was at least eight weeks ago. It could just be the common cold, and you're taking longer than usual to shake it."

Violet broke out into another round of coughs, as if to emphasize Dawn's statement.

"Thankfully, whatever you have, it hasn't been passed on to Solace," continued Dawn. "However, I think it's best to take a blood test and start figuring out what's going on here."

"Okay." Violet took another gulp of water.

Dawn nodded with an approving smile and went to retrieve a trolley from the corner of the room.

Gus's eyebrow quirked. "Are you sure?"

"Yeah, why?" Violet asked.

"You did hear the part where Mom said 'blood test,' right?"

"What about it?"

Gus gave an exaggerated shrug. "Am I the only one who remembers the kicking and screaming last time?"

"She's just had a baby, Gus." Dawn snapped on some latex gloves. "You'd be surprised how much having a child can change a person."

He slowly nodded his head. "Actually, I think that explains a lot."

"What does that mean?" Violet narrowed her eyes at him as Dawn cinched a tourniquet above her elbow.

"You've been a little . . . how should I describe it?" Gus looked up at the ceiling and tapped one finger on his chin.

"*Grizzly bear* is how I'd describe it," said Autumn, who was now clacking away on her laptop.

"Yep, I think *grizzly* just about sums it up," agreed Gus.

Violet huffed. "I am not like a grizzly bear."

"Oh yeah? What about the time Gus was playing peek-a-boo with Solace?" Autumn countered.

"What? I was fine."

"Right up until he scared her. You practically snatched her out of his arms and chewed him out with a voice from *The Exorcist*."

Violet rolled her eyes. "That was one time."

"Okay, what about the time Autumn dropped Solace's pacifier on the ground?" interjected Gus. "When you realized she was going to give it back without washing it, you practically accused Autumn of giving her Ebola."

"Are you saying I'm not allowed to be concerned about germs?" Violet said, putting her free hand on her hip.

"I'm not saying that at all," said Gus, "but I think you're forgetting that Solace is not as fragile as you think she is. She's tough like her mom, for starters, and my mother has made sure she's been getting her vaccinations when they're due. Don't let the nose ring and hippie facade fool you. My mother is a doctor first and a tree-hugger second. But even with that, it was a drama all in itself for you to let Mom come near Solace with the needle."

Violet frowned and shot a sidelong glance at Dawn, who was preparing the syringe and collection of vials. "It's normal for a new mom to be concerned about the well-being of her child, right, Dawn?"

Dawn finally looked up from her work to give Violet a tight-lipped smile.

"Face it, Vi," said Autumn. "You've definitely amped up the aggro. The only person you haven't abused yet is him"—she pointed to Sagan as he sauntered in—"and that's because he hasn't been anywhere near her."

Sagan held up his hands defensively. "Don't bring me into this. I don't know anything about babies. I'm afraid I'll drop her or something. And I definitely don't want to be on the receiving end of *'Hurricane Violet'* if something like that were to happen."

"Okay, I get it." Violet groaned. "I need to tone it down a little."

Autumn scoffed.

"A little? How about a lot?" said Gus.

"Fine. I promise to make an improvement." Violet bit her lip as Dawn wiped a swab over the crook of her elbow. She screwed up her nose, still hating the tangy odor of antiseptic, as the evaporating alcohol cooled her skin.

"Ready?" Dawn asked.

Violet nodded and barely flinched at the small sting. Gus was right; she had changed. During her pregnancy, Violet had definitely freaked out any time it was necessary to do a blood test.

And Dawn was right too; becoming a mother had changed Violet in so many other ways. From the moment she'd heard Solace cry for the first time in the delivery room, her whole universe had realigned—Violet would conquer worlds for her child.

But she supposed she had become a little over-the-top in the small things.

Her gaze flicked to the others. As much as she could excuse her behavior by saying she was protecting her baby, she knew full well the others loved Solace too and would never harm her. In fact, if it wasn't for Gus, Autumn, and their families, neither Violet nor Solace would have a warm bed to sleep in, full bellies, or a safe environment to call home. A twinge of guilt stabbed at Violet's stomach. When she was Solace's age, she'd already been passed between several social workers and foster parents.

"All done." Dawn removed the last vial of blood and the needle in Violet's arm before taping some gauze over the small wound.

"Thanks, Dawn."

"Don't mention it." Dawn folded Violet's arm to enclose the gauze in the crease of her elbow.

"No, really," said Violet. "I'm really grateful for all you've done for Solace and me."

This time, Dawn's smile was relaxed and genuine.

"Same to you, Gus and Autumn. I don't know how I would have coped with going through pregnancy and delivery without your support."

"Aw, shucks," said Gus at the same time Autumn said, "You're welcome!"

Violet smiled, hopped off the bed, and made her way over to Sagan. "I also owe you a huge thanks."

His brow creased. "Why? I haven't done anything."

"Yes, you have. That day on the road at Brookhaven, you distracted the guy with the gray beard long enough for us to escape. At the time, I didn't know I was pregnant, but if it wasn't for you, Solace and I wouldn't be here today. You saved us both."

Sagan shoved his hands in his pockets. A corner of his mouth tugged up, and he gave a small nod of his head. "Consider us even. I wouldn't be here either if you hadn't found me and driven me here."

"What do you mean, found you?" Violet said. "You were

standing in the middle of the road. I almost hit you with my car."

Sagan smirked. "Yeah, well, it couldn't have caused more damage than—"

A distant scream grabbed everyone's attention. For a second, no one moved.

"That's Skye!" Dawn exclaimed.

In an instant, they all rushed out of the infirmary. Autumn ran ahead, but Violet and Sagan had overtaken her by the time they cleared the gardens and were speeding toward the house.

Skye's screams grew louder. Then, suddenly, they cut off.

A surge of panic and adrenaline rushed through Violet's core, pushing her to run faster, *faster.*

Whatever was going on, her baby was in there.

4

MOUTH-BREATHING CHIHUAHUAS

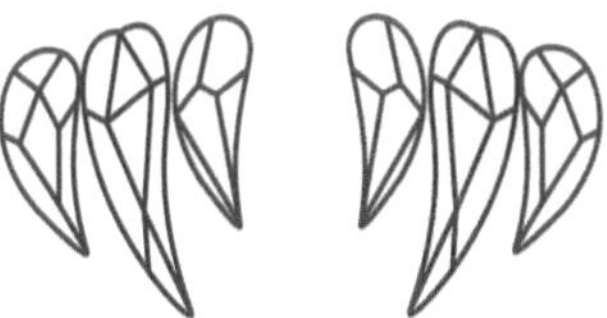

Nathan hit the ground with a grunt as the two Erathi hunters dumped him onto the cold hard floor of his cell. The Metallikite door clanked shut, followed by the whir and beep of the keypad lock—a feature of every cell door in Tempecrest.

With an agonizing effort, Nathan rolled onto his back. He rubbed his eyes with the heels of his hands, trying to quiet his mind, to erase the images of his last battle and dismiss the heaviness weighing down on him—the dense fog of self-loathing.

He tentatively prodded at his thigh, where four claw marks carved a line from his hip to the top of his knee. His accelerated healing had kicked in while he was in Veniri form in the arena, and the ragged flesh had already begun to scab over. In a day or two, it would be nearly fully healed, but Diamantium always left its mark. He was going to have an epic scar, much like the mottled scarring over his heart from his fight in the lava-lake arena. More and more of their Lycan opponents were now being bestowed with Diamantium-tipped claws.

The door clanked open again, followed by a thud and an *ooph* as two more hunters threw Thane into the cell next to his.

"You okay?" Nathan asked after the hunters left.

"Yeah." Thane groaned, gingerly standing and stretching with a pained grimace. "Do those morons think that throwing us around after a fight is doing us a favor?"

Tio scoffed, leaning against the bars of the cell adjacent to Thane's. "I'd say they're acting out on their small-Erathi syndrome."

"Small-Erathi syndrome?" repeated Nathan.

"What's that?" asked Thane.

"You know, it's like small-dog syndrome. They always try to make out that they're bigger and meaner than everyone else. It's the same with the Erathi, only they haven't figured out that on the shifter totem pole, they're way down at the very bottom."

"I would have thought the Yranum were at the bottom," said Thane.

"Nope." Tio shook his head. "They have healing abilities that benefit not only them but also others. That makes them special. The Erathi, on the other hand, have no abilities—at least, none that compare to the rest of us. They're just a bunch of mouth-breathing Chihuahuas, but instead of picking a fight with a pack of dogs, they're taking on a pack of lions."

"And what about you?" asked Nathan. "Where does your race sit on the totem pole?"

Tio's expression turned pious. "Duh! At the top."

Both Nathan and Thane laughed.

"What?" Tio's face dropped into a frown. "We're the strongest and the biggest and—"

"And the most pigheaded and vainest and most destructive," said Thane.

"Hey!"

"It's true, kid," said Nathan. "I admire your loyalty, but your race hasn't got the greatest reputation either."

"Whatever." Tio collapsed onto his cot with an adolescent huff, mumbling under his breath. After a few moments, the murmuring was replaced by an electric crackle.

Nathan rolled his head to find Tio sitting on his cot in full shifter form. While he'd seen other Jiovis shifters with copper, pewter, or rose-gold colored flesh—even metallic cobalt—Tio's transformed flesh was a deep gold, riddled with the elaborately designed flesh manipulations typical of his race. His face had been sculpted into an overemphasized skull, with an organic design of whirls and curls accenting his brow and cheekbones. Two tusks protruded from the edges of his mouth. Embellished on his bicep was the Jiovis symbol for Jupiter.

Tio's forearms rested on his knees, his focus on one of his hands. Bright orange blood dripped from his fingers and collected in a puddle on the floor between his feet.

"Lost another finger?" Nathan inquired. "What's that bring the tally to? Eight or nine?"

"Soon to be fourteen. I'm about to lose a hand." Tio's voice was tight with pain. "That stupid mongrel flung an iron sword at me. He heated it up first with one of those wall-mounted flamethrowers, and some of the molten metal fused to my hand. I need to cut out the iron before I get rust rot."

"Flame torches and molten metal . . ." Nathan groaned and rocked his head from side to side on the stone floor. "That reminds me too much of the lava-lake arena we did seven weeks ago. Or was it eight weeks? Ugh, I'm losing track. They used to throw us into the arena every three or four weeks. Now it feels like once a week."

"Yeah, that lava one was brutal," said Thane. "The rain-forest theme for this one wasn't too bad, although it wasn't all that great when my opponent decided to scurry up a tree like a little spider monkey."

A loud crackle of lightning erupted again in Tio's hands. He didn't cry out, but his features twisted in obvious severe agony. The ability to regrow his limbs like an axolotl had become a convenient talent for Tio since his arrival at Tempecrest. He'd boasted he could even add extra limbs and appendages if he wanted to, contemplating whether it would aid or hinder him in the arena.

The Jiovis flesh was called Metallikite—the same material the hunters used for their chains, handcuffs, and prison bars. Metallikite could only be described as a "living metal"—and its properties were astounding. It gave the Jiovis the ability to mold their flesh into highly decorative sculptures, an extremely painful process similar to how some Erathi Pacific Islander and African cultures adorned themselves with tribal tattoos and scarification. It was even possible to trade colors to enhance decorative features. Nathan couldn't help shuddering when he spotted a few different-colored accents in Tio's decorations. The equivalent would be him grafting someone else's flesh onto his, just for aesthetic purposes.

Tio's flesh was as intricate as a baroque frame. Along with the skull-like features of his face, his torso had been molded to look like armor, with elaborate patterns mixed with three-dimensional moldings of skulls, teeth, spikes, and bones. Based on the warmongering culture of the Jiovis, Nathan knew the design was meant to terrify onlookers.

One standout feature of Tio's design—Nathan had observed it on every Jiovis—was a solid neck shield, also highly decorated. But the shield wasn't golden like the rest of Tio's skin; it was silver with a light green tinge, very much like the green-tinged bars that held them all captive.

Unfortunately for the Jiovis, the Erathi hunters had found their own depraved uses for Metallikite. They would flay their Jiovis captives, peeling back layer after layer of the living-metal flesh until their victims died a prolonged and agonizing death. The Erathi had discovered that once the Metallikite was cured, it would fade to a silvery green and become nearly impossible to destroy. Even a Jiovis could not damage cured Metallikite.

After about half a minute, Tio extinguished the lightning and admired his handiwork, wiggling his new fingers. From fingertips to wrist, his skin was now smooth and polished like a golden mirror—not a single sculpted adornment remained.

Tio sighed. "I'd only just finished this hand's new modifications yesterday. Now I'll have to do it all over again."

Thane snickered. "Typical clanger. Losing a hand isn't a problem, so long as you look pretty doing it."

"Shut up, slith." Tio grinned, his metallic gold skin darkening back into the rich obsidian of his human form. Once he'd fully hazed, he cocked an eyebrow at Nathan. "Oi, Nathan? You still alive?"

A corner of Nathan's mouth twitched up into a half grin. "Yeah, kid. I'm still alive."

"Are you going to lie there all day?"

"Maybe." Nathan shrugged. "It's just as comfy as the cots."

"You're right about that. How much damage did you cop this time?"

Memories flickered through Nathan's mind's eye. "Almost a little too much." He hefted himself up into a seated position. Every muscle screamed in pain. "Not sure how much more of this I can take."

Thane stood up and gripped the bars that separated them. "Don't say that," he said in a hushed voice. His wide eyes gave away his panic. "You can't give up now. Not after all we've been through. We're getting out of here. You hear me?"

Nathan nodded. "Yeah, I hear you. I'm not as young as I

used to be, that's all. You and Tio are still nimble and spry. It's taking me longer and longer to snap back, especially with the frequency of these battles." He dragged his hands down his face. "We've gotta figure out how to get out of here. Before they kill us. We came too close to fighting each other this time. One day our luck is going to run out, and they'll toss just the three of us in the arena to battle it out."

"If I had access to a computer, I could get us out." Tio gestured to the digital locks. "I'd only need five minutes to override the system and unlock this whole facility."

Nathan quirked an eyebrow.

"Sure you could, kid." Thane rolled his eyes.

"Of course I could! I could also get us all new IDs and passports and any other paperwork so these Erathi scum would never find us again."

"Anyway"—Thane cleared his throat and turned back to Nathan—"just promise me you won't give up."

Nathan nodded but didn't voice any guarantees. It wasn't worth telling Thane what he really thought their chances were. Not when Thane still had the hope to continue on.

He pushed himself onto the edge of his cot and rubbed at an itch on his shoulder. A jolt of fear clutched at his chest as his fingers brushed over a glassy texture. He'd discovered the small patch of crystal a few months ago. It had started out as just a pinprick but was gradually getting bigger—first growing to the size of a flat thumbtack, then a postage stamp, and now bordering on the area of a playing card.

He quickly checked the other patch he'd found on the back of his calf. It too had grown, and it looked like another was starting to form on his ankle. He rotated the joint, and the crystallized skin sparkled as it captured the overhead light.

Nathan sucked in short, shallow breaths. *What's going on? What do these patches mean? Am I sick? Is it nothing?* Whatever it was, he wouldn't be able to hide it for much longer. It was a wonder no one had mentioned anything about the crystal patch on his shoulder yet.

"So, Thane, you think you're up for it again?" Tio grinned and wriggled his fingers. Little crackles of electricity danced over his skin.

"Why not? May as well add a bit more agony to my day." Thane sauntered over to the bars between his and Tio's cells and lay down on his side, facing Nathan.

Tio crouched by Thane's head. He leaned in as much as the bars would allow. "It looks much better than yesterday."

"You think it's working?"

"Actually, I think it might be. We've only done about eight rounds, but the colored ink's almost gone, and the black sections look like they're fading a bit."

"I'll take your word for it," said Thane, "It's not like I've got access to a mirror. We may as well keep going."

"How about I try a higher current this time? You know, to try and speed things up."

Thane waved a hand. "Sure, just get on with it."

Reaching through the bars, Tio hovered his fingers over the crystal scorpion tattoo on Thane's neck. "Ready?"

Thane winced. "Yep."

Tio's hand glowed a brilliant orange, and golden electricity hummed and sparked between his fingers. Thane hissed as the electricity connected with his skin.

Nathan couldn't help wincing too, especially once the stench of burning flesh reached his nose. He'd been the victim of a Jiovis shifter's electricity only a handful of times, and none of them had made him want to volunteer for the experience again.

Back when Thane had come up with this improvised tattoo-removal method, Nathan had thought the idea ridiculous. Getting tattoo ink through Veniri hide was one thing, but removing it would be much more difficult—which Thane had found out the hard way after many failed attempts with the standard Erathi laser removal treatment.

Thane's groans rose over the fierce crackle of Tio's efforts. Even from where Nathan was sitting, he could make out small bolts of light shooting from Tio's index finger into Thane's neck with a monotonous *zap-zap-zap*. Tio hadn't been joking when he'd said he had tight control over his power.

Thane's grunts of pain grew even more anguished as time went on. His legs writhed, and his knuckles turned white from gripping the bars. Nathan couldn't help admiring Thane's determination. Whatever the reason he wanted to get rid of the tattoo, Nathan was certain it had something to do with Violet.

"There," said Tio after a few minutes. "That should probably do it for today."

"Finally," Thane gritted out.

"Hey, you wanted this, remember?"

"Yeah, yeah." Thane pushed himself up, cupping the area of his tattoo with one hand, and lay back down on his cot with a final groan. "It's going to itch like a mother tomorrow."

Just then, a mechanical click and whir announced the opening of the main door to the prison block. All heads turned as a group of hunters—two men and a woman—entered. They sauntered down the hallway of captive shifters until they reached the barred door of Nathan's cell.

The two males, one bulky and brunet and the other a bit shorter and leaner with light brown hair, leaned on the bars and grinned. Their hunter amulets swayed on black chains around their necks, both with three of the ten vials filled.

"Here he is, Nika—the slith of the hour, in the flesh," said the brunet hunter.

The young woman pushed her way between the two males and peered through the bars. "He doesn't look like much."

The smaller male chuckled. "Don't let that fool you. This slith made us a lot of money tonight. Right, Quill?"

"Hell yeah. I told you Axel's mongrel wouldn't beat this slith. And I told you"—Quill elbowed Nika—"you should have placed a bet of your own. Hestus and I are going to be celebrating with our winnings later."

Nathan scoffed.

The brunet hunter frowned. "What're you laughing at, slith?"

In reply, Nathan just shook his head. Gambling was another part of Erathi culture he just hadn't got a handle on yet. Every Erathi had something to prove and, in their mind, everything to gain.

"So," said Nika, "does anyone know why Uncle Ty decided to bring sliths into Tempecrest?"

"Nah, I haven't heard anything," said Hestus.

"Who cares?" Quill threw his hands up. "Tempecrest has become way more interesting. There's only so many fights you can watch with mutts before things start to get boring. Uncle Ty should have brought in the sliths ages ago."

Quill leaned on Thane's cell door. "This slith's not too bad either."

"Yeah, this one's my favorite," said Hestus, moving to join him. "Did you see how he sliced the mutt's head off before cutting out his heart?"

The two proceeded to recap their favorite play-by-play, but the woman, Nika, remained at Nathan's cell. She quickly glanced at the two other hunters, then gestured for Nathan to come closer.

Nathan narrowed his eyes at her. She may have been a woman, petite and pretty, but he didn't for a second think she wasn't capable of slitting his throat just for fun if she wanted to. He dropped his gaze and ignored her.

"Psst." Her hiss was barely audible over the two, now arguing, males. From the corner of his eyes, Nathan glanced at Thane, who was surreptitiously eyeing the woman while trying not to divert the two guys' attention.

"Psst."

Nathan flicked his gaze back to Nika, and again, she gestured for him to come forward. *What is this chick's deal?* As casually as possible, he got up and approached her.

She opened her mouth to speak.

"Hey! Get away from my sister!" A hand shoved Nathan back. Quill's face appeared between the bars, his expression dripping venom. "If you ever come near my sister—"

"Back off, Quill." Nika gave him an elbow to the ribs. "I can take care of myself, remember?" She held up her amulet in front of his nose. Four vials were filled: silver, teal, magenta, and orange.

Quill scowled down at the amulet and crossed his arms over his hefty chest.

"He's just worried about you, sis," said Hestus. "We both are. When you took off, we just—"

"Yeah, well, I'm back now, so you can both drop the 'protective big brother' facade. Besides, I just wanted a closer look. I still don't get what the big deal is."

Nathan almost laughed out loud. He was about to go sit back down, but Nika's intense expression held him in place.

"Well, he won't be a big deal for much longer," said Quill. "Uncle Ty's got some decent plans for the slith's big finale. It's gonna be so epic that the buy-in price is through the roof!"

Nathan froze. *Finale?*

"Hestus and I are gonna pool our money," continued Quill. "Whaddya say, sis? You want in?"

Nika shook her head. "Nah. It's not really my thing."

"Seriously? Come on. It's bound to be awesome!"

"So?" Nika shrugged one shoulder. "Just because crazy Uncle Ty's become bored with his pets doesn't mean I have to squeal like a girl about it."

"Crazy's an understatement," said Hestus in a low voice.

"True," added Quill. "Ever since he's come back, he's been all 'spangle this' and 'spangle that.' I mean, if I hear one more thing about his precious spangles, I swear I'll—*ooph*."

Hestus had elbowed him in the gut. "Shut up, Quill!"

"What? What'd I say?"

"We're not supposed to talk about what Uncle Ty's been up to, let alone in front of these guys." Hestus shot a glare at Nathan, who couldn't help giving him a knowing smirk.

Hmm . . . spangle. What could that be in reference to? If Matthias Branstone thought they were precious, it was probably something really bad.

Hestus shoved Quill toward the exit. "Come on, let's go before you accidentally let something else slip."

"Seriously? It's not like I gave them the passcode to escape or anything."

"Hey, Nika, you coming?" Hestus called back once they'd reached the main door.

She turned to follow, but not before slipping a scrap of paper to Nathan. When the door finally clanged shut behind the three hunters, followed by the mechanical whir of the lock, Nathan cautiously unfolded it.

Midnight. Be ready. Make sure you and the other slith DON'T MOVE!

5

WHAT ARE YOU?

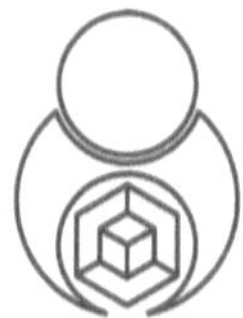

MY BABY'S IN THERE! MY BABY'S IN THERE!

Violet's sprinted up the garden path leading to Autumn's home, every beat of her heart flooding her limbs with panicked energy. Sagan appeared in her periphery as he overtook her and disappeared through the back door.

Close behind, Violet leaped over the threshold and skidded to a stop in the kitchen. Her hands flew to her mouth.

Skye lay sprawled on the tiled floor, her eyes open but lifeless. Deep crimson pooled beneath her from a gaping gash in her throat, and a smeared handprint on the wall marked where she'd tried to catch herself before falling to the ground.

Violet's numb mind struggled to comprehend what she was seeing, only vaguely registering Autumn, Gus, and Dawn as they rushed in behind her. Autumn's screams were other-worldly. Dawn tried her best to staunch the bleeding, but Violet knew even Dawn's talents couldn't bring Skye back.

Cruz lay in his own ruby-red puddle in the foyer, crumpled behind the still-open front door.

Just as Gus ran over to his Uncle Cruz, a loud bang forced Violet's attention to the hallway. Her whole body jolted as if shocked by an electric surge.

That noise had come from Solace's bedroom!

Violet shot down the hall, but before she could reach her daughter's doorway, a man in a black suit sailed out of it. His flailing arm slammed into Violet's chest as he crashed into the opposite wall, the force of the blow making her slide backward a couple feet.

Sagan exploded out of the room after him. He slammed his knee into the man's chest, then—before the man could even double over in pain—elbowed him in the face, took a handful of his hair, and yanked. The man stumbled headfirst into the other wall with an incredible crash. Drywall cracked and crumbled to the ground at his feet.

The man pulled his head out of the new hole in the wall, shook off the white dust, and hurled himself back at Sagan, throwing power punch after power punch. Sagan ducked and weaved until a fist collided with his jaw. His head snapped to the side as his whole body spun with the force of the man's right hook.

The man's victorious grin was even more eerie beneath the white dust mask. In a blink, he produced an unusual knife with a deep-magenta blade—Violet didn't see from where.

With an overhead strike, the man sliced the air toward Sagan's head. Sagan blocked the deadly assault with his forearm and countered with his own crystal dagger. A beam of sunlight streaming through the skylight glinted off the crystal and magenta weapons with each lunge and swing.

Solace's cries rang out over the cacophony of the vicious fight. Violet scrambled to her feet and desperately waited for a gap in the fierce melee so she could shove past Sagan and run into her daughter's bedroom.

Her heart stopped in her chest.

A blonde female, also in a black suit, was lifting Solace out of the crib. The glass door leading into the garden was wide open, and a black van waited in the driveway at the end of the garden path.

"Put my baby down!" Violet roared.

The woman threw a glance over her shoulder and sneered. Then she turned and fled out the glass door.

With a speed she didn't know she possessed, Violet sprang. Reaching out, she latched on to the woman's ponytail. The blonde's head snapped back as Violet's other arm wrapped around her torso, trying to shield Solace from the impact as they all smashed to the dirt.

As soon as they hit the ground, Violet jumped onto the woman's hips and tried to pull Solace from her arms, but the woman's grip was relentless.

"Give me my baby!" Violet's scream barely drowned out the shrill cries of her distressed child.

The woman hissed through her teeth and bucked, clutching Solace even tighter. She was surprisingly strong and agile, even with Violet straddling her and a screaming baby in her arms.

Cold fear flooded Violet when she realized her baby was on the verge of being either crushed or ripped to pieces. *What should I do? Should I let go? What should I do?*

Without warning, the woman's head flew forward and connected with Violet's nose. Tears sprang to her eyes, along with stars and blinding pain, and her hold on Solace began to falter. In desperation, she let go with one hand and reached for the switchblade in her back pocket.

Before the woman could kick free, there was a subtle *shnik*, and Violet plunged the switchblade into Blondie's bicep.

The woman's shriek drowned out Solace's hysterical

cries. Blondie's iron grip unfastened as she attempted to pull the switchblade out of her arm.

With triumph, Violet pulled her baby free and pressed the precious bundle tight to her chest. "Shh. I've got you." She stumbled up the garden path, still half-blind and a little dizzy from the headbutt. She blinked, hoping to clear her vision, but it only brought another wave of pain crashing through her skull.

Come on, Violet! Now is not the time to lose focus! She needed to get her baby to safety. *Who are these people? Why are they trying to steal my baby?*

Violet had almost reached the end of the pathway by the time her vision began to clear. But in her disorientation, she'd headed straight for the intruders' van.

No! She needed to get away! To escape. To hide.

As Violet veered to the side, her own dagger sped past her periphery and embedded in a tree trunk to her left. Instinctively she flinched away, but the sudden movement caused her to trip. Twisting herself in the air, she managed to land on her back. The bone-cracking *thud* was nothing compared to Solace's screams slicing through her eardrums. *Did I hurt my baby?*

Violet looked up, and her eyes widened in horror. The woman was looming over her. Blood dripped from the wound on her shoulder, but instead of crimson—or even teal—it was a bright magenta.

"What are you?" Violet whispered.

Her insides turned to granite. If this woman wasn't a human, that meant she was a shifter . . . and Violet knew in her soul she wasn't capable of overpowering a shifter.

The woman's mouth curled into an evil grin. She raised her hand, palm up and fingers splayed. Pink smoke began collecting in a nebulous bubble several inches above the woman's hand, and within seconds, the undulating magenta bubble morphed had solidified into the shape of a dagger, much like the one Sagan's opponent had used.

Fear choked Violet, making it hard to breathe. "NO!" she shrieked. She hated how hopeless, how defeated she sounded. *How on earth can I protect my baby against someone who can literally pull weapons out of thin air?*

With her pulse pounding in her ears, she scrambled to her feet, turning her back on her attacker to run for her life.

Then she screamed.

Fiery agony sliced through the back of her thigh as the dagger's blade buried itself deep. She collapsed to her knees. Pain and panic eclipsed her last surge of adrenaline, and her body began to shudder.

"No," wailed Violet. "Stay away from us. Stay away from my baby!"

The woman stalked over with confident strides.

"You can't have her!" Violet screamed. "You're not taking her!"

"I think you'll find that we are," said a deep voice at her back.

Violet whipped around to see a pair of shiny black shoes and black trousers. She craned her neck back to meet the eyes of a second man in a black suit. He reached down to Violet's screaming baby.

"Nooooo!" Violet clung tightly to Solace, but the man's strength easily surpassed her own. His grip was like iron. Violet wrestled him for a moment, doing her best not to hurt her child, but then Blondie socked her in the face with a hard fist. White lights exploded across Violet's vision, and her baby was wrenched from her arms.

A gurgling cry escaped Violet. *I let her go. I let my baby go . .*

The man turned his back to her and strode toward the van.

Violet made to run to her baby, but Blondie had a firm grip on her, dragging her back.

Exhaustion crashed into Violet, and she stumbled to the ground. She couldn't summon the energy even to try to get back to her feet. Instead she clawed through the soft grass on her elbows and forearms, the sting from the knife still lodged in her leg only a dull hindrance.

The guy opened the van's passenger-side door, and both he and Solace disappeared inside.

"Give me back my baby!" Violet shrieked.

A cold chuckle came from Blondie. "Pathetic," she said, stepping over Violet.

White-hot rage ignited in Violet's core, and her face contorted into a scowl. "I'll show you pathetic," she said through clenched teeth. She swiveled onto her side, reached back to the magenta knife in her thigh, and yanked it free. Then she pushed herself up from the ground and pounced onto the woman's back.

Unleashing all her rage, Violet hooked one arm around the struggling woman's neck and plunged the blood-red tip of the dagger into her chest. Savagely. Over and over and over . . .

An enraged shriek tore from the woman's throat. Hot, sticky magenta liquid splattered over Blondie's chest and coated Violet's hand.

Blondie latched on to the arm around her neck and tried shaking Violet off, but Violet refused to be thrown—to be defeated. She held fast to the dagger now embedded in the woman's chest. The blade ground against bone.

"Give me back my baby!" Violet screeched again and again, drowning out the woman's agonized wails.

Blondie collapsed to her knees.

Violet's attention whipped to the van as the engine roared to life. With a scream of frustration, she tore the magenta dagger from the woman's chest and rushed to the van's tire, burying the blade deep in the rubber. The tire released a sharp hiss when she yanked the knife free.

"No!" shouted the woman behind her.

Violet yelped as something ropelike cinched around her waist and yanked her back. Gravel bit into her flesh as she was dragged away from the van. She tore at the tight restraint, but whatever it was, it seemed impossible for her fingers to pry it loose.

Blondie was still on her feet but bent over, bracing herself on her knees. Her black jacket had been torn to shreds, and magenta gore oozed everywhere, mingling with the torn flaps of fabric. The woman swayed a little as she looked down at the carnage of her own chest.

Violet guessed she'd gotten close to a dozen stabs in before she was thrown off. Any human would be struggling to remain standing. But as for a shifter with magenta blood . . . Violet had no idea if any of the stab wounds were fatal.

Blondie held the magenta handle of a whip in one hand. She tugged hard, and the whip squeezed tighter around Violet's waist.

"Stop playing around," the man called from the van. "Just kill her and let's go."

The woman's fierce gaze bore down on Violet.

Violet whimpered, her fingers clawing at the whip now cutting into her flesh. She glanced up at Blondie, then froze. Terror leached into her veins, polluting every last shred of hope.

The woman's face rippled as her features began to change. Her skin turned molten black—the color of cooled lava. Hairline fractures appeared all over her tarlike skin, growing wider, revealing slivers of molten magenta light. It reminded Violet of volcanoes and apocalypse movies where the earth's crust would split to spew fiery magma.

Streams of magenta blood still oozed from the stab wounds in the woman's chest, the blood sizzling where it dripped into the magenta fissures. When the woman opened her eyes, small magenta flames ignited in each of her eye sockets.

Get up! Violet's mind screamed. *Run!* With panicked desperation, Violet began hacking at the whip with the dagger.

The woman lunged.

In full shifter form, Blondie pinned Violet to the ground like a predator would its prey.

Violet's scream ripped through the air, raw and piercing. "Get off me!" She kicked, bucked, and flailed her arms.

The shifter caught the arm that held the dagger. She opened her mouth wide, then bit down on Violet's forearm.

Violet's whole world narrowed until only the acute pain of the shifter's teeth in her arm remained. It was as if a raging inferno were seeping into her from the shifter's bite, setting her veins on fire, replacing her blood with lava. The agonizing heat spread throughout her entire body.

Violet screamed and writhed, all thoughts and fears for Solace gone. Only the infernal torment existed now. She was no longer Violet. She was pain incarnate.

The shifter hovered over her, once again wearing that twisted smirk. She raised one hand, and magenta fire ignited in her palm. The flames licked down her wrist and toward her elbow, reflecting in the shifter's bloodlust-filled eyes. Her lips moved, but Violet's screams drowned out whatever the woman was trying to say.

Violet wished she would just shut up and deliver the death blow—this agonizing existence was too much to bear. Darkness clouded the edges of her vision. If the shifter didn't kill her soon, Violet was sure the pain in her body would extinguish her life.

The shifter's fiery palm drew closer to Violet's face.

Suddenly, the woman's head snapped unnaturally to the side. The magenta fire in her eyes went out, and she fell out of Violet's view.

Instead, Sagan's face filled Violet's fading vision. His skin was mottled with cuts and bruises, and crimson blood dripped from his head and mixed with the magenta blood on his clothes. His icy eyes were laced with worry.

Blackness consumed the remainder of Violet's sight.

She embraced the emptiness.

AERIFORM COMMUNICATIONS

A BRIGHT TEAL LIGHT ENGULFED NATHAN'S WORLD. HIS INNER eyelids shuttered open and closed, adjusting to the intense exposure of the condensed Venusian beam. A tingle in his skull intensified into painful vibrations as smaller shards of Diamantium sliced through his scaled head, adorning his brow bones, cheekbones, and chin. His canines and premolars lengthened and sharpened. After a moment, his forked tongue slashed out between a triple set of protruding fangs.

Nathan's jaw locked open in a long, guttural roar. His body writhed and flailed, the chains his only tether to the world—

"Nathan, wake up," hissed a voice from the dark. "Psst, Nathan? You awake?"

Groaning, Nathan rubbed at his eyes and face. "Yeah, Thane. I am now."

Thane released a breath. "You were having a nightmare again."

"Sorry. Did I wake you?" Nathan allowed a few moments for his groggy mind to clear. He blinked, but the lights in the cell block had been turned off hours ago. The darkness was the same whether his eyes were open or closed, which made his dreams—his memories—as bright as day against the black.

"Everything okay?" Thane pressed.

"Yeah, I'm fine." A flash of intense blue light danced across his mind's eye, and the memory of his own screaming echoed in his ears. "It's nothing. Go back to sleep."

Nathan hadn't told Thane about the hunters who'd captured him last year and tried to harvest his crystal bones. Verbalizing that memory was something Nathan still couldn't bring himself to do, especially after his encounter with Aphrodite, the hunters' light cannon that blasted condensed Venusian beams on restrained Veniri captives to ensure they didn't return to human form upon death. A Veniri's skeleton was made of Diamantium crystal, whether alive or dead, in human or shifted form—but it was only in shifted form that the large Diamantium shards protruded from the flesh in glittering spires. The hunters prized the Veniri crystal bones, fashioning them into weapons and other tools to aid their grotesque trade.

Still reeling from the nightmare, Nathan absentmindedly scratched his shoulder, not realizing what he was doing until his fingertips glided over the crystallized patch. The familiar tingle of fear washed over his skin, blanketing him in a cold dread.

As he stared into the black, the night stared back. In moments like these, his thoughts quickly began to spiral into hopelessness. He'd seen firsthand how captivity could break a man. He wouldn't, couldn't allow himself to plummet into his abyss of despair now. Thane was relying on him to keep it together. So was Tio, regardless of his arrogant exterior.

But despite his best efforts, tendrils of Nathan's deepest fears crept closer with each passing day, threatening to take hold of him, strangle him. Soon—very soon—he wouldn't have the strength to pull himself away.

Nathan rolled over, and something crinkled in his pocket. He fished out the piece of paper Nika had given him. It was too dark to read the words, but he could see them clearly in his mind.

Midnight. Be ready. Make sure you and the other slith DON'T MOVE!

A growing hope fluttered in his chest. The logical part of him wanted to shred it to bits; it was likely a trap. And yet maybe it wasn't . . .

He snorted. Of course it was a trap. After all, it was a damn hunter who'd given him the note.

But even if it was a trap, what did he have to lose? At the rate things were going in this gladiator hellhole, he was a goner anyway. He might as well find out for sure. Maybe he'd be able to find an escape for Thane and Tio. And if he died in the process . . . hopefully the others could find another way out by themselves.

There was no way of telling what time it was. It wasn't as though shifter gladiators had the privilege of a clock or anything. Hunters could show up at any time, but only for two reasons—to deliver the disgusting slop they considered suitable to feed shifters, or to retrieve the next combatants for the arena.

At night, in the dark blacker than pitch, Nathan had no choice but to wait, with only his building anxiety for company.

Suddenly, a beep—followed by a whir and clank—shattered the silence: the telltale sounds of the cell doors being unlocked. But it wasn't just one door; it was all of them, and there were at least a hundred cells lining both sides of this particular corridor. A few moments later, a chorus of eerie screeches echoed through the inky dark. Nathan didn't need to see to know that all one hundred cell doors had just automatically swung open.

His blood thrummed in his ears. It was almost as deafening as the silence. But things weren't silent for long.

"Oi!" called a Lycan from several cells down. "Wake up! The doors are unlocked!"

A few sleepy answering mumbles rolled up and down the cells. The mumbles turned into confused and cynical comments, and then the collective voices peaked into a tumult of shouts.

"Nathan?" Thane's voice was barely audible over the hysteria. "Tio? You guys awake?"

Before either answered, the hallway lights flicked on. Nathan's eyes slammed shut against the painful, glaring light as the rest of the inmates objected with collective groans and yells.

"What's going on?" Thane shouted over the commotion.

"Not sure yet." Nathan shielded his face with his forearm while his eyes adjusted. Squinting, he glanced around. Most of the inmates were now out of bed, peering out of their cell doors with quizzical expressions and making speculations with their neighbors. After a few seconds, someone tentatively stepped out of his cell. When nothing happened, another Lycan inmate stepped out. Then another.

Finally, someone yelled, "The outer door is open!"

All heads swiveled to the main door of the cell block. Sure enough, their gateway to freedom was wide open.

Without hesitation, a stampede of frenzied werewolves rushed the main doorway. The desperate shifters bottlenecked in the cell block's corridor, pushing and shoving with cries of "Move it!" and "Get out of the way!"

"Thane!" Nathan called out urgently. "Stay put! Tell Tio not to move!"

He couldn't blame anyone for not questioning the how

and why of what was going on. Any captive dog will charge straight for the exit if it's cooped up for too long.

A Lycan stumbled and fell at the doorway of Nathan's cell, and the others trampled over him without a backward glance. The rush of inmates seemed endless. Werewolf after desperate werewolf rushed past, elbows and knuckles clipping against cell bars and sending discordant clangs throughout the prison block. Dozens of bare feet stamped and shuffled over the stony floor.

Eventually the cacophony of voices and slamming bodies died down as the crowd thinned out. Before long, even the straggling Lycans, those unfortunates who'd gotten trampled, limped out after the others.

Finally, only Nathan, Thane, and Tio remained. The frenzied commotion continued at a muted level in the outer hallways.

Is it just our cell block that unlocked? Are any of the other hundreds upon hundreds of Lycans running through the halls?

By now, the hunters were more than aware that at least a hundred of their captives were on the loose. Bellows, roars, and howls outside the cell block had reached a violent crescendo, suggesting that the chaos had turned into a bloodbath.

"Come on," said Tio. "Let's get out of here before the doors shut."

"Wait." Nathan held up a hand.

Tio stopped in his tracks just outside his cell. Thane hadn't moved; his brows were knit together in a skeptical frown.

"We need to stay here," Nathan said.

"What?" exclaimed Tio.

"Why?" demanded Thane.

"Because . . ." *Because why? Because a little piece of paper told me to?* Nathan scanned everywhere—the walls, the ceiling, the floor—for something, *anything* to validate Nika's note.

"Come on. Let's go." Tio bounced on the balls of his feet. "What are we waiting for?"

"Not yet." Nathan flexed his hands, then closed them into fists. His eyes swiveled erratically, searching, searching . . .

"Nathan?" Thane's sharp tone betrayed his own anxiety. "What aren't you telling us?"

After a slight hesitation, Nathan handed him the note.

"Who gave this to you?"

"That female hunter. Nika."

"It's a trap," said Thane, studying the small piece of paper. "It's gotta be a trap."

"What is it?" Tio glanced at the note over Thane's shoulder. "You're joking, right?" Tio's questioning eyes held Nathan's. "You mean to say you've been making friends with the hunters? Why didn't you say anything?"

Nathan shook his head. "I don't know her. I'd never seen her before today."

Tio's incredulous eyes widened. "You'd never seen her before, yet you think she's trustworthy?"

Thane cursed and began to pace in a circle. "This is insane."

Nathan glanced at the open door to the cell block, only about twenty cells away. Lycans and hunters blurred past the opening. Harrowing death cries echoed through the abandoned space around him, slicing through Nathan's indecision. "You're right. There's no point waiting here. Let's go."

Nathan hadn't even reached his cell door when dust sprinkled down onto his head. Shielding his eyes, he looked up at the stone ceiling. An irregular panel of rock shifted above, then was pulled away, leaving a dark void. Half a heartbeat later, a face appeared.

"Hey, it's her," said Tio.

"Hurry up. We don't have much time." Nika threw down a rope, and the end coiled at Nathan's feet. When he didn't move, Nika frowned. "What's the deal? Do you guys want out or not? It makes no difference to me, slith."

Nathan put his hands on his hips. "Who are you? Why are you helping us?"

"Wouldn't you prefer to discuss this after we get out of here?" She wiggled the rope for emphasis.

"How do we know we can trust you?" Thane called up.

"Sagan sent me."

Nathan was taken aback. *Sagan?* "Do you mean Sagan Branstone?"

"Seriously?" Nika looked at him as if he'd just grown a second head. "How many Sagans do you know?"

Nathan and Thane exchanged a glance. Nathan had often wondered what had happened to that young hunter who'd helped him escape from having his bones harvested. Could Sagan still be trusted?

"Soooo, are we doing this?" Tio looked between Thane and Nathan. "Can we trust her?"

A vexed groaned came from above. "Figure out your trust issues quickly. Our window to escape is closing."

Thane gave a sharp, decisive nod.

"Done," confirmed Nathan. "Tio, you're up first."

"Whoa, whoa," Nika protested. "Hold up. I'm only here for you two sliths. Sagan never said anything about a clanger."

Nathan crossed his arms. "Either we all go, or none of us do."

Nika swore. "Fine. Get your asses up here."

After all three shifters had climbed the rope, Nika led them through several stone passages. She held a lantern over her head to illuminate their way. Judging by the light's magenta tinge, the lantern was powered by a Magneii shifter's energy core.

Nathan shook his head. Typical hunters. Why use a standard flashlight when you can incorporate shifter body parts into everyday items?

"What's the deal with these tunnels?" Tio crinkled his nose. "It smells like ass in here."

Nathan rolled his eyes. Trust Tio to remind them all of his adolescence in the midst of a prison break.

Nika scoffed. "That's probably because these tunnels haven't been used in years and years. Tempecrest was a prison in the Dark Ages and was abandoned for about a hundred and fifty years before the hunters took over. These passageways were used by the original prison wardens."

At the end of one of the passages, Nika passed her lantern to Nathan, then pressed her hands against the rough stone wall. A large panel inched outward, and bright light streamed in, bringing with it only silence from whatever lay beyond.

Nika took a second to peek through the crack. "The coast is clear." She pushed the rugged door wide enough for them all to step out into a modern white hallway lined with a number of nondescript doors. "Stay close. Don't let anyone see you."

She darted to the left, and the others followed, with Nathan at the rear. After several more stark hallways—these hunters sure liked their labyrinthine corridors—they rounded another bend and came to a T-intersection, where Nika stopped short. She held a finger to her lips. Voices drifted from around the corner to the left.

"I say we gut him," said a male voice.

"Tempting" came another male voice. "But I'm not sure the consequences are worth it."

"What consequences? If we do it quick and fast, no one will know it was us."

"No, *please*," a new voice said. "There's no need to be rash." That familiar, slimy whine set Nathan's teeth on edge. He leaned in over the top of Nika, Thane, and Tio to get his own look at the conversation.

Three hunters were crowded around someone they had backed against the wall. The hunter in the center was pressing a Diamantium dagger against the victim's cheek—Kronan's cheek.

It took every ounce of Nathan's self-control to stay silent and hidden. To not jump out and drive the hunter's deadly blade into Kronan's flesh.

Just as Kronan's begging began to pitch up into hysterical screams, the crackle of a radio cut through the commotion. Behind the voice on the other end, it wasn't difficult to hear the distinct sound of rioting.

"Copy that," replied one of the hunters. "We're on our way."

"Hear that, slith? Looks like you get a free pass today," said the hunter with the dagger.

The one who'd answered the radio began moving off. "Come on, we better take the stairs."

The other two hunters threw several last threats at Kronan before following their companion down the corridor, their chatter and footsteps gradually fading away.

Nathan backed away from the corner. For several agonizing seconds, there was silence. Then, as one, Nika, Thane, and Tio flinched and waved for Nathan to move farther back. As quietly as possible, they all scrambled to hide in a nearby alcove.

Kronan shuffled past their previous hiding spot. Thankfully, rather than turning in their direction, his defeated form kept walking up the hall in the opposite way the hunters had headed. The soft *pat-pat* of his footfalls was agonizingly slow.

Everyone waited, like statues, not daring to move as the foot-steps retreated farther and farther away.

"I think it's safe," Nika finally whispered. Before anyone could protest, she darted out to check both directions of the intersection. Without a word, she gestured for them to follow, then vanished around the left corner. Thane, Tio, and Nathan shared a silent glance before they hustled to catch up.

Nika was waiting for them at the end of her chosen passage. Thane and Tio went after her, but just as Nathan was about to follow, he spotted Kronan rounding the corner in the opposite direction. His feet felt rooted to the spot. He glanced at the receding backs of Thane and Tio, then to the far corridor where Kronan had disappeared.

Something dark stirred in his gut.

He was already halfway up the hall Kronan had taken when his brain kicked in. *What the hell am I thinking?* But it was too late now. He *had* to keep following Kronan—had to figure out what he was doing here. Every instinct inside him demanded it.

He reached the end of the hallway just in time to see Kronan turn another corner, this time to the right. Nathan hurried to follow, his anxiety spiking higher and higher the farther he got from the others. He should turn around. He should go back and find them.

But he didn't. He kept after Kronan, maintaining his distance, reaching each intersection just in time to see the next turn taken. Finally, Kronan stopped outside a door, turned the handle, and went inside

Nathan bolted and caught the door just before it latched closed. Peering through the gap, he looked into what appeared to be a large storage room. Kronan was heading down a narrow walkway between metal floor-to-ceiling shelving. Cardboard boxes; fat, dusty books; and piles and piles of newspapers and geographical magazines were crammed onto the shelves.

When Kronan was a safe distance ahead, Nathan slipped inside. He wasn't sure if the door would lock closed behind him, so he grabbed a magazine and shoved it in the doorjamb.

A voice called out from the other side of the storage shelves. "There you are. What took you so long, slith?"

Nathan froze. That was Matthias Branstone's voice.

"Nothing," said Kronan after a slight hesitation.

"Hmm, really?" Without even seeing him, Nathan could just imagine Matthias's shark grin as he asked, "Then what happened to your face?"

"I . . . fell." Kronan patted his cheek, smearing the teal blood that trickled from a small cut beneath his eye.

A gravelly guffaw joined Matthias's laugh. "Whose crystal blade did you 'fall' on this time?"

Nathan knew that voice too. He crouched down and peered between the stacks of newspapers. Sure enough, a slightly overweight hunter with a gray beard stood next to Matthias. Wherever Matthias was, his right-hand man, Axel, was close by.

The storage room the two men and the Veniri stood in was like a museum. Every inch of the back wall was covered in framed artifacts—obsidian arrowheads, ancient keys, golden coins, Aztec sacrificial knives carved from jade. Other relics, too big to be framed, were stored in pristine white cabinets that lined the walls. The glass shelving and back-lighting enhanced an impressive collection of antiquities Nathan couldn't even begin to guess the names of.

Matthias and Axel stood at a large white counter in the center of the room, facing Nathan's hiding spot. Both men wore white cotton gloves as they handled a collection of ancient-looking golden books. Various scrolls were bundled at one end of the counter, and at the opposite end sat a square chest about six inches high and a foot long and deep.

The chest was open, though Nathan couldn't see the contents from where he crouched. When Kronan rounded the counter to join the other men, Matthias hastily closed the lid.

Kronan pursed his lips. "Master, if I was privy to what it is you seek, I'm sure I could be of some assistance."

Nathan cringed at Kronan's use of the word *master*. Clearly Kronan's groveling wasn't yet a thing of the past.

Matthias patted the top of Kronan's head with a gloved hand. "All in due time, my little slith."

Kronan scowled when Matthias turned back to the counter.

"I have other uses for you in the meantime," added Matthias. He opened one of the golden tomes and, as gently as possible, carried the hefty relic over to a tall, narrow platform in front of the hanging wall artifacts. After placing the open book on an easel, he carefully covered it with a glass display case, completing the exhibit.

When Matthias moved out of the way, Nathan squinted, but the only thing he could make out on the open pages was a double-spread image of some kind of creature with wings.

"What kind of other uses?" Kronan asked.

"Something along the lines of—" Matthias waved a hand, as if trying to pluck a word from the air "—communications."

Kronan frowned. "Communications?"

Matthias shared a sly grin with Axel, who had picked up several of the scrolls and was walking them over to one of the cabinets behind Kronan. "Yes, I've been waiting on a message." He let his words hang in the air, pinching each fingertip of his white gloves as he slowly removed them. "From your queen, no less."

Kronan's eyes flickered with shock, but his features soon

smoothed into a neutral mask. "You've . . . spoken with her? With Her Majesty? When?"

It was Nathan's turn to frown. Since when did the Veniri queen converse with the likes of Matthias?

Matthias leaned against the counter and inspected his fingernails. "Yes, I spoke with her not too long ago. We organized an arrangement, and you see, I've upheld my end of the deal. But . . . I've yet to hear from your *queen*." He spat that last word as if it tasted bitter.

The Veniri queen speaking with a hunter was one thing, but for Queen Idalia and Matthias Branstone to be making deals together . . . the thought made Nathan's stomach churn.

"I . . . I can help. Yes," confirmed Kronan. "I can leave at once and take a message to her, then return with a reply as swiftly as possible." He bowed his head, much lower than necessary.

"Hmm, that is one idea," mused Matthias.

Nathan held back a scoff. If Matthias was even considering Kronan's suggestion, he was more stupid than Nathan had given him credit for.

"But I have a better idea," added Matthias.

Kronan began to wring his hands, his eyes darting about the room.

A split second after Nathan realized what was about to happen, Axel jumped Kronan and wrapped an arm under his chin. With a flash of crystal, the hunter plunged a Diamantium dagger into the curve between Kronan's neck and shoulder. Kronan let out a startled cry, his hands latching on to Axel's arm, trying to pry it away from his throat, but the gray-bearded hunter held firm.

All the while, Matthias simply waited, silent, until Kronan's struggles began to weaken.

"Call your queen." Matthias's tone was clipped, all signs of lighthearted banter gone.

Nathan blanched. He doubted Matthias meant for Kronan to get out a cell phone and dial the queen's number. *How does Matthias know about our aeriform way of communication?* But then he felt stupid for even thinking the question. If Queen Idalia had been liaising with Matthias, of course she would rather relinquish centuries-old Veniri secrets than leave the safety of the hive to converse with a hunter face-to-face.

Kronan fought Axel's grip for a few more seconds before gurgling out, "I can't." The words turned into a wail of agony when Axel yanked on the dagger still buried in his neck.

"Don't bother telling me you can't," warned Matthias, "because I know you can. She's somehow connected to you, isn't she?" He gestured to the teal rivulets of blood running down Kronan's suit. "It's got something to do with your blood. That much I know. So . . . how much needs to be spilled before you can call your slith queen, huh?"

Kronan didn't answer, but Nathan knew that look creeping over the Veniri's face.

Don't do it. Don't do it. Don't do it.

"Do you need to be alive for it to work?" Matthias asked.

Kronan nodded at once, then immediately winced—most likely because of the knife in his neck, not because he was divulging ancient Veniri secrets.

Coward, thought Nathan.

"What are you waiting for?" Matthias pressed.

Kronan kept his mouth shut, but his face was pale.

"If you don't call your queen right now, Axel will slice you open from jugular to navel," Matthias said softly, but even from where Nathan crouched, he could see the storm clouds building behind Matthias's placid mask.

Without another moment's hesitation, Kronan—unlike any other loyal, self-sacrificing Veniri would have—called upon his Divine Oath connection with the Veniri queen.

Every muscle in Nathan's body tensed as a tendril of teal smoke began to billow from Kronan's wound. No one but the queen dared to instigate an aeriform connection. If Kronan was lucky, she wouldn't answer.

Matthias's fingers tapped faster and faster on the counter with each passing second as the blue vapors swirled lazily in the air. "Where is she?" he eventually asked through gritted teeth.

"She . . . she might be indisposed. Or busy. Maybe sleeping."

Depending on Matthias's knowledge of Veniri culture, it was possible he knew Kronan's blabbering was all nonsense. Whether asleep or not, the queen was very much aware she was being called upon.

Another heartbeat passed. And then another. Until finally Matthias waved a dismissive hand and said, "Kill him."

"NO!" Kronan screamed. "Please, you need me!"

Matthias shoved his face into Kronan's, their noses millimeters apart. "You are of no use if you don't even—"

"What is the meaning of this?"

The room fell silent as all eyes turned to the female figure in the blue mist. Queen Idalia, as usual, was dressed to both intimidate and seduce. Thousands of pearls formed the rigid outline of a ribcage over her torso, the daring design teasing glimpses of her pale skin underneath; one wrong move, and everyone was in for a peep show. A lace choker and ruffled sleeves complemented the decorative chest piece, and the pearl theme continued onto her face, with lustrous dots lining her eyes and lips, spilling across her nose, and swirling over her brow and cheeks.

"Who dares to plague me with their presence?" The queen looked at each of the hunters but scarcely spared a glance for Kronan, despite his outstretched arm to her.

Matthias chuckled, but Nathan still caught the venomous

tone behind it. "Forgive me, Majesty, but our meeting is necessary and couldn't wait any longer."

Idalia glared at him. "And why would you think that?"

Matthias placed his hands on his hips. "Remind me how long it's been since you promised to contact me on the whereabouts of"—he shot a sidelong glance at Kronan—"that particular object we spoke about?"

Fury flashed across Idalia's features before her face smoothed into a guise of composure. "Hmm." She tapped a finger to her lips. "I'm not sure I recall a conversation about a particular object." Her apparition drifted over to the gold tome exhibit and gazed at the winged creature with an expression of nonchalance. "This object . . . is it important?"

"Of course not," said Matthias slowly. "I'm merely upholding our trade agreement. I supply you with what you want, and you give me what I want."

"What I want? Are you sure? Because I believe I'm still waiting on a particular Erathi, Gloria Chambers."

Nathan froze. *Gloria Chambers?* Fear zapped down his spine like a bolt of electricity.

Matthias scratched at the stubble on his jaw. "Yes, well, that woman has proven to be difficult to track down, even for my men. What's your infatuation with her anyway? Surely there's more to this world than trudging to the ends of the earth looking for one measly woman."

Idalia glided over to him, laid a smoky teal finger on Matthias's cheek, and dragged it down to his jaw. "Really? And what more is there? What more could the likes of you possibly offer me?"

Despite the alluring smile that played on the queen's lips, Matthias's eyes narrowed. He pointed to Kronan, now slumped in Axel's grip. "Take a closer look at that slith. He's your cousin, is he not? If you don't give me what I want, I will end him. Right here. Right now."

Idalia fluttered her fingers in an offhand gesture. "Do whatever you like with him."

"No," wheezed Kronan. "Your Majesty, please."

The queen ignored him and turned her back on Matthias.

Matthias's face screwed up with rage. His fists clenched and his body shook. "Don't cross me, slith, or I'll hunt you down. I will send every last hunter out to find you, and I'll tear every last blood-soaked shard from your wretched body."

Idalia cast him an imperious glance over her shoulder. "We're finished. Don't contact me again." With a flurry of blue, her apparition vanished, and the remainder of the teal mist dissipated.

Matthias roared out a torrent of foul abuse, punching and swiping at the empty air in a vicious tantrum. All the while, Kronan was screaming, begging for Idalia to save him, but his cries were cut off when one of Matthias's punches landed square in the Veniri's face. Axel released Kronan and let him tumble to the floor. The faint rise and fall of Kronan's chest confirmed that he was still alive—for now, at least.

Matthias slumped against the counter and let his head drop into his hands.

"Do you think she figured out what it is?" Axel cleaned the blade of his Diamantium dagger with his white gloves.

"Perhaps, or perhaps not. She probably figures if I want it, it's something worth keeping in her possession." Matthias raked his fingers through his hair before throwing his arms down in frustration. "After five millennia, the shifters have practically forgotten all about the spangles, or at least their history . . . and what they're rumored to be capable of."

He opened the chest on the counter, and Axel came to stand next to him.

"Well, you have four of them at least," said Axel.

"Four is not ten," said Matthias, as if he were speaking to a moron. "I need all ten."

Axel shrugged. "We know where the teal one is. That slith queen playing coy confirmed that. And we know where the purple one is—we just need to figure out how to get it, considering none of us have any gills. As for the orange one, well, apparently the clangers' prince keeps it on his person— at least, that's the word on the street. I've got one of my boys tailing him, and he'll send word when the time is right." Axel twisted a strand of his gray beard between his fingers. "Although, we do have a clanger here now. What about the idea of using him as bait?"

Matthias shook his head. "No. That would only work if he was a member of the royal family. This one's just a boy Hestus and Quill picked up at a video game arcade."

"Hmm . . . still, that only leaves the gold, black, and emerald ones."

"Yes, thank you for that insightful rundown." Matthias's tone dripped sarcasm. "In the meantime, the new plan to acquire the teal one is—"

Nathan jerked as a sharp pain in his ribs snatched his attention away from Matthias and Axel's conversation. He looked down to find a Diamantium dagger digging into his side, held by a livid Nika.

"What the hell?" she mouthed, yanking on his arm and forcing him to follow her quietly out the door.

When they were several paces down the hallway, she whirled on him. "Have you got some kind of death wish? I swear, if I didn't have explicit orders from Sagan, I would've left you here to rot. Do you have any idea how freaking hard it was to find you?"

Nathan didn't bother answering. Yes, following Kronan was possibly one of the stupidest things he'd ever done. Nevertheless, he'd found vital information.

But . . . what the hell was a spangle? And why did Matthias want them so badly?

Nika swiftly led him back through the hallways. They had to pause once or twice to wait for hunters to pass by, but on the whole, the corridors were still empty. Perhaps things weren't yet under control with the Lycan escapees.

Finally, the two of them reunited with Thane and Tio in another unused part of Tempecrest, based on the rugged stone walls and dusty, uneven flooring. Thane's expression as they approached was a mixture of curiosity and annoyance.

"I'll explain later," Nathan promised.

Ducking into a large stone room, Nika stepped up to the edge of a round hole in the floor. She glared pointedly at Nathan and inclined her head to the black opening. "You first."

"Seriously?" Tio asked. "You want us to go down there?"

"Do you want out of here?" Nika retorted.

"Yeah, but . . ." Tio's nose scrunched up as he studied the hole. "Is that what I think it is?"

Nika rolled her eyes. "Get over it. These sewers haven't been used for hundreds of years. Besides, it's the quickest way to the boat."

At the mention of a boat, all three shifters scrambled down through the ancient latrine and through the sewer tunnels.

Only once Tempecrest Island was a distant speck on the watery horizon did Nathan finally feel free.

7

SHATTERED BEYOND REPAIR?

EVERY MUSCLE IN VIOLET'S BODY ACHED—NO, BURNED. IT WAS as if every cell, every molecule, sparked into a blaze whenever she moved. She knew she ought to stay still, but her stiff body desperately needed a stretch. She groaned; even stirring slightly sent flames of pain licking down her spine.

"Hey, it looks like she's finally awake."

Her fuzzy mind couldn't quite place the familiar voice. She tried to open her eyes, but exhaustion weighted down her lids. *Maybe I should just go back to sleep.*

Then an image of a blonde woman burning with magenta fire flashed in Violet's mind, bringing with it the memory of extreme, agonizing torment.

Pain. So much pain.

She sat up and immediately regretted it, doubling over as the inferno roared to life inside her. *What is wrong with me?*

"It's okay, Violet. You're safe now," said Gus.

A hand touched her shoulder, and she flinched away, but the searing pain only intensified. She whimpered and wrapped her arms around her chest.

"Try to relax," Gus said.

Heeding his advice, Violet attempted to calm her thoughts and body. She referred back to some of the grounding exercises her psychiatrist in high school had shown her when she was still dealing with PTSD symptoms after being kidnapped.

She closed her eyes.

Breathe in. One, two, three.

Breathe out. One, two, three.

Squeezing her eyes tighter, she tried to understand what was happening, to analyze the torture her body was feeling. Her instinct was to flee, to run away from the pain and, if she couldn't escape, to scream and curl up in a ball. But the more she fought against the agony, the more she realized she was fighting against herself. The intense suffering was foreign, and yet it was somehow a part of her. It was . . . strange. Unlike anything she'd ever encountered before.

Changing tactics, she tried embracing the pain instead. Slowly at first, and then almost all at once, the torment vanished. It was as if the moment she succumbed to the fiery agony, her body was able to absorb the pain and dissolve it.

With a sigh of relief, she lay back against her soft pillow and slowly opened her eyes. She was lying in one of the infirmary beds. Gus was perched on the edge of the mattress, and Sagan stood close by.

"Hey, guys. What happened?"

Sagan and Gus glanced at each other, their expressions serious.

A wave of panic crashed through Violet. She shot up, looking around wildly. "Where's Solace?" The guys refused to meet her gaze; sorrow and grief hung thick and tangible in the air. "Where is she?" Violet demanded, clenching her hands into fists.

"I'm so sorry, Violet," said Gus. "She . . . they took her."

"No." Violet's voice was barely a whisper. Deep despair

settled on her chest, squeezing the air out of her lungs, stopping her heart. She clutched at the fabric of her shirt. "Noooo . . ."

The memory reel of what had happened flashed in her mind.

Skye screaming.

Skye's and Cruz's bodies.

So much blood.

Solace screaming.

People in black suits.

Solace screaming.

A blonde woman kidnapping her daughter.

Magenta fire.

Severe, burning pain.

Darkness.

Uncontrollable sobs racked Violet's entire body. Skye and Cruz were dead. Murdered. Gone.

And her baby—her daughter had been taken. Snatched from her arms.

A gaping void grew in her chest, erasing her, eating her from the inside out. All she wanted was to have her daughter back, safe in her arms.

When the tears began to roll, Gus pulled her into a bear hug, and Sagan rested a gentle hand on her shoulder. Several minutes passed before Violet was able to speak, to even attempt to articulate the competing questions and thoughts churning in her head. She wiped the stream of tears away with her sleeve, but more continued to pour down her face. "How long have I been out?"

Gus grimaced.

"About two days," said Sagan.

Violet's jaw dropped. "What?"

Helplessness consumed her. *Two days* had passed since Solace had been taken. How could she possibly track down her daughter? She didn't know where to start. She didn't even know who had taken her.

"You've given us quite a scare." Gus gave Violet a sad but warm smile. "Mom and I have been keeping a close eye on you while you've been out." He gestured to Violet's arm, where an IV was attached with medical tape. "When you didn't wake up after a few hours, we figured it was best to take precautions."

Nodding was all Violet could manage. Emotional numbness washed over her, hollowing out her insides. Flashes of half-formed plans to get her child back warred with the steady onslaught of crippling grief. She allowed Gus to plump up her pillows and vaguely registered that he was checking her temperature and blood pressure. For the past nine to ten months, this vital checkup had become so familiar it was as if she'd memorized a dance.

"Any improvement?" asked Sagan.

Gus's brow creased, and his lips pressed into a thin line. "Hmm . . ." He picked up the chart at the end of Violet's bed and scribbled down some notes.

"What's wrong?" Violet asked dully.

Gus scratched his chin with the back of the pen. "I don't want to confirm or deny anything just yet, at least not without a blood test. Hopefully that will shed some light on your situation. In the meantime, you should try to eat. I'll go get Aunt Skye—I mean . . ." A blanket of grief enveloped the room as Gus fumbled to correct himself. "I mean . . . I'll let Mom know you're awake."

He gave Violet a quick hug, then disappeared.

Sagan sat in the chair by her bed. "How are you feeling?"

Solace is gone. My baby is gone . . . Violet wiped away a rogue tear and swallowed hard, forcing her despair down, down. She needed to be strong. She needed to be strong to find Solace. "I'm . . ." She was what? Devastated? Breaking on the inside? Shattered beyond repair? But then she realized Sagan was referring to her physical injuries. "I'm fine. At least . . . I think I am." The fierce pain hadn't returned, but somehow she could still sense the fiery inferno coiled up deep inside her; it was just waiting.

Waiting? Violet almost scoffed at how stupid that idea was. *Waiting for what?*

She pushed the thought aside. "How are you?" she asked Sagan.

He dismissed her question with a shrug. "Fine."

"I'm serious."

He met her gaze. "Let's just say I've been worse." Several cuts over his lips, brow, and face were either scabbed or almost healed, and faint yellowish bruises could still be seen around his eye, cheeks, and jaw. He pointed to Violet's face. "I'm not the only one who managed to get a collection of battle scars."

Violet raised a hand to her cheek, and her fingers brushed against gauze and medical tape. She winced at the sudden pain in her forearm. More bandages covered her left arm from wrist to elbow, and a scattering of small cuts marred the underside of her right.

"You fought hard, Violet."

Tears stung her eyes and blurred her vision. "Not hard enough." She had given it everything, and yet her child had still been taken away from her.

Sagan was kind enough not to reply.

Blinking away her tears, Violet asked, "That woman in the suit, what happened to her?"

An intensity flashed behind his ice-blue eyes. "I'm sorry, Violet. While I was checking if you were okay, she managed to escape."

A flicker of rage ignited in Violet's belly, but intense

exhaustion doused it into a smoldering ember. "What about the guy, the one you fought in the house?"

Sagan raked his fingers through his hair, then dropped his hand to the black chain around his neck. "I've dealt with him. No need to worry about him anymore."

Violet's nod was somber. "They were shifters . . . weren't they?"

He heaved in a lungful of air before nodding. "They were all Magneii. In the same way werewolves are linked with the moon and the Veniri are linked with Venus, the Magneii are linked with Mars."

"Oh." Violet allowed herself a few seconds to let that sink in. "What do these aliens from Mars want with my baby?"

Sagan shook his head. "They're not aliens, just like werewolves aren't aliens. All the shifters are supernatural entities, whether they're linked with the moon, Mars, Venus, Saturn, or any other celestial body in the solar system. They just know how to utilize energy from their associated planets to fuel their transformations and abilities. But as for why they took Solace . . . I have no idea."

Violet pressed back into the pillow and stared at the ceiling. "How?" She fisted the sheets in her hands, gripping the fabric tight. "How did they even know about Solace?"

"We have reason to believe it was Macie who told them."

Violet was taken aback. "What? The midwife? But . . . why?"

"Macie and her husband were relatively new to Maple Shire, and other than helping out in the infirmary, they kept to themselves. But after Solace was kidnapped, we found Macie and her husband dead in their bedroom." He fiddled with the black chain. "It's possible Macie got spooked when she saw Solace shift in the delivery room and contacted someone—we're not sure who. She probably wasn't counting on a group of Magneii showing up instead."

Violet's breaths quickened. "Are you telling me that Macie, my midwife, called in a bunch of psychos to assassinate my daughter? Are you telling me that Solace—"

"No." Sagan leaned forward and placed his hands on top of hers. "I'm not saying what you're thinking. I think she's still alive."

"How do you know for sure?" Her voice cracked, and a tear rolled down her face.

"Because if they wanted Solace dead, why go through the trouble of taking her with them?" He raked a hand through his hair, then slumped back into his seat with a huff. "I just haven't figured out why they took her. Solace is important somehow."

"Of course she's important!" Violet started to kick her sheets off. "We need to go find her."

"Hang on, hang on." Sagan held his hand up. "Two days ago, you took an epic beating from a Magneii shifter, you woke up from a coma less than an hour ago, and Gus is still concerned about your current state. We can't go and—"

Violet scoffed. "I'm fine, okay? I don't need you or Gus holding me back!"

Sagan gently but firmly took hold of her shoulders to stop her from getting out of bed. His pale blue eyes were fierce, but his words were soft and calm. "Don't talk about Gus like that, especially after what his family has had to deal with the past few days. Not to mention the lengths both he and his mom went through to make sure we didn't lose you too."

His words felt like a punch in the face. Violet dropped her gaze to her lap and began stroking the scar between her thumb and forefinger where Solace had bitten her.

Sagan was absolutely right. She wasn't the only one who had lost someone. Shame bubbled up in her gut as she recalled Skye's and Cruz's butchered bodies in their own home. The blood-smeared walls. Their open, glazed eyes. Violet wrapped her arms around herself and hunched over. While she still had the hope of finding her daughter, Autumn would never see her parents again.

She dared to meet Sagan's eyes. "Skye and Cruz?"

"We buried them yesterday. I'll take you to them when you're ready to see them."

About a minute passed before Violet finally found the courage to say, "I'm sorry."

Sagan gently squeezed her shoulders, then released her. "It's okay." After a few heartbeats of silence, he held out her switchblade. "Here. I found this."

"Thanks." Violet palmed it, the familiar dips and curves of the pearl-and-gem-encrusted handle fitting comfortably in her hand. It was originally a gift from Nathan, from when he'd first started training her in self-defense. Violet wasn't sure why she kept it—a constant, painful reminder of his betrayal—but she still couldn't bring herself to throw the switchblade away. Carrying it with her everywhere had become too strong of a habit.

"That woman, the Magneii, she had a pink knife . . ."

"Do you mean this one?"

Violet's eyes grew wide as Sagan held up a dagger. Its handle and blade were a deep magenta, and an organic swirling pattern along the flat of the blade seemed to pulse with a dull glow when Violet took it. The thing that surprised her most was how tangible—how *material*—it was.

She turned it over and over in her hands. "It's . . . real. But she created it. I saw her. It formed in her hand out of nothing."

"Yeah," confirmed Sagan. "I've seen it happen a few times. One minute a shifter is empty-handed, and the next there's a throwing axe being hurled at my head."

"If the knife's real, why didn't it work?"

Sagan frowned. "What do you mean?"

"I stabbed her. With this knife. But she . . ."

"Didn't die?"

"Right."

Sagan didn't look surprised. "The Magneii have an energy core in their skulls, right behind their eyes. It powers their abilities, such as fire and accelerated healing. The best ways to kill them are to cut off their heads or damage their power core."

"Oh." Violet studied the magenta dagger. She held up her own switchblade and found the release button with her thumb. *Shnik.* The teal blade flicked out from the center of the pearlescent hilt. She held up the two weapons, side by side. The pattern on her own teal blade was similar in style, except for the two emerald-green and deep-magenta veins that wove through the teal.

"What?" Sagan asked. "What's wrong?"

"Nothing. Except . . . that's weird. These used to be black." She ran her thumb along the line of black gemstones embedded in the switchblade's hilt. Two of the gemstones were now glowing, one teal and the other magenta.

Sagan's pale blue eyes narrowed at the gems.

"Sagan," Violet said in a quiet voice.

"Yeah?"

"I want you to teach me how to fight."

"But you already know how to fight."

She shook her head. "No, I've been taught how to defend myself. I want to learn how to *really* fight. I want you to teach me how to kill someone."

Sagan opened his mouth to speak, but before he could get a word out, Dawn bustled in. She greeted Violet with a warm smile and a hug. "I'm so glad to see you're awake."

Dawn fussed for several minutes over Violet's chart, dressings, and cuts, asking questions to gauge her level of discomfort. During the consultation, Gus came in with a dinnerplate piled high with food. Sadly, it wasn't as homey as a meal prepared by Skye would have been, but Gus's father, Lazareth, had stepped in to take over the cooking, and it was clear he was doing his best to fill the void.

While Violet ate, Gus and Dawn swapped notes regarding Violet's current state. They both agreed she could be discharged from the infirmary after she'd had her bandages changed.

Dawn patted Gus on the shoulder. "Mind if I leave this in your capable hands while I go check on"—she shot a quick glance at Violet—"our more delicate patients?"

Interesting, Violet thought. It wasn't like Dawn to be cagey.

A sudden tingle grew under her tongue, and she stopped chewing for a moment as she waited for the bizarre sensation to pass. Maybe it was a reaction to flavor overload after not eating anything for a few days, or a side effect of whatever pain medication Dawn and Gus had her on.

After Dawn left, Gus pulled over a trolly of medical supplies.

"So, Dawn has you looking after patients by yourself now, huh?" Violet observed.

"Sort of. She's got me doing the more basic stuff I've done a million times already. A few of the neighbors got caught in the crossfire during the attack, and now it's like the infirmary has a revolving door. Burns, broken bones, cuts, scrapes, post-traumatic jitters, nightmares—we've been getting all sorts. The community leaders have been trying to calm things down by saying Macie and her husband were once involved with a violent gang and their past finally caught up with them, but still, everyone's shaken. And on top of everything, three travelling women showed up in the midst of all the drama, desperate for medical attention. Mom's been run off her feet, so I'm trying to shoulder some of the load. Besides, it helps to . . . you know . . . keep busy."

He cleared his throat and occupied himself with a pair of latex gloves. Before he'd finished putting them on, he turned back to her, and his eyes narrowed with concern. "Your cheeks are flushed." He pressed the back of his hand against her forehead. "Geez, you're burning up. Are you feeling okay? Hot, maybe?"

Violet shook her head. "I don't feel hot. I feel fine." Recalling the odd sensation under her tongue, she added, "I was a little tingly before."

Gus frowned. "It might be worth getting you some antibiotics, just to be safe." He snapped on the second glove. "All righty, how about some fresh bandages?"

When the old bandage on Violet's forearm was removed, she inspected her wound. The mangled flesh had the bumpy appearance of an acid burn and was edged with pink scar tissue. Once Gus had applied the new dressing to his satisfaction, he removed the IV from Violet's hand and gave her the all-clear to leave.

Sagan walked her back to her room at Autumn's place. Stepping back into the kitchen nearly broke Violet's heart. Of course Skye's and Cruz's bodies were gone and all the blood stains had been cleaned away, but the pristine walls and floor couldn't erase the memories of carnage from Violet's mind.

Her ultimate challenge was walking past her daughter's empty room. She couldn't, *wouldn't* look inside. When she collapsed in a heap of misery and tears a foot away from the nursery door, Sagan offered to retrieve some fresh clothes for her.

The next day Violet struggled to find a new routine, one that didn't involve changing diapers, midnight feeds, and frequent cuddles with Solace.

It killed her that she couldn't just go out and turn the world upside down to find her child. She'd lost count of how many times she'd sat in her jeep with the keys in the ignition, ready to search—*needing* to search. But how? Was she supposed to drive around and shout Solace's name out the window? Even going to the police wasn't an option. She could just imagine the officers' expressions: "Yes, Mister Officer, the blonde woman transformed into some kind of monster that looked like it crawled out of a volcano. And the van with my kidnapped baby drove in that direction— although, I can't be too sure of that, because I passed out and was in a coma for two days."

Until she came up with a plan that didn't include plastering missing-person posters of her Veniri infant all over the state, she needed to keep herself busy. The best solution she could come up with to keep her roiling grief and despair at bay was getting involved in the community, cleaning up the devastation of the attack. Violet had received many hugs and condolences from her Maple Shire neighbors, and most of the children would give her flowers when she'd cross paths with them. As far as everyone else knew, Solace had sadly been an innocent victim in Macie's "gang war attack." A little memorial for Solace had been placed near where Skye and Cruz were buried, but Violet couldn't bring herself to go see it.

The outdoor pavilion had become the new eating area for everyone. It housed about ten banquet tables with bench seating, carved from trees from the bordering forest. The area was usually reserved for weddings and other celebrations, but since the attack, the community families had banded together to contribute potluck dinners, baked goods, and homegrown produce, ensuring everyone was looked after and provided for.

Two days after waking up from her coma, Violet noticed

how hard it was to track down Autumn. Her larger-than-life, dreadlocked friend had become a ghost. At breakfast, Violet caught sight of her snatching food from the buffet table. She called her name over the noisy morning conversations, but Autumn made no sign of hearing her before hurrying away.

"Give her time," said Lazareth, who was sitting at the same table. "Autumn's dealing with her grief as best she can. We all deal with grief a little differently." He wrapped an arm around Gus and hugged his son tight. "She'll join us when she's ready."

After breakfast, Violet wandered around the compound, searching for any task to distract her racing mind. She came across the little building Cruz had built to be Autumn's computer lab. The curtains were drawn, but light gleamed out of a gap in the fabric.

She stopped just before she knocked on the door. When Lyla died, all Violet had wanted to do was curl up under her blankets and be left alone to mourn. Maybe Lazareth was right and the best thing to do was give Autumn her space. Perhaps Dawn had some jobs for her to do in the meantime.

As she searched the infirmary's halls for Dawn, a cacophony of chattering, cooing, and crying stopped Violet in her tracks. The door to one of the multi-bed ward rooms was open, and she couldn't resist poking her head in for a peek. About a dozen cots lined the room's walls, but only three were occupied, all by women bouncing, nursing, or singing to their babies.

Tears pricked Violet's eyes; the gaping void in her chest became unbearable. What she wouldn't give to have her daughter back in her arms.

Dawn stood in the middle of the room, her vintage blonde bob lit up like a halo by the sunlight streaming in through a large window. She gave an exhausted smile when she saw Violet, and gestured for her to enter.

"Hello, Violet. Let me introduce you to Yumiko, Pradhi, and Genevieve." Dawn gently took the baby from Yumiko and coaxed Violet to have a closer look. "This little guy here is one of our 'delicate' patients."

Violet's eyes bugged as flickers of iridescent blue began to ripple over the baby's smooth skin. "Wait . . . is he . . . ?" Before she could utter another word, the baby had completed his transformation.

"Yes, he's a Veniri." Dawn nodded and smiled. "In fact, all three of these babies are."

Pradhi, Yumiko, and Genevieve all shared concerned looks.

"It's okay," Dawn reassured them, but only after she'd explained that Violet had also given birth to a Veniri baby did the three mothers' expressions and postures relax.

"Where's your child?" Genevieve asked.

"She's . . ." Violet struggled to hold back the torrent of tears pressing against the backs of her eyes. "She was taken." Absentmindedly, her fingers brushed against the small bite mark on her hand.

All three mothers shared a wide-eyed look.

"She?" Pradhi asked.

"But that's impossible," blurted Yumiko.

"Not impossible," Dawn said, handing the baby back to his mother.

Violet rocked from one foot to the other as the women gaped at her with mixed expressions of shock and awe.

Genevieve stood up from her bed and came over to Violet. "Would you like to hold him?"

Violet gaped at the precious bundle in Genevieve's arms. "Are you sure?"

Tucking a lock of wavy auburn hair behind her ear, Genevieve smiled kindly. "He's just been fed and needs a burping. You'd be giving my arms a rest."

After hesitating for a few moments, Violet gently took the baby in her arms. Her heart instantly ached; the infant felt about the same size as her own daughter. "I'm guessing he's about ten weeks old?" she asked, her voice unsteady.

"You'd be correct." Genevieve climbed back into her bed, visibly exhausted. She snuggled against her pillows and pulled the blankets up. Two of her fingers sported small bandages.

With Genevieve's permission, Dawn proceeded with a typical vitals check, then marked her findings on the chart at the end of the bed. Violet took a seat in one of the empty chairs and placed the wriggling baby over her shoulder, just as she used to do when burping Solace.

About twenty minutes later, when both mother and child had fallen asleep, Dawn laid a hand on Violet's shoulder. "Come on, it's lunchtime."

Violet and Dawn strolled through the gardens toward the pavilion, crossing paths with several members of the community. A woman herded about half a dozen sheep out of their way, and a group of rowdy kids with swimmers and towels barreled past. The youngest child halted when she saw Violet and ran over to give her a hug and a heartfelt "sorry for your loss."

"You're really good with children." Dawn smiled after the young girl bounding off to catch up with the others.

Violet, unsure how to respond, shoved her hands in her pockets and stepped off the path to make way for a man carrying a large wooden crate. The heavenly aroma of freshly picked strawberries drifted in his wake.

"If you think you're up to it," continued Dawn, "I do need an extra hand in the infirmary, especially with Yumiko, Genevieve, and Pradhi. Technically, their presence isn't a secret, but I've been keeping it on the down low. I don't need medical help, but . . . do you remember when I told you about human women being kidnapped and forcibly impregnated by Veniri?"

Violet grimaced. "Yeah, I remember."

"Well, I have a friend who works in helping these enslaved women escape their Veniri captors, and she sent Yumiko, Genevieve, and Pradhi to me. Aside from helping them rehabilitate, there's also some daily assistance they need, with all the diapers, laundry, bottle sterilizations, and—"

"Yes!" exclaimed Violet, a little too loudly. She gave Dawn a sheepish smile, then at a more suitable volume, added, "Yes, I'd love to help out. With whatever the mothers or their babies need."

"Are you sure? Because I wouldn't want you to feel—"

"I'm sure. Don't worry about me. I just want to help."

Dawn studied her for several seconds, her gaze analyzing but kind. Finally, she nodded and laid a hand on Violet's shoulder. "Thank you. You know, it's funny, all the mothers are suffering from the same flulike symptoms you did, and just like you, they acquired them not long after their child was born. I wonder if it has something to do with . . ." Dawn stared off into space and tapped a finger against her lips, then paused and shook her head. "I'm sorry. I'm sure the last thing you need is me babbling on about some kind of medical anomaly regarding inter-shifter pregnancies."

"It's fine. I don't mind." Violet did her best to give Dawn a reassuring smile.

She startled Violet by pulling her into a swift, sudden hug. "Thank you, even though I know you're not fine. Thank you for your help today." She kissed Violet on top of her head. "Let's find the others and get some lunch."

The pavilion was buzzing with people by the time they arrived. Violet paused at the bottom step of the wooden platform. "You go on ahead. I'll have lunch back at the house."

Dawn's frown was subtle. "Are you sure?"

"Yeah. I think I'm a little peopled out at the moment. Maybe I'll just skip lunch and go straight for a nap."

"Okay." Dawn nodded in understanding. "I'll come and check on you when I'm done."

Leaving Dawn behind, Violet meandered back through the floral-scented paths and along the edge of the gravel driveway. As she rounded the garden that bordered the house, she stopped dead in her tracks at the sight of an unfamiliar car parked in the driveway. A group of people stood by the car. She spotted Gus and Sagan first.

Then her eyes locked with another familiar face.

Rage tore through her like a hurricane. She sprang forth.

"Violet! Stop!" yelled Sagan.

His words scarcely registered. In a second, she'd reached the group of people and launched into the air. Her victim's eyes widened a split second before she collided into him. As they crashed to the grass, Violet's hands wrapped around Thane's throat.

"Stop!" Someone grabbed her from behind and yanked, breaking her hold on Thane's neck.

Thane sucked in a gulp of air.

The rage inside Violet boiled over—she was livid he was still breathing. Her fury ignited, to her surprise, quite literally.

Several cries broke out as aquamarine flames burst to life in her hands. They crackled just above her skin but, astonishingly, didn't burn her.

A cough from Thane recaptured her attention.

She grabbed the hands on her waist that were dragging her back, away from Thane. Instantly a man screamed, and the hands disappeared.

Thane sat up, clutching at his throat, heaving in lungfuls of air, but Violet immediately tackled him back to the ground. She punched his face. Again and again. Left fist, right fist.

More yelling erupted behind her.

Thane's shock had worn off. His eyes bore into hers, her flames reflected in his golden-brown eyes, but he didn't even try to block her pummeling. He wouldn't fight her. He would probably even allow her to kill him.

She hated him even more for it.

"VIOLET! DON'T!"

Something solid crashed into her side and sent her rolling over the grass. Breathing hard, she scrambled to her feet.

Sagan, the one who had tackled her, jumped up too. He eyed her burning hands and backed away, careful to keep himself between her and the man she desperately wanted to tear apart. Thane had managed to half sit up, his hand still wrapped around his throat.

"Violet?"

She snapped her head toward the voice, recognizing that calming tone.

Nathan.

Bitter betrayal slammed into her.

At the same moment, stabbing pain tore at her flesh from the inside.

A guttural scream ripped through Violet's vocal cords. She threw her head back and writhed, searching in vain for relief, blinded by the endless torment. Panic quickly chased away her remaining anger. *What's going on? What's happening to me?*

When the agony finally began to fade, something glittered in her periphery. She held up her arms and gaped at the texture of her iridescent magenta flesh—no, not flesh. *Scales.* Foot-long crystal shards protruded from her elbows, and even more jutted up elsewhere on her body: her shoulders, torso, legs. Her clothes hung off her body in tatters, torn to shreds by the crystal spires.

"What's happening to me?" Violet's voice cracked as cold fear constricted her lungs. She glanced at the onlookers, but they answered only with wide, shocked eyes and small gasps.

No one said anything.

A tingle under her tongue appeared with overwhelming force. Then, like a whip, a forked tongue lashed out of her mouth. An alarming number of vibrant flavors engulfed her —molasses, pipe tobacco, mint, nutmeg, sour apple, jasmine, ginger, rhubarb. It was all too much. Her hands clamped over her mouth.

Pure terror raced through Violet's veins.

This wasn't natural. She wasn't natural.

Something bit into her chest, and numbness began to trickle through her body. Sagan was pointing what looked like a handgun at her.

She glanced down, expecting to see a bullet wound. Instead, a small metal dart was embedded in her scales below her sternum. Fury began to boil inside her again as the numbness continued to spread, paralyzing every limb until she had no choice but to fall to the ground. Within seconds, Violet was completely immobile.

Faces peered down at her. Sagan, Gus, Nathan, Thane, and two strangers all towered over her prone, rigid body.

She tried to scream her fury, to force herself to move. But her lips wouldn't work; every muscle refused to obey her desperate commands. Nothing, not even a whimper, escaped her.

Gus heaved a deep breath. "Can someone please tell me what the hell just happened?"

8

ITTY-BITTY DIAMANTIUM-TIPPED NEEDLE

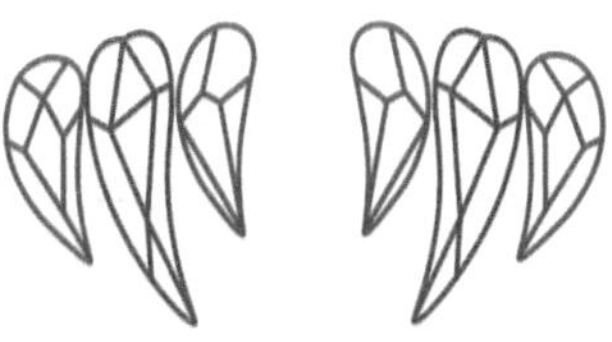

"So, what now?" Gus said again. "Nathan?"

"What?" A few silent seconds passed before Nathan tore his eyes away from the paralyzed Violet. "Why are you all looking at me?"

"Uh, maybe because you're the most experienced in this kind of thing," said Thane.

"Me? I've never seen anything like this. Surely Sagan's had more experience, with the number of shifters he's encountered."

Sagan threw up his hands. "I haven't seen anything like this before either."

The room fell back into silence. One by one, everyone's attention returned to the unmoving girl on the bed.

After Sagan shot Violet with the tranquilizer dart, he, Nathan, Thane, and Tio had carried her through a secluded path to the community's medical facility, where they'd found a spare bed in a private room. Nika had followed and was now hovering just outside the open door, her dubious glare fixed on Violet.

"We can't keep her like this," Gus said, breaking the silence. "We can't just keep her sedated until we figure out what's going on."

"Or can we?" mused Tio.

In answer, Violet's eyes once again ignited with teal flames.

Gus grimaced. "That's definitely a no."

The blue flames sparking in Violet's eyes set Nathan's teeth on edge. She shouldn't be like this. She shouldn't be incapacitated as if she were a dangerous animal. And she certainly shouldn't be able to manifest crystal shards, blue flames, or any other shifter attributes. How did this happen? Or rather, *who* made this happen?

Fury bubbled up in Nathan's chest until he finally snapped. He rounded on Thane, took a fistful of his shirt, and shoved him up against the wall. "You bit her, didn't you?" he roared.

With a ferocity Nathan wasn't expecting, Thane shoved him back, using the momentum to pivot so that Nathan became the one pinned.

"No," said Thane, his voice a deadly whisper. "I would never. You think I want her to have this life? Or even risk killing her?"

Nathan's jaw clenched and unclenched as he let Thane's words sink in.

It was true; a human could become a shifter from a bite. But unlike what happened in the movies, the shifter's bite was usually too toxic, and the human almost always died. If turning humans was as simple as biting them, his race wouldn't need to rely on kidnapping and impregnating human women to raise the number of female Veniri.

Nathan saw the truth in Thane's golden-brown eyes—the gold flecks startlingly bright, almost overpowering the natural brown. With a jolt, Nathan realized he'd known the young Veniri was innocent all along. No, the person who really deserved blame was himself. He'd wanted to keep Violet well away from the shifter world—believed she was safer in her ignorance. But look how badly that had backfired.

"Then if you didn't bite her, who did?"

"As if I would know," Thane growled. "I've been locked up with you the whole time."

It took a second for Nathan to relax his grip on Thane's shirt, then a second more to pluck up the courage to make eye contact. "You're right."

Thane studied him, testing Nathan's sincerity with his eyes instead of a lash of his Veniri tongue. Then, with a firm nod, he released him.

"Sheesh," said Tio after a beat of awkward silence. "For a minute there, I was getting some serious Tempecrest flash-backs. I'm glad everyone's hearts remained in their chests."

Gus's eyebrows skyrocketed. "Tempecrest? What's that? Actually, come to think of it, who are *you*?"

Tio chuckled. "Right. Sorry. With all the excitement of Thane getting his ass kicked by your resident flamethrower here, introductions have been neglected." He patted himself on the chest. "I'm Tio, and you are?"

"Gus."

Tio raised one hand for a high five. "Put 'er there, Gus."

Gus stared at Tio's palm. "Right. What about her?" He turned his attention to Nika.

"Oh, that's Nika," said Tio. "Don't mind her. She's not one for chitchat. Also, don't let the cute factor fool you. She's more of the don't-feed-after-midnight type."

Nika glared daggers at him.

"See what I mean?" Tio tilted his head and pointed a

finger at Gus. "You know, you kinda look familiar. Have we met before?"

Gus frowned and shook his head. "No, I don't think so."

"You sure? Because I'm not one to forget a face."

Nathan ignored the rest of Tio's continuing babble; he'd had lots of practice during their travels from Tempecrest. Though the journey had been long and tough, following the tricky path Sagan had texted to Nika was vastly preferable to being a slave in the gladiator arena.

At least ten minutes had passed since they'd brought Violet into the ward room, and other than the flames shooting from her eyes, she had yet to show signs of the paralysis wearing off. Even without the flames, Nathan could still see the raging fury in her stare—the frustration and fear.

"I suppose I could start with a blood test," Gus finally said. "That's all I can think to do at the moment, unless Mom comes up with a better idea." He frowned. "Hopefully she'll be here soon."

He asked Violet for permission to draw some blood. When no flames flared from her still-open eyes, he took it as an okay. He disappeared from the room, then returned a few minutes later pushing a trolly stocked with medical supplies. After putting on some latex gloves, he wrapped a tourniquet around Violet's arm. "Okay, Violet, here comes a little pinch." He angled a needle into the crook of her elbow.

A thought struck Nathan just as a small metallic *ting* rang out.

"What the . . . ?" Gus held up the snapped tip of the hypodermic needle. Mumbling something about cheap equipment, he reached for a new one.

"Actually," said Nathan, "I just remembered. Based on the scales and Diamantium spikes, chances are needles won't be able to pierce Violet's skin anymore."

Gus's jaw dropped. "That's . . . crazy. How am I supposed to—"

"Give me a second," said Sagan. He rushed out of the room, then came back a minute later with a small needle in his hand; its tip glittered under the lights. "Try one of these."

Gus's eyes widened. "Do I want to know why you have a diamond-tipped needle with you?"

"Old habits." Sagan shrugged. "Just try it."

Nathan glanced down at the impression of a hunter's amulet hidden beneath Sagan's shirt. No need to guess as to what "old habits" referred to.

This time, the needle glided smoothly into Violet's arm, like a skewer testing a perfectly cooked cake. Thane let out a small hiss as blood immediately gushed into the attached glass tube.

"Hey, it worked," said Gus.

"Ugh," said Tio. "I think I'm going to be sick. Tell me when it's over." His hand clamped over his mouth as he rushed out into the hallway.

Nathan shook his head. The Jiovis shifter could handle having his arm cut off and regrown, but pull out an itty-bitty needle and he was running for the exit.

After a couple minutes, Gus finished filling the last vial, then held a sample up to the light. "There's something about this that already seems a little unusual." He narrowed his eyes. "The color is . . . different."

He handed the vial to Nathan, and Thane and Sagan crowded around for a closer look.

Nathan's eyes grew wide. The liquid inside was a rich magenta swirled with a vibrant teal. Only upon closer inspection did Nathan spot a tiny vein of crimson.

"What is going on?" Thane asked. "What's happening to Violet?"

Nathan floundered for an answer. "I . . . can't even begin to guess. Sagan, any ideas?"

Sagan looked just as clueless as the others. "Can't say. I've never seen or heard of anything like this."

"Hopefully"—Gus plucked the vial out of Nathan's hand—"in a few hours, the blood test results will be able to shed some light."

9

TROUBLE WRITTEN ALL OVER

Violet blinked. Finally, the paralysis was starting to wear off. If only she could move her hands to rub her dry eyes, but no luck on that front yet. Blinking would have to do for now.

Boy, was Sagan going to get the tongue-lashing of his life once she regained the ability to speak.

"Here, Violet, I got you an extra blanket," said Gus. "It's starting to get a little chilly."

Warmth covered Violet's body. She tried to at least murmur her thanks, but still, only her eyelids would obey her command.

Her panic had mercifully died out, especially after Dawn shooed everyone out of the infirmary room a few minutes ago. Now, Gus was filling his mother in about what had happened. From her prone position, Violet couldn't see Dawn's face, but she could imagine the doctor tapping her lips with one finger as she processed the particulars of Violet's new condition.

They didn't say so in as many words, but Violet could tell

the two of them were a little fearful as, in hushed voices, they began brainstorming ideas to discover what was wrong with her: X-rays, MRI scans, tissue samples, ongoing observational tests. Some of the procedures they mentioned sounded painful—maybe even a little extreme.

Hello? Violet tried to say. *I'm still here. I can hear you, you know?* Didn't she have the right to be part of the conversation? It was her body, after all.

As she waited, immobile on the bed, turmoil and rage and helplessness seeped into every corner of her conscious thoughts. She hadn't been able to save her daughter—couldn't even try to look for her now that she was gone. In the one way she'd promised she never would, she'd failed Solace, and on top of everything, Violet was morphing into some kind of unknown, dangerous monster. Everything—even her own body—had spun out of her control.

And now, of all the freaking places on the planet, Nathan and Thane had shown up here.

Blue flames flared from her eyes, and her breathing doubled in speed. It was the only outlet she had for the writhing fury that fought against the drug paralyzing her body.

"It's okay." Dawn stroked Violet's hair. "You're safe."

Safe? Thane was here. Thane, who had kidnapped her and her best friend, Lyla, when they were sixteen. He'd been there when Lyla was murdered and Violet was left for dead. And then the sicko had tracked her down and invaded her life when she was in college, all while keeping his true identity hidden. Only after she'd fallen for him had she seen that damned tattoo and unlocked the truth.

And as for Nathan . . . ?

Tears gathered at the corners of her eyes.

When Lyla died, Violet's only tether to this world, to this life, was ripped away. But Nathan had taken her under his wing. He'd offered her a place to stay when no one wanted her. He'd helped rebuild her shattered existence, not just by giving her a home but by teaching her self-defense so she could overcome her fears and leave her trauma behind.

When the nightmares of her captors plagued her, he'd always assured her she was safe. Even at her lowest, he was there, as a shoulder to cry on or just a silent, calming companion as she coped with her grief. Nathan was her anchor.

Violet had always hated the term *father figure*. It made her think of cheap knockoffs, like bootlegged movies or fake designer purses with the brand name spelled incorrectly—the original, authentic version could never be beaten. Violet didn't know who her real father was, but when she imagined what the best father in the world would be like, Nathan came pretty close.

But the day she found out who Thane really was—the day she'd fled to Nathan, only to find him standing in the kitchen with the man who'd kidnapped her and allowed her best friend to be murdered—all of that was dashed to pieces.

An endless stream of tears ran down her face. Someone dabbed them away with a tissue, then tucked the blanket tighter around Violet's body. A few moments later, Dawn's face appeared in Violet's periphery.

"Violet, I've just sent Gus on an errand, but I've realized it's been a while since I checked on the mothers and their babies." She placed a hand on Violet's cheek, her fingertips resting on her temple. "I'll return as soon as possible, all right?"

Sure, I'll be fine, thought Violet, hoping her blinking somehow communicated the mental reply.

Dawn smiled. She gave Violet a peck on the forehead and disappeared.

Immediately, Violet regretted Dawn's departure. There

was nothing left to distract her from the turbulent fire stirring deep in her core. Thankfully, the burning wasn't as intense as it had been; it was as if the towering flames of her anger had died down to a slow molten churn, just waiting for the next eruption.

The air around her shifted. Violet couldn't see, but she could feel that someone had entered the room and was standing near her bed. Whoever it was, they didn't step into view, remaining still and silent.

A patter of footsteps came in a few minutes later, followed by a feminine voice Violet didn't recognize. "Oh, there you are, Thane."

Thane? What is he doing here? Violet scowled. *Oh, hey! I can move my eyebrows.*

"I've been looking everywhere for you," said the female voice again.

"Well, you found me." Thane's voice was monotone, very different from what Violet remembered about him. A silent second passed. "What do you want?"

"Just wondering what you're doing."

Thane didn't answer.

"So, are you thinking what I'm thinking?"

Thane's sigh dripped with disdain. But disdain for what? For the woman he was talking to? Or was he just not in the mood for talking? "I'm not sure I want to know what you're thinking, Nika."

Nika? That was the name of the girl that new guy, Tio, was talking about.

"Well, think about it. Have you seen anything like that happen? I know I haven't. And if you ask me, that shifter—or hybrid or whatever that thing is—has trouble written all over it."

"She. Not *it*," said Thane, a dangerous edge in his tone.

"Whatever. The point is, something needs to be done before this all blows up in our faces."

Violet's heart began to thud faster. She didn't like where this conversation was going. With a surge of desperation, her fingers twitched.

There was a scuffle of shoes, followed by a loud *thud* against the wall and a feminine *ooph!*

"And what is it you think 'needs to be done,' Nika?" Thane hissed.

"Careful, Thane. Don't forget it's because of me that you're not still rotting in Tempecrest."

Thane growled. "You think I owe you? Is that it?"

Nika's hard tone matched Thane's. "I'm not cashing in, if that's what you're worried about. But what you should be worried about is that shifter on the bed."

For a few moments, no one said anything. Violet kept flexing her fingers. Sensation had started to creep into her toes, so she began to wiggle those too.

"Let me make this crystal clear," Thane said. "If you ever go near Violet, if you even look at her in a way I don't approve of . . . I will end you."

Nika scoffed. "You can try, slith. But I'm telling you, whatever is going on with that shifter, it's not right. So don't come running to me when all hell breaks loose. And another thing"—a *crack* of skin smacking against skin resounded through the room—"don't ever touch me again."

Heavy boots stomped out, then faded down the hall.

Silence.

For a moment, Violet assumed Thane had left with Nika, though she still hadn't regained enough mobility to move her head to check. Fingers, toes, eyebrows . . . *ugh!* That wasn't enough! She needed to get out of here.

Once again, anger and frustration ignited the teal flames in her eyes, covering her world in a wash of light blue.

"Don't worry, Violet."

Startled, Violet extinguished her flames. *He's still here?*

"No one is going to hurt you. I'll make sure of that."

10

UNFAMILIAR SOUL-TRAILS

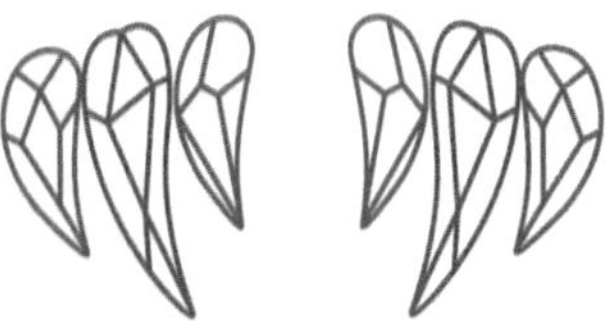

Nathan had assumed he'd be relieved to finally reach Maple Shire, especially after trekking from what felt like one side of the country to the other.

His profound elation at seeing Violet had twisted into crushing guilt the moment she'd looked in his direction. Nathan couldn't shake the memory of the mighty rage in her eyes. When she'd bolted across the driveway, he'd been certain he was the target of her fury, but she'd sailed right past him to pummel Thane instead. Nathan hadn't known whether to feel relieved or wretched. In the end, shock eclipsed all else when, after just one call of her name, her wrathful eyes had turned to him, and she'd hazed.

She'd hazed.

But she didn't just have crystal shards and scales; she had *magma and fire.*

How could that be?

The blazing eyes and hands were a telltale Magneii ability, yet Violet's flames were teal, not magenta. Nathan couldn't even begin to imagine how Violet had acquired dual abilities. It was unheard of. Impossible.

When Nathan left the infirmary, Sagan had filled him in on the Magneii attack that had resulted in four murders and the destruction of Maple Shire's peace. When Nathan had demanded Sagan take him to the scene, the young Erathi led him back to the gravel driveway next to one of the community houses.

Sagan pointed. "Four days ago, this is where—"

"Don't." Nathan held up a hand. "Give me a chance to get an impression of what happened first."

In reply, Sagan gestured for him to proceed, then planted his hands in his pockets.

Nathan inspected his surroundings, just as he'd done for countless crime scenes when he was a detective. Scuff marks, tire treads, and long grooves of what may have been finger drags were still visible in the gravel, and small clumps of upturned earth marred the grassy area on one side of the drive, perhaps caused by a scrimmage. Several yards away, beyond the grass, Nathan spied a gouge mark in the trunk of one of the garden trees. The straight, unsplintered score suggested it wasn't made by a claw but rather a knife or blade.

Nathan's tongue whipped through the air. The remaining scents were a little stale, but he would make do.

Though the daytime sky hid the stars beyond, his tether to Venus remained strong. Closing his eyes, he angled his face toward the planet and tuned in to the melodic hum of energy that radiated from above. His body quickly responded to Venus's beckoning, and thin inner membranes slid over his still-closed eyes.

When he opened his outer lids, the world remained the same. Then he lashed out his Veniri forked tongue, and it completely transformed.

A variety of neon, smoke-like trails mingled in the once-empty air over the lawn and driveway. Just as the phosphorescent tendrils began to fade, he flicked his tongue again, and they pulsed back to life. Nathan immediately registered the essence of a few unfamiliar soul-trails among the flavors. They coursed from the house and along a garden path until a large concentration collected over the lawn by the driveway. The soul-trails briefly tangled with another, but there was something amiss. Something didn't quite add up, almost as if there was a void among the entanglement.

Nathan zoned in on the collective mass of soul-trails. He heaved in a lungful of air, then expelled a foggy puff of Venusian energy. The subtly glowing cloud dispersed among the phosphorescent wisps, latching on to the strongest emotional echoes of the past.

With another gust of energized breath from Nathan, the mist revealed a frozen image: a woman, her arms wrapped around . . . nothing. But her fierce expression and the angled formation of her body suggested she was trying to drag something—or someone—away.

Violet!

The void was Violet. Of course Nathan couldn't track her. Years ago, unbeknownst to her, he'd put Veniri poison glands in her lower back to act as a shield, to protect her from being tracked by any Veniri.

The luminescent scene before him began to fade. He flicked his tongue and it pulsed back to life, allowing him to study it further.

It was clear the woman was determined to keep the void —Violet—from reaching the remaining soul-trails of a man walking toward the van. In the man's arms was—

"A baby?" Nathan spun around to stare at Sagan in shock.

"Yeah."

Nathan's gaze flitted between Sagan and the void in the misty impressions of the woman's arms. "And Violet? She's . . ."

"The mother. Yes."

Nathan scrubbed his face with his hands, then locked his fingers together on top of his head. "How is this possible?"

Sagan quirked an eyebrow. "I'm not going to explain the birds and the bees to you."

"No, I mean, who . . . ?"

In answer, Sagan's lips pinched into a thin line.

Nathan groaned. "Thane. But . . . if he's the father, that means"—his knees almost buckled—"the baby is Veniri."

Sagan slowly nodded.

"Does Violet know?"

"She knows."

How did it come to this? Nathan had failed. He'd failed to protect Violet, to shield her from the world he'd tried to leave behind. All that effort to keep his true self hidden from her, and now . . . "She must've lost her mind the first time the baby shifted."

"Not really. It was a surprise, yes, but it wasn't the first time she'd seen a Veniri in shifted form."

Nathan looked up. "What?"

Sagan filled him in on what had happened after Violet found Thane in their kitchen and fled, how she'd discovered Sagan standing in the middle of the road, and together, they'd escaped a trident-wielding hunter and a Veniri.

Nathan pinched the bridge of his nose. That Veniri must have been Kronan. Too bad that scum hadn't met his demise in Tempecrest.

"I'm not sure if I should've told you all this, especially since Violet can't speak for herself at the moment. I figure she'd want the choice whether or not to reveal who her daughter's father is."

"Daughter?" Nathan's eyebrows shot to the sky. "Are you sure?"

"Definitely."

"But Veniri females are—"

"Rare. I remember you telling me."

Turning back to the phosphorescent trails, Nathan scratched at the stubble along his jaw. "A Veniri girl changes everything."

"I thought it would. Can you track her?"

Nathan lashed out his tongue again. The soul-trails from the pair who'd left in the van streamed down the long driveway and faded out of sight. "It would be complicated. For starters, we're dealing with Magneii. Even if they hadn't left in a vehicle, they're not as easy to track as the Erathi. Besides, I haven't actually met . . . What's Violet's daughter's name?"

"Solace."

A heartbeat passed before Nathan said, "Wow." That name, that *word*, was fundamentally what Violet wanted out of life: a place to call home, a family who loved her. Safety. Peace. *Solace.* "Unfortunately," he continued, "because I haven't met Solace, I haven't got a stable impression of her soul-scent."

Sagan moved to his side, staring with him toward the forest where the van had disappeared. "So what do you suggest?"

"Well, kidnapping aside, it's the presence of Magneii that concerns me. Magneii don't just randomly show up out of the blue and decide to kill and kidnap. They're not warmongering or predatory—they're mercenaries. Someone sent these shifters to kidnap Violet's daughter. If we can find who's been writing the checks, chances are we'll also find Solace."

11

"WHAT THE HELL" KEEPS COMING TO MIND

VIOLET SHOOK HER STIFF ARMS AND SWUNG HER LEGS OVER THE edge of the bed. It was great to get the blood flowing back into her limbs.

"How are you feeling?" Dawn asked.

"Physically? Not so bad. Mentally? The phrase 'What the hell?' keeps coming to mind. Emotionally? . . . Let's not go there."

"As far as we can tell, you're healthy." Gus ripped the blood pressure cuff off her arm.

Violet groaned and rubbed her eyes. "Then what's wrong with me? How is it that I'm all of a sudden . . . fiery? And not in the metaphorical sense."

"You also grew crystal shards," added Gus.

"Yeah, I remember." Violet winced and rubbed her elbows. "Those really hurt. But seriously, last I checked, I was just an average, non-superpower-wielding human. What's the deal?"

"I think it's safe to say you're definitely a shifter, but as to what kind . . ." Dawn's lips pressed into a thin line.

"Without a doubt it has something to do with that

Magneii attacking you," said Gus. "But that doesn't explain why you've got Veniri attributes as well. From what the others have said, you're really lucky to be alive. Humans normally die from a shifter bite. It's really rare that one survives. But even if we set that mystery aside, we still don't know why you're a Magneii and a Veniri—and a *female* Veniri at that."

"What do you mean?" Violet asked.

"Veniri females are extremely rare," said Dawn. "Apparently only one in every hundred Veniri born is female. I don't know if you noticed, but all the Veniri infants currently in the nursery are males."

Violet's eyebrows shot up. "But what about Solace?"

"Like I said, you're really lucky," said Gus.

"But hang on. I wasn't born Veniri, nor was I bitten, so . . ."

Gus's eyes suddenly grew as round as saucers.

"What?" Violet asked.

Gus didn't say anything. Instead, his gaze fixed on a point far away.

Dawn laid a hand on Gus's cheek. "What're you thinking?"

Shaking his head to break the trance, Gus bolted out of the room. Before he disappeared into the hall, he called over his shoulder, "I have a theory, but I need to check the blood test results again, before I can confirm anything."

Violet turned back to Dawn, who gave her a reassuring smile.

"Try not to worry yourself too much," said Dawn. "With some further testing, observations, and precautions, we'll soon find some answers—maybe even a cure."

"A cure?" Violet was surprised by how much that concept troubled her. Yes, okay, before the day started, she didn't have flames burning from her eyes or shards of crystals sprouting over her body. Was that super freaky? Heck, yes! But for the first time in her life, she felt powerful. As if maybe, just maybe, she could take back control from all the things that had been making her life hell.

So the idea of having her newfound abilities taken away . . .

Thane's face flashed in her mind.

She couldn't shake the discomfort of knowing Thane and Nathan were now close by. She was bound to run into one or both of them as soon as she left the infirmary. How long did they intend to stay? Hopefully not long at all.

But what really gutted Violet was being taken off duty from helping out with the Veniri babies and their mothers.

"It's not because we don't trust you," explained Dawn. "It's just that we don't know yet the extent of your powers—let alone the extent of your control. And God forbid . . ."

Violet hung her head, not needing Dawn to finish her sentence.

Once Dawn had rattled off a number of tests and an examination schedule, she deemed Violet fit enough to leave the infirmary.

Violet stepped out into the fresh evening air. *Evening?* The day was over already? The moon shone bright in the navy sky above. The absence of city light pollution meant the Maple Shire heavens were vibrant with stars. The Milky Way —a mottled band of color—was a photographer's dream. It had been ages since Violet used her camera; she'd left it behind when she fled Nathan's. Any photo she'd taken of Solace had been on her phone. Maybe one day she'd invest in a new camera, but that was way, *way* down on the list of her current priorities.

With a heavy sigh, Violet weaved through the orchard and past the beehives. The soft melody of an acoustic guitar, along with the scent of smoke, reached her just as she came across a few families roasting marshmallows over a campfire. Their invitation to join in was tempting. When was the last time she'd done something so relaxed and carefree? But she had other plans first. It was about time she became reacquainted with Autumn.

Rounding the corner, she bumped into someone coming the other way.

"Sorry," said Violet and the other person simultaneously.

She froze.

Thane was looking down at her, wearing the same shocked expression she was.

She couldn't bring herself to do or say anything, considering the last time she was this close to him, she was raging on him with her fists. Not a bruise, cut, or any proof of her abuse was evident on his face, which surprised her—every ounce of her strength had driven those strikes. But then she remembered he was Veniri. *Does that mean they don't get hurt like humans?*

"Hey, Violet." Thane wrapped a hand around the back of his neck.

"Hey," she mumbled.

"How are you?"

"Fine."

A muscle twitched in Thane's jaw.

The two stood stiffly, awkward tension rising as the silence dragged out.

Thane opened his mouth, but whatever he was about to say was interrupted by a chorus of giggles from behind Violet. Two teenage girls paused in their laughter to openly ogle Thane. Only when they passed did they resume their giggling, flicking glances at him over their shoulders. All the while, Thane's eyes never left Violet.

She huffed. Hugging her arms around her torso, she stepped around him and continued down the path.

"Violet?" he called after her.

She glanced back, not sure what had compelled her to stop.

"I just want you to know that I can explain . . . everything. But . . ." His mouth hung slightly open.

A few seconds passed as Violet waited for him to collect his thoughts.

"I'll leave it up to you to figure out when—or even if— you're ready to hear it."

Violet couldn't bring herself to respond, not even with a nod or a shake of her head. Instead the smoldering inferno in her chest flared to life. She hugged herself tighter and turned her back to Thane.

She needed to find Autumn.

Thankfully, Thane didn't follow her as she trudged up the path to Autumn's little computer hut. When she reached the door, she gently peeked her head in, hoping to find any sign of her dreadlocked friend.

"Whoa," Violet said under her breath. Unlike the dark hacker labs Violet had seen in movies, this place was well-lit with white light. Several desks lined the large room's perimeter, and computer screens of varying sizes were *every-where*, mounted on the walls. A number of power cords led back to a massive black box in the corner of the room. The box was covered with red, green, and amber flashing lights. Violet could only guess it was a server of some kind.

Sitting at one of the desks, surrounded by about seven screens, was Autumn. Her legs were folded up on the swivel chair she was on, and her cheek rested on top of her knee. Flickering images on the screens reflected garish colors onto her face. Other than the low hum of the electrical equipment, the familiar *clack-clack* Violet always associated with Autumn was the only sound in the room.

Violet took another tentative step inside. She spotted a

stretcher bed by Autumn's desk and recognized the rumpled band shirt Autumn wore when she slept. No wonder Violet hadn't seen much of her friend. When was the last time Autumn had even left this room?

Dreadlocks spun as Autumn whipped her head to the doorway. Her eyes momentarily widened, then narrowed into a subtle frown.

Violet couldn't disguise her own shock at Autumn's gaunt cheeks and dark-rimmed eyes. Hesitantly, she stepped forward and gave her friend an unsure smile. "Hi."

Autumn swiveled back to face the screens. "What are you doing here?"

Another flicker of heat added to the fire in Violet's chest. "Seriously? We haven't seen each other in what feels like forever, and after everything that's happened, the first thing you say to me is 'What are you doing here?'"

Autumn dropped her feet to the ground and pinched the bridge of her nose. "Don't be so dramatic. It's only been two days. Besides, I've been a little busy, okay?"

"Busy? Too busy to even come and see if I'd woken up from my coma?" She gestured to the stretcher bed. "Have you even bothered to leave this room?"

"Geez, Violet." Autumn smacked a hand down on the desk, hard. "Not everything is about you, you know?"

"What do you mean by that?" Her hands balled into fists, and the molten anger inside her began to surge.

"I mean, ever since I met you, everything's been about you." Autumn stabbed a finger at her.

Violet floundered for a response. "I . . . I don't understand. How has it been all about me?"

Autumn put on a dramatic pout and said in an overemphasized whine, "Poor Violet doesn't know who her parents are. Poor Violet gets knocked up, then finds out her boyfriend is a kidnapping maniac. Poor Violet has daddy issues with the only guy who ever gave a damn about her. Poor Violet failed in protecting her own daughter—"

Violet darted forward.

Crack!

Autumn's head snapped to the side before Violet even registered she'd backhanded her friend. Mouth gaping in horror, she curled her stinging hand against her chest. *What did I just do?*

Autumn covered her cheek with her fingers, her face hidden by dreadlocks.

Seconds dragged by.

Violet bunched her hands into fists, the molten anger within her demanding to ignite. It took all her effort to fight it back. To distract herself from the rage, she scanned Autumn's screens. Two flickered through surveillance footage of various locations within Maple Shire. Another displayed online news articles with random mugshots and images of people Violet didn't recognize. But the big screen in the middle captured her full attention.

A wave of shame and understanding slammed into Violet's center. She placed her hands on her burning cheeks. "Oh, Autumn . . ."

The screen displayed several stills of CCTV footage from the inside of Autumn's house, capturing the macabre images of Skye and Cruz only seconds after their deaths. Violet spotted herself in one of the screenshots, as well as Sagan— paused in mid-fight with the male intruder in the black suit. Another capture showed the woman entering Solace's room. The zoomed-in images of the man and woman had been cleaned up and enlarged, their blurry faces looking out at Violet from yet another computer monitor.

Violet dropped her hands to her sides, and her shoulders drooped. "Oh, Autumn. I'm so sorry." Submerged in her own grief over the loss of her child, she hadn't seen that Autumn had been drowning. Shame knotted her insides. Of all people, she should've recognized Autumn's anger and harsh words as the result of deep anguish. She knew what it was like to lose someone forever. To never be able to see a loved one again.

"It's taken me ages," said Autumn in a soft voice, "but I've finally found the people who killed my parents." She looked Violet square in the eye. "And I think I know where they've taken Solace."

HELIX HOAX

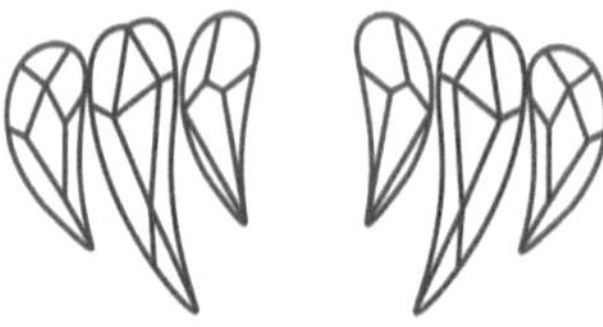

NATHAN TOWEL DRIED HIS HAIR. AFTER ALMOST A YEAR IN Tempecrest, even the small freedom of showering and putting on fresh clothes felt like a luxury.

He wrapped the towel around his waist, then wiped down the condensation on one of the mirrors in the men's communal bathroom. He couldn't remember the last time he'd looked in the mirror. Tilting his head from left to right, he examined the subtle changes: a little more gray in his dark hair, new hollowness to his cheeks, a scruffy salt-and-pepper goatee along his jaw—he'd tried his best to keep his beard trim in Tempecrest, but Diamantium blades weren't the best tools for the job. The most alarming change was his eyes. There was something more wizened behind his tawny eyes— maybe even wild—about them. Was it because he'd spent so long fighting for his life? Or was this just a part of getting old?

He unboxed the brand-new safety razor Lazareth had kindly donated to him and inserted a new double-edged blade. Then he sprayed a puffy mound of shaving cream onto his fingertips and smeared it over his chin. A flash of reflected light caught his eye.

Realization sent an icy chill shivering through his body.

The glimmering light had come from *him*. The crystal patch on the back of his shoulder had grown; it was now spreading down along his bicep. Light gleamed off the polished facets when he rotated his shoulder. He tapped at the area with his fingernail, and it made a melodic *ting-ting-ting*.

What is going on?

It wasn't the first time he'd asked himself that question, but it was clear he could no longer pretend he didn't want to know the answer.

He reached down to check his leg, and his heart sank. What had started as a small patch on the back of his calf had expanded over his shin and down to his ankle. He straightened and spun to check the other side of his body but, in doing so, knocked the can of shaving cream off the sink.

With lightning speed, Nathan reached out and caught the can. It burst with a *bang* and a *pffffssshhhh!*

"Damn it!" White foam leaked out in fat dollops, expanding like something from a demonic horror movie. The mess all over the sink and floor was unbelievable. He glanced down at the mutilated hunk of metal in his hand. He didn't even think he'd squeezed it that hard.

A few minutes and about five extra towels later, he finally had the shaving foam explosion under control.

"So, this is where you've been hiding."

Nathan looked up as Tio leaned on the sink next to his. The teenager raised an eyebrow at the small mountain of towels.

"Uh, there was a malfunction with the shaving cream." Nathan nodded toward the twisted metal in the sink, then, with a jolt of panic, realized he hadn't put a shirt on yet. He snatched his button-up and shoved his arms through the sleeves, glad Tio was standing on the other side of his crystallized shoulder.

"Right . . . malfunction, huh?" Tio sounded dubious as he picked up the can between his thumb and index finger. He dropped it back in the sink with a clatter and leaned against the wall. "So, where have you been all day?"

"Here and there." Nathan finished buttoning his shirt. "I've been trying to make sense of why a small group of Magneii would attack a place like Maple Shire."

Tio grimaced. "Those shifters are messed up. They'd sell their own mother for the right price."

"No kidding. So, what about you? What have you been up to?"

"I met this chick named Autumn. She has a sick computer den, by the way. And get this—it turns out she's the legendary *Helix Hoax*, one of my hacker buddies from way back."

"Oh, really?" Nathan almost chuckled—what did "way back" mean for a sixteen-year-old? He remembered meeting Autumn, Gus's dreadlocked cousin, and seeing her computer tech all over the room when he'd moved Violet into her dorm, so it didn't surprise him much to hear about the girl's "legendary" status. He had been a little surprised, however, to find out Maple Shire was Autumn and Gus's hometown. It was good to know Violet had found a home with friends after she'd fled Brookhaven.

"Yeah, anyway," continued Tio, "I put two and two together when I remembered I once supplied her and her buddies with some fake IDs. I knew I'd seen that Gus guy before. And come to think of it, the same goes for that hybrid-shifter girl. Can you believe it? I've met Helix Hoax *in the flesh*. Who knew she was a dreadlocked hippie chick out in the middle of hicksville? Who knew she was a *chick*? You know, I'm pretty good behind the keyboard, if I do say so myself, but Helix Hoax—she's a beast! There ain't a hacking forum out there that isn't talking about her. And what's more, she's set me up with my own tech. Geez, it's good to be back in front of a screen."

"And keeping out of trouble, I hope," said Nathan.

"Trouble? Me?" Tio sniggered. "Aw, it hurts that you don't know me at all."

Nathan grinned and shook his head. "Just don't get caught, kid."

Tio scoffed. "I never do."

"Never, huh?"

"Er, I mean, I never get caught *online*."

Nathan barked a laugh and mussed Tio's hair. "Yeah, yeah, you're a real angel in disguise."

"Hey!" Tio swiped at his hand. "Watch it! Touch the hair again, old man, and I'll take you on. Your 'Dog Shredder' rep doesn't scare me."

"You had to bring that up." Nathan groaned. "I'm trying to put Tempecrest behind me."

Tio quirked an eyebrow. "Good luck with that. I'll probably still have nightmares about it well into my twenties."

"Yeah, well, we can't go back and erase what's been done. We can only move forward. We have to learn from our mistakes and promise ourselves to do better."

"Riiiight," drawled Tio. "Is that Shakespeare or something?"

Nathan shook his head and gave Tio a good-natured pat on the shoulder. "One day when you're older, it might make some kind of sense to you."

Tio just smirked at him—a smirk that explicitly said, "Okay, Boomer."

"Look, all I'm saying is, nightmares or not, I'm just glad I'm out of there."

"Agreed," said Tio. "You know, for a little hick town, this place ain't too bad."

Nathan chuckled. "Compared to Tempecrest, anywhere isn't too bad."

"Yeah, I suppose you're right."

Since the remnants of the shaving cream had been washed down the sink, Nathan made do with what little remained on his face to finish shaving. The new razor was a dream, gliding smoothly over his jaw. He was almost done when he realized Tio had gone silent.

"What's up?" Nathan asked, rinsing the razor.

Tio shrugged a shoulder. "Nothing."

"Come on, kid. I've spent almost a year being two cells down from you. I know that look. Something's up, so spill."

Tio sighed and raked a hand through his raven hair. "I, uh, finally got in touch with my brother."

"That's great."

Tio's expression became somber.

"That is great, right? You'll finally get to see your family again, and I'll finally get to meet this big brother you keep talking about. What was his name again?"

"You don't understand. It was my fault I got caught. I didn't stay put like I was supposed to." Tio crossed his arms. "Believe me, this reunion isn't going to be a joyous occasion. My brother is going to kick. My. Ass."

"Aw, come on." Nathan nudged Tio's arm. "I'm sure it won't be that bad. If he is angry, I bet it's to hide the fact that he's been worried sick about you. It's a big brother's job to look out for his younger siblings."

Tio chewed his lip. "I wish that were true. But in my family, I'll be punished to ensure I've learned my lesson."

"Well. I'm all out of encouragements." Nathan sucked in a breath through his nose. "So . . . good luck, kid." He grabbed his belongings and headed for the exit.

"Wait!"

Nathan paused in the doorway.

Tio winced. A few seconds passed before he spoke. "Will you, uh, come with me when I meet up with my brother?"

"Of course."

The young Jiovis's face broke into a wide smile, his shoulders sagging with relief.

"When's the rendezvous?" Nathan asked.

"I'm waiting on a confirmation."

"Just let me know when and where, and I'll be there."

13

HERE KITTY, KITTY

VIOLET TURNED THE KEY IN THE IGNITION, AND THE JEEP'S engine roared to life.

As soon as Autumn had revealed she'd found Solace, anything she said afterward turned to white noise. When a map appeared on Autumn's computer screen, Violet committed a single name to memory—*Rivermyre*. Then turned and ran out of the room. Her friend's confused shouts, quickly muffled as the door swung closed, had fallen on deaf ears.

Violet booted up the GPS and typed in Rivermyre. The suburb was located across the river from where she'd gone to college. She recalled hearing a few details about it; some fancy-shmancy developer had bragged that Rivermyre would be a utopia, featuring ostentatious high-rise accommodations with killer views, extravagant cafés and restaurants, and a shopping district with hundreds of designer stores.

But halfway through construction, the developer went bust. Now, Rivermyre was a deserted wasteland of half-finished apartment buildings, known as the City of Silence.

The cold voice of the GPS announced it would be a two-hour journey. *Two hours?* Frustration ramped up Violet's heart rate. Forget the road rules—she was going pedal to the metal. As soon as she got there, she would have all guns—or rather, hands—blazing. After all, with her new arsenal of crystal blades and a triple set of fangs, she was practically invincible. One way or another, she was bringing her daughter home. *Tonight.*

Just as she was about to put the car into gear, the passenger-side door opened, and Sagan slid in.

"What are you—?" Violet cut herself off as both the back doors opened too, and Tio and Nika jumped into the backseat. "What the hell? What are you guys doing here?"

"Coming with you to get Solace back," Sagan said.

"How did you know that's what I was doing?"

"We saw you leaving Autumn's hut and heard her shouting after you," said Nika.

Violet shot a questioning glare at Tio.

"What? I was coming out of the bathroom when I saw these two trailing you like you'd just stolen their wallets. When they told me what you were up to . . ." He flashed a toothpaste-commercial grin. "Count me in on this rescue mission. I'm here for the backup."

"I don't need the backup. I'm just going to get my daughter back."

"And you're not going without me," said Sagan.

Violet was about to argue, but her words fizzled when she saw the severity in his eyes. "Fine," she blurted. "You can come. But as for the rest of you, get out."

Tio's protests erupted full force, and Nika glared daggers as she said, "I'm coming too."

Violet narrowed her eyes at her. "Why? So you can find your opportunity to 'do what needs to be done'?"

Nika grinned, obviously not missing the reference to her conversation with Thane, but all she said was "Where my cousin goes, I go."

Violet's jaw clenched. What were the chances Sagan would kick his own cousin to the curb?

"Besides," added Nika, "I'm already over this little village's Kumbaya crap, and this little road trip seems promising for some action."

"Yesssss! Road trip!" Tio fist-pumped the air.

Violet turned her attention to him. "You need to stay here, Tio."

"What? Why?"

"Because I hardly know you, and you're just a kid, and I don't need to be looking out for you if things go south," Violet gritted out.

"Then how come Nika gets to come? You hardly know her. And for your information, I've done time at Tempecrest Island—as a *gladiator*. If things go south, you're gonna need me."

He held up a hand and wiggled his fingers. Violet almost jumped and her jaw dropped as bright orange electricity crackled over his palm. What was he? A shifter, for sure, but she'd never heard of an electricity ability. How many kinds of shifters were there?

"Yeah, yeah, you're a badass," drawled Nika. "Come on, let's go already."

The idea of taking orders from Nika made Violet's hands clench on the wheel, but she'd been delayed too long already. She released the brake and sped down the driveway, then onto the road toward the interstate. The forest whipped past, and gravel rumbled under the jeep's tires.

For a few minutes, everyone fell into silence. The presence of the others nagged at Violet, but at least Sagan tagging along gave her some scrap of peace. She knew she could rely on him. As for the others? Well, there was no point in worrying about it now.

"So," piped up Tio, "the idea of this trip is to get your kid back, right, Violet?"

"My daughter, yes."

"What was her name again?"

"Solace."

"Right. And is it true that Thane's the father?"

Violet drew in a long breath through her nose. *What is with the twenty questions?* She didn't bother answering, but sadly, that didn't stop Tio from badgering her.

"He doesn't know, does he?"

When no one said anything, Tio's laugh shattered the silence. "Hoo boy. I hope I'm there when someone finally tells him."

Violet glanced at Sagan, who shrugged a shoulder and shot her a look that seemed to say, "Don't blame me. I didn't bring him."

It was going to be a long car ride.

* * *

Violet slowed the car as she drove over the bridge into Rivermyre.

"Whoa," said Tio.

"Whoa" was an understatement. While the city lights behind them lit up the car's rearview mirrors like the fourth of July, the ghost city ahead was dark and ominous. The eclectic array of skyscrapers gradually blacked out the misty moonlit horizon as Violet steered the jeep onto the offramp.

The entire cityscape was as one would expect a city to be —with traffic lights, crosswalks, street signs, ground-floor cafés, and stores with tall glass windows. Yet everything was empty; there were no signs of a living soul. All this place needed was a fog machine and glowing eyes peering through the shadows to make the perfect setting for a horror movie.

"So, which one of these buildings is your daughter in?" Tio asked.

"I, um . . ." Violet grimaced. "I don't know." She continued down the same road she'd pulled onto from the freeway. The giant buildings towering on either side looked nearly completed, minus panels of glass in the upper levels. Other buildings farther along were still early in their construction, with moonbeams shining straight through their monstrous skeletons.

"You do realize any one of these spooky buildings would be perfect for a kidnapper's hideout?" said Tio. "Maybe just pick one and knock on the door and see who answers. There's one—*Xabat Biogenetics Research Inc.* They sound friendly."

"Not helping," said Violet.

She turned down a side street, hoping to find a change in scenery. Nika and Tio leaned forward into the front seats to take advantage of the limited illumination the headlights offered for their path ahead.

Violet scanned the area, searching for a clue, anything to prove Solace was close by. But each street was the same as the last: empty shops, unlit streetlights, grass and weeds sprouting from the cracks in the sidewalk, overgrown shrubs in the garden islands dividing the road.

Violet was beginning to regret running out on Autumn so soon. There was nothing here. No one. Searching every one of these buildings would take months.

"There!" Nika yelled.

"Where?" Violet's pulse spiked, and her eyes darted along the darkened storefronts.

Nika leaned forward and pointed. "I saw something over there."

"I don't see anything," said Tio.

"It went down that street."

A surge of adrenaline pumped through Violet's veins as she hit the gas.

"What did you see?" Sagan asked

"I think I saw . . . There! It turned into that street on the right." Nika slapped Violet on the shoulder. "Drive faster! We don't want to lose it."

Violet yanked on the wheel, and the car lurched around the corner.

Several silent seconds ticked by as they all peered into the darkness. Frustration started to churn in Violet's gut. Was Nika having them all on? Was she really here to help find Solace, or was this just a game to her?

"I think you're imagining things," Tio said.

"I'm telling you, I saw something," Nika growled.

Violet's chest heaved, her hands gripping the steering wheel so tight her knuckles felt ready to bust. "Just face it, Nika! There's nothing here!"

"Hey! Don't yell at me. It isn't my fault you decided to take a joyride without getting all the information first."

"This isn't a joyride! Autumn said Solace is here. I'm getting my baby back."

"Oh, really?" came Nika's snide response. "And where exactly did Autumn say your baby was?"

Violet opened her mouth to retort, but there were no words.

"See?" Nika leaned back. "Like I said, this is just a waste of time."

"Seriously?" Violet spun in her seat to look at her. "If that's what you think, why didn't you mention it two hours ago? Why did you even bother coming in the first place?"

"Violet. *Stop*," Sagan exclaimed.

She rounded on him. "Don't tell me what—"

"The car! Stop the car!"

Just as Violet registered that Sagan was pointing ahead, something banged against the front of the jeep.

Everyone lurched forward with the sudden impact. Violet slammed on the brakes, and the car screeched and jolted to a stop.

"What the hell was that?" Violet said.

"I'll check." Before anyone could react, Tio was out of the car.

"Tio, get back in here," called Sagan, just as Nika jumped out too. Sagan released an exasperated breath. "Stay here, Violet. I'll go check it out."

Forget that. She was sick of sitting on her ass while everyone told her to wait and stay put. She opened the door and stepped out before Sagan could say another word.

"What was it?" Violet walked over to the alleyway entrance where Nika and Tio were standing.

"I think it went in here," said Tio.

Violet peered into the murky shadows. A gentle wind stirred up a flurry of leaves and scattered debris, which tumbled into the alley to be absorbed by the dark.

"There!" Tio pointed. "Do you see it?"

Violet studied the area where Tio was pointing. An icy chill tremored through her body as ghoulish yellow eyes peered out from the black.

Holy crap. They were in a horror movie.

Sagan stepped into Violet's periphery. With a subtle *click*, a beam of light shone into the alley. Trust Sagan to be the always-prepared-boy-scout type.

"I think it's a cat," Nika finally said.

"Aw, Violet, you hit a cat?" said Tio.

"Seriously?" Violet's shoulders sagged. *All this drama over a stupid alley cat?*

Sagan's flashlight revealed a furry feline face—tan with rounded black-tipped ears—peeking out from behind a dumpster about ten paces in. Its yellow eyes were much less creepy under the light.

"Poor kitty," cooed Tio. "Are you okay? Did the mean Violet girl hit you with her car?"

"Tio, don't," warned Sagan.

But Tio was already three "here kitty, kittys" in when the animal began to move out from behind the dumpster. He stopped mid-word when the "kitty" came into full view.

Violet's eyes grew wide. Her heartbeat sped up to double time.

"Guys, I don't think that's a cat," said Tio.

Nika shot him a glare. "No kidding, moron."

The animal in the alley was like a leopard, but where the spots should be, large porcupine-like quills sprouted along its back. A murky-green crocodile tail dragged on the ground behind it, lined with spikes that continued up the creature's spine. The beast glared at the group with two predatory eyes —and then four more yellow eyes opened on its face.

Sagan grabbed Violet's arm and pulled her back, which was just as well, because not only was the spiky leopard thing starting to move toward them, but Violet's fear had clutched her in an iron grip.

A low growl rumbled from the creature as it advanced.

"Guys, get back in the car," Sagan commanded.

As one, all four of them turned and ran. But everyone slid to a halt when three more of the spiky leopards prowled out from behind the jeep to block their path. The three new creatures paced back and forth in front of the vehicle as a fifth jumped onto the jeep's hood.

Sagan and Nika drew their Diamantium weapons, and Tio's hands flickered with electricity. Violet struggled to keep her fear at bay. The creature on the hood stood solid, its hackles raised, as the four on the ground began to circle Violet and her companions.

"What are those things?" Violet asked. "Are they shifters?"

"No," said Sagan. "Definitely not shifters."

"I've never seen anything like them," added Nika.

Terror squeezed Violet's windpipe as the beasts circled closer. They began to growl. One bared its teeth, the bright light of the moon flashing on the white fangs and strings of drool.

"Nika, take that one. Tio, take the one over there. And, Violet, take the one in front of you. I'll deal with the last, then finish off the one on the hood."

A whimper escaped Violet. *I can't do this. I can't do this. I can't do this.*

"You can do this!"

She flinched at Sagan's commanding bark. She must've said that out loud.

"Violet, are you with me?"

A deafening rush roared through Violet's ears, drowning out Sagan's words. He was saying something about fire. Or was it fear? Her mind could only comprehend the leopards' fangs, the claws, the quills, the savage yellow eyes. Her mind screamed for her to run, but everywhere she turned, a leopard mutant blocked her exit.

Then one leaped into the air.

She screamed.

The snarling open jaws came right for her. She covered her face and crumpled into a ball, waiting for the teeth to sink into her flesh. When no pain followed, Violet looked up.

Tio had jumped in front of her and was wrestling with the beast, which had clamped its jaws on his arm. The night erupted with vicious growls, snarls, and shouts from the others.

Violet's flight mode kicked into overdrive.

She ran.

Her shoes beat against the pavement. Her lungs burned with labored breaths. The growls and snarls echoed behind her.

Someone was shouting her name, but all she comprehended was her fear screaming, *Run! Run! Run!*

Soon the pounding of her feet was joined by more footfalls behind her. Whatever was chasing her was catching up fast.

She pushed her aching legs. *Faster! Faster! Faster!*

In a flash, two of the creatures flew past on either side. They bolted several feet ahead, then, with synchronized grace, spun to face her.

Violet pulled up short.

Fangs, claws, quills, yellow eyes. She needed to run, but which way? She couldn't outrun these things.

Sagan roared at her over the vicious showdown still going on at the jeep. "Violet!"

The two spiky leopards slowly stalked toward her.

Sagan yelled again. "Use your fire!"

Fire?

Her mind snapped out of the fear that had eclipsed all rational thought. She'd forgotten about her new abilities.

Violet backed up a few steps as the creatures inched ever closer—they'd be upon her in moments. She held up shaky hands. But nothing happened. No fire, not even a spark.

The six-eyed mutants took another step closer.

Maybe she needed to say her ability out loud for it to work. "Fire!"

Again, nothing. *What on earth?* How had she made her fire powers work last time?

The creatures were now so close their humid breath warmed her outstretched hands.

Again, the irresistible urge to run overwhelmed Violet's mind, but just as she turned to sprint away, the ground beneath her shook. The leopards froze in their tracks. Their growling died out, then turned into whimpers. Violet tried to run, but the rumble beneath her feet rapidly grew into a violent quake, and she fell back into a heap on the ground.

The spiky leopards turned and bolted, but the asphalted road exploded in front of them before they'd gone more than a few yards.

If Violet had been afraid before, it was absolutely nothing compared to the paralyzing terror that slammed into her as a giant wormlike thing shot out of the ground right before her eyes.

Thousands of razor-sharp fangs filled its gaping round maw, which was wide enough to swallow Violet with one bite. Scorpion tails rose threateningly from the two massive antennae on its head, and rows and rows of millipede-type legs lined the sides of its grotesque body. With heart-stopping speed, a slimy tongue tipped with a huge crab claw shot out and captured one of the leopard creatures around its middle. The feline's agonized squeal ended abruptly when the crab claw crunched down hard. Bones cracked, guts squelched, and the leopard went limp. Then the mutant worm whipped its tongue back into its mouth along with its prey.

The second leopard tried to make a run for it, but one of the scorpion-tailed antennae surged forward and pinned it to the ground. The leopard let out an ear-piercing shriek, writhing in a futile attempt to escape the scorpion stinger.

Once the first leopard was gulped down, the second followed shortly after. Then the worm's insectile eyes found Violet.

Its mouth opened wide.

Violet scrambled back, but she hadn't even made it two feet before the creature's tongue flew toward her. With a scream, she blocked her face with her arms.

Just as she expected the crab claw to crunch down on her body, an almighty roar thundered in her ears and reverberated through her chest.

Violet peeked through her arm shield to find her world bathed in a teal glow. Her hands were coated with flames, which sizzled the tongue to a charcoal crisp before the creature could whip it back into its mouth. Violet cringed back as the monstrous worm let out another earth-shattering shriek.

One of its scorpion stingers lunged toward her.

Someone grabbed Violet from behind and dragged her back—only a split second before the stinger smashed deep into the ground where Violet had been sprawled.

"Get up!" Sagan commanded as he pulled her to her feet.

A second stinger plummeted to the earth, missing Violet by inches as they turned and ran. Sagan had a tight grip on her upper arm and half dragged her behind him, his speed was way too fast for Violet to keep up.

Another boom of exploding asphalt sounded at their backs, jolting the earth so that Violet almost stumbled. But Tio appeared at Violet's other side to steady her and rush her toward Nika, who was standing by the jeep surrounded by the corpses of the three other leopard mutants.

They were just a few feet away from the jeep when the earth burst open directly in their path, and the worm's head sprang out with a roar. Violet, Sagan, and Tio skidded to a halt as a stinger hurtled toward them.

But a breath before the stinger's deadly point could make impact, a gleaming streak of metal cut across its path, neatly severing the scorpion tail from the antenna. The stinger crashed to the ground, and the worm shrieked and flailed, spraying putrid brown gore from its antenna stump.

Violet glanced down at the severed scorpion stinger that still twitched on the ground, then over to what had severed it: a metal ninja star, now embedded in the concrete wall.

The roaring stopped when the worm set its sights back on Violet.

A person in a hooded jacket appeared in front of her. The mysterious figure held up one arm as the worm's remaining scorpion stinger sped downward.

Another streak of metal blasted from a contraption on the newcomer's arm. With a faint *clink-clink-clink*, several more ninja stars shot through the air and sliced through the incoming stinger, sending more screams and more brown goo out into the night.

The hooded person aimed their star launcher at the beast's eyes next. More flashes of metal rocketed forth to blind the worm, which began flinging its head from side to side, bashing against the ground over and over—whether from the pain or to try and dislodge the stars, Violet wasn't sure.

The hooded person bolted toward the creature, nimbly dodging the worm's head as it slammed into the ground. As the head rose, Hoodie latched on to one of the antennae stumps and swung themselves up so they were riding the monster like a bucking bronco. With one hand still holding tight to the stump, Hoodie produced a sword with the other, which they thrust deep into the raging beast's head.

The worm roared and flailed one last time before it crashed to the ground. Hoodie gripped the sword with both hands and drove it farther into the worm's flesh. With a final twitch, the beast moved no more.

Violet's ears rang from the sudden void of noise.

"Who on earth is that?" Tio asked.

No one answered. All three stood motionless, stunned and breathing hard, as they watched the hooded person retrieve their metal stars from the dead worm's body.

Tio walked over to the star still wedged in the concrete wall. With a bit of effort, he pried it free, then brought it over to Violet and Sagan. The projectile had six-points, each blade shaped like a grim reaper scythe.

Sagan took the star from Tio to inspect it more closely. That was when Violet noticed Tio's other arm hugged tightly against his chest.

"Tio, you're hurt!" she exclaimed. Her stomach churned; "hurt" was an understatement. Half of Tio's hand was missing, and the majority of his forearm was a mangled mess. Bright orange liquid covered his arm and clothes in streaks and splatters.

A nauseating shame washed over Violet when she recalled how Tio had intercepted the spiky leopard while she'd been in the depths of uncontrollable panic.

Tio shrugged but immediately winced from the movement. "Don't worry about it. I'm Jiovis. It's nothing I can't handle."

Violet couldn't find the words to reply. How does one respond to someone who'd willingly volunteer to be mauled by a mutant leopard?

Tio's attention shifted to something behind Violet. "Nice of you to join us, Nika." His tone dripped sarcasm.

"Hey, don't blame me if I don't have a death wish when it comes to Godzilla worms." She inclined her head to the hooded figure. "Who's our new friend?"

The hooded person looked up as if Nika had called their name. They removed the sword from the worm, sheathed it in a scabbard strapped to their back, and jumped off the creature's lifeless body before sauntering over to the motley group.

As they came closer, Violet realized Hoodie was a girl, possibly around her own age. She was of Asian descent, and her raven-black hair had a bright purple gradient at the ends. She must've had an affinity with gradated colors, because on closer inspection, her leather jacket was a midnight-blue-to-black ombre.

Sagan took half a step forward as she approached the group. "Who are you?"

Hoodie didn't answer, coming to a stop in front of Tio. Her eyes trailed up and down the tall Jiovis shifter.

Tio frowned in confusion, then shared a glance with the others as Hoodie brushed a hand over the orange splatters on his shirt and inspected the orange blood on her fingers.

She then moved to stand in front of Violet. The girl leaned in close, an uncomfortable inch from Violet's nose, and stared deep into her eyes, as if searching for something. Then she took hold of one of Violet's wrists and held it up.

"What is she doing?" Tio asked under his breath as Hoodie inspected Violet's hand.

Finally, Hoodie dropped Violet's wrist and moved over to Nika. The hunter glared at her, but that didn't stop Hoodie from looking her up and down too. After a moment, she reached out and took hold of Nika's amulet.

"Hey! Watch it." Nika slapped the girl's hand, and the amulet bounced back into place against her chest.

Hoodie cocked an eyebrow. An amused smile played at her lips as she *pishh*ed before turning her attention to Sagan. Instead of facing him, as she'd done with the others, the girl first walked around Sagan in a slow circle. When she finally did stop in front of him, Sagan crossed his arms and met her gaze head on.

Hoodie made a show of folding her arms too. Sagan frowned and put his hands on his hips. She did the same, then copied him again when his arms dropped to his sides.

Sagan frowned with a soft gruff, to which the newcomer replied with a smirk. Then she tapped at the hidden amulet under Sagan's shirt. It wasn't hard to see he was trying to restrain himself from slapping the girl's hand away as Nika had.

"Who are you?" he asked again.

She smiled. "I am . . . wondering what two hunters are doing with a Jiovis and . . ."—she pointed to Violet—"whatever type of shifter she is."

In a flash, something flitted out from within the girl's hood. Another creature, about the size of a soda can, darted around Sagan's head.

"What the—" Sagan swatted at it, but it managed to swoop out of the way each time, tittering and chattering in a voice similar to a parakeet. When it held still long enough, Violet could just make out what looked like a tiny monkey with beetle wings.

The little monkey finally ceased agitating Sagan and went to land on its owner's shoulder, folding its wings up neatly beneath an iridescent beetle carapace on its back. It pointed a tiny clawed finger at Sagan and chattered in a way that made Violet think it was scolding him.

The girl in the hoodie crossed her arms. "This is Toffee, and she's wondering why the one with ice in his eyes would steal from us."

Sagan blinked; it was the closest Violet had ever seen him to being startled.

"Steal from you? I'm not a thief."

The girl stepped forward until she was uncomfortably close to Sagan's nose. "Then when were you planning on giving this back?" She snatched his wrist and held up the hand with the throwing star.

"You could've just asked for it," Sagan countered.

"All right. May I please have my star back?"

"On one condition."

The girl frowned. "Which is?"

"You tell me your name."

The little monkey-fairy chattered. Hoodie shared a glance with it, and then the little creature shrugged.

Raising her chin, the girl looked down her nose at Sagan. "I'm Umbra. And you?"

"Sagan." He held the star out to her.

Plucking it from his fingers, Umbra raised her arm with the launching contraption, then with a subtle *click-clack*, loaded the star back in. Without a word, she turned and stalked off.

"Wait," Violet called after her.

Umbra didn't slow down. Only the little monkey on her shoulder turned back to look at Violet, who was now running after them.

"Can you help us?"

"I did help you. I just saved all your asses," Umbra said without stopping. "Go home. You shouldn't be here."

"Please," said Violet. "I'm looking for my baby."

Umbra stopped and faced her. "They took your baby?"

"Yes." A small seed of hope began to sprout within Violet's chest.

"Is your baby like you?"

"Like me?"

"Does your baby make flames like the Magneii but with the color of the Veniri?"

Violet shook her head. "No, she's just a Veniri."

Umbra's eyebrows shot sky high. "She?"

Violet nodded.

"Then it is too late for your baby. There's no point trying to get her back—not unless you want to become one of these failed Xabat Lab experiments." She pointed to the giant worm and mutant leopard corpses. "Go home, hybrid. And don't come back."

Umbra reached out to a cable hanging down the side of one of the buildings. In one smooth motion, she put her foot in a loop at the end, yanked on the cable, and shot up, disappearing into the night.

14

IT'S TIME TO STOP MOPING

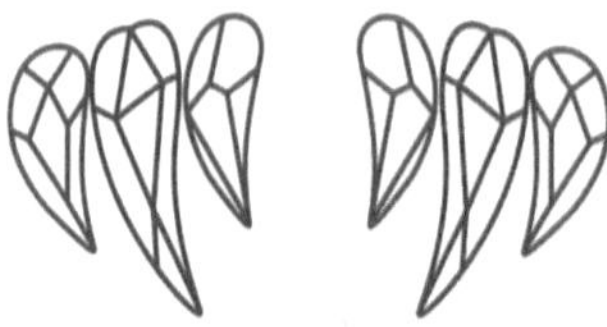

NATHAN LEANED AGAINST THE WALL AND WAITED. THE BACK door of the house where Violet lived was the one place he figured she would eventually show up.

No one had seen Violet since she'd arrived back from a trip to the city.

Earlier that night, when he hadn't been able to sleep, Nathan had gone for a walk only to find a battered Sagan and Nika half carrying Tio to the infirmary. All three had been covered in a concerning amount of red and orange blood mixed with some kind of brown slime.

Sagan had filled in Nathan on their failed mission to rescue Violet's child. Apparently, it had become clear during the car ride home that Tio couldn't regenerate his hand after being attacked by a leopard-crocodile-mutant thing.

Dawn had concluded that something in the leopard's saliva might be preventing Tio's healing ability from kicking in. In the end, Tio decided to treat it the same way he would rust rot and elected for an amputation. With a clean cut, he would be able to grow a new arm for himself.

After Gus had patched up Sagan and Nika and administered painkillers, Nathan decided he needed to go check on Violet. Sagan told him she'd refused to get out of the car, even after she'd refused to get in the car in the first place and he'd been forced to throw her over his shoulder and lock her in the jeep's cargo area to bring her home.

The jeep was empty when Nathan checked, and Lazareth —who was up preparing community meals for the next day —had told him Violet hadn't returned to the house yet.

So Nathan waited. It was the middle of the night, and usually that wouldn't have stopped him from using his tracking abilities, but since he'd made Violet immune to tracking, there was nothing for him to do except wait for her at the house.

But what if she didn't come back? What if she'd left in another desperate attempt to try and rescue her child?

What if—

"What are you doing here?"

Despite Violet's harsh tone, relief washed over Nathan. The incandescent security light above the back door shone its pale yellow hue over her blotched, puffy eyes. Her shoulders were hunched, and her arms wrapped tightly around her waist.

Nathan casually slid his hands into his jacket pockets. "Waiting for you."

"I thought I told you I didn't want to see you ever again."

"Actually, I recall you saying that you would kill me."

"So take a hint."

The cold distrust in her gray-blue eyes pierced Nathan deep. She'd never looked at him like that, not even when she'd been wary of him the first time they met. His mind went blank with the attempt to form a response.

Seconds passed. A small swarm of moths bumped against the glass bulb of the security light with a subtle *tink-tink-tink*, keeping the complete silence at bay.

"We need to talk," he finally said. "There's a lot I need to explain."

When he tried to continue, Violet shook her head and snorted with disgust. She stormed up to the door and shoved it open.

"Violet, wait." Nathan sidestepped to block her entry.

Violet barked a humorless laugh. "Dream on, moron. I'm not talking to you. Ever."

She tried to shoulder through, but Nathan stood firm. Even though he wanted to, he couldn't blurt out everything he'd promised he would say to her the moment he escaped Tempecrest—and there was no way he could force her to forgive him—but there was something he *could* do to help her get what she desperately wanted. "If you want to get your daughter back, you need to learn how to use your new abilities."

Her jaw dropped. "How did you know about Sol—" She groaned. "Did Gus tell you? Sagan?"

"I know what happened at Rivermyre."

She exhaled with annoyance and took several steps back. "Look, if you're here to give me a lecture, I don't want to hear it. I got enough lectures during the car ride home. I get it, okay? It's all my fault. It's my fault Tio got hurt. It's my fault we went in blind. And it's my fault my baby—" A sob strangled her words.

Nathan tried to approach her, but her hand flew up in his face.

"Don't!" Despite the tears streaming down her cheeks, her scowl had turned deadly. "Don't you come near me."

"Violet—"

"Look, whatever the others told you, it changes nothing between you and me. Now get out of my way."

Nathan didn't move. Instead, he pushed aside his own

hurt and focused on what needed to be done. "Do you want to get your daughter back?"

Her scowl faltered.

"Do you?" he pressed.

"Of course I do." She practically spat the words at him.

"Then training you is even more urgent. If you want to get her back, you can't go in half-cocked like you did tonight. You need to learn to control your abilities. It's time to stop moping and—"

"I haven't been moping," Violet snapped.

Nathan continued as if she hadn't interrupted. "—drop your sour, sooky attitude and get to work. Sulking isn't going to get Solace back. Now get changed into clothes you don't mind getting ruined, and meet me at the pavilion."

Violet opened her mouth to retort, but Nathan turned and headed down the path. He didn't even glance back to make sure she was following his orders.

* * *

As Nathan rested his back against the outer wall of the pavilion, a soft breeze brushed over his face and twisted through his hair. It was longer than he usually kept it, but he hadn't had a chance to find someone to cut it for him since escaping Tempecrest. Encroaching memories of his imprisonment began to infect his consciousness, but he shook his head and pushed those thoughts away.

Instead, he focused on Violet. The vicious scowl she'd given him earlier flashed in his mind, followed by a sharp pang in his chest.

How had it come to this? He'd tried his darnedest to protect her, to keep her away from his world. And yet Violet had somehow contracted not only Veniri abilities but Magneii abilities as well. Not to mention she was now a mother to a Veniri child—a daughter, no less. In the Veniri world, any female was automatically considered royalty. Did that mean Violet was also a Veniri royal, even with the Magneii abilities? Either way, Nathan hoped Queen Idalia would never find out about Violet and Solace. She would have them hunted down and slaughtered just to eliminate any challenge to her throne.

His worries heightened when he recalled what Gus had told him earlier—theories on how it could be possible for more humans to become hybrid shifters. If Gus was right, and if this information ever began to spread, all hell would break loose for all shifter races. It could mean a global war.

Nathan dropped his head in his hands and rubbed his eyes. On top of everything else, he wasn't sure how much longer he could take Violet hating him.

He'd considered leaving, especially since it was clear Violet had moved on; she didn't need him anymore. Gus and his family had embraced her as one of their own. Sagan was keeping a watchful eye. And there was no chance Thane would leave her anytime soon, especially if he found out he was a father.

But Nathan had promised Tio he would stick around until the kid's brother arrived. In the meantime, he could at least help Violet learn to use her new abilities—give her a fighting chance to get her daughter back. Maybe he could even play a more direct role in rescuing Solace. And if that still wasn't enough to earn Violet's trust and forgiveness, he would leave, and she could continue her life without him.

Not wanting to suffocate in his melancholy, he tilted his face toward the inky sky and closed his eyes. His inner melody, a soft tune only he could hear, thrummed comfortingly in his ears. He pivoted, knowing, even without opening his eyes, that he was facing Venus; the music in his soul had swelled to a full orchestra.

He stood still and quiet, absorbing the Venusian beams. The revitalizing energy buzzed from his core and radiated out to every cell in his body. Despite how chaotic life could be, his link with Venus was refreshingly constant. Whether day or night, sunny or cloudy, in the midst of summer or the depths of winter, as long as Venus was in the sky overhead, Nathan could tap into his connection with the planet. Only during a superior conjunction—when Venus's orbit took it to the opposite side of the Sun from the Earth—was he cut off from its power.

He was about to stop absorbing the Venusian energy when a beam *latched on to him*—or at least, that was what it felt like. His inner creature roared to life, and without his consent, his body began to haze.

Instant panic shot through him as he tried to regain control, to maintain his human appearance. There was no mistaking the ragged sound of tearing fabric as several shards erupted from his legs and arms. If he couldn't hold back the haze, his clothes would be torn to shreds within seconds. Crystal blades shot out of his elbows, and his smooth skin turned into iridescent scales that shimmered under the pavilion's floodlights.

A cold, paralyzing fear gripped his throat, choking him, as he watched the scales ripple and fuse into a faceted crystallized surface, much like the patches that had been spreading on his shoulder and calf.

What is happening to me?

With every ounce of focus he possessed, he tried to force his arms to haze back into their human form. After a slow, brutal effort, his scales gradually reappeared, erasing the crystallized surface. Then, several torturous seconds later, the scales themselves smoothed into human skin, and his shards melted back into his flesh.

His ragged panting was almost deafening. He stared at his

arms, rotating them back and forth to examine them from every angle, trying to convince his racing mind that the crystals were really gone. That he was back in control.

A heavy *thump-thump-thump* came from the wooden steps at the opposite end of the pavilion.

Nathan hurriedly composed himself just as Violet came into view. She'd changed into a black tank top and ripped denim shorts. Her dark brown hair was tied back into a high ponytail. Though the scowl was still etched onto her face, it was less poisonous than before.

"I'm here," she said, crossing her arms.

"Uh, great." Nathan rubbed his clammy palms on his jeans. "Great." *Come on, pull yourself together!* "Great."

"So you keep saying." Violet raised an unimpressed eyebrow. A moment passed before she added, "I know what you are."

"Oh, yeah?" He knew there was no point playing dumb. He'd been a fool for trying to delay the inevitable.

"You're a shifter. A Veniri."

"How did you . . ? I mean . . ."

"What, you thought I would never find out?" She crossed her arms. "I had a suspicion while all you guys were talking around me when I was paralyzed, and you confirmed that suspicion just now."

Nathan made a silent "oh" with a nod of his head. He couldn't hold her gaze. She was bound to demand why he hadn't told her. Perhaps she was trying to picture him in shifted form. He froze. *Damn it, what if she asks me to haze?* "You must have a lot of questions."

She regarded him with a steady gaze.

Nathan waited, preparing for whatever she would ask him.

But with a flippant wave of her hand, she said, "Whatever.

Can we just get this training thing over with so I can go to bed?"

"Fine, let's make sure you get that full eight hours," he said, with a little more bite than he intended. "Have you forgotten your daughter is counting on you?"

The stricken look in Violet's eyes made Nathan immediately regret his words. There was no excuse for his lashing out like that, no matter how much her keeping him at arm's length hurt him.

"Violet—"

She turned her face away, clearly not ready for his apologies.

Nathan sighed and raked a hand through his hair. This training session was off to a terrible start. Maybe it wasn't such a good idea after all. Besides, even if he knew how to train a Veniri—which he wasn't entirely convinced of—he still knew nothing about how to train a Veniri-Magneii hybrid. He mentally rifled through his childhood memories for something of use—some trick or scrap of advice to make this easy —but unfortunately, most of the memories of his own training were a blur, considering he'd begun at about six years old.

Maybe he should just start with the basics.

"I'm sure by now Sagan's filled you in on some things. So what do you currently know about the Veniri?" he asked.

"I know they're ugly, scaly creatures who kidnap and kill young girls."

Nathan *hmmph*ed a humorless laugh. "Yep. That's pretty much it, in a nutshell. Anything else? Keep in mind that you're now just as ugly and scaly as the rest of us."

Violet's scowl deepened, but after a few seconds, she added, "Their blood is blue, and they use their crystal spikes as weapons."

"Do you know what the crystal is called?"

She nodded. "Diamantium. Sagan said it's what your skeleton is made of. Actually, I suppose it's what *my* skeleton is now made of." She stared off into the distance, her eyes widening as the concept washed over her.

Nathan asked her a few more questions, and Violet's attitude thawed a little more with each answer.

Sagan had been pretty thorough with his description of the Veniri—as expected from someone who'd hunted them for most of his life. But there were still a lot of things even a seasoned hunter would never know.

"All right, let's get your hazing under control," said Nathan.

"Hazing?"

"Yeah, you know, changing. Transforming. Shape-shifting. Hazing."

"Oh, shifting. I know what that is. Why don't you just call it shifting?"

Nathan shrugged. "I wasn't there when the decision was made."

"Well, we can move on to the next lesson, 'cause I already know how to 'haze.'" Violet wiggled her fingers to make air quotes.

"Oh, yeah? Then what's the story I hear that you didn't use your abilities at Rivermyre?"

Violet opened her mouth to retort but said nothing.

Nathan stifled a smirk when she clamped her mouth shut again. "Close your eyes. I want you to focus on the 'shifter' part of you. I want you to listen—"

"Do I have to do it with my eyes closed?"

"Just do it."

With an adolescent grumble, Violet complied. "Fine. My eyes are closed. Now what?"

"Focus on the 'shifter' part of—"

"You already said that."

Nathan slowly sucked in a breath and massaged his temples. This shouldn't be so hard. He'd trained Violet before. What had changed?

He inwardly groaned. How could he even ask that? *Everything* had changed.

"Are you doing that thing where you pretend to strangle me?" Violet asked, her eyes still closed.

"I have never done that, and you know it."

"Whatever you say, old man."

"Hey, keep it up, and I'll have no problem doing it for real."

The corner of Violet's mouth twitched.

A tiny ripple of relief washed over Nathan. It was good to know they could still banter the way they used to, but he didn't want to get his hopes up yet. Knowing Violet, it would take much more than a half-hour training session to get her even close to trusting him again.

"Focus and listen. Tune your ear to your inward melody."

"'Inward melody'? That sounds dumb. What kinda—" Her whole body went stiff. "Whoa . . . I think . . . I can hear it."

Nathan almost shouted "hallelujah." Finally, a breakthrough. "Okay, good. Pay attention to that melody." He waited for about a minute before saying, "Now, let the energy wash over you. Very slowly, tune your body to that melody, then haze."

Violet's face screwed up, and her hands balled into fists at her sides. She squirmed uncomfortably and clenched her jaw, most likely because of the pain Nathan knew came from hazing.

Teal flames ignited all over her body, then disappeared. Diamantium shards sliced out from her flesh, then just as quickly glided back in. Scales rippled all over her exposed skin, then burned black and split, revealing molten magenta fissures that soon turned to glowing teal. The teal flames returned to lick across her arms and face, flickered to magenta, and then just as quickly flashed back to teal.

Shock rooted Nathan in place. *What on earth? This isn't right.* "Violet, stop!"

More shards burst from her shoulders and collar bones. Magneii flesh rippled back into scales.

He needed to do something. But what? "Stop!"

"I . . . can't . . ." she gritted out through Veniri triple fangs.

"Concentrate!" Nathan demanded. "You must regain control."

A few more agonizing seconds passed, then finally, Violet hazed back into human form and collapsed to the ground.

Nathan rushed to her side. "Are you okay?" He took hold of her arms and helped her up. "Violet?"

"I'm okay." She dragged in several deep breaths. "What just happened?"

"I think . . ." Nathan floundered for an answer. "Well, it looked like both your Veniri and Magneii components were fighting for domination."

Violet grimaced. "Oh."

Nathan rubbed at his jaw. "Hmm . . . I wonder . . ."

"What?" Violet stood a little straighter. "What is it?"

A few seconds passed before Nathan was able to articulate his musings. "The way I see it, there's no doubt you're a hybrid, but it might be possible to control your Veniri and Magneii sides individually."

Violet chewed on her lip. "Are you saying I might be able to shift . . . I mean haze . . . into a Veniri *or* a Magneii *or* whatever my hybrid version is?"

Nathan tilted his head from side to side as he considered the possibility. Then he shrugged. "Sure. I don't see why not."

Violet's hands flew to her cheeks. "In that case . . . I'm not sure if I should be saying 'cool' or 'damn.'"

Nathan almost chuckled—until he realized she might be

on the verge of one of her overwhelming meltdowns. He braced himself for her to flee, as she usually did when things became more than she could handle. It had taken a lot of work for her to get her panic attacks under control. Was she still doing the exercises her school psychologist had recommended? Did she still get panic attacks at all?

A pang of sorrow pricked his heart. Violet had been through so much since he last saw her. How much of the woman before him did he really know?

Violet's hands dropped from her face. The determination blazing in her eyes reminded Nathan of the moment he'd given her a switchblade and told her he was going to train her how to use it.

She squared her shoulders and looked him directly in the eye. "What's next?"

Nathan couldn't help but grin. There was the Violet he knew.

15

DOWNRIGHT DIRTY FIGHTER

THE NIGHT AIR WRAPPED AROUND VIOLET, TURNING THE FILM of sweat over her skin into a blanket of ice. The residual adrenaline of her Veniri and Magneii-hazing overload still trembled through her body.

But that energy was nothing compared to the surge of excitement she'd felt when Nathan had suggested she might be able to learn how to control not one or two but *three* versions of her new abilities. She remembered how powerful she'd felt when Nathan began teaching her how to use her switchblade. Back then, she'd felt like no one would ever be able to take advantage of her again. But with the prospects of gaining control of her abilities, she would be able to find her child and obliterate anyone in her path. She would be unstoppable.

"What's next?" she asked.

"We change tactics." Nathan grinned at her.

She almost grinned back before the stinging memory of his betrayal stifled it. How could she stand to be anywhere near this man? All along he'd known who and what Thane was, even when her own memories had eluded her.

She had trusted Nathan.

Nathan's betrayal had cut deep, and talking about it would only reopen the wound. As much as she still didn't want to have anything to do with him, there was no denying she needed him. She needed to learn how to harness her powers. To save Solace.

"I think if you learn the inner workings of both your Veniri and Magneii side individually," Nathan continued, "you should be able to fit together the hybrid parts of each seamlessly. I'll be able to teach you all about how to be a Veniri, no problem. You'll learn how to haze, heal, track, distinguish other's intentions and emotions, and even fight like a Veniri. But for your Magneii side . . ."

"I'll teach you how to use your Magneii abilities," said a new voice.

Both Violet and Nathan spun to find Sagan leaning against a tree at the edge of the nearby path. Next to him was his cousin Nika.

"How long have you guys been standing there?" Violet asked.

Sagan shrugged a shoulder.

"Long enough to see you go shifter crazy," said Nika with a grin.

Violet wasn't sure she felt comfortable with the expression Nika was giving her, but apart from her warning to Thane, Nika hadn't actually done anything to cause Violet any further concern. At least not yet.

"But you're not Magneii," Violet said to Sagan. "What makes you think you can teach me?"

"I've dealt with enough of them to learn how they react in various situations. The least I can do is show you how to counter a hunter's attack. Plus"—he grimaced—"I also know a little about their anatomy."

A few seconds of silence passed before Violet caught on to what Sagan meant, and she made a voiceless "oh."

Nathan cleared his throat. "Well, I suppose it's the best we've got, short of kidnapping a Magneii and forcing them to train you."

"Great," said Nika. "When do we start?"

Sagan gently nudged her with his elbow. "You're not staying."

"What? Why?" Nika retorted. "You want her to learn how to *not* die, right? Besides, I think I'm qualified enough to help out, wouldn't you say?" She pulled an amulet from under her shirt and held it up in Sagan's face. Violet couldn't make out the image on the amulet, and she didn't understand its significance. All she could tell was that it was made of black metal and had four colored strips—silver, teal, magenta, and orange—that glowed subtly in the night. "Anyway, last I checked, your amulet—" She reached for the black chain around Sagan's neck.

With vicious speed, Sagan slapped her hand away. The poisonous glare he gave his cousin was enough to make Nika stand down, or at least decide not to make a scene in front of Violet and Nathan.

"It's fine," said Violet. "She can stay. I think we can all agree I need as much help as possible."

Sagan's expression became unreadable. Nika's grin was impish.

* * *

Violet had wanted to put off seeing Autumn as long as she could, but her friend hunted her down at breakfast the next morning and dragged her to the computer hut.

"Violet Chambers! You're an idiot!"

Violet crumpled deeper into her swivel chair as Autumn continued to lecture. The brutal scolding might have only lasted about five minutes, but it felt like half an hour.

". . . Tio lost an arm . . !"

Violet cringed. She'd wanted the ground to swallow her up when Sagan told her Dawn and Gus had amputated Tio's arm. But it was such a relief to find out Jiovis shifters had regeneration abilities. Tio had already been sporting a new arm at breakfast.

". . . You left without me . . !"

Trust Autumn to add FOMO to her lecture list. Violet almost snorted a laugh.

". . . We've lost the element of surprise, and now I won't be surprised if Xabat Labs will be expecting our next visit."

"Xabat Labs? I doubt it," cut in Violet. "We drove past that building, and it was nothing but an empty shell. No one was there."

"Exactly! Don't you think that would make the perfect cover to hide away some kind of secret facility? A place where no one goes but is also in a perfect location that's central to the city and surrounding towns? If you hadn't run off on me so fast, I would have told you their real facility is *underground*."

That revelation was like a punch to Violet's gut.

Autumn pulled up a model of Rivermyre on her computer screen, then zoomed in on a three-dimensional structure several stories below the city's surface. The image rotated on the screen, showing at least four different levels with a few offshoots that might have been connected with elevators or tunnels.

Violet's eyes bugged. "That was underground this whole time? Along with that . . . that worm thing?"

"Oh, yeah, I heard about that." Autumn quirked an

eyebrow. "A giant worm? Really? Are you sure you guys didn't smoke some crack on the way?"

Violet shot her a look that made Autumn raise her hands in surrender.

"Anyway," continued Autumn, "these plans are the latest I could find, but they're already years out of date. I have no idea what's inside. As far as satellite imagery is concerned, it may as well be a black hole; there's no evidence on the surface of anyone living in Rivermyre. But I dug deeper, and there's definitely something heavy duty going on, judging by the electrical and data drain I'm finding. I've uncovered an epic firewall surrounding the place. It's incredible. Unlike anything I've seen. It's as if there's a total void or some kind of virtual camouflage, so even when someone stumbles across it, there's nothing to see. But I found that when I—" She plunged once again into her technological lingo. And to think Autumn thought Gus and Dawn needed subtitles.

"English, please."

"Okay, okay." She pointed to another screen, which looked to Violet like nothing but lines upon lines of colored text. "I've been developing a new code to break into their network. Once I'm in, I'll be able to see what's going on, and from there I should be able to override the system to figure out how to get us in and Solace out."

"Great," said Violet. "That sounds easy enough. So how long will it take?"

"Violet, you need to understand that I'm dealing with a highly sophisticated security network here—beyond military grade. First I'll have to finish writing the code, and then I'll have to consider—"

"How long?"

"I'm not going to say, only because I don't want to get your hopes up or dash them to bits. But the moment I've broken in, you'll be the first to know."

After a heartbeat, Violet slowly nodded, doing her best to ignore the rolling wave of hopelessness in her core. It was difficult to maintain her composure, to not allow the information overload to consume her. "Who are these people?" Violet shook her head, dumbfounded. "Who is Xabat, and what do they want with my baby?"

"I don't know, Vi." Autumn reached over and took Violet's hand. "But once I crack into their system, hopefully we'll get some answers. In the meantime, I suggest you keep up your training with Nathan and the others."

"How did you know about that?"

Autumn shrugged. "There's not a whole lot I don't know." She clacked for half a second on her keyboard, and the screens filled with multiple camera views of places around Maple Shire, including the living areas of her and Gus's home. A few of the views showed different angles of the pavilion.

"So, I suppose you also know that I can now—"

"Shoot flames from your eyes and sprout crystal spikes? Heck yes! That footage was epic!"

Violet *hmmph*ed. "I don't *shoot* flames from my eyes. It just kinda . . . ignites."

"Yeah, well, the looks on everyone's faces was priceless. And by the way, that was a decent beating you gave Thane."

Violet chuckled.

Autumn held up a finger. "Question. How come your clothes don't burn when you're on fire?"

Violet blinked. "I have no idea. I hadn't thought about that. Come to think of it, my hair doesn't burn either." She inspected the ends of her hair. Not a singe or even the scent of smoke. "Which is convenient, because I'm pretty sure I would have burned off my eyelashes and eyebrows ages ago."

"Hmm . . ." Autumn chewed on her lip in thought. Then she shrugged. "It's just as well. Being butt naked would make your training sessions with Nathan and Sagan a lot more awkward."

"Ain't that the truth."

Autumn grinned when Violet covered her burning cheeks.

Returning her attention to the computer screens, Violet asked, "How long have you had the cameras?"

"I had CCTV installed when we came home from college," Autumn explained. "Because, you know, after Bessie . . . I still don't know who killed her. And with the video surveillance, I sleep better at night. Well, I did sleep better before . . . you know."

Violet nodded, grief settling in her stomach like a stone when she thought of Bessie, their bubbly friend from college. The night she was murdered, Bessie had been staying over in Violet and Autumn's dorm room while Violet was out late studying. Autumn had woken in the night to find Bessie's throat had been slashed.

Autumn had changed after that. She'd become more withdrawn and had spent countless hours on her laptop typing away with intense urgency. It was Autumn's parents who had helped reassure her and forced her to spend more time in the real world.

"Uh, Autumn?"

"Yeah?"

"I'm sorry. And not just for running off on you." Violet paused to push aside her pride. "Yesterday when I slapped you, I was out of line, and I—"

"It's my fault." Autumn turned to look her square in the face. "I shouldn't have said those things. I used you as my punching bag. I know you didn't come here looking for a fight. But . . . when my parents . . ." Autumn's gaze dropped to her lap. A tear, and then another, fell onto her hands.

"I understand." Violet reached out to wrap her arms around her friend. "I'm so sorry."

"I'm sorry too," said Autumn, hugging her back.

* * *

Violet fell into a solid routine of training with Nathan, Sagan, and Nika every night at the pavilion after the majority of Maple Shire had gone to bed. Each morning, she would wake up stiff, sore, and seriously regretting pushing her body so hard. But whenever she reached the threshold of wanting to quit, she only had to think of her daughter to keep going. Fear for Solace—the constant, terrifying questions of where she was and who had her—was, at times, crippling. Thankfully, the avalanche of new information, skills, and lists upon lists of things to remember helped occupy her mind.

It was hard to believe only a week ago she'd woken from her coma. With her growing strength and muscle, she was losing the remnants of her pregnancy body. Her stomach flattened, but her stretch marks remained. In a way, Violet was thankful for the marks; it was a reminder Solace was once a part of her, that she was still a mother.

Along with the toned body, she'd also gained greater control over her hazing. With practice, the Veniri and Magneii forms were becoming second nature, although a smooth transition into her hybrid form was still a little tricky. At first it was as if the two parts were at war with each other, but gradually Violet wrangled them under her control. Her hybrid form of magenta scales with teal magma fissures was swiftly becoming her preferred option.

Locating the positions of Venus and Mars and utilizing their energy became more natural all the time. Nathan said developing her connections with the celestial bodies would be easier at night, yet Violet was becoming increasingly aware of her connections with them during the day too.

The hardest part of her training was comprehending her new anatomy and abilities. Crystal spikes, scales, flames, fangs, poison glands, and energy orbs were all foreign concepts that belonged in a sci-fi movie, and a forked tongue that could taste emotions was just the icing on the cake. With her taste and olfactory senses enhanced, Violet's knowledge of flavors had increased exponentially. Yet remembering what they all represented was next to impossible. Even though—thankfully—each emotion's flavor was the same for everybody, the variety and complexity of emotions seemed inexhaustible.

"It's important to decipher each specific flavor within the emotional bouquet," Nathan had said to her one night. "Train your palate to distinguish even the most complicated of flavors. For example, if you sense vinegar, don't just assume the person is suffering from melancholy. What kind of vinegar is it? Balsamic vinegar represents sadness, cider vinegar represents grieving, and white vinegar represents depression. And what if you sense sweetness? What kind of sweet is it? Sticky like syrup? Artificial like candy? Natural like fruit? Also, don't fall into the idea that if a flavor tastes good, it must represent a 'good' emotion. Jealousy tastes like marshmallows, and truthfulness tastes like bleach."

He'd been giving her a list of new emotional referents every night, to the point Violet was mentally reciting them in the shower, at mealtimes, and even in her dreams.

One part of controlling her abilities was learning how to master her own emotions. They usually flared out of control when her dark thoughts spiraled around Solace, or if she happened to cross paths with Thane. Most of the time, only her eyes would ignite, but if things got too overwhelming, flames would burst from her hands too, and she would get an agonizing, searing pain in her elbows. Nathan had told her that was when her elbow blades were about to slice through her flesh.

As Violet gained more control over her abilities, she discovered how to take small advantage of them. When helping Lazareth in the kitchen, if she kept her hands aflame while she was washing the dishes, the water in the sink would stay hot for longer. She just needed to remember to turn down the heat when cleaning anything plastic. There was also a time the hot water ran out while she was showering, and her Magneii flames kept her from catching a chill.

Learning how to be an adequate shifter had Violet feeling incompetent on so many levels. Yet there was one aspect of her training she felt right at home with: the fighting. Each training session usually ended with a sparring match against Nathan, Sagan, or Nika. Sometimes Gus would come, dragging Autumn along to check out Violet's progress and cheer her on. Most nights Violet would spy Thane watching from several meters away. As far as she knew, he still wasn't aware of Solace's existence. Apparently, he'd figured the training sessions were necessary to prevent Violet from accidentally burning or skewering someone.

Nathan had her learning how to fight Veniri-style. "With your previous self-defense training, I taught you how to fend off other Erathi. As Veniri, our biggest defenses are the blades from our elbows and knee spikes."

He'd acquired a pair of boxing pads and was teaching Violet a variety of sequences to get her used to landing blows with her elbows and knees. At first, Violet couldn't quite get her head around it. What was wrong with just throwing a power punch? But with every passing night, her movements became less awkward, and the cracks and thrusts of her elbows against the pads became more robust.

Sagan's role was to teach her how to defend against

hunters and anyone else who knew Veniri and Magneii weaknesses. It was some comfort to know she now had the tough Veniri hide that was practically impenetrable except by a Diamantium weapon. The fact that Diamantium was actually bones still made her squeamish, and she shuddered at the memory of the Diamantium-tipped crossbow bolt the gray-bearded hunter had used to shoot Sagan. If she wasn't on her guard—Sagan drilled into her—one day she could be diced up and have her own bones forged into similar weapons.

Sagan's fighting style was very different from Nathan's. Sagan would kick, throw punches at, and use makeshift practice weapons on Violet's vulnerable areas over and over, forcing her to instinctively react to protect her head and torso.

Much like a human, stabbing a Veniri's heart was lethal, but it wasn't the stabbed heart itself that killed them; rather, it was puncturing one of the several nearby poison glands. "The poison glands feed into a few small shards located here, here, and here." Nathan pointed to Violet's collarbones, the tops of her shoulders, and her lower ribs. "The poison is highly corrosive, like acid. Once a gland is punctured, it melts away your surrounding organs within seconds." He went on to explain that flesh reacted differently to the poison. "In dire circumstances, the glands can be cut out and used to cauterize wounds."

Nika had scoffed at this statement. "When would Violet ever need to cut out a gland for cauterizing?"

Nathan didn't answer. The guarded expression on his face made Violet curious about what exactly he wasn't saying.

Other than her heart, Sagan told Violet she needed to protect her head. The Magneii were hunted for their Luxiums, energy orbs with an infinite lifespan. The hunters used them to power flashlights, vehicles, power plants, high-tech weapons, and everything in between. The Luxium was located in the Magneii's skull, right behind their eyes.

"If you can light your eyes on fire, then you definitely have a Luxium," said Sagan. "If the Luxium is damaged, the Magneii dies instantly. In a fight, a hunter usually tries to cut their head off to reduce the risk of damaging the Luxium. Otherwise, a strong, direct hit between the eyes gets the job done."

As for Nika, Violet wasn't exactly sure what her job was. If anything, training seemed to be Nika's excuse to use her as a punching bag.

"Don't take your eyes off Nika," said Sagan while Violet and Nika circled each other for a sparring match. "Watch where she looks. Take note of even the slightest movement."

"Use your other senses as well," Nathan cut in. "Now would be a good time to taste her intentions."

The tingling sensation in Violet's mouth grew stronger, and she allowed her tongue to change into its whip-like form. As instructed by Nathan, she lashed it out, snakelike, and braced herself for the chaotic rush of flavors.

Nika took advantage of Violet's sudden disorientation to land a solid punch to the side of her head. Violet growled, her ear ringing.

"What are the flavors telling you?" Nathan called out.

"Uh . . ." Violet shook her head, trying to clear the ringing and make sense of what she was tasting. "I think—"

Nika attacked her with a three-punch sequence to the head, followed by a knee below the belt.

Violet ground her teeth, biting back her groan of pain. Where Nathan and Sagan had a level of honor, respect, and restraint during sparring, Nika was a downright dirty fighter. Violet was glad she wasn't a guy, but that knee to the groin still hurt like a mother.

"Come on, Violet. Concentrate," demanded Nathan.

Nika hooked another punch at her ribs, but Violet managed to block the blow at the last second.

"Knees. Remember to use your knees," Nathan reminded her.

"I know," Violet gritted out.

Again, Nika came at her, landing more blows around her head and stomach. When Violet managed to throw a punch of her own, her fist only cut through the air.

"Elbows!" Nathan shouted. "Your shards aren't out, so it's safe to crack her with an elbow."

This time when Nika charged her, Violet aimed an elbow strike at her face. The blow landed but not as hard as she would have liked, as the other girl sidestepped at the last second. Nika then countered with a swift jab-cross-jab to Violet's diaphragm.

Violet stumbled back, giving herself space to return some air to her lungs. The hunter laughed maliciously.

"Nika," Sagan warned.

Nika ignored him.

"You're enjoying this too much," Violet said in a low voice.

Nika shrugged and tucked a loose strand of hair behind her ear. "You want to learn how to survive in this world, slith. Don't expect me to go easy on you." Before she'd even finished speaking, she slammed a fist into Violet's jaw.

Violet wiped her mouth, surprised not to find any blood. Then she remembered her tough Veniri hide. It was a shame that even though her flesh was hard to cut, she still felt every slap, kick, and punch with as much intensity as when she was a human.

Nika laughed again, and Violet's body began to shake from frustration and rising fury.

Nika rushed her, but this time Violet was ready. She

blocked an incoming punch to her head and, using the blow's momentum, swung Nika's arm out. In the same swift move, Violet hooked her hands around the back of the hunter's neck and yanked her into a headlock. Nika grunted with surprise, then with pain as Violet slammed one knee and then another up into her opponent's belly.

"That's it! Dig your elbows into her collarbone. Don't let her break through your defenses," urged Nathan.

Violet's strength drained as Nika writhed. She managed to land two more knee strikes, but the hunter connected a few painful low punches as well. Pivoting on her heels, Violet used the centrifugal force to throw Nika to the side, then finished the move with a kick to her ribs.

A cheer erupted from both Nathan and Sagan.

Violet couldn't help but give Nika a victory grin. "How d'ya like me now, hunter?"

Nika's air of foolhardy arrogance had disintegrated, especially after she shot a pointed look at the cheering spectators.

Violet's grin faltered at the cold bitterness in Nika's eyes.

"Great job, Violet," said Nathan. "How about we call it a night?"

"We're not finished yet," Nika said, then lunged.

For the first time, Violet's kneejerk reaction was to lash out her snakelike tongue before she braced for the collision.

The pummeling was endless. Every bit of training abandoned Violet; pure instinct overtook her blank mind as she blocked and parried as many of the vicious blows as possible. As Violet's endurance began to wane, Nika's assault only became more intense.

"Nika, slow down," Sagan called out.

More shouts followed, but Violet had to tune them out, focusing all her attention on keeping up with the never-ending flurry of attacks.

Violet managed to block most of the punches, then

spotted an opening and ducked under Nika's incoming fist. Nika sailed past her but spun back around almost instantly, locking Violet in place with a ferocious glare.

Run, everything inside Violet screamed. *Run.* To avoid being attacked again. To avoid being a victim again. It was what she knew best. Throughout her entire childhood, she'd run from every foster home. She'd run when she discovered Thane's true identity. She'd run when Nathan betrayed her. And at Rivermyre, she'd done nothing but run.

Then the image of her daughter sprang to mind.

The molten heat in Violet's chest churned.

No more, she thought. *No more running.* The inferno in Violet's chest spread through her whole body, igniting the flames in her eyes and over her hands.

Nika's expression turned greedy. "You think a little fire is going to save you?"

Violet ignored her and lunged.

The hunter dodged.

Violet stumbled, colliding with nothing but air. She spun and rushed again. Nika sidestepped but not before swinging a punch at Violet.

"You're allowing your anger to take control, Violet," Nathan shouted. "Pull yourself together."

Violet half turned to tell him to shut up, but instead she *ooph*ed when Nika's fist sank into her stomach. As she reflexively hunched forward, the hunter met her with a mighty uppercut to the jaw. The blow snapped Violet's head back, and she slammed to the ground, winded by the impact.

Violet cried out from the searing agony radiating through her face. As she tried to refill her empty lungs, she cupped her chin and was surprised to find it sticky. Her hand came away covered in a viscous teal liquid streaked with magenta.

She was bleeding. But how?

In confusion, she looked up at Nika. The hunter's eyes glittered at the sight of Violet's unique blood.

In a split second, Nika pounced on Violet and pinned her to the ground. Pain sliced across Violet's cheekbone as the hunter's fist came down onto her face.

She screamed.

As Nika pulled her arm back for another blow, Violet spotted a row of crystal shards sparkling across her knuckles.

I KNOW WHAT CINNAMON MEANS

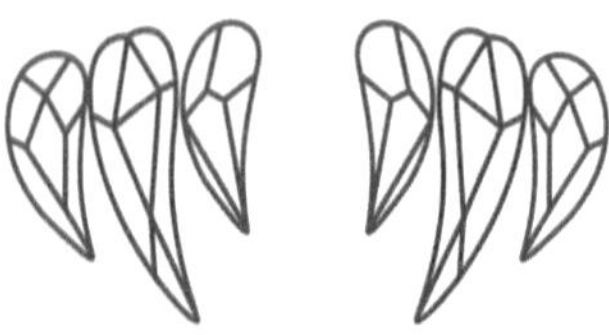

VIOLET'S SCREAMS RIPPED THROUGH NATHAN'S EARDRUMS. IT took half a second before his mind comprehended what he was seeing. *Is that blood? Violet's blood?*

Before he could react, a blurred form shot past him.

Thane rushed in and wedged himself between Violet and Nika's cascade of punches. Blotches of teal began to bloom over his shirt.

Nathan lunged forward just as Sagan intercepted Nika's final punch by grabbing her arm. Collectively, the two of them dragged Nika back as she writhed and bellowed, struggling against them tooth and nail.

"Nika, stop!" Sagan demanded. "What the hell is wrong with you?"

Nika's arm broke out of Sagan's hold, and her flailing fist clipped Nathan's arm. He hissed at the sudden pain and streak of teal along his bicep. Catching her wrist, he inspected the offending fist.

His blood sizzled with rage when he spotted the Diamantium knuckle-buster. He dropped his hold on the hunter as if she were infected with the plague and, instead, focused all his attention on Violet. She was still curled on her side, with Thane crouched over her unmoving form.

"Violet?" Thane gingerly rolled her onto her back.

She coughed.

Nathan's spark of relief died when he saw the gore that coated Violet's face and the amount of blood she coughed up. She blinked slowly, as if waking from a drug-induced sleep. Thane carefully helped her into a sitting position, then placed his arms under her back and knees and lifted her off the ground.

Violet groaned again and mumbled something Nathan didn't quite catch.

"What did she say?" he asked.

Violet mumbled again; Thane's expression became stricken with horror.

Cinnamon.

That single word plunged the knife of shame further into Nathan's chest.

Thane fixed Nathan with a deadly, accusatory glare. "How could you let this happen?" He didn't wait for Nathan to answer. Instead, he gently bundled Violet tighter into his arms and carried her away.

"See, she's fine," said Nika as Thane left. "Now she can get a lesson on healing herself."

Nathan's anger boiled to the brim. His knuckles cracked from the intense pressure of his clenched fists, and he didn't need to look down to confirm his elbow blades were out. Savage tremors racked his entire body.

He set his sights on Nika. "You filthy—" His mouth erupted with fangs. "You're going to pay."

Nika's eyes grew wide. She at least had the intelligence to appear afraid.

But before Nathan could spring forward, Sagan's

Diamantium dagger bit into his neck. When Nathan tried to step around him, Sagan stood firm.

"Move out of my way, *hunter.*" Nathan spat the last word, as if it were the foulest thing he'd ever tasted.

"No," said Sagan, his tone void of emotion.

"If you don't move out of my way, I will rip your throat out as well as hers."

Nika laughed. "Good luck, slith."

Sagan's blade didn't budge even a hairsbreadth.

Nathan's disbelief that Sagan was defending his cousin rooted him in place even more than the knife. Clearly it didn't take much for an ex-hunter to revert back to their cold-blooded ways. Nathan took half a step, but Sagan's dagger pressed deeper into his neck.

It took everything in Nathan's power not to unleash his attack on Sagan. He released a guttural growl. "Violet said . . . she scented . . ."

"I know," said Sagan in a voice low enough only Nathan could hear. "I know what cinnamon means."

Nathan's rage faltered. Tearing his murderous gaze away from Nika for the first time, he saw the icy savagery behind Sagan's calm facade.

"Leave her to me," said Sagan.

Nika scoffed. "Seriously? What's the big deal? I thought we were here to train her."

Nathan's anger flared again, but he reined it in when he read the pleading message in Sagan's eyes. With a slight dip of his head, Nathan took a step back.

Sagan turned to his cousin.

"Aw, come on, cuz." Nika rolled her eyes. "Don't look at me like that. I didn't do anything that wasn't done to us in our training. That was nothing compared to what your father put you through."

"You are not my father," said Sagan, the words slow and deliberate, "and Violet is not me."

"Gee, Einstein, thanks for clearing that up for me. This whole time I've been so confused." Nika's laugh was without humor. "Lighten up. She has to learn."

"Yes. She has to learn how to become a shifter. Not a hunter."

"Well, duh! But if Violet's going to stand any kind of chance against a hunter, then it's best—"

Sagan sprang forward into Nika's face. "You don't get to make those decisions," he hissed, a slight tremor in his voice. "You don't know the first thing about what's best for Violet."

Nika's smirk wavered. "But . . . she needs to learn. She's . . . just a slith."

"She's more than you'll ever know." Sagan's back was ramrod straight, his neck and shoulders tense. Raw emotion glittered behind his icy eyes.

Nika's bewildered expression melted, leaving behind cold granite. "Don't tell me you're choosing her over me."

Sagan gave a sharp shake of his head. "Of course not. You're my cousin. But you crossed the line, Nika. You can't let it happen again."

"Oh, really?" Nika put her hands on her hips and narrowed her eyes. "And what if it does? What are you going to do about it, huh? Are you going to punish me like Grandpa?"

"No. But if you hurt Violet like that again—"

"You'll what?" The challenge in her eyes was lethal.

A second passed. Then, with one swift move, Sagan grabbed hold of Nika's amulet and slammed the handle of his dagger onto the decorative face. The crack of glass rang out into the night.

Nika let out a shrill cry, her eyes wide with horror, as liquid dripped from the amulet in Sagan's hand and pooled onto the ground. Four colors—silver, teal, magenta, and orange—merged into a small puddle between their feet.

"There's a reason we left the hunters. It's best you remember that," said Sagan.

Nika looked back up at him, her expression unreadable. Then she yanked her amulet from his hand and stormed off into the night.

SPEAKING OF HURLING

VIOLET HAD ONLY A HAZY, DISTANT AWARENESS THAT SOMEONE was carrying her. Lights flashed past her half-open eyes, and it took her brain a moment to register that they were fluorescent bulbs on the ceiling of a hallway. Who had her? Where were they taking her?

She groaned. And why did she feel as though she'd just come out of a blender?

"It's okay, Violet. We're nearly there."

The molten heat that had been burning in her gut lately turned to ice when she recognized that voice.

"Put me down," she demanded.

"I'm taking you to Dawn," said Thane.

"I don't care. Put me down now."

"Ten more feet."

"I said *now*." Violet tried to buck out of his arms, then immediately regretted it when stabbing pains shot up both her sides and all along her back. The sudden pain shocked her so much that she sucked in a sharp breath and held it until the agony subsided.

All the while, Thane's grip around her remained solid. "Three more steps and the doc will have you taken care of."

A muffled groan was all Violet could manage in reply. She hated the soothing effect his voice still had on her, even now —but that was nothing compared to the chagrin she felt when she realized how tightly she'd been clutching his shirt. Her surge of disgust as she removed her hands almost muted the physical pain.

"We need some help here," Thane called out.

Violet caught sight of Gus's and Dawn's shocked expressions as Thane set her down on a stretcher bed.

"Violet? What happened?" Dawn rushed over and immediately began assessing Violet's condition.

Gus set his sights on Thane. "What did you do?"

Thane gaped at him for a moment. Then his eyes narrowed, and his hands balled into fists. "I didn't do this," he said, his voice dangerously low.

For several seconds, he and Gus had a staring showdown.

Violet decided she'd better intervene before Gus became pulp at the end of Thane's fist. "I'm okay, Gus."

Gus just shook his head before stepping around Thane to help his mother.

Several Steri-Strips, a bottle of medical glue, and a mountain of dirty swabs later, Violet gingerly slid off the stretcher. She was going to have some epic bruising in the morning. "Thanks, Dawn," she said, wincing slightly as Dawn helped her back into her shirt.

Thane had stepped behind the curtain divider when Dawn asked Violet to undress so she could assess the damage to her torso. But Violet was certain he hadn't left altogether. Her suspicion was confirmed when Dawn pushed back the curtain to reveal Thane hunched over in a chair by the door, his forearms resting on his knees. Patches of teal blood were still evident on his shirt, even after Gus had addressed Thane's cuts.

Gus handed Violet a small vial of some funky-looking liquid. "Before you turn up your nose, this is a Veniri painkiller I've concocted."

"Really?"

"Yeah, I, uh . . ." He donned a sheepish expression. "I've had a few chats with Nathan, and I figured if Mom can develop a formula specifically for Veniri babies, I ought to be able to come up with some Veniri painkillers. Especially since Nathan told me that most human—or rather, *Erathi*—medication is useless for shifters."

Dawn patted her son's shoulder, pride evident in her beaming smile.

Violet took the vial, but she couldn't stop her face from screwing up once she caught a whiff of the rancid odor.

"I've made sure to use nothing that would be harmful to a Veniri."

"What about a Magneii?" Thane asked.

Gus swiveled, almost as if he'd forgotten Thane was there. "Uh, actually"—he rubbed the back of his neck—"I'm not one-hundred-percent sure on the details of the Magneii shifters yet. I'll admit, it might need a little tweaking."

"She shouldn't need it," interjected Thane. "Compared to the Erathi, the Veniri and the Magneii have accelerated healing abilities. Granted, it can be painful, but give her a day or two, and she'll be back to one hundred percent. That's if Nathan and Sagan don't stand by and let her get an ass-kicking again."

Violet opened her mouth to retort, but Thane was already throwing more questions at Gus.

"How do you know that stuff won't cause more damage? Who have you tested it on?"

Gus winced and cleared his throat. "I, uh, haven't tested it on anybody."

Thane's jaw dropped open. "And you expect Violet—"

"It's okay, Gus. I trust you." Violet gave her friend a reassuring smile. Then, before she or anyone else could talk her out of it, she chugged down the contents of the vial. The taste was a thousand times worse than the smell, but Violet forced her gag reflex into submission. Even so, she couldn't help grimacing.

Thane's expression and body went rigid—with fury or concern, Violet wasn't quite sure. She'd be able to figure it out with a lash of her tongue, but when it came to Thane, knowing his emotions felt a little too . . . intimate.

"Thanks for the painkillers, Gus. I'll let you know how it goes."

"Actually, before you go, I need to talk to you about . . . um . . ." Gus shot Thane a sidelong glance.

Thane huffed out a small breath. "I'll wait out in the hall."

Only after Dawn closed the door behind Thane did Gus say, "I think I may have figured out how you became a hybrid shifter."

Violet's eyes bugged. "How?"

"Well, I've been working on this theory. To be a shifter, you have to either be born one or be bitten by one. Right?"

"Yeah."

"Clearly you weren't born one. So that leaves the shifter bite."

Violet frowned. "But if a shifter bites a human, doesn't the human generally die?"

"Yeah."

"And I have two shifter abilities. To go along with your biting theory, I would have to have been bitten by two different shifters."

Gus grinned. "Exactly. Not one but two bites."

Violet blinked several times. "I think you lost me."

Gus reached over and gently held up Violet's arm. "At first I thought that blonde Magneii injured you with her flames." He pointed to the scarring on her forearm that looked like an acid burn. "But I had a closer look when I was replacing the bandages. She bit you, didn't she?"

Flashbacks of that day flickered through Violet's mind as she stared at the raised flesh. "No way." Her words were barely a whisper. In the chaos of the fight, waking up from a coma, then dealing with the aftermath of losing Solace—as well as Skye and Cruz—some of the finer details had become blurry. It made her feel stupid now that she was thinking about it. That day was the only time she'd ever encountered the Magneii, so of course that was when she'd contracted her shifter abilities.

"But I've never been bitten by a Veniri, so that doesn't explain that side of things. Or why I'm not dead."

Gus held up her other hand.

Violet's mouth dropped open, and she stumbled a step back. It had been staring at her this whole time. She *had* been bitten by a Veniri, by her own daughter.

"My theory is," said Gus, "the reason you didn't die when Solace bit you is because half of her DNA is yours. But I think her bite still affected you. Do you remember when you had that cold for weeks after she was born? What if it wasn't a cold? What if her bite somehow changed you? What if she gave you Veniri abilities, and those abilities were dormant until the day a Magneii bit you?"

Silence flooded the room for a few heartbeats. Violet brushed her fingers over the small Veniri bite mark between her thumb and forefinger, then looked over at Dawn, who had been quiet the whole time. "Is it possible?"

Dawn nodded. "I certainly believe Gus's theory is plausible. I even convinced all three mothers down the hall to get their blood tested. Of the three mothers, two confirmed that they had been bitten by their children. Those two also went through a phase where they thought they had a bad cold, and when we compared their blood to the blood we took from you before the Magneii attack, we found some similar anomalies. It's likely they've also developed Veniri abilities, but those abilities are currently dormant."

"So those mothers will one day be like me?" Violet asked.

"Perhaps," said Dawn. "Perhaps not."

"The only way to test it would be to have a shifter from another race bite them," said Gus. "They'd likely become dual shifters, like you."

"Okay . . . so if we don't die from a bite from our own children, how is it I survived the second bite?"

"That's where my theory gets a little hazy," admitted Gus. "Maybe the bite from Solace somehow protected you. Or maybe, statistically speaking, you're one of the rare lucky ones who can survive a shifter bite."

Violet squeezed her eyes shut and rubbed her temples.

"I know it's a lot to take in," said Dawn. "Gus and I are here for you. And we are doing our best to find more answers."

"Do the mothers know? I mean, are they aware that it's possible for them to acquire shape-shifting abilities?"

"No," said Dawn. "In fact, we think it's best this information stays between us. If this leaked to the wrong people, who knows how dire the consequences might be."

Violet and Gus nodded in agreement. Then, after an outpouring of thanks for their help, Violet left the room. Much to her displeasure, Thane was still waiting for her in the hallway.

"You shouldn't have drunk that stuff," he said.

Violet rolled her eyes. "I feel fine. Besides, the last thing Gus would do is poison me."

"Maybe not intentionally. Don't get me wrong, he and his mother know what they're doing when it comes to the Erathi, but they're not all knowing when it comes to shifters."

"Oh, yeah? And I suppose you're the 'all knowing' one, huh? Considering you're a Veniri. Right?"

Thane blanched. "How did you . . . Did Nathan tell you? Or was it Sagan?"

"No one told me."

He regarded her with a creased brow. "Then how?"

Without answering, Violet began walking toward the exit. As if she was going to mention that her baby shifting was the tip-off. No way was she ready to tell him about Solace.

Just when she began to think he'd leave her alone, she heard Thane's footsteps behind her, and he appeared in her periphery.

"Whatever Nathan or Sagan or anyone else told you, I can explain."

"Just forget it. I'm not in the mood for a backstory chat. Oh, and another thing. Just because it turns out you're a Veniri doesn't mean you get to start making decisions for me."

Thane scoffed. "Of course not. All I'm trying to say is, you're a shifter now. Not only that—you're a hybrid shifter. Do you have any idea what that means? From what I know, a hybrid is unheard of. Shifters don't survive a bite from another race. Don't you see? You're special. When the news starts to spread, others will come from far and wide to try to hunt you down and take what you have. You need to be careful. That elixir Gus gave you might be a painkiller for your Veniri side, but who knows? It might make your Magneii side vulnerable."

It was Violet's turn to scoff. "And you know all about what makes me vulnerable, don't you?"

Thane crinkled his nose and raked a hand through his beach-blond hair. Violet half expected him to bark an insult at her and storm away. But he didn't. He kept walking beside her in silence, matching her brisk pace.

She shot a sidelong glance at him. He was hunched forward, his hands deep in the pockets of his jeans. A small part of her wanted to apologize for her prickly attitude, but then she reminded herself she should be glad he was feeling just as miserable as she was. Her head swam with all the raging insults she wanted to hurl at the man who had lied to her and watched her best friend die.

Violet froze. Speaking of hurling . . .

Her hand flew to her mouth. In a flurry, she spun and sprinted back down the hall toward the ladies' bathroom. Judging by the thumping footfalls that followed her, Thane was right on her tail.

She shoved the bathroom door open, ducked into a stall, and expelled Gus's revolting medicine from her stomach. The taste was even more wretched on the way back up.

"Don't say it," said Violet when she'd stopped gagging.

"I wasn't going to." Despite the rank smell Violet was creating, Thane was holding her hair out of the way and handing her paper towels when she needed them.

After rinsing her mouth out and splashing water on her face, Violet gripped the sides of the sink. Her head drooped to her chest.

"How are you feeling now?" Thane asked.

She winced. *Why is he still here?*

"Your stomach might feel better, but how does the rest of you feel?"

When she thought about it, she was pain free. Gus's painkiller had worked. "I'm fine. There's no pain." She lifted her head to tell Thane where he could shove his doubts about

Gus's medicine, but instantly, she was overcome with a dizzy spell.

Thane caught her before she could crack her head on the sink. "Violet?"

"I'm fine. I just . . . whoa." The room began to spin. "I feel like I drank way too many tequila shots."

The next thing Violet knew, she was back in Thane's arms. The dizziness lasted as long as it took him to carry her all the way to her bedroom.

When he gently laid her down on her bed, he asked, "Feeling any better?"

Violet stared at the ceiling, trying to maintain her nonchalance in the face of Thane's close proximity. "Yeah. This room isn't spinning. Maybe the bathroom is broken."

Thane chuckled, catching her off guard. She couldn't remember the last time she'd seen him smile, let alone laugh. *That's because you haven't seen him in almost a year, and you've been avoiding him like the plague*, she told herself.

His chuckles died down, and for a second, they just looked at each other. For the first time, Violet noticed the golden flecks that used to be in Thane's irises were absent, leaving them a drab brown.

"I think I just need to sleep it off," she said, trying to ignore the feelings stirring in her core.

Thankfully, Thane took the hint and stood up. "In that case, I'll leave you to it, Ronda Rousey."

Violet frowned. "Who and what now?"

"She's a famous Erathi fighter."

Violet blinked.

"Never mind," Thane said with a smile. "See you in the morning."

Violet stared at the door long after he'd left, contemplating: *Did he forget to turn the light off, or did he remember I prefer to sleep with it on?*

SWAROVSKI CRYSTAL STATUE

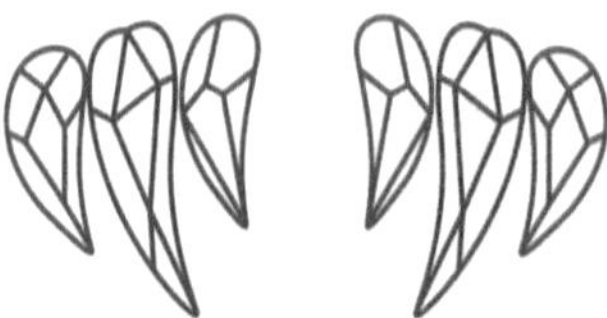

After Nika stormed off, Nathan and Sagan sat in contemplative silence on the edge of the pavilion platform, looking up at the night sky.

"I'm sorry I didn't end up helping you with your mission," Nathan finally said. "I got a little caught up."

Sagan frowned. "What mission?"

"The Veniri queen's assassination."

"Oh, right. That one." Sagan hissed out a long sigh. "That feels like ancient history now. At the time it felt like it was my ultimate goal in life. But now . . ."

"Yeah, I know what you mean. I felt the same way. It took me a while to drop the obsession of plotting to kill Idalia."

"I haven't decided not to kill her. My sister will get her justice. And you're definitely still going to help me."

Nathan huffed a laugh. "Fine."

"But first we help Violet and Solace."

"Of course. Violet and Solace first."

"How long has your skin been like that?" Sagan asked, catching Nathan off guard.

His insides turned to granite. "Like what?"

Sagan fixed him with a don't-bother-lying-to-me look. "When you were about to attack Nika, I saw your chest was crystallized. Last time I checked, you had scales."

"Last time?" Nathan quirked his head to the side. "Do you mean the time your sociopathic father made you stab me in the chest, just for funsies?"

A mix of emotions swiftly crossed Sagan's face, and Nathan mentally rebuked himself for prodding at what was clearly still a sore point for both of them.

"So, what's going on?" Sagan asked again. "Since when do sliths grow Diamantium skin?"

"They don't." Nathan shrugged. "I, uh . . ." There was no point trying to make something up; Sagan was way too in tune with his BS radar. "I don't know what's going on. And from what I can tell, I don't think it's Diamantium. It's . . . different."

Sagan's eyebrows shot up. "How do you mean?"

Nathan tilted his gaze to the stars, searching for the right words. "Well, Diamantium is rigid. The other stuff is somewhat flexible."

"Show me."

"Now?" Nathan glanced around.

Sagan rolled his eyes, as if Nathan were a toddler throwing a tantrum. "*Show me.*"

Nathan reached for the top button of his shirt, then hesitated. "You know this is weird, right? You're basically asking me to undress—"

"Just do it," Sagan snapped.

"Okay, okay."

* * *

When Sagan dragged Nathan into the infirmary, they interrupted Dawn and Gus busily clearing away a mound of bloodied swabs. Nathan's chest constricted when he recognized the teal-and-magenta combination. So much blood . . .

"How's Violet?" he asked.

"Aside from looking like Frankenstein's bride, you mean?" Gus's expression was hard.

Nathan's shoulders hunched. There was no excuse—no worthy explanation. Once again, he'd failed to protect Violet.

Dawn laid a hand on his shoulder. "If it helps, none of her injuries were permanent, and with a little rest, I'm sure she'll be back to one hundred percent in no time. And even though you might be blaming yourself for what happened, just know that Violet wasn't blaming anyone."

Nathan crossed his arms. "You're letting me off the hook way too easy, Dawn. But thanks."

Dawn gave him a kind smile, then glanced between Nathan and Sagan. "I have a feeling that's not the only reason you're here."

Sagan closed the door and flicked the lock before turning to Nathan. "Show them what you showed me."

"Wait!" Gus held up both hands. "If this has anything to do with butts or junk, I'm outta here. I'm definitely not qualified for any of that."

"August Farrow!" Dawn rounded on him with a stern look of disapproval.

"Relax." Sagan leaned back against the door. "Do you think I would be here if it was anything like that?"

Nathan raised a hand. "Uh, I also wouldn't be here if it was anything like that."

"Good point," said Gus.

Dawn tutted, cutting the conversation off before it became any more awkward. "What do you need to show us, Nathan?"

A hush fell over the room as Nathan stripped off his shirt.

"Whoa!" Gus's jaw dropped. "What is that? Is that a Veniri thing?"

"No . . ." Dawn's forehead crinkled in a thoughtful frown as she moved closer. The patch now covered Nathan's entire shoulder, along with the area beneath his collarbone, and was heading toward his sternum.

"Have you seen anything like this before?" Nathan asked.

"Never. Do you mind if I . . . ?" She gestured to the crystal flesh.

Nathan shrugged. "Sure, go ahead."

Dawn pressed the crystal patch with one fingertip, and it dimpled like skin under the gentle pressure. Nathan had to hold back his shock at the sensation; he could swear he felt every tiny ridge in the texture of her skin.

Gus moved to stand next to his mother. "What is it?"

Dawn shook her head. "I can't begin to imagine. What happens when you haze? Does it still affect your scales?"

Nathan hazed from the waist up. There was no point in ruining another pair of pants if he didn't have to.

"Hmm . . ." Dawn studied the still-crystallized flesh inter-woven with his scales, then examined the area on his calf. Nathan tried to suppress his horror that the crystallized surface on his leg had started to wrap around his ankle and head up toward his knee.

By the time Nathan finished explaining the details of how and when he first noticed the patches, the group had already begun to speculate about possible causes and hypothetical cures, with Gus furiously scribbling notes on a clipboard.

Had Nathan's stress and anxiety in Tempecrest brought about some kind of physical manifestation?

Was there a genetic anomaly in Nathan's DNA that had recently been triggered?

Had Nathan picked up a rare disease in Tempecrest?

Was this some kind of Veniri autoimmune disease?

Was Nathan being possessed by a Veniri demon?—that was Gus's question.

Was Nathan progressing to the next stage of the Veniri's evolutionary process?—that was also a Gus question.

"Actually," said Nathan, suddenly struck by a memory, "now that I think about it, there was something unusual that happened right after"—he shot a pointed look at Sagan—"Aphrodite."

At the mention of the hunters' light cannon, Sagan's eyes widened.

"You said that no one had survived long enough to know the full effects of Aphrodite," said Nathan.

"No." Sagan's features hardened.

Gus's head swiveled between them. "Care to elaborate?"

"The Aphrodite is a tool the hunters use in harvesting Diamantium," Sagan replied. "It's a light cannon that sends out a condensed, artificial beam of Venusian light that forces the Veniri to haze and expose their shards. The Aphrodite also ensures the Veniri doesn't shift back into human form even when they . . ." He winced. ". . . even after they die."

Gus's pen hovered over the clipboard as his mouth formed an "oh."

"And this *Aphrodite* was used on Nathan?" Dawn asked.

"Yes," confirmed Nathan and Sagan at the same time.

"And you think things started to change after that?"

Nathan nodded. "Yes."

"What kind of changes do you recall?"

Gus proceeded to scribble as Nathan answered. "The first thing was that I couldn't haze out of Veniri form. That was when Sagan helped me to escape the hunter's bunker. After that, I discovered I can jump higher, run faster, and punch harder. And then there's my elbow blades." He held up one of his arms and released the Diamantium blade from his elbow.

The crystal shard ran parallel to his forearm, the tip just shy of his wrist.

Gus's eyes bugged. "Whoa. Cool."

"I used to get an agonizing pain right before my blades sliced out from my elbows. But now I feel nothing."

"That doesn't sound too bad to me," said Gus.

"Believe me, it's bad," said Nathan. "The blades are a defense mechanism. If I'm in danger or a heightened emotional state, they can automatically release. The pain used to warn me, and I could pull myself under control before the blades appeared. Now it's next to impossible for me to contain them."

Dawn gazed into space, her index finger tapping her lips.

"What're you thinking, Mom?" Gus asked.

"Hmm, I'm not sure yet. The only way to confirm anything is with more observation and testing."

Without any further delay, Gus and Dawn checked and recorded Nathan's vitals, took photos and measurements of the crystallized patches, and drew blood samples. Nathan gritted his teeth when Dawn cut out a small section of the crystallized skin with a Diamantium-edged scalpel. She also collected a small section of his scales to compare under the microscope later.

The last thing they did was draw up a schedule for Nathan to come see them every day.

Not even twenty-four hours later, however, Dawn and Gus had some disturbing news.

"Now, just to clarify," began Dawn, "this is just what we've discovered since we saw you last night. Further tests need to be performed before we can confirm anything."

Nathan nodded, trying to ignore the sinking feeling in his gut. "Just give it to me straight, Dawn."

She gave him a tight-lipped smile as Gus opened a little box and pulled out two glass microscope slides.

"As you'll see, the sample on the left is your scaled flesh, and the other is the crystallized flesh." Gus held up what looked like a little flashlight. "I borrowed this from Sagan. It's a smaller and much less powerful version of what you guys called the Aphrodite. Take a look at the scales."

As Dawn switched off the lights, Gus slipped the slide into the microscope and gestured for Nathan to look into the eyepiece.

The image Nathan saw looked like a lumpy mound of playdough randomly hatch-marked by deep crevices.

"What you're seeing is actually your flesh, or rather your un-hazed skin," explained Gus.

Nathan frowned into the eyepiece. "I thought you said they were scales?"

"I did. As you would probably expect, when your body isn't reacting to Venusian energy, it reverts back to its human state, right?"

"Right," said Nathan.

"Now, watch this."

A teal light appeared at the edge of the image. Where the light washed over the skin, the lumpy mass rippled with an inner glow, then began to warp until the hatch pattern morphed into hundreds of glowing circular cells. But when Gus pulled the flashlight away, the glowing cells reverted back to their original state.

"You've just witnessed what your flesh looks like at a microscopic level when it hazes," explained Gus.

Nathan whistled. "I've never seen it from that perspective before. It looks pretty awesome."

"Wait till you see this." Gus pulled out the slide and replaced it with the second one. "This is a sample we took from the edge of the crystallized patch. You'll already notice some differences."

"Yeah, you're right," said Nathan, looking into the eyepiece. This image had the same lumpy playdough-like texture, but tiny flecks of iridescence glittered across the surface.

"Now, this sample hasn't been exposed to Sagan's flashlight yet," said Gus. "Watch what happens."

Again, the teal beam of light shot over the skin sample; again, the lumpy mass began to glow, undulate, and transform into hundreds of shimmering circular cells. But this time the cells began to stretch and split into thousands of tiny shards, with tiny rainbow flecks reflecting off each splinter. When the light disappeared, the splinters shifted back into the lumpy mass, but the glittery particles seemed a little bigger than before.

"What just happened?" Nathan asked.

"We're not sure yet." Gus exchanged a look with Dawn. "But we have a theory based on these next slides."

Nathan kept his eye on the microscope's eyepiece as Gus slid in slide after slide.

"This sample of your scales was exposed to the Venusian beam for one minute. This next slide, ten minutes. This slide was thirty. The last, an hour."

With each slide, the iridescent glitter fragments gradually took over the lumpy skin texture—until, in the last slide, the skin had completely disappeared.

Nathan tore his gaze from the microscope, his heart pounding against his rib cage. When Dawn turned on the lights, the slideshow almost felt like a daydream.

"You said you had a theory. What is it?"

"Well, nothing's confirmed yet," Gus hedged.

Nathan rubbed his eyes with the heels of his hands. "Just spit it out."

"We believe that the more your body is exposed to Venusian energy, the more the crystal will spread, until eventually . . ."

"Eventually I'll be all crystal," said Nathan when Gus didn't finish.

"Yes."

Dawn stepped up beside Gus. "We also believe it could affect your shifting abilities—as in, there could be a chance you won't be able to haze back into human form."

A few seconds of silence passed as Nathan let that sink in. "How long?"

"We don't know," said Dawn. "We're still in the very early stages of figuring out what's going on. But from what we've already seen, we assume the crystallization process takes effect only while you're in Veniri form."

"So you're saying I can't ever shift again. I have to stay in human form for the rest of my life if I don't want to . . . to become a life-sized Swarovski crystal statue."

"Well, technically, you would be a life-sized Diamantium statue—"

Dawn elbowed Gus to make him shut up. "At the moment, we're only speaking in hypotheticals. There's no guarantee this condition is a death sentence."

"Do you seriously believe that?"

Dawn's lips pressed into a stern line. "I'll admit I'm concerned about how far this crystallization will spread and what will happen if it starts to affect your muscle tissue and your internal organs, or even your . . ." She paused for several heartbeats. "Perhaps your brain may one day be affected too, if it hasn't been already. I might even say, if you are determined to continue shifting into Veniri form, you might want to consider putting your affairs in order."

* * *

"So, what did Gus and Dawn have to say?"

Nathan looked up. "Huh?"

Sagan quirked an eyebrow. "Gus and Dawn. What did they say?"

"Oh, um . . . they're not too sure what's causing the crystallization. More tests need to be done, at least before anything can be confirmed."

"What needs to be confirmed?"

. . . consider putting your affairs in order.

After a slight hesitation, Nathan shrugged. "Not a whole lot."

"Riiight." Sagan crossed his arms, studying him.

Seconds dragged by, but Nathan couldn't think of anything to say or do to break Sagan's pale, icy gaze or the building tension. Hopefully, the others would arrive soon to get the training session underway.

After the whole "Nika beating the crap out of Violet" incident, Violet had been adamant about continuing with training. She'd assured him that Gus and Dawn had helped her heal fast, and after all, it was *her* baby somewhere out there. It took a bit of hounding and the addition of some new training rules—such as coming up with a safe word—before Nathan had been okay with moving forward.

"Hey, sorry I'm late." Violet crossed the pavilion to join them.

Seeing the cuts and bruises on her face made Nathan inwardly cringe—Diamantium always left its mark. But the injuries already looked about a week old by human healing standards, and they even seemed to have improved significantly since Nathan spoke to her at breakfast. Perhaps it was the Magneii side of her that aided in the lack of scarring.

Thane arrived a few seconds later and took a seat on the edge of the platform—much closer than he'd watched prior to the Nika incident. He'd warned Nathan earlier that if anything else happened to Violet, it would be Nathan's skull skewered on the end of his elbow blades.

Trying to ignore Thane's ever-attentive gaze, Nathan suggested they start with a warm-up before getting into more fighting techniques.

"Actually, can we try something else?" Violet asked.

"What do you have in mind?"

"That blonde Magneii shifter, she made this." Violet pulled out a subtly glowing magenta dagger. "I swear she made it out of thin air, and she made a whip the same way. Have you heard of this? Is it a Magneii ability?"

Nathan took the dagger and examined it. "Yes, I have heard of this ability. And no, it's not just the Magneii. Any shifter can learn to do it. It's called light forging."

Violet's eyes lit up. "Can you teach me?"

He twirled the weapon in his hand. The blade was razor sharp—clearly forged by a master. "I guess I can teach you the basics."

"Basics?" Violet frowned. "Why only the basics?"

"Uh, well . . ." Nathan scratched the top of his head. *How do I explain this?* "Think of light forging like it's a piano. Anyone can bash on the keys to make sound, but it takes a lot of training and hours upon hours of practice to play it effectively. You start by playing 'Chopsticks' before you can work your way up to 'Flight of the Bumblebee.'"

"Okay, well, let's get into it then."

"All right." Nathan handed her the magenta blade. "In that case, the first step is focusing on a beam of celestial light, then condensing it into a tangible mass. To do that, as always, you need to tune in to your inner melody and locate a beam."

Nathan tried to explain the next few steps with as much clarity as possible. Violet listened intently to his instructions while Sagan and Thane watched in silence.

It didn't take her long to locate a beam, and after a few

tries, a small bundle of teal light about the size of a sesame seed began to hover several inches above her hand. The mass grew into an undulating pea-sized globule.

"Whoa." Despite the bead of sweat trailing down her temple, Violet's whole face lit up with a smile. "I did it."

Sagan and Thane moved closer to inspect the tangible blob of light.

"Now, that's cool," said Sagan.

Nathan silently shared a glance with Thane. The look on the younger Veniri's face held all the shock Nathan was suppressing. Never had he seen anyone forge their first light globule so fast. Either Violet had severe determination or she was a natural. Perhaps having the power of two shifter races enhanced her forging abilities. Who would even know? Every time Nathan thought he was beginning to understand Violet's hybrid capabilities, she threw him a curveball that left him flustered.

Violet flicked her gaze at Nathan. "What now?"

"Well, you've managed to pull off the hardest step. Now you practice your control by molding the light into specific shapes, starting with a sphere."

She mastered the sphere in record time, and Nathan told her to add a flat surface, then another. After about half an hour, a small tetrahedron hovered over her hand. She was determined to add a fifth side, but her body had become tense all over, and her face and neck were flushed and covered in a sheen of sweat. If she pushed herself any harder, she was at risk of bursting a blood vessel.

"I think we should call it a night," said Nathan. "You don't want to overexert yourself."

Once he convinced her to reverse the process by removing one flat surface at a time, she released the blob, and it instantly solidified and dropped into her hand like a small obscure pebble.

Thane shook his head in disbelief. "That was amazing."

"Um . . . thanks." Violet's smile didn't quite reach her eyes, and it disappeared as quickly as it had come. She turned back to Nathan. "Can we do this again tomorrow?"

Nathan shrugged. "I don't see why not. But like I said, practice, practice, practice is what will lead you to master the skill."

"And then what?" Violet asked.

"I suppose the sky's the limit, or perhaps your imagination is the limit. Light forging can be used for a number of things aside from weapons—building purposes, medical purposes, jewelry, and . . ." *Blocking memories.* He couldn't bring himself to say that last one out loud—not when the last person he'd light forged a memory block for was Violet.

He'd sealed away the memories of her kidnapping and everything she'd witnessed about the Veniri shifters who had captured her and murdered her best friend. For three years, the memory block had been a success, minus one small detail: Thane's neck tattoo.

If only Thane had heeded Nathan's command at the time and stayed away from Violet. If he'd left her alone, things would have panned out completely differently. For everyone.

19

HEAVENS HAVE MERCY

VIOLET WAS HEADING DOWN THE INFIRMARY HALLWAY AFTER visiting Gus when a baby's cry stopped her in her tracks. Almost against her will, her gaze drifted to the doorway of the nursery.

Any day now, the three mothers and their Veniri babies would be transferred to their new safe location. Dawn had done all she could for them; the children were healthy, and none of the three women had any flulike symptoms, something Dawn had been keeping an eye out for since the revelation about Violet's bite from Solace. As far as Dawn was concerned, unless the mothers were bitten by another shifter, there were no more concerns about their welfare.

Since Skye's passing, Autumn had taken over contacting the shifter safe houses on behalf of the mothers and their Veniri children, though she never spoke about it. Violet knew not to ask for details. The fewer people who knew the locations, the safer the mothers and their children would be.

Another wail from the crying infant tore through Violet's psyche.

She should leave. But the infant's cries refused to let her go. Tears pricked her eyes, blurring the world around her.

The ache for Solace had turned into a black hole, with a gravitational pull so fierce Violet was starting to believe she would never be able to escape it. This grief was much greater than when she found out her own mother had abandoned her at the hospital after she was born. Greater than when her best friend Lyla was murdered. Even greater than when she found out Thane and especially Nathan had betrayed her.

Violet hastily wiped her tears away and peeked into the nursery. Dawn was doing her rounds with the mothers and their babies, as well as having a cuddle or two. The infants had grown so much, even after a few days. How much had Solace grown since she last saw her?

Violet tore herself away from the scene of mothers who hadn't had their children ripped away from them.

She needed to see Autumn.

Eyes now dry, she hurried over to the exit and bumped into Sagan, who was on his way in.

"Hey," she said.

"Hey." Sagan nodded to her. "I'm getting some of my stitches out."

"Oh, right." With some effort, Violet pushed down her rising shame when she recalled how Sagan's stitches were a result of their disastrous trip to Rivermyre. She hurried to change the subject. "How's Nika? She hasn't been coming to the training sessions, and I haven't seen her around since that night."

Sagan's eyes narrowed sharply before his expression smoothed back into neutral.

"You've told her I'm fine, right?" Violet asked when he didn't respond. "I'm practically healed already, and the pain wasn't that bad. Gus has been working on developing a painkiller for Veniri shifters. The first trial gave me a raging hangover the next morning, the second gave me a wicked case of the hiccups, and the third, well . . . let's just say I told Gus I resigned from being his guinea pig until he worked on it a little more."

Sagan softly snorted.

"So?" Violet pressed.

"What?"

"Where's Nika?"

With a sigh, he buried his hands in his black jeans pockets. "Listen, about Nika . . . she's a little more complicated than most, even in the hunter world. She tends to take things a little harder than necessary."

"Yeah, but even though things got a little out of hand, she doesn't have to avoid me completely."

"Violet, Nika is gone."

"Gone? When?"

"That night, after your sparring match. When I went to check on her, her things were gone."

Violet frowned. "When were you planning on telling me?"

"Don't worry. It's a classic Nika thing to do. When she gets pissy, she runs off, and when she's done sulking, she comes back."

"Okayyyy," said Violet, dragging out the last syllable. "So when are you expecting her back?"

A few beats passed before Sagan answered. "I'm not sure."

"Well, let me know when she returns." Violet headed for the exit.

"What are you up to now?" Sagan called after her.

"I'm going to see Autumn. She's been doing some heavy research to find Solace and those Magneii shifters who killed her parents. I thought I'd see if she has any news."

"If you wait until I get my stitches out, I'll come with you."

About fifteen minutes later, Violet and Sagan found Autumn at her usual spot, surrounded by computers. She greeted them with a tired smile; other than the dark circles still around her eyes, she was looking a lot less like the poster child for doom and gloom.

"Hey, Autumn," said Violet. "Any progress?"

Autumn tilted her head from side to side. "A little bit of *yes*, and unfortunately a big lot of *no*." Violet and Sagan flanked her as she turned back to her screens. "My last attempt to break through the underground facility's firewall failed, so I'm working on a new angle."

Images, maps, and several other items Violet didn't understand popped up onto one screen or another, and Autumn pointed to a large block of text and symbols. "This is the new firewall-cracking code I've developed, and I have high hopes it'll work this time."

Violet's eyes bugged. She had no idea what she was looking at.

"So, what does this mean?" Sagan asked, pointing to a progress bar currently at 98 percent.

Autumn grimaced, twiddling one of her dreads. "When that hits one hundred, we'll know if my code successfully cracked the firewall. It's been running for days—since you guys took off to Rivermyre. It might be a few hours longer before we possibly hit the jackpot."

At that moment, Tio sauntered into the computer hut and grinned at everyone. "Hey, we have visitors."

Autumn swiveled her chair to face him, and they immediately dove into a complex conversation about whatever it was the two hackers had been fiddling with that morning. Violet glanced at Sagan, who shrugged and gave her a don't-ask-me look.

"Yeah, yeah, I'll work on it in a minute." Tio waved Autumn off, then turned back to Sagan and Violet. "Do you guys have any lunch plans? Mine's on its way. There should be enough to share."

"No thanks," said Violet. "I've got some stuff I need to work on." After her light-forging session the night before, she was keen to continue building on what she'd learned, especially since she could already see herself getting better. She'd been growing more attuned to her connection with Venus and Mars, even during the day, and had managed to add a fifth side to her light mass that morning before break-fast. "I better get going, but let me know if you make more progress."

"Wait, I almost forgot." Autumn jumped up from her chair, ran to the corner of the room, and came back with what looked like a scrap of paper. "I found my mom's phone, and I was going through some of her photos . . ." She bit down on her trembling lip. "Anyway, I know this can't replace the real thing, but I thought you might like it anyway."

Violet's hand flew to her mouth, and tears immediately flooded her eyes. Her heart was about to shatter into a million pieces.

"What is it?" Sagan asked, coming to look over her shoulder.

Autumn stood on Violet's other side. "Last week, I figured it might be worth broadening my search for Solace in several government databases, just to be safe. But for an accurate search, I needed a recent photo of Solace. And, well . . . this is the one I used."

Violet couldn't take her eyes away from the smiling little girl in the photograph. She remembered the day the photo was taken, and even recognized the adorable pink dress Skye had made and embellished with hand-stitched butterflies.

Tears began to stream down her cheeks. "Autumn, you

have no idea what this means to me." She pulled her friend in for a hug.

"Aw, don't cry, Vi." Autumn wiped away Violet's tears with her thumbs. "You're gonna make me cry. Rein it in, girlfriend. Sagan's too macho to handle our estrogen-fueled emotions."

Sagan scoffed, gaining a laugh from both Violet and Autumn.

Sniffling, Violet wiped her eyes and held the photo out to Sagan. "What do you think?"

He nodded with a slight smile. "She's beautiful."

Autumn's face broke into a wide grin. "See? I was right when I said you and Thane would make beautiful babies."

"What did you just say?" said a voice behind them.

Violet spun. Every cell in her body froze.

Thane stood in the doorway, his eyes wide and his mouth slightly open. The tray of food clutched in his hands began to tilt forward, making the plates slide, and he fumbled a little before managing to set it down on the closest desk. Breathing hard, he took a step closer to Violet.

"Oh no," whispered Autumn from behind her.

Thane's eyes bore into Violet's. "What did Autumn mean?"

Violet's mouth opened, but no words came out.

Thane continued to walk toward her, decreasing the chasm between them. "Am I . . . a father?"

Her mouth clamped shut as she took in the raw emotion on his face—a reflection of the emotional turmoil that had possessed her the moment Solace was taken. No matter what he'd done or what she felt for him, seeing it tore her apart inside.

Violet nodded.

Thane collapsed to his knees at her feet, his head in his hands, his shoulders heaving. Then, without warning, he reached out and hugged her. His hands dug into the small of her back as he buried his face in her stomach, trembling.

Violet stood still as a statue. She'd never planned for this moment. She'd never expected this moment would happen—or rather, she'd desperately hoped it wouldn't.

Telling Thane would've meant admitting Solace was not just hers—she was also half his. It hurt too much to face the idea that something still tethered her to him—to the man she'd fallen in love with, had once even thought about spending the rest of her life with, only to discover he'd lied to her, taken advantage of her, and been at least partially responsible for Lyla's death.

He and that stupid scorpion tattoo had haunted her dreams for years. And yet . . .

A small, almost forgotten feeling pierced her emotional stronghold, bringing with it memories of her time with Thane after she'd bumped into him that first day at the coffee shop: snippets of conversation, laughter, the indescribable sensation of his arms around her body. He had encouraged and challenged her, listened to her. Back then, she would've sworn he'd *understood* her. Being with him had made her feel free. Happy. Safe.

Her world zoned in on Thane, the man she once loved.

The father of her child.

His grip on her was as tight as ever, even when his whole body was racked by shuddering sobs.

What was happening? Was Thane . . . crying? What should she do?

In Violet's experience, men didn't cry. They were always stoic or unsentimental, viewing tears as a weakness despite causing so many to be shed by the women and children in their homes. Even when the fights, the abuse, and the addictions had reached an abominable level, not one of them had been reduced to tears.

Violet flicked out her whip-like tongue. A myriad of pungent flavors rippled through her senses: rhubarb, lotus flower, champagne, rosewater, pine needles, and seaweed, all tinged with the stickiness of nougat and the tang of cider vinegar. Her mind raced as she tried to decipher each associated emotion. Rhubarb represented shock, and rosewater suggested Thane was feeling overwhelmed. The champagne indicated feelings of inadequacy, yet lotus represented immense joy. Violet couldn't quite recall what pine needles and seaweed meant, but these flavors were strong enough to rival her own emotional rollercoaster.

A small part of her still wanted to scream and rage and kick Thane off of her, to demand he leave her and her daughter alone. But . . . she couldn't. She couldn't bring herself to push him away, not when the presence of nougat and cider vinegar made it clear Thane's heartbreak and grief were soul deep. All she could do was kneel down in front of him, tears blurring her vision until they eventually spilled down her cheeks.

Thane wiped his own tears on the collar of his shirt and took a deep, shaky breath. "How is he?"

"He?" Her brows furrowed.

"Yeah. How's the baby?"

Violet slowly shook her head. "Not a he."

"A girl?" Thane's eyebrows shot up to his hairline, then he buried his face in the crook of his elbow. "A girl?" he repeated over and over under his breath. "A girl . . ?"

Violet frowned and folded her arms. "Is there a problem?"

"No!" Thane gripped her folded forearms and said in a gentler tone, "You don't understand. I have a daughter. A girl. It's . . . it's almost impossible." He started to laugh quietly and shake his head.

For half a second, Violet was confused by his reaction,

then she remembered that having a Veniri daughter was beyond rare.

"What's her name?" he asked. "I assume you've given her one?"

Violet nodded. "I named her Solace."

His entire face lit up, erasing all evidence of his tears. In contrast, Violet couldn't help feeling that by giving him her daughter's name, she'd also given up a tiny piece of her soul.

"Solace." Thane looked around the room expectantly. "Where is she? Can I see her?"

Violet's lip began to tremble as she struggled to control fresh tears. Her gaze dropped to the small bite mark on her hand. "She's . . . not here."

"Is she, like, napping or something?"

"No. I mean, she's . . . gone." Violet almost choked on the last word. "Which is what Autumn has been working on this whole time. And why Nathan's been training me to control my abilities."

Thane stiffened, his eyes widening with horror. "So, last week, that trip to Rivermyre . . ."

Violet nodded. Then, before she could hold back, she recounted the whole story of how Solace had been kidnapped.

By the time she'd finished, Autumn, Tio, and Sagan had gone back to working on the computers, leaving Violet and Thane to themselves, still sitting in the middle of the floor. During their conversation, Violet had handed Thane the photo of Solace, which he held reverently between his fingers as if it were a priceless relic.

Other than the intermittent *clack-clack*ing of keyboards and the hushed conversations between the other three, Thane and Violet sat for several minutes in silence. Strangely, it didn't feel awkward. It was almost companionable, much like when they first met. Before . . .

Violet shot a sidelong glance at the crystal scorpion tattoo on his neck. As usual, the potent concoction of rage and heartbreak churned in her chest, threatening to choke her. She hated everything about what that tattoo meant to her.

Weird. It didn't seem as clear or bright as she remembered. Had her intense feelings made the image more vibrant in her mind? She squinted. The black geometric lines were now a dull gray, and barely any color remained in the fractal crystal design. Was the tattoo fading?

Thane rubbed his neck, blocking her view. "I can still feel it, you know."

"Feel what?" Violet almost held her breath, unsure where his statement was heading.

"I can still feel it when you look at me."

A heartbeat passed. Blood rushed to Violet's cheeks the second she recalled the photoshoot with Thane in her college dorm room. She'd needed help with one of her photography assignments, and during the session, Thane had told her he could sense her looking at him. She'd thought he was going nuts at first, but after a small test, it was hard to deny he could literally feel her gaze.

"Why didn't you tell me?"

Violet blinked several times at Thane's sudden question.

His brown eyes met hers. Was it her imagination, or were the golden flecks in his irises more prominent than they were a few minutes ago? "Why didn't you tell me sooner about Solace? I mean"—he gestured to the doorway—"if I hadn't walked in on your conversation, were you ever planning on telling me?"

"I . . ." Violet shifted uncomfortably, scrunching her knees up to hug her legs. "No," she finally admitted.

Thane stared at her for a long time, his expression unreadable. Violet could have sworn the gold in his eyes dimmed.

A thousand excuses bounced around her skull as she tried to anticipate his questions, his accusations, but he didn't say anything. Instead, his lips pressed into a thin line, and he slowly nodded.

Eventually, his gaze dropped back to the photo. "As much as I hate to admit it, I think I can understand your reasoning."

Instead of the vindication Violet had expected, an intense wave of shame washed over her. She bit the inside of her cheek, hard, and dropped her chin to her knees, staring intently at the pattern in the carpet.

"Violet?"

"Yeah?" She allowed herself a second or two to work up the courage to meet Thane's gaze.

His expression was hard, and this time, his eyes were edged with steel. "I promise," he said, slowly and deliberately, "I will do everything in my power to get our daughter back."

Our . . . The word reverberated through Violet's head.

In that moment, Violet remembered the emotional meanings of pine needles and seaweed. Pine needles represented deep, abiding love, and seaweed expressed Thane's sheer determination.

A high-pitched squeal yanked their attention to Autumn doing a happy dance in her swivel chair. "I'm in!" She fist-pumped the air and hooted. "I've finally weaseled my way in. I knew it! I knew it would work this time."

Tio whooped as Violet and Thane scrambled up from the floor.

"Whoa." Sagan gave a low whistle.

Image after image was flying up all over Autumn's screens: architectural plans, all sorts of schematics, various files and scanned paperwork, ID photos of staff dressed in white lab coats and security uniforms. Violet could barely comprehend all the new information. The one thing that tied all the documents, images, and uniforms together was a logo of an X with wings over the words *Xabat Biogenetics Research Inc.*

"No way," said Tio. "So back at Rivermyre when I joked about knocking on that Xabat building's door to ask for your daughter back, it wasn't a joke after all."

Violet blanched.

"Do we know what this mysterious facility is all about yet?" Thane asked.

"I'm not sure." Autumn slowly shook her head as she flicked through several more documents. "Maybe . . . something to do with, I don't know, biochemistry? Genetics? Umm . . . maybe Aunt Dawn would know. This seems like something she would understand." Autumn pointed to a screen displaying what looked like a lab report, then clicked on another file.

A gruesome parade of photographs immediately flooded the monitors.

With a screech, Autumn covered her eyes and spun in the swivel chair until her back was to the screens. Violet gasped, her hand flying to her mouth as ice-cold terror replaced the warm blood in her veins.

If horror and fear were tangible beings, one was now squeezing Violet's throat, and the other had an even tighter grip on her heart. She couldn't move. She couldn't tear her eyes away from the photos—though God knows she wanted to. She *needed* to. But the more she stared, the more her fear froze her in place. Never, as long as she lived, would she be able to forget the ghastly images.

And those people have my baby!

"Ugh . . ." Tio sounded as if he was about to gag. He slouched forward, one arm wrapped around his torso. "That's . . . messed up."

Sagan and Thane had become like twin statues on either side of Violet, but she barely registered their presence.

"They've got to be some kind of experimental facility," said Sagan.

"Yeah, but what kind of psychos experiment on . . . on children?" said Tio.

A heavy silence settled over the group.

As if waking up from a coma, Violet disjointedly said, "That girl at Rivermyre, Umbra, the one who killed the Godzilla worm. She mentioned something about failed Xabat experiments."

Tio reached for Autumn's abandoned keyboard. He clicked a thumbnail of a video file, which filled the screen and immediately began to play. It showed a man strapped to a bed with multiple IV lines injected into his chest. Several scientists surrounded him, discussing the procedure they were about to perform.

Even Autumn was curious enough to peek past her barrier of arms and dreadlocks.

Tio skipped the video ahead several minutes to a scene erupting in chaos. The man on the bed was now screaming and writhing, fighting the bonds on his legs, on his wrists, and across his forehead. The IV tubes were now filled with different colors of heaven knows what. Scientists darted around in a flurry, shouting and yanking out tubes. Colored liquid and vibrant red blood sprayed all over the flailing man's chest.

A wrist strap snapped. Then the other. The man's writhing turned into violent tremors. His chest expanded, blowing up like a balloon, until his skin began to split.

Violet stopped breathing as the doomed soul on the bed began to morph into a thing of nightmares—a creature Violet was unfortunate enough to have seen in person.

"No. Freaking. Way," breathed Tio. "That guy's the Godzilla worm."

Heavens have mercy.

"Are you serious?" Thane pointed to the screen. "That's the thing you guys encountered at Rivermyre?"

"That thing was a man." The horror in Sagan's voice echoed Violet's own disbelief.

The ear-splitting roar on the screen morphed into a sound that still rang crystal clear in Violet's memories. The Godzilla worm grew and grew. Thrashing and wreaking hell, it finally pounded through the wall and out of the camera's view, leaving bodies and carnage in its wake.

The screen went blank, and the computer hut was plunged into silence.

"Do you guys seriously think Solace is in that place?" Thane asked.

A small whimper escaped Violet. Her eyes burned, whether from her refusal to blink or her need to burst into tears. Knees buckling, she collapsed on the ground beside Autumn, who sat hunched over her knees, hands locked tight around the dreadlocks on either side of her head.

Tio clicked on another file. When he scrolled through the images, something caught Violet's attention.

"Wait! What's that?"

Tio clicked on the thumbnail, and an employee's photo filled the screen.

Violet's world spun. She pointed to the photo of the smiling woman in the lab coat. "That's Macie, my midwife."

Tio clicked through to another photo that showed Macie's husband. "It looks like both of them were scientists at Xabat for a number of years, and then about a year ago"— he pointed to a section of writing—"both of them were fired. But it doesn't say why."

Sagan leaned closer to one of the screens, zoning in on a

photograph of a group of people in white lab coats fanned around the gore on a hospital bed. He pointed to a grinning man standing front and center in the group.

"Oh no." Sagan's whispered words sent a chill down Violet's spine.

"Who is that?"

Sagan ignored Thane's question as he pushed past Violet to access the keyboard. "Please no," Sagan breathed, his eyes darting over a document. "I know what this place is trying to do. They're experimenting with animals and humans to somehow bioengineer shifter abilities for the human race."

"In that case, mystery solved as to why Macie and her husband were also killed during the Magneii attack," said Autumn.

"What do you mean?" Violet asked.

"The way I see it, they were kicked out of this secret science society. A brand-new shifter baby would've been the perfect ticket for them to try and weasel their way back in."

Violet sucked in a sharp breath. The sudden need to vomit was intense.

Sagan went back to scrolling through the file of staff documents. Face after face flashed across the screen. After a few seconds, he growled in frustration and typed something on the keyboard. The search pulled up a single document, this one without a staff photo.

Sagan turned away from the screen, his eyes wide and glassy. After taking half a step, he stumbled into the wall by Autumn's desk, then slid down to the floor in a heap.

"I don't understand," said Thane.

"Yeah." Tio peered at the screen. "What are we looking at?"

Violet's own terror was amplified by the fear radiating off Sagan. She scanned the document. It looked like a simple employee file for one of the top scientists in the facility. None of it made sense—until she recognized the last name.

"Branstone?" she said aloud.

All heads swiveled to Sagan except Violet's. Instead, her eyes bored into the grinning scientist at the front of the pack in the photo Sagan had singled out.

"Yeah," Sagan finally said. "The director of Xabat Biogenetics is Renard Branstone. My grandfather."

20

ZHIVOTZA

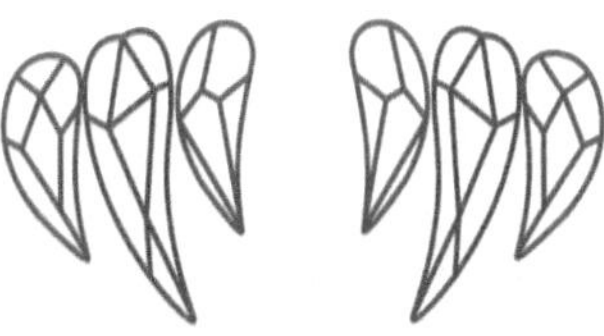

"GRANDFATHER, HUH?" NATHAN'S RHETORICAL QUESTION WAS met with somber silence from the group, but his heavy mind was elsewhere anyway. He'd hardly slept last night, still unable to shake Dawn's words.

. . . consider putting your affairs in order.

Nathan had been checking in with Gus at the infirmary when Tio had run up and vehemently told him they all needed to check out what Autumn had discovered. The kid had manhandled Nathan and Gus down to Autumn's computer lab before either of them could protest.

Nathan was trying his best to absorb all the new information quickly, but it was hard enough trying to figure out what the hell Autumn and Tio were even showing him. Autumn's computer den was straight out of a sci-fi movie. He cast a sidelong glance at Gus, who was intently studying a number of lab documents on the computer screens.

Thane, Violet, Tio, and Autumn were all watching Nathan with a mix of wide eyes, crossed arms, lip biting, and dreadlock twirling. Sagan was slouched against the wall with his head bowed, very much in contrast to his usual nonchalant hunter pose. It reminded Nathan of when Sagan and Matthias had captured him to harvest his Diamantium shards. Even though it had been Nathan getting tortured, there was a moment where Sagan looked as if he was the one going through hell. And now, his defeated expression suggested a whole other level of torment.

Everyone was waiting on him. Expectant. But for what? Why did he have to be the go-to guy whenever something came out of left field? Just like when Violet manifested dual shifter abilities, he had no more insight than anyone else into what was going on, let alone what needed to be done about it.

Nathan scratched at the new stubble along his jaw, then released a lungful of air. "What makes you so sure that this guy"—he pointed to the photo of the smiling group of people in lab coats—"Sagan's grandfather, has Solace?"

Autumn, Tio, Violet, and Thane responded all at once.

"Whoa, whoa. Stop!" Nathan waved his arms to get everyone to shut up. He turned to Gus, who just shrugged his shoulders.

"Don't look at me," said Gus. "I didn't catch any of that either."

Nathan grunted. "Autumn, start at the top. What's this about you and Tio hacking into government databases?"

Gus chuckled. "Once a cop, always a cop, huh?" His grin crumbled under Nathan's withering stare.

"Government databases or not, I did what I had to do to find Solace. And the shifters who killed my parents." Tears glittered in Autumn's fierce eyes.

Nathan crossed his arms. "Look, I get it. Believe me, Autumn, you're talking to one of the best in the revenge business. But even if we find Solace in there, there's no guarantee we'd be able to escape a facility like this."

Autumn's expression hardened. "We're doing this," she said through gritted teeth. "With or without you."

Nathan opened his mouth to shoot back a response, then quickly bit back the words. Arms dropping to his sides, he leaned on the edge of Autumn's desk and turned his attention to the computer screens. Maps, building plans, staff ID photos, experimental lab reports—this was all way beyond his capabilities. He was just a small-town cop who morphed into an overgrown reptile every once in a while. Except now . . .

. . . consider putting your affairs in order.

He shook his head. "Whether I help you or not, I have a feeling the person you have to convince is Sagan. This is his grandfather—his family—we're up against."

A heartbeat of silence passed before Sagan said, "I don't need convincing. We can't allow Violet and Thane's daughter to remain with Renard Branstone." His haunted eyes met Nathan's. "We need to get her out of there as soon as possible."

Everyone turned back to Nathan—again, waiting for him. To give them answers? The all-clear? Assurance they could pull off this mission unscathed?

Why rely on him so much?

An impossible weight settled in his core. If Dawn was right, there wasn't much time left for anyone to rely on him.

Violet stepped forward. "Please, Nathan. I know that I . . . well, that this is something you don't have to get involved in. But it would mean a lot to me if you helped us . . . helped *me* rescue Solace."

Nathan's breath hitched. Was there any point even trying to pretend he would ever deny Violet the chance to get her baby back? It was a sure bet he would need his Veniri abilities. And if it came to it, well . . . helping reunite Violet with her daughter wasn't a bad way to end things.

"All right." Nathan stood up. "If we're going to do this, we have to give it everything we've got. We find Solace and get her out of there."

Violet's small smile broke through Nathan's darkness like a rainbow; when she spoke, every hushed syllable was worth a ton of Erathi gold. "Thank you, Nathan."

He gave a sharp nod. "We'd better get started."

The tension in the room broke as the group scattered into action.

"First things first," Tio called out over the chaos, "we need IDs, which means photos." He dragged Nathan over to a wall.

"Watch it, clanger," gruffed Nathan as he tried to unlatch Tio's bone-crunching grip from his bicep. "What are they feeding you here? Iron?"

Tio chuckled and held up a camera. "Stop whining, slith. Now, usually I tell people to look like they just lost fifty bucks, but for you, well . . . resting I'm-about-to-kick-your-ass face should work too."

"Resting what?"

"Don't blame me. Violet was the one who came up with the term."

Nathan humphed just as the flash went off.

Tio grinned down at the camera display. "Perfect."

Just then, a shrieking alarm blared through the room, and everyone clamped their hands over their ears.

"What the hell is that?" Nathan demanded.

Autumn rushed over to her computer, and a few seconds later, the wailing stopped. "The perimeter has been breached."

Everyone shouted at once.

"Breached?"

"What perimeter?"

"Does Mom know you installed these alarms?"

"I think everyone on this side of the hemisphere knows now. Sheesh! Did you have to make it so loud?"

Nathan pushed his way through the group to reach Autumn. "Who breached it?"

Ignoring the initial influx of questions, she continued typing. "It looks like one of the boundary lines in the forest has been tripped. Give me a sec, and I'll pull up the live camera feed." She paused her typing when surveillance video feeds from around the compound came up on the screens. "There." She pointed to a couple of feeds that showed a section of forest bordering the compound. Four very large figures were weaving their way through the trees, heading straight to the residents' buildings.

"Shifters." Without even needing to check, Nathan knew both his elbow blades had been released.

"What kind?" Violet asked.

"Who are they?" Gus's brow creased as he glanced around at everyone. "They could just be lost, right? They could just be out for a casual, nonthreatening stroll. Or maybe they're . . . is that guy holding a spear?"

"There's no need to panic." Everyone turned to Tio, who winced. "It's just my older brother and his, uh . . . friends." Frowning, he added, "He's a few days early."

* * *

Nathan scanned the dense forest for any flicker of movement. "Are you sure this is where you said you'd meet your brother, Tio?"

"Pretty sure" came Tio's voice a few steps behind.

"Yeah, but are we sure this is a good idea?" Gus asked for what might have been the hundredth time.

Autumn groaned. "If you're scared, you should just go back to the house."

"I'm not scared. I'm just . . . I'm not scared, okay?"

"Uh-huh, sure."

"Whatever. Just shut up, Autumn."

"You shut up."

"How about you both shut up," hissed Violet.

A hush fell over the group. If Nathan hadn't been so on edge he would have been grateful for the brief interlude from Gus and Autumn's incessant arguing.

Violet and her friends had all insisted on coming, although Nathan would have vastly preferred they'd stayed in the computer lab. Arguing would've been pointless. Besides, he hadn't had enough rope on hand to tie them all up so they'd stay put—although in hindsight, he could've used some of the several thousand power cords lying around Autumn's den.

"Anything?" Thane stood in Nathan's periphery, as still as a statue.

"Not yet," said Sagan from Thane's other side.

"Maybe they've left," Violet said in almost a whisper.

The tension in Nathan's torso bubbled and churned. His tongue lashed out, the dimming rays of the afternoon sun glinting along the pink whip before it returned to his mouth. Mentally canceling out the emotions of his nervous companions, he focused on the flavors that remained. "Nope. They're definitely still in there. Tio, what's your brother doing? Why isn't he coming out?"

"Um . . . I'm not sure. Maybe he wasn't expecting me to have company."

"Maybe we should just go in and find him," suggested Violet.

"No," said Tio, a little too harshly. "My brother might find it threatening if we go in. He needs to come to us."

"Are you sure we're meeting your brother?" Gus asked. "It sounds like you're describing a Bengal tiger."

"Yeah, well . . ." Tio's words morphed into a groan. "My brother's a bit of an old-school Jiovis."

Nathan's pulse spiked. "Well, then it would be helpful if you stopped hiding and got out here where he can see you," he gritted out, fighting hard to prevent his elbow blades from slicing into view.

There was a soft *swish-swish* as Tio stepped through the grass, and half a second later, he pushed in between Nathan and Thane.

Nathan had detected the strong presence of apricot, the emotional flavor of dread, when he'd tested the air earlier. It almost certainly belonged to Tio. Only the young Jiovis knew what was waiting for them beyond the barrier of trees.

Tio suddenly stiffened.

"What's going on?" Nathan demanded.

"I'm not sure," said Tio, "but something's definitely put him on edge. One of them, maybe all of them, have been hurt."

"What makes you so sure?" Nathan asked.

"Because I smell blood. Jiovis blood."

Both Thane and Sagan readjusted their stances.

Nathan couldn't help sniffing the air, even though he knew it was useless; his sense of smell wasn't like that of the Jiovis and the Lycans. "You better call out to him. Assure him that we're not a threat."

Tio looked as if he were waiting for the ground to swallow him whole. "My brother's going to be so pissed that I got myself kidnapped in the first place. And it's my fault he had to go out of his way to come and get me."

"Really?" Gus said through clenched teeth. "Is now the time you wanna sink back into your teenage insecurities?"

"Why didn't he just send someone else to come and get you then?" Autumn asked.

Tio shrugged in defeat. "Because it's his duty. I mean, our

mother would have made him come and get me. Let's just say, it would have been more convenient for my brother if I'd stayed kidnapped."

Thane scoffed. "Glad I'm not the only one with brother issues."

Tio rolled back his shoulders and huffed. "Let's get this over with." He took a step forward; called out a few clipped, guttural phrases; then waited.

"Get ready," Nathan said in a low voice to Thane and Sagan, "just in case."

Both nodded, and along with Nathan, they strengthened their stances, prepared to strike like vipers.

Tio called out again, this time with a slightly longer phrase. Nathan wasn't fluent in the Jiovis language, but he recognized at least one word: *friend,* or rather *harmless being.* The description almost made him chuckle. There was nothing harmless about Thane, Sagan, or himself. Even Violet wasn't someone to contend with.

A harsh voice shouted to them from the forest.

Nathan froze and scanned the trees, straining his ears. A faint crackle of twigs, a rustle of leaves, and then—

His eyes narrowed.

Four hulking figures traipsed out of the woods. Every inch of their exposed metallic flesh gleamed in the slowly setting sun.

"Oh no," said Tio.

"What's wrong." Nathan closed in behind him as Thane and Sagan flanked Tio's other side.

"There's a lot of polished metallic skin."

"Why is that bad?" Violet asked.

"It means they've recently taken a lot of damage," said Nathan. "The patches of glossy skin are where their flesh has regenerated."

The Jiovis shifter who led the group had gold flesh, very

similar to Tio's Jiovis form. Two of the others were silver—or maybe pewter—and the last was copper. Horns, skulls, needle-tipped spikes, and paper-thin blades protruded from every shifter, alongside more decorative swirls, geometric patterns, scales, ripples, and dimples. Each warrior's pattern was unique, with the only shared feature being a solid silvery-green-tinged neck shield.

The shiny polished patches stood out even more starkly against the intricate designs. The golden shifter's entire left arm was glossy and smooth, either due to a fresh amputation or severe flesh wounds from shoulder to fingertip.

"Oh boy," said Gus in a hushed tone. "Who else thinks this was definitely a bad idea?"

The golden shifter's heavy stomps halted a yard from Tio. He planted the base of his spear into the earth with a dull *thud*, then looked the young Jiovis up and down, peering at him from behind a fierce golden mask. Its living-metal design of sharpened teeth bordered the shifter's mouth, and a highly detailed pair of skeletal hands framed his eyes with bony thumbs and forefingers.

Tio began to speak, but the golden shifter took no notice. Instead, he turned his gaze on Nathan, then slowly scanned the other members of the group.

Nathan glanced back at the "spear" in the golden one's hand, and as recognition slowly dawned, the blood in his veins turned to ice.

"Nathan?" Thane said in a low tone.

"Yeah?"

"Are you looking at what I'm looking at?"

"Yeah. That's not a spear."

Rather than a typical blade, the spear-like shaft boasted a decorative metal head with a glowing orange orb floating at its center. Surrounding the orb were several metal semicircles and rings, like a kinetic solar system sculpture, but most striking of all was the Jiovis symbol for Jupiter etched into the metal above it. The symbol glowed a fierce orange even richer than the orb itself. Nathan recalled various rumors about the glowing orb containing the blood of the first Jiovis king; a drop of blood from each royal successor was supposedly added during every coronation ceremony.

Thane released a heavy exhale. "We're screwed."

Nathan slightly tilted his head. "It's a possibility."

The golden Jiovis finally responded to Tio, his voice a deep rumble with a rich accent. Then he eyed Nathan and directed a few phrases toward him and the rest of the group.

Tio turned, his face pinched in a grimacing smile. "So, guys"—he gestured to the Jiovis shifter towering over him—"this is my older brother. And you should probably know that, um . . . that he's—"

"En'gorr Droth, the crowned prince of the entire Jiovis race?" Thane offered.

Several gasps erupted from the trio behind Nathan, along with a hissed, "Did he just say *prince*?"

Tio pursed his lips and nodded.

"No way," Gus blurted out.

"That information would have been handy before now, Tio." Nathan huffed, glancing between Prince En'gorr and the royal Jiovis scepter.

"Yeah, Tio. Why didn't you tell us?" Thane asked. "Or should I say Prince It'thio Droth?"

Tio's bottom lip protruded in a mournful pout. "I hate it when people call me by my full name."

En'gorr spoke again, and he and Tio began to converse. Nathan's Jiovis translation skills were getting a thorough workout, but before he could make much sense of anything, Thane groaned.

"What now?" Nathan asked.

"Uh, well . . ." Tio winced. "My brother's not really

impressed that I'm . . . how should I put it? That I'm *mingling* with sliths and Erathi."

"No kidding," growled Thane.

The prince jabbed a finger at Sagan, and Tio rubbed the back of his neck. "He's especially confused as to why there's a hunter with us."

"*Confused* wasn't exactly the word he used," amended Thane.

Sagan slowly raised his hands. "Tell your brother I'm not here to harm anyone."

In reply, En'gorr curled his lip into a sneer. He stepped forward until he was eye to eye with the hunter. Without even a flinch, Sagan raised his chin to expose his neck—the Jiovis's customary sign for submission—and steadily held the prince's fierce gaze.

For several agonizing seconds, En'gorr stared Sagan down.

Tio translated En'gorr's vicious statement: "The Erathi whose men slaughtered my warriors looked a lot like you."

Sagan stood solid, even as En'gorr's eyes began to glow a vibrant orange and a crackle of amber electricity ignited all over the prince's head.

Nathan grabbed Thane's shoulder to hold him back just as Tio clasped En'gorr's arm, speaking urgently in the Jiovis language too fast for Nathan to have a chance at deciphering. Tio gestured to Sagan, then at Nathan and Thane.

En'gorr's eyes never left the young hunter, and for several long seconds, every muscle in Nathan's body braced for the worst possible outcome.

Finally, the raging electricity died down. Even the intensity in En'gorr's expression diminished. He eyed Sagan for a second longer, then with a *tsk*, took one step back and turned his attention to Thane and Nathan. They also raised their chins to expose their necks.

En'gorr spoke as Tio translated. "My younger brother tells me it was you who helped him escape from the hunters' prison. To express my thanks, my warriors and I extend our peace to you"—he shot a venomous glare at Sagan—"for today."

Nathan nodded. "Tio, tell your brother—"

He cut himself off as Thane responded in the Jiovis tongue. Nathan's eyebrows shot up, and even Tio's face slackened in shock. It was difficult to see the prince's expression behind his mask, but Nathan could sense his surprise. It was one thing to understand the metal shifters' language, but when had Thane learned to speak it? More importantly, who taught him?

The prince inclined his head slightly when Thane finished.

"What did you say?" Autumn whispered to Thane.

En'gorr's attention abruptly shifted to Autumn, the intensity in his gaze almost palpable. After a moment, everyone else in the group warily turned to her too.

"Uh, Autumn, why is he looking at you like that?" Violet asked.

Autumn's jaw hung open. "I don't know."

The Jiovis prince spoke, his gaze still locked on Autumn.

Tio translated: "A few days ago, a large group of Erathi hunters ambushed and raided our camp. Many Jiovis shifters lost their lives, but so did many of the Erathi filth. Eventually, myself and three of my warriors were all that remained, and we were overpowered and chained. But before my three warriors and I escaped, Matthias, the leader of the hunters, spoke to me."

Nathan, Sagan, and Thane all readjusted their stances.

"He was looking for something," En'gorr continued. "He believed the object he was after was in my possession, but his men turned our camp upside down and never found it. He screamed and threatened, demanding I tell him where it was hidden. To begin with, I didn't understand. But soon I began to realize what he was looking for. Up until that moment, I had assumed the heirloom he described was just another trinket, passed down from father to son.

"The hunter and his men did not find it because it was stolen from me many months ago." Tio paused the translation as En'gorr pushed past Nathan to stand toe to toe with Autumn. "Stolen by you."

Gus groaned and dragged a hand down his face.

Autumn's eyes grew as round as saucers as the hulking prince stooped to her eye level.

"Autumn, what did you steal?" Violet asked.

Autumn grimaced, and her face turned white as a sheet. "I didn't steal anything. Is he kidding?" She shot a desperate glance at Tio. "I've never met this guy . . . this shifter . . . this *prince* before in my life."

Nathan leaned closer to Thane and Sagan. "Do either of you know anything about this?"

"Nothing," said Thane.

Sagan shook his head.

"Tio, is there a chance your brother could be mistaken?"

Crossing his arms, Tio studied Autumn as he asked the question in Jiovis. En'gorr shook his head and barked a reply.

"There's no mistake," said Tio, frowning. "He says he knows without a doubt it was you."

En'gorr stood up straight, and behind the living-metal teeth of his mask, it almost looked as if he was grinning. "Zhivotza."

Tio's eyes bugged.

"Oooh-kay. This is new," said Thane.

"What?" Autumn's gaze danced around the group. "What did he just say?"

"Wait a second. I've heard that word before." Violet

squinted and tapped her forehead. "But I can't remember where."

"What does it mean?" Gus asked.

Violet shook her head. "No idea."

"Tio," said Autumn through gritted teeth, "you better tell me what your brother just said, or I swear I'll—"

En'gorr's entire being began to ripple. The decorative armor melted and morphed into softer human flesh, and the metallic gold hue shifted to a rich ebony. Once the hazing was complete, a tall mountain of a man stood in front of Autumn.

Her hand flew to her mouth.

"Oh," said Violet, her lips barely moving. "You've got to be kidding me."

"Aw, hell no!" exclaimed Gus. "I knew it! I just knew you'd find yourself seriously screwed one day, Autumn!"

"Wait a minute, so you do know him?" Nathan asked.

"How do you guys—" began Thane just as Gus burst into hysterical laughter.

"How do we know him?" Gus said between maniacal cackles. He jabbed a finger at En'gorr Droth. "This is the guy from the UV party with the green dragon body paint. He tried to kill us!" His mirth abruptly died on the last two words.

"Wait," interjected Tio. "That was you guys?"

Gus ignored the question and rounded on Autumn, releasing a barrage of nonsensical insults.

"Hey!" Nathan stepped between them. "That's enough." He grabbed Gus by the shoulder and manhandled him away from Autumn, who was now hiding behind Violet—except Autumn's fearful expression was directed at the hulking En'gorr, who was still in human form.

Violet's face was calm, and her hands remained by her sides, but teal flames had already ignited over her palms.

En'gorr's eyes panned between Autumn and Violet's hands. To Nathan's surprise, the prince didn't seem angry or even hostile. Instead, his expression held only curiosity and a hint of amusement.

"Somebody had better start explaining what's going on." Nathan pushed Gus over to Thane and Sagan. No one said a word. With an impatient grunt, Nathan pointed to Tio. "Explain."

Tio shuffled his feet. "I wasn't actually there. I just heard about what happened when my brother and his guards came home from the club that night. All I know is they had an altercation with some people and something was stolen from my brother."

"An altercation?" Gus yelled. Both Thane and Sagan clamped a hand around his biceps before he could take another step. "Altercation, my ass! This guy attacked us! He attacked Autumn. He had his hand around her throat and was trying to kill her!"

"Hold on," said Nathan. "He had his hand around her throat?"

Gus turned his glare on Nathan. "Yes! And when I tried to stop him, he threw me up against the wall and gave me a concussion. And then—"

Nathan held up a hand. "Wait, go back." He turned to Autumn. "Are you sure it was your throat he grabbed?"

Autumn looked at him as if he'd just suggested she grow a second head. "I'm pretty sure."

It was Nathan's turn to grimace. Thane sucked in a breath through his teeth and half squinted one eye.

"What?" Violet looked between Nathan and Thane. "What does it mean?"

Nathan scratched the top of his head. "Well, if he was holding on to Autumn's throat, then the good news is he wasn't trying to kill her."

"What?" exclaimed Autumn, Gus, and Violet in unison.

En'gorr puffed out his broad chest, and Tio chuckled.

"You've got to be kidding!" Autumn stepped out from behind Violet. "That guy had a strong grip on my neck. If that's the good news, then what's the bad news?"

"Uh . . ." Nathan rubbed the back of his neck and turned to Thane. "Do you wanna explain?"

"No way." Thane shook his head in big sweeps. "Nope. All yours, buddy."

"It's really bad, isn't it?" said Violet.

"Well"—Nathan tilted his head from side to side—"it depends on how you look at it."

By now, En'gorr and Tio were discussing something in their language. Even the three other Jiovis warriors were conversing in hushed tones.

Autumn stamped her foot. "Just spit it out, Nathan."

"You know how generally in the Erathi culture, when . . . uh gee, how do I explain this?" Nathan sighed. "Okay, look. When a guy likes a girl, he usually starts with the small stuff, like asking for her phone number or taking her to the movies, and then eventually . . . uh, you know." He made an incomprehensible gesture with his hands.

"No! I have no idea what you're saying," exclaimed Autumn.

Nathan groaned and dragged a hand down his face. "Okay, let me put it this way. When a Jiovis guy likes, well . . . what's usually a Jiovis girl, instead of starting with the hand holding, they go straight to their version of 'down on one knee.'"

Violet's hand flew to her mouth.

"No way!" Gus threw his head back and guffawed.

Autumn looked at everyone in turn. "What am I missing? I don't understand."

Nathan's grimace deepened.

"He was hitting on you, Autumn," said Thane. "Not only was he hitting on you, he was basically proclaiming his . . . undying commitment to you."

Gus nearly doubled over with laughter.

Autumn's eyes bugged. "What do you mean 'his commitment'? The dude was cutting off my air supply."

"Yeah, well, the Jiovis shifters are not only fierce warriors but also fierce lovers," said Nathan.

Autumn paled.

"Uh, sorry," said Nathan after a beat. "That statement didn't help, did it?"

With lips pursed as if she'd bitten into a lemon, Autumn shook her head.

"I don't get it." Violet waved a hand over her throat. "Why the neck? How is that significant?"

Thane pointed to the Jiovis warriors. "See those silvery-green shields over their necks? Those shields are made from Metallikite, which is the strongest metal known to man and shifter. The Metallikite protects the Jiovis's most vulnerable organ: their heart."

Violet's brow wrinkled in confusion.

"Anatomically speaking," Thane went on, "while the Erathi hearts are located in their chest, the Jiovis shifters' hearts are located in their throat. Much like the Erathi, the Jiovis heart is considered the most vulnerable organ, both physically and emotionally. So when a Jiovis proclaims their love for another, they clutch their chosen partner's heart as a sign they will protect their lover's most sacred and delicate organ."

A pregnant pause fell over the group as the new information settled in.

Violet was the first to break the silence. "So, that word he said . . . what he called Autumn . . ."

"Zhivotza?"

"Yeah, that one. That's what he was calling her back at the UV party."

Thane nodded. "The Jiovis's sense of smell allows them to confirm pretty much straightaway who their . . ."—his gaze flicked to Autumn—"life partner is. *Zhivotza* means 'drug' or 'medicine,' as well as 'life source.' It's also used as a term of endearment for a Jiovis's soulmate."

A whimper escaped Autumn, and her head fell into her hands.

At that moment, one of En'gorr's silver warriors released an agonized groan, then collapsed to the ground with a heavy *thud*. The copper one knelt by his fallen companion's side before looking up at En'gorr with a concerned expression.

"He needs help." Gus broke free from Thane and Sagan, but before he could reach the fallen shifter, the second silver Jiovis drew a sword and blocked his path.

Sagan immediately bolted between Gus and the tip of the shifter's blade.

Nathan threw his arms out—one to block Thane and the other to stop Violet and Autumn from running to Gus's aid— as a flurry of shouts erupted around him. Autumn was shouting after her brother, Gus was demanding that they take the wounded shifter to the infirmary, and both Tio and Thane were yelling in Jiovis, presumably explaining Gus's sudden action.

The competing voices only grew louder until En'gorr roared a Jiovis command. In an instant, everybody grew silent.

"Please, we only want to help." The thundering rush of adrenaline in Nathan's ears muted his own voice. "Tio, please tell your broth—His Highness that there is a medical clinic here where he and his companions can rest and recover."

Tio, who was clamped on to the prince's arm that held

the scepter, slowly spoke, gesturing to Gus and then in the direction of the compound's infirmary.

The silence that followed was deafening. Nathan's thumping heartbeat threatened to crack a rib.

Finally En'gorr nodded and signaled to his men. The silver one with the sword threw a final glare at Sagan, then sheathed his weapon to go help the copper shifter raise and carry their comrade.

En'gorr leaned into Nathan's face and spat out several harsh words.

"He said—"

"No need to translate," Nathan cut Tio off. "I know a threat when I hear one."

"Not threat," said En'gorr Droth. His eyes narrowed. "Is promise."

DIRTY LITTLE SECRET

"Hey, Autumn," said Thane from the other end of the dinner table, "wanna tell us the story of when you stole something from the Jiovis prince?"

Violet, along with everyone else at the table, stopped eating and turned to Autumn.

"Actually, I'd like to hear that story too," added Tio.

Autumn met Thane's and Tio's gazes with a cool expression. Her ability to not crumble under scrutiny never ceased to impress Violet.

Nathan and Gus had gone to the infirmary with the four Jiovis shifters while Lazareth had rounded up the rest of the group—Violet, Autumn, Sagan, Thane, and Tio—and insisted they all have some dinner at his house. Conversation had remained at a minimum until Thane finally became the one brave enough to dive into the topic that was doubtless on everyone's mind.

After an extended pause, Autumn exhaled a long breath. "Fine." She dug into her jacket, pulled out a gold clutch, and put it on the table. "Here's my dirty little secret."

Violet recognized the clutch as the one Autumn had taken

with her to the UV party—the night that had gone horribly wrong. She took the clutch and opened it, then instantly had to blink against the bright orange light coming from inside.

"Whoa, it's . . . pretty." Violet pulled out what looked like a glass coaster, about the diameter of a soda can and maybe a quarter of an inch thick. The source of the orange light was a series of etchings along the outer third of the disc, leaving the center transparent and pale. Fascinated, she ran her fingertip along the glowing dots, lines, and squiggles. "What is it?"

"That's a spangle," said Sagan, and Autumn nodded.

"A spangle? What's that?" Violet asked. Thane and Lazareth looked similarly confused.

Sagan held his hand out, and Violet gave him the disc. "My father has been searching for these for as long as I can remember. From what I understand, his obsession has gone beyond insane." He inspected it closely, flipping it over to view each side. "This is the first time I've seen one up close."

"You've seen others?" Autumn's eyebrows flew up to her hairline.

"Two others," admitted Sagan. "The silver one and the pearl one."

"Whoa." Autumn stared off into the middle distance, lost in some faraway thought.

Sagan quirked an eyebrow. "How did you even find out about these?"

She shrugged. "I came across the term *spangle* on one of the hacking forums."

"Oh, yeah," said Tio, "I remember those forums. But . . ." His forehead creased into a frown. "If I remember correctly, those forums were full of conspiracy nutters rambling on about hacker urban legends and myths."

"Yeah," said Autumn. "I began dabbling in the conspiracies just for something to do. There are only so many social media accounts and government facilities you can hack into before things start to get boring."

Lazareth chuckled. "Only our Autumn would find things like that boring." He stood up and began clearing everyone's empty plates.

Autumn grinned before continuing. "Anyway, I decided to search further into some of these legends, and I came across several forums where whispers of these special types of discs had begun to circulate. There were a whole bunch of rumors on what these discs did and what kind of information might be on them. As far as anyone knew, there was only a handful of them, and it was like searching for a pot of gold at the end of the rainbow.

"So, of course, my not-so-humble self thought, *Challenge accepted*. The only catch was that these discs couldn't be obtained online. You had to physically find one, or in my case—" she cleared her throat "—convince your friends to go to a UV party to steal it from the guy who turned out to be the biggest dude in the room, and who happened to have a penchant for choking girls."

"You forgot the part where he also turned out to be the prince of a shifter race associated with Jupiter and developed an epic crush on you," said Tio.

Violet groaned. "That night was the worst. How did you even know he was going to have the spangle with him?"

"I didn't, but I figured it was worth the risk. I wasn't sure when my next opportunity would be."

"*Risk* is an understatement," Violet grumbled.

"Yeah . . ." Autumn's tone was regretful. "There was no way I could have foreseen how that night would go. And I never would have guessed he would one day show up at my place."

"So what's on the disc?" Thane asked.

Autumn shrugged. "I have no idea. It's not like I can plug

it into a USB port or load it into a DVD drive. Either I haven't yet come across the correct hardware to read it, or I've been led up the garden path, and all I managed to steal from Tio's brother was a glorified paperweight."

"Hey," Tio interjected, "that 'glorified paperweight' has been in my family for generations. It's practically a Jiovis relic and might one day be mine—you know, if my brother unfortunately meets his demise."

"Do you know what it does?" Violet asked.

"Um . . ." Tio eyed the spangle, which still rested in Sagan's hand. "I can't say that I do, and to be honest, this is the first I've heard of anyone making this much fuss over it. En'gorr just treats it like you would a brooch or a key ring. It's just a trinket he's carried around with him since our father passed away."

"Do you know what it does, Sagan?" Thane asked.

Up until that moment, Sagan had been staring at the spangle in contemplative silence. "I don't know what they do. But I do know if my father gets his hands on all of them, it'll be bad. Really bad. I've heard him say that the one who holds all the spangles holds the power to change worlds."

"Worlds?" Tio quirked an eyebrow. "As in plural?"

Sagan shrugged. "My father has a longstanding reputation of not outgrowing the stories we were told as children."

"How many spangles are there?" Violet asked.

"It's believed there are only ten, one for each of the shifter races."

Thane's brows furrowed. "And you said your father only has two of them?"

"Two that I've seen, but that was a few years ago. Who knows if he's acquired more since."

"Well, it sounds like he's hellbent on getting all of them," said Violet, "especially if he was willing to attack Tio's brother's camp."

Sagan grimaced. "Then pray he never finds Maple Shire. I don't want to find out what he plans to do if he succeeds in collecting all of them." He put the orange spangle on top of the golden clutch and slid it across the table to Autumn.

Lazareth had just begun serving dessert when Nathan walked in with Tio's big brother—although *big* was an understatement. En'gorr Droth was enormous. Even if he was Tio's family, the guy set Violet on edge, especially when flashbacks of the UV party flickered through her mind.

Nathan went over to the kitchen counter, where Lazareth had set out the night's dinner dishes, and En'gorr's attention immediately landed on Autumn. Violet's dreadlocked friend shifted slightly in her seat.

Having the somewhat uncouth adoration of a Jiovis shifter would be bewildering for anyone. Shifters of any sort would complicate any human girl's love life. Violet was beginning to be glad she didn't have to deal with that kind of situation when a sudden thought made her breath hitch.

She shot a glance at Thane. By now it was common knowledge he was a Veniri, but she'd never seen him in his shifted form. Nathan's Veniri side sometimes surfaced when he was really agitated, and he'd hazed several times during their training sessions. Even Tio had joined them during training a few times and had shown her his metallic Jiovis form.

But Thane was—in her mind at least—still human. She peered at him as he ate his bowlful of Lazareth's famous fig-and-lychee cheesecake. No telltale sign showed he was a Veniri. No scales, no glittering spikes, no claws, no—

His golden-brown eyes met hers, and a slight smile played on his lips.

After a heartbeat, Violet's cheeks grew warm, and she broke eye contact. *Damn that stupid thing where he can feel me looking at him. How long was I staring?*

She sank down in her seat as Nathan plonked two loaded plates of food onto the silky oak tabletop and sat down, leaving the spare seat next to Tio vacant. En'gorr still stood by the dining room doorway.

"Sit. Have some food." Nathan gestured to the unclaimed plate.

En'gorr glanced back over his shoulder.

"Your men will be fine," Nathan said. "Dr. Dawn and her son will take good care of them."

En'gorr looked down at Nathan and only said, "Why?"

Nathan frowned. "Why what?"

En'gorr inclined his head in the direction of the infirmary. "Why help?"

"To tell you the truth. I don't actually know." Nathan shrugged. "But what I do know is, whether Erathi, Veniri, or even Jiovis, it makes no difference to Dawn and her family. They're good people."

Even Violet was still trying to figure Dawn out. Every time she learned something new about the shifter world, Dawn already knew ten times more—not to mention her in-depth medical knowledge of several shifter races.

En'gorr just grunted in response as he scanned the table. His expression this time was different, almost inquisitive.

"Come on, whaddya say?" Nathan pushed the plate of food a little closer to him.

Again, the prince inclined his head toward the infirmary. "They eat."

"Don't stress. I'll ensure they're fed once their treatments are done," said Lazareth.

After a second, the prince nodded and sat down next to Tio. His eyes landed on the orange spangle still sitting on the golden clutch by Autumn's elbow.

For the first time ever, Violet could have sworn Autumn's

cheeks developed a red hue. She held the spangle out to him. "I suppose I'd better return this."

En'gorr made no move to retrieve the spangle. Instead, he shook his head and spoke. Once again, Tio translated. "Too many of my men have died because of that thing. Either keep it or destroy it, but whatever you do, make sure Matthias Branstone never gets ahold of it."

Autumn hesitated before nodding and placing the spangle back on the clutch.

Violet caught Nathan eyeing the orange disc, his brow wrinkled in thought. For a moment, he looked as if he was about to say something, but then he shook his head slightly and turned his attention back to En'gorr.

"Hungry?" Nathan held out a knife and fork, but En'gorr pushed them away with a grunt. Violet watched in awe as En'gorr's arm hazed into a metallic gold, and he pressed his unshifted hand into the gold skin as if it were made of cookie dough. After pinching off a small handful, he fashioned a golden set of utensils from the malleable flesh, then stabbed at his food with his brand-new fork.

"Like I said earlier," Tio said to Nathan, his expression apologetic. "My brother is kind of an old-school Jiovis. Using someone else's eating utensils is usually against our customs."

"Oh," said Nathan with raised eyebrows, still holding the disapproved cutlery.

Autumn wrinkled her nose. "I don't know if that's really cool or really gross."

"How come I've never seen you make your own cutlery, Tio?" Thane asked.

Tio shrugged. "Maybe I'm just too lazy."

"If you don't mind me saying," Thane continued, "even though you're brothers, I can't help but notice there's a big difference between you two."

Tio nodded, then shot a glance at En'gorr. "Being the

crown prince, En'gorr didn't have as much freedom as me. I wasn't under the microscope as much as he was."

En'gorr grunted a few Jiovis words, seemingly in agreement.

"Our parents made sure En'gorr's childhood was focused on politics, dining etiquette, war strategies—basically, anything that wasn't focused on training him to be the next mighty ruler of our race was considered a waste of time. As for me, I was brought up by my nanny, who had what some might call an unhealthy fascination with the Erathi. I was practically raised on cheeseburgers, Erathi pop culture, and *Friends* reruns. My nanny didn't really prioritize the ancient traditions of our culture."

"*Friends* reruns, huh?" Autumn quirked an eyebrow.

"Yeah, that's where I learned most of my English," said Tio with a grin. "Out of the seven languages my brother knows, English is his newest addition. He can understand most of what you guys say, but he's still in the early stages of speaking it. That's why he makes me translate for him."

En'gorr rounded a flinty glare on his brother and said something in a sharp, reproving tone. Thane and Sagan shared a glance, and Thane covered a grin with his hand.

Tio scowled at En'gorr, who had resumed eating his dinner, then grabbed his empty dessert bowl and stood up. "I'm gonna get a second serving of cheesecake. Anyone else want some?"

Both Sagan and Thane threw their hands up, and Nathan demanded there be some left over once he finished his dinner.

Tio placed bowls of dessert in front of Thane, Sagan, and himself, then grabbed a can of whipped cream from the fridge. The three passed the can around, each swirling ample mounds on top of their cheesecakes. En'gorr looked on with interest. Before Tio was half-finished with his own dollop of sweetness, the can was snatched out of his hand.

Ignoring Tio's protests, En'gorr turned the can over and studied it from every angle, then upended it and sprayed a small dot onto his mashed potatoes. By the time the Jiovis prince scooped up a forkful of mashed potato and cream, all eyes were glued on him.

Everyone watched with building tension as En'gorr's eyes grew wide. Then in a flash, the whipped cream can was back in his hand, and everything on his plate swiftly became coated in a thick layer of white: the honeyed carrots, the slow-cooked pork belly, the sesame chicken salad, the mixed green and cucumber salad with ginger yogurt . . .

"I've never seen anything like that in my life," said Autumn.

Violet couldn't stop staring. "Neither have I."

A chorus of chuckles went up from the table before everyone returned to their meals. Only Tio didn't join in; he glared daggers at his brother and shook the now empty can in irritation. "Gee, thanks, bro. Next time you may as well chug it straight from the can."

En'gorr responded in Jiovis, and Tio rolled his eyes as Thane chuckled again.

"What did he say?" Violet asked.

"A Jiovis version of 'challenge accepted,'" Thane answered.

After a few minutes, Lazareth left to take some meals to Dawn and the others, and Autumn pulled out her laptop. Before long, she and Tio had their heads bent together, quietly discussing some new hacking strategy.

Gus joined the group just as Nathan and En'gorr were finishing up their own helpings of dessert. Unimpressed with finding only a tiny sliver of his dad's cheesecake left, he compensated by retrieving some apple crumble with ice cream and a new can of whipped cream. En'gorr's eyes lit up, and he eyeballed the can until Autumn finally said, "You'd better give it to him, Gus."

Gus reluctantly handed over the can, then watched in slack-jawed shock as En'gorr downed the contents.

"So, how are the patients?" Nathan inquired.

"Fine," Gus said around a mouthful of dessert. "The shifter who collapsed, um . . . what was his name?"

"Urg'vhul," said Tio. "Not to be confused with his twin brother, Tyor'vhul, the other pewter shifter."

"Er, yeah." Gus winced. "Anyway, he's now stable, all tucked up and sleeping. The others are resting too. They took a bit of convincing to change back into human form—treatment's easier without all the metal plates and blades all over their bodies—but Mom's pretty good at getting her own way." He turned to En'gorr and patted the regal man's shoulder. "What about you, buddy? Your guys have all been tended to. We should get you to the infirmary to see if you need any treatment."

En'gorr Droth glared at the offending hand on his shoulder, and Gus removed it to gesture to the doorway.

"No," said En'gorr, then tilted his head back and sprayed whipped cream into his mouth.

Tio dropped his face into his palm and mumbled under his breath—something about regretting bringing out the cream in the first place.

"How long until the other Jiovis shifters recover?" Sagan asked.

"Don't know for sure. Mom's worried about Urrrg . . . um . . ." Gus turned hopelessly to Tio.

"Urg'vhul."

Gus nodded. "Right. Mom thinks it's best to keep an eye on him for a few days."

"No," said En'gorr.

All heads turned to him.

En'gorr patted a fist on his chest. "Jiovis strong. Leave at sunrise." He raised the can to his mouth again, and a hiss of frothing cream filled the ensuing silence.

Tio and Autumn exchanged a look.

"Looks like I'm pulling an all-nighter to get you guys prepared before I leave," Tio said with a burdened sigh.

En'gorr looked over at him and said something in Jiovis, and Tio replied in the same tongue, gesturing to the laptop. The two conversed as En'gorr looked at the screen, then he barked a phrase that startled everyone at the table.

"Seen this." En'gorr pointed to the screen.

Tio looked at him in confusion. "That's the Xabat Biogenetics logo. You've seen this logo before?"

His brother nodded. "Erathi have on clothes. On cars. On boxes."

"Boxes?" cut in Sagan.

En'gorr's eyes narrowed. "Alive Jiovis. Not escaped. Put in metal boxes."

Thane hissed out a breath and turned to Sagan. "What does that mean? I thought he said it was your father who led the attack?"

Sagan frowned, clutching the black chain around his neck that peeked above his shirt collar. "It sounds like my father and my grandfather might have called a truce."

"And that En'gorr's men have become the new lab rats for Xabat Biogenetics," added Autumn.

Tio and En'gorr had been conversing in their own tongue while the others were talking. When En'gorr turned his attention to Violet, flashbacks of his meaty hands pinning her shoulders to the ground made her stiffen. She couldn't stop herself from slowly reaching for the switchblade nestled in her jeans pocket.

"Your baby." He pointed to Tio's laptop. "They take?"

A pang of grief stabbed through Violet's chest. "Yes."

With a decisive nod, En'gorr stood up, the wooden chair legs screeching along the floor. "Xabat kill my warriors. They take your baby." His lip curled in a snarl. "We kill Xabat."

* * *

It took Violet a while to settle into the idea of En'gorr's involvement in the rescue mission, even after Tio explained that his brother had a sacred duty to avenge his slain warriors. Nathan, Thane, and even Sagan were just as shocked at the Jiovis prince's involvement. Apparently, it was rare for shifter races to intermingle, let alone work together. The fissures between the races ran too deep. Yet here they were: Veniri, Jiovis, Erathi, a hunter, and who knows what Violet was now, all working together.

Sagan's family—and by extension, Xabat Biogenetics—had caused too much damage for too many shifters. Now, the damaged were banding together.

Even Autumn seemed to be warming up to the Jiovis prince. He usually had a lost-puppy expression when Violet caught him staring after Autumn, but he must have said or done something to win her over, because Violet noticed them huddled together in deep conversation more than once.

As for the rest of the group, morale was pretty decent, even though they were up to their eyeballs in planning Solace's rescue mission. Autumn and Tio were the masterminds, constantly *clack-clack*ing on their computers, working their magic to ensure everything fell into place.

At first, the plan had seemed ludicrous, even with the staff IDs, makeshift uniforms, hazmat suits, cliché hacker's van, second transport vehicle, and ongoing training sessions. But after hours of weeding out as many hypothetical problems as possible, Violet was beginning to believe they had a solid chance of retrieving Solace and safely escaping Xabat Biogenetics . . . at least in theory.

Two nights after the Jiovis shifters arrived—on the two-week anniversary of Solace's kidnapping—the team decided they were ready.

Violet sat waiting in the back of a Chevy Impala, impatiently bouncing her knees. "What's taking them so long? How much more stuff can they fit in that van?"

"No idea," Sagan said from the driver's seat. Va'atuu, the copper Jiovis shifter, was in the passenger seat. He didn't bother answering, or even acknowledge she'd spoken.

Violet stifled a groan and threw her head back against the headrest. "This is crazy. Tell me honestly, Sagan, do you think we'll succeed this time?"

He swiveled in his seat to face her. "One thing I know for sure is that we'll all do our damndest to get Solace safely out of there."

Violet gnawed on her lip. He hadn't really answered her question, but she wasn't sure if she was ready for his honest answer.

"You know, I envy Solace," Sagan said quietly.

"Envy?" Violet frowned.

"Yeah. She's been taken from you, but no matter what, every decision you've made, whether good or bad, has been aimed toward getting her back." He heaved in a deep breath and stared into the blackness beyond the car window. "My mother disappeared when I was a kid, and if I were to believe what I've been told, she abandoned me. But I would do anything—I would ransom the world—if it meant I could have my mother back."

After a few beats of silence, Violet said, "Thank you. I'm grateful to have you here. And if it means anything, I hope you find your mother one day."

Sagan gave her a small smile and turned back to face the front.

Another minute or two passed, and Violet was once again finding it difficult to keep her fear at bay. Tonight. There was a chance she was going to see her baby *tonight*. She needed to go, to shout at Sagan to start the car. Now! Before her head exploded with gruesome what-ifs and images of failed scenarios.

Her breathing quickened, and her fingers drummed faster and faster on her thighs. She needed to calm down. She needed something to take her mind off things.

Forcing her thoughts away from the spiraling worry, she began to recall her last few training sessions with Nathan. As per her request, they had been working on light forging. In Violet's unshakable opinion, that female Magneii's light-forging ability had been the key to kidnapping Solace. Violet could still feel the constricting grip of the whip that had stopped her from saving her baby.

Focus! She held up her hand, and the moon's dim light glinted off her fingertips. She couldn't see either Venus or Mars in the sky tonight, but closing her eyes, she was still able to tune in to what Nathan called "the melody."

Her breathing began to slow as she tapped into the energy emitting from both planets, narrowing her attention on the center of her cupped hand. Nathan's calm instructions echoed in her mind. The first step was to focus on the beam of light itself, then concentrate the light into a tangible mass.

A small glowing dot of marbled teal and magenta began to hover several inches above her palm. Violet's temples started to prickle with sweat as the tiny mass grew to the size of a pea, then a grape. A bead of moisture rolled down the side of her face just as it reached the size of an apple.

She released a slow breath and gently rolled her stiff shoulders. Gathering the first bit of tangible light was the hardest step. The next few phases of light forging came a little easier, especially since she'd been using every spare moment to practice. She had a jar full of light-forged pebbles and oblong shapes back home to prove it.

But the uber complex shapes of weapons, swords, knives, or whips still presented a challenge. Apparently, one could also forge the likes of a gun, but without gunpowder, such a thing would only be useful as a paperweight.

With all the extra training she'd been doing on her own, Violet could now make a twenty-sided polyhedron without too much thought. She'd essentially mastered the basics; the next step was to experiment.

An image formed in her mind, and the floating polyhedron of light began to elongate and flatten, its edges sharpening until the ethereal bundle resembled a throwing knife. Once her forging was complete, Violet studied her work, marveling at the marbled pattern of glowing teal and magenta along the blade.

Hmm . . . I wonder . . .

She focused again on a new image, and a second passed before the throwing knife began to split in two. Finally, she had a teal blade and a magenta blade rotating around each other above her palm.

"You're really good at that," said Thane.

Violet flinched and whipped her head toward his voice. In the same instant, the two blades hurtled in his direction. He managed to dodge just in time, and the knives embedded themselves in the half-open car door with a loud *thwunk*.

"What was that?" Sagan asked. Both he and Va'atuu turned around in their seats.

"Um . . ." began Violet.

Thane's face appeared in the doorway, his wide eyes darting between Violet and the knives in the door. After a moment, his expression turned apologetic. "Sorry, there's no room in the van. The other three Jiovis shifters took the spare seats in the back, but"—he looked again at the light-forged blades—"I can go see if someone wants to swap."

"Too late," said Sagan. "The van's already leaving."

He was right. As the van pulled past, Violet caught sight of Nathan in the driver's seat and Gus and Autumn in the two passenger seats.

Sagan started the car. "Get in, Thane."

Thane hesitated for half a second before sliding in next to Violet. As soon as he was inside, Sagan revved the Chevy's engine and raced after the van.

Violet kept her eyes glued to the back of Sagan's headrest, although she was highly aware of Thane in her periphery. Anxiety started to make her stomach churn.

A couple of metallic twangs from Thane's direction made her glance to the side. He'd removed the teal and magenta daggers from his door and was flipping them over in his hands, examining each of them.

"These are some decent blades. I meant it when I said you're good at this."

"Thanks." Violet started to turn toward the window, but then a hand appeared in front of her. Both the throwing knives rested in Thane's open palm.

"Keep them," she said with an indifferent wave. "I can always make more."

Thane hesitated for a few seconds before he withdrew his hand.

Violet's cheeks grew warm. *What is wrong with me? Why didn't I just take the knives? After all, I was the one who sent them flying at him in the first place!*

And now that she'd said he could keep them, what did he think that meant? Did he consider it a gift—a sign she was thawing toward him? Or did he think she was an arrogant light forger who could "always make more" whenever she felt like it?

She squeezed her eyes shut to stop her mind from over analyzing every detail of the last few minutes. The fact that Sagan and Va'atuu had probably been listening in as well made her stomach twist with embarrassment.

"So, you still have an affinity for daggers, huh?" Thane asked.

"Yeah, I suppose." Violet frowned. Affinity for daggers? What did he mean by that?

"Do you still have that star-blade?"

She turned to him. "Star-blade?"

"Yeah, the one you stabbed me with before . . ." Thane cleared his throat. "When you left my place that day."

A rush of emotions hurtled through Violet's insides along with the memories of "that day." The day she saw his scorpion neck tattoo he'd been hiding from her with concealer. The day all her memories from her kidnapping and Lyla's murder returned. The day she realized Thane was one of her kidnappers. She'd stabbed him with her switchblade, and his agonized roar had followed her as she ran out of his apartment building.

"Yeah, I still have it." Her switchblade suddenly felt heavy in her pocket.

"Can I see it?"

"Um . . . sure." She dug out the knife and handed it to him, although she wasn't sure how much he could see it in the darkness; as far as she knew, Veniri didn't have enhanced night vision.

A second later, she heard the subtle *shnik* of the blade being released.

"Wow, this is cool," said Thane.

"Why did you call it a star-blade?" Violet asked.

"Nathan didn't tell you when he gave it to you?"

"No."

"Oh, that's right. You didn't know anything about shifters at the time." He paused for a few seconds. "I'm not exactly sure why they're called star-blades, but I do know they all have two things in common."

"And what's that?"

"The first is this." He held up the switchblade. For a second, Violet wasn't sure what he was referring to in the darkness, but when he repositioned the dagger in his hand, Violet's eyes grew wide.

Along the handle of her switchblade were ten black gems, three of them now glowing. One was teal, one magenta, and the third was orange.

"A star-blade lets you know what kind of shifters are close by," Thane explained.

"Say what?" Violet exclaimed, but then a memory struck her. "Actually, come to think of it, I do remember a time at college when there was a teal light coming from it. The night Bessie died."

"Yeah, about that . . ." Thane's tone had taken on a cautious edge. "That might have been me."

"You?" Violet's jaw dropped. She'd been scared out of her mind when she realized someone had been following her back to her dorm.

"There was a strong scent of cinnamon in the air that night. You were up late, studying at the library, and, well . . . I wanted to make sure you were all right." Thane's words came out in a rush.

Violet blinked, taking a moment to allow his statement to sink in. "You knew Bessie was going to die that night?"

"No," Thane blurted. "Not at all. I thought you were the one in danger. And from what Autumn said, the killer was in fact after you. So I kept an eye on you, I followed you from the library back to your dorm—"

"Can I have it back?" Violet held out her hand.

"What?"

"I want my switchblade back."

"Oh." He passed it to her handle first.

Violet snatched it off him, then turned her body to face her window. It was too dark to see anything outside, but the glowing light of her switchblade cast her reflection against the glass, as well as illuminated Thane's forlorn posture behind her.

Violet couldn't deal with the information Thane had just dropped on her. Not now. Not on the brink of getting her daughter back. Why was it that every time one of her friends had been murdered, Thane was around?

The rest of the car trip passed in somber silence. When they finally came to the bridge that connected the city to Rivermyre, adrenaline began to surge through Violet's veins. She stared up at the looming ghost city in front of them, her fists clenching at her sides.

Sagan pulled up next to the van at the end of the bridge's exit ramp. Once everyone had exited the vehicles, Autumn handed each of them an earpiece.

"Can you hear me?" Autumn's voice buzzed in Violet's ear.

When everyone confirmed they could hear her loud and clear, Autumn took a deep breath. "Let's go get Solace."

22

CORPSE DIVING

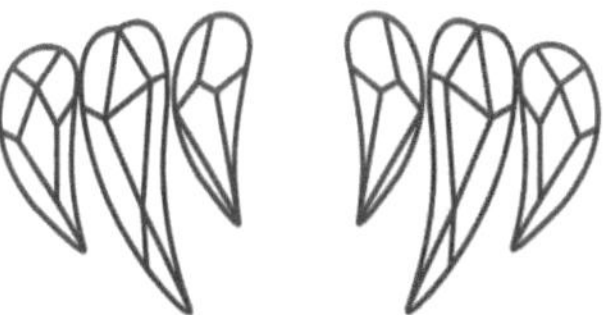

Nathan almost gagged. The vile stench was unlike anything he'd ever experienced.

"Oh, wow, it's still here" came Violet's muffled voice as the group approached the massive corpse in the middle of one of Rivermyre's abandoned streets.

Nathan had seen the footage of the man-turned-worm experiment, but the monster on Autumn's screen hadn't even come close to the reality. The actual thing was much more hideous and much, much bigger. Bile bit at the back of his tongue, closely followed by shame. This creature had once been a man. Nathan's detective instincts were fighting to take over. Whatever was going on in the facility beneath his feet, it was clear the experiments Xabat Biogenetics carried out were criminal, devoid of any moral compass. No wonder they were hiding under an abandoned city.

Sagan and Violet pointed out the remains of the leopard mutants that still littered the ground.

"They look a lot more mangled than when we were here last," said Sagan.

Upon closer inspection, the mutants had hunks of flesh

missing from their bodies. A few bones were exposed and looked as though they'd been gnawed on.

"You guys better keep your eyes open," Tio's voice crackled through the earpiece. Before the team entered Rivermyre, Tio had pinned a small camera on the front of all their shirts so he, Autumn, and Gus could have eyes on the group even from the safety of the van.

"I vote we get this over with quickly." Nathan slid his arms into the backpack Autumn had given him.

"Agreed," said Violet, putting on her own backpack.

The group skirted around the giant worm, then stopped at the edge of one of its tunnels—a giant hole in the road. The ominous void was surrounded by a mixture of dirt and rubble, but the rich earthy aroma did nothing to abate the stench of death. Thankfully, Autumn had acquired some disposable hazmat suits to protect Violet, Nathan, Thane, and En'gorr from whatever filth they might find in the tunnel's depths. Sagan and the other Jiovis warriors would remain on the surface to guard the entrance.

Violet peered down the hole. "I'm not sure I like this idea anymore."

"This is the best way in," said Autumn. "Unless you want to face off with the electric fences, razor wire, and armed security guards. Also, based on the facility's schematics, that worm thingy escaped from near the experimental labs, so one of its tunnels should lead you straight there."

"Just don't forget to turn on the ultrasonic seismic displacement sensor when you get in so we can map the tunnels and tell you which one to take," added Tio.

Sagan cracked several glow sticks, which all illuminated green, then threw the lot down the hole. They landed with a soft thud several feet down.

Thane gestured to Violet. "Ladies first."

Violet scowled. "Why? So you can just follow me again? How about you go first?"

Thane visibly bit back his response by sucking in a breath, then stepped to the edge of the hole and jumped in. Violet quickly followed.

Nathan turned to Sagan. "Do I want to know what that was about?"

Sagan shook his head.

"That's what I figured," said Nathan and leaped into the worm hole.

* * *

"Is everyone okay?" Nathan asked when all went quiet in his ear.

"Yeah," came Sagan's voice through the earpiece. "That was the last mutant. For now."

Nathan almost sighed with relief. Based on the raucous snarling, howls, and bellows that had streamed through his earpiece not long after he and the others dropped into the tunnels, he'd expected the worst. Over the commotion, Sagan had managed to yell that a pack of mutant animals had found them.

"What's the damage?" asked Gus.

"Minimal for us. Can't say the same for the mutants. Umbra showed up and helped us finish off the last few."

Nathan frowned. "Umbra?"

"Yeah, you remember that samurai chick I told you about?" cut in Tio's voice. "The one who killed the worm and saved all our asses last time?"

"Oh, right." Nathan turned to his immediate companions. "We better hustle. Who knows how many more mutants are up there." *Or down here.* But he thought it best not to verbalize that thought.

The four of them picked their speed up, following Autumn and Tio's directions through the grimy passageway. Every now and then, one of their flashlights would illuminate a rotting animal carcass or other putrid reminder of the creatures that resided in the tunnels.

"Hopefully, there's not another one of those Godzilla worms down here," said Violet.

As they rounded another corner, Nathan stopped short. The stench slammed into him first, then every cell in his body recoiled at the sight before him.

"What the . . ." breathed Thane.

"Ugh, I think I'm going to be sick." Violet leaned over and hugged her stomach at the same time Autumn's, Gus's, and Tio's cries of disgust erupted through the earpiece.

Nathan panned his flashlight beam over the hundreds of slime-covered animal carcasses piled almost as high as his waist. He glanced at his companions; their faces were either screwed up or covered with an arm in an attempt to block out the smell. For a second, no one moved.

"What is it?" Sagan asked. While Autumn, Tio, and Gus had access to the camera screens back in the van, Sagan and the other three Jiovis shifters were still blind to the tunnel group's progress.

"It looks like we've found the Godzilla worm's . . . garbage pile," said Nathan. "Autumn, I think you've given us a wrong turn."

"Bad news," Autumn answered. "I haven't. The most direct route to the lab is straight ahead."

"You've got to be kidding!" Violet's head whipped violently from side to side. "There has to be another way. There has to be!"

"Not that we can find" came Tio's voice through the earpiece. "Sorry, guys, it looks like you're going corpse diving."

Nathan's pulse quickened, and his eyes flew to Violet. Flashbacks to her panic attacks and PTSD episodes rained down on his consciousness as he watched her heave in one deep breath after another of the putrid tunnel air.

But she didn't freeze—didn't crumble.

During her high school years, working to move past her traumas had been an upward battle. In the last few weeks, Violet had been knocked down in more ways than one—cruelly, brutally—and yet she'd managed to find the courage to get back up and continue fighting her demons.

Nathan couldn't have been more proud of her.

"Ready?" said Thane. There was no impatience in his tone, no pressure to hurry up. If Violet wasn't ready, Thane would wait until she was—Nathan was sure of it. Despite the young Veniri's mistakes, he always looked out for Violet, no matter what.

A few moments passed before Violet raised her chin and rolled her shoulders back. Looking straight ahead at the pile of corpses, she gave one firm nod. "I'm ready."

En'gorr grunted and trudged to the front of the group to take the first few steps through the carnage.

Nathan swallowed the lump in his throat. "Let's just try not to think about it."

But not thinking about it was next to impossible. The path ahead was slick—Nathan didn't want to know with what. Almost every step squelched or popped as something gave out under his weight, driving him almost thigh deep. White bones gleamed in the light of his flashlight—leg bones, rib bones, skulls—far too many of them still covered with meat in varying stages of decay. Shredded fur, feathers, reptilian hide, and who knows what else hung from the corpses in clumps and scraps.

Is that a human hand? A shudder rolled down his spine. A

surprising amount of the carnage resembled human features. *Try not to think about it.*

He paused and glanced back. "How're you guys doing?"

Violet moaned through tight lips, her arms held out to the sides like a tightrope walker.

"I'll just be glad when this is over," came Thane's tense tone a few steps behind her.

"Mmm-hmm," agreed Violet. With her next step, she lost her footing and began to windmill.

Thane hustled up to her and wrapped an arm around her waist, bracing himself against the slimy wall. "I got ya." The two wobbled until Violet regained her balance.

"Ugh, that could've been much worse if—" Violet cut herself off with a blood-curdling scream. Eyes wide, she pointed at the carcasses near Nathan.

For a second, Nathan had no idea what had brought on her reaction—until something latched on to his leg.

Cold terror shivered down his spine.

He yanked his leg back, but the more he yanked, the more the creature who clung to him began to surface. Within seconds, a skeletal form had risen from the fetid mound up to its waist.

In a blur, Thane stumbled over to Nathan's side, and with their combined efforts, they finally managed to shake the creature off. Nathan couldn't believe the strength of something so emaciated. It was humanoid in appearance, but so much about it wasn't even remotely human. Its skin was a mismatched patchwork of either scars or animal hide. Chunks of hair—or was it fur?—were missing, leaving the majority of its skull bald. The disfigured lips resembled a beak, and both its arms were not only covered in grime but also speckled with needles that reminded Nathan of pin feathers on a baby bird.

What the hell is this?

"Help." It dragged the word out on a raspy wheeze. One spindly arm reached out to where Nathan and Thane sat in a paralyzed heap against the tunnel wall. The creature had its back to Violet, who was still a few feet away. Both her hands were clamped over her mouth, and the whites of her eyes shone under the collective beams of their flashlights.

The creature slumped forward, as if holding its body up was an excruciating effort. For several agonizing moments, the only movement was the creature's chest rising and falling with each wet breath. Then it reached out again. "Please . . ."

Something was clutched in the creature's scraggy fist. Slowly, the bony fingers uncurled until the item rested freely in its flat palm.

Driven either by blatant curiosity or by the desperate expression in the creature's eyes, Nathan took a step closer.

Thane clamped a hand on his shoulder. "Don't."

"It's okay," Nathan reassured him, then took another step. Despite his own warning, Thane kept close to his side.

An arm's length away, Nathan leaned down. The creature had slumped even farther against the mound of muck, its head resting on the shoulder of its outstretched arm.

Nathan shone the flashlight on the object in its hand. It was a photograph. A wedding photograph of a smiling bride and groom—the groom's eyes eerily similar to the creature's.

"Tell my wife I'm sorry." It—*he*—heaved a laborious breath. "I tried . . . to come home . . . Tell her . . . I'll always love her." He lifted his hand, offering the photo to Nathan.

After a slight hesitation, Nathan took it.

Fast as lightning, the deformed man latched on to Nathan's arm and yanked it down into his own wasted chest. It wasn't until the life in the man's eyes grew dim that Nathan realized his elbow blades were unsheathed.

"What just happened?" said Sagan's voice through the earpiece.

Nathan couldn't answer. Nobody answered. The shock that engulfed everyone devoured several long, stretching seconds.

The Xabat Biogenetics logo was visible on the ragged material hanging limply off the man's collapsed figure. Nathan looked down at the wedding photo again. This man was another of Xabat's abominable experiments. What had Xabat done to him?

"We must go." En'gorr's rich baritone rumbled toward them from a few feet away.

Nathan hung his head. As much as he hated leaving the man in the fetid carcass mound, they needed to focus on getting Solace out of this godforsaken laboratory.

Nathan and his three companions continued in silence. Tio kept giving them directions while Autumn did a search on the wedding photo. Apparently, the man had been having a rough time with their finances and applied to a too-good-to-be-true job advertisement, only to end up in a missing persons file.

After what seemed like an eternity, Nathan's flashlight illuminated a concrete wall. "I think we found the facility," he said into his mic.

"Awesome," Autumn's voice crackled in his ear. "Take a left. Then, as per the ultrasonic sensor, there should be some kind of opening through the concrete wall somewhere."

"I think we found it." Nathan swept his flashlight beam over a pile of rubble obstructing their path. "Judging by the damage, it looks like this is where the mutant worm broke out."

"Do you want us to go through the rubble?" Violet asked.

"Yes," said Tio.

Violet crossed her arms. "And how do you suggest we do that? It's not like we brought an excavator."

With a grunt, En'gorr pushed his way forward and got to

work. Within about a minute, he'd cleared away enough chunks of cement to create an opening wide enough to squeeze through.

"Oh." Violet's eyes bugged as En'gorr disappeared through the gap. "So, no need for an excavator when you have a Jiovis prince with you."

Nathan and Thane chuckled, and Tio's laughter joined them through the earpiece.

"The room on the other side doesn't seem to have any kind of security footage—at least, not any I can find," Autumn informed them. "I can only assume it's an abandoned section of the facility. But abandoned for what reason, I can't say. Be careful, guys."

23

CAN'T HIDE IT, FLAUNT IT

VIOLET'S BOOTS LANDED ON HARD TILE AFTER SHE FINALLY squeezed through the rubble. They'd emerged into what may have once been a staff bathroom, based on the broken sinks, smashed stalls, and shards of mirror scattered among the chunks of concrete littering the floor. The path of destruction led into the next room via a Godzilla-worm-sized hole in the wall. It looked as if this corner of the underground facility had been abandoned for several weeks, if not months. Perhaps the colossal damage caused by the worm's jailbreak had been beyond what the facility was willing to repair.

"We're in," said Nathan into his mic.

"Sweet. Now for the wardrobe change," said Autumn.

All four stripped off their disposable hazmat suits and dumped them into a pile. It wasn't part of the plan, but Violet went ahead and set the trashed suits on fire. In the blink of an eye, the crumpled clothing was reduced to ash, replacing the fetid tunnel odor with the far less unpleasant smell of smoke.

Once that was done, Violet pulled out a lab coat from her backpack, along with a fake ID tag Tio had made. She bundled her brown hair into a tight bun on top of her head, then put on a pair of royal-blue-framed glasses to complete the disguise. The other three donned makeshift security suits. Tio had managed to fabricate the Xabat logo and other embellishments based on the staff photos in the lab's database.

"Okay, now's the part where you guys need to be super careful," said Autumn. "The last thing we need is for one of you to get caught."

Following Autumn's directions, the four entered a hallway and swiftly made their way to the next junction.

"Wait," Autumn warned. "Some people have entered the corridor you were about to turn into."

Violet's pulse thudded in her ears as she waited with the others for Autumn's next instructions.

"Just wait a little longer . . . oh no. It looks like they're not turning off. They're headed straight for you."

Nathan hissed through his teeth.

"Can't hide it," Violet whispered, adrenaline buzzing from her chest to her fingertips. "Better flaunt it." Nathan shared a raised eyebrow with Thane as she added, "Follow my lead."

She raised her nose and brandished an ice-queen expression before sauntering into the corridor. The others hustled to catch up, falling into step on either side. About halfway down the hall in front of them, the group of Xabat employees was still headed their way.

"That's it," encouraged Tio, "just act like you belong there."

Violet desperately tried to control her trembling nerves. She needed to keep it together. Solace was relying on her. *I can do this. I can do this.*

She tried to imagine herself as the embodiment of confidence and intelligence—a woman on a scientific mission. A force to contend with. She may as well have been the CEO of Xabat herself.

After a few more steps, Violet began to believe her own facade.

When the group of Xabat staff came closer, she had to force herself not to ogle them; instead she simply tilted her chin up and set her sights on the direction she was heading. Keeping her expression nonchalant, she inclined her head to the group the moment they were about to pass by.

But when the man in the front caught her gaze, her heart nearly stopped.

She'd just locked eyes with none other than Renard Branstone himself.

"Guys! It's Renard," squeaked Tio.

A cold rush flooded Violet's veins, but she managed to tear her gaze away, keep moving, remain in character.

The next few seconds felt like an eternity. Violet waited and waited for someone to shout at them, raise an alarm, start shooting.

But . . . nothing.

She released a sigh of relief when they finally rounded the corner.

"You're clear," said Autumn on a sigh.

"That was way too intense," said Tio.

"Understatement," added Gus's voice.

The team resumed following Autumn's directions until she ordered a halt several junctions down. "There's a door around the next corner, and it's guarded by four guards."

Violet dared a peek and spied the four guards standing firm. Behind them was a pair of metal doors barricaded with a crossbar and secured with a handprint scanner and a keypad.

Damnit. They'd run out of luck. They couldn't just fake their way past these guys.

"What's the plan?" Nathan whispered into the mic.

Before anyone could answer, En'gorr stepped out into the hallway.

All four security guards' heads—and weapons—whipped toward the Jiovis prince. When En'gorr was about four feet away from them, they fired. A bolt of blue electricity shot out of each gun-like device. Luckily for En'gorr, being a Jiovis meant the four crackling beams of energy didn't affect him in the way the guards were likely expecting.

The guards all paused their streams of blue electricity and looked at one another uncertainly, which gave En'gorr enough time to blast two guards with his own burst of crackling orange lightning, throw a third into the concrete wall, and headbutt the fourth with a skull-breaking *crack*.

"Never mind," said Nathan when the fourth guard collapsed beside his unconscious buddies. "Uh, Autumn . . . ?"

"It's all good. En'gorr hasn't raised any alarms," said Autumn.

"Yet," added Tio.

"Based on the schematics, this is the door we want. I need one of you to get closer to the keypad with your cameras so I can get a better look at it."

Violet and the other three huddled around the mechanism.

"Hmm," Autumn buzzed in their ears after a few seconds.

"What's wrong?" Thane asked.

"This lock might take me a few minutes to crack."

"Can't you just work your magic like you did with the security cameras?" Violet asked.

"It's not that simple. Firstly, the security cameras are on a completely different network. Secondly, this door and its lock aren't even on the electrical schematics. I'm going to have to—"

Violet nearly screamed as a thunderclap of orange lightning struck the door only inches from her arm, leaving a black scorch mark fanned out over the metallic surface. The glass screen of the handprint scanner was shattered, and the keypad's lights had gone dead.

"Sheesh, En'gorr! A little warning next time," Tio rebuked. "You're lucky you short-circuited the backup alarm as well. Otherwise, you'd all be hightailing it out of there."

"Agreed." Nathan laid a hand on En'gorr's shoulder. "How about you keep the rest of us updated when you're about to do something that could get us all killed?"

En'gorr simply glared at him, then yanked the doors' metal bar out of its brackets and dropped it to the floor with a reverberating *clang*.

Violet whirled around, expecting more guards to close in on them, but no one appeared from around the corner. Maybe luck was still on their side.

Nathan pinched the bridge of his nose. "Tio, what's the chance you can speak some sense into your brother?"

Tio responded in Jiovis, but En'gorr's only reply was to shove the double doors wide open.

Violet's jaw almost hit the ground when she saw what was inside. Her heart felt as if it had stopped—as if it would never beat again. "Autumn, please tell me you don't think Solace is in here."

"I have a hunch that she is" came Autumn's solemn reply. "Schematically speaking, this is where Xabat keeps all their captives and their, um . . . live experiments."

The room beyond contained rows upon rows of cages, most of them occupied by a huge number of different animal species. Many looked deadly, including several marine animals in large water tanks along the length of one wall. Upon closer inspection, every caged creature was tagged or cuffed with the Xabat logo and a serial number.

"Whoa, that place has more animals than a rainforest," said Tio.

As the group of four moved deeper into the room, the types of captives became more unusual—or rather, more unnatural. The number of aberrations and cross-species features grew with every passing occupant, each one more gruesome than the last. At the far end of the room, the row of cages turned a corner, and a wave of nausea nearly made Violet retch.

This new row of cages contained humanoid creatures. Each wore a simple camo-green gown with a Xabat logo on the sleeve.

"Those gowns they're wearing—it's like what that man in the worm tunnel had on," Nathan pointed out.

Almost all of the humanoid captives were in varying stages of experimentation, much like their animal counterparts, but every one met Violet's stare with the same deadened expression. Their silence was even more eerie.

"Oh, wow," said Autumn. "I'm cross-referencing all of these inmates, and the ones whose human features are still recognizable are a match to a lot of missing persons files."

Violet felt as if she could hardly breathe. There was no way they could rescue all these people. They didn't have enough getaway vehicles, to begin with.

"Autumn, where in this damned hellhole would a baby be locked up?" Nathan asked.

"Try farther on. Based on the security camera footage, there seem to be a few specialized cells in the back corner."

Nathan led the way through the silent once-humans until they reached an alcove with about ten rooms. Each had three concrete walls, with the front face made entirely of glass. The immediate cells were empty, but a soft female voice drew the team deeper into the alcove. It was singing an uncanny song

—something about a boy making friends with his echo in a well.

"What's that?" Sagan demanded. "Who . . . is singing that song?"

"It's just one of the captives," said Thane.

Violet didn't catch Sagan's response. Her pulse was pounding in her ears, and her heart had leaped into her throat, cutting off her voice, her breath. "There!" she managed to choke out, pointing to the cells at the far end of the alcove. She hurtled forward, eyes stinging with tears, and flung herself against the glass.

On the other side was a baby cradle with the most beautiful sight Violet had seen in an eternity. *Solace!* Finally—*finally*—she'd found her daughter.

The delicate child was fast asleep, her tiny fingers curled over the top of her blanket. Her little chest rose and fell with each breath.

"Is that her?" Thane's low voice held a note of uncertainty. "Is that Solace?"

Violet nodded, an overwhelming mixture of joy, love, anxiety, and eagerness coursing through every nerve and making it impossible to think straight. Her hands were splayed over the glass, and she began to bounce on the balls of her feet in barely restrained hysteria. "Yes! That's her!"

Gus's whoop came through loud and clear, and Autumn began to coo over how much Solace had grown in the short time she'd been gone.

Violet pressed against the glass, half expecting it to swing open. When it held fast, she scanned up and around the edges. Her elation began to fade as she studied her daughter's prison more closely—there were three concrete walls, one glass wall, but no door. "Autumn, how do we get in?"

A heavy silence passed.

"Autumn, how do we get her out?" demanded Thane.

"Just give me a second," said Autumn.

With every passing moment, Violet began to give in to her rising panic. To come so far and not be able break Solace out of her cell . . . *No!* Violet couldn't, *wouldn't* let herself think about that.

Without warning, Thane began pounding Veniri-formed fists against the glass. Unable to resist, Violet followed suit. She pummeled the barrier as hard as she possibly could, her breath coming in sharp, shallow pants, misting up the glass in front of her face.

"Come on!" Thane barked, changing from punches to powerful kicks.

"Guys, stop!" Nathan called out.

"There's no point," said Tio. "You're never going to break it."

Suddenly, a section of one of the concrete walls broke away, revealing a hidden door.

Violet almost cried in relief. "Wow! I knew you could do it, Autumn!"

"Um . . . that wasn't me," Autumn said.

The world could have imploded beneath Violet's feet, but that wouldn't have been anywhere near as terrifying as Renard Branstone stepping triumphantly into Solace's cell.

"No!" screamed Violet. "No! No! *No!*" With each word, she bashed her fists against the glass. "Stay away from my baby!"

With a cruel grin, Renard reached into the crib, raised the sleeping Solace into his arms, and gently rocked her from side to side.

Violet's screams were unintelligible. Thane stood as still as a statue, staring dumbfounded at the man who held his daughter.

Flames and crystal shards erupted over Violet's entire body. Clouds of sparks exploded around her fists every time she beat them against the glass with all the force she could muster. But the pounding wasn't working. She needed to change tactics.

Allowing her shifter instinct to take over, she held her hands out in front of her, palms up. The melody of her Veniri and Magneii energy screamed through her veins, and within a heartbeat—the fastest she'd ever achieved—a light-forged two-handed mace appeared in her grip. The instant the weapon was complete, she hammered it against the glass again and again.

"GIVE! ME! MY! BABY!" Each word coincided with a reverberating *boom* as the glowing teal-and-magenta weapon collided with the barrier.

An almighty wail pierced Violet's eardrums, drowning out her own desperate cries. Someone must have set off the alarm. But her focus remained fixed on her child.

"We've got to go," Nathan yelled over the screeching siren. He shoved Thane out of the alcove, but Violet completely ignored his shouts. Her fiery form continued to thrash against the glass between her and Renard, whose intense, calculating eyes watched her with a cold kind of wonder.

"Come on!" roared Nathan.

"NO! I'm not leaving!" shrieked Violet. "My daughter is right there! I'm not leaving without her!"

Nathan bared his teeth. Braving her teal flames, he snatched her arm and dragged her away. Her wrathful screams rivaled the deafening sirens.

With Thane's help, Nathan hauled the kicking and screaming Violet back through the menagerie of animals and human experiments. The Xabat captives hollered, yelped, and squealed. Some hammered against the metal bars, while others huddled in a corner of their cage.

Violet didn't give any of them a second glance. She was fighting her own hysterics, as well as the strong hands gripping her arms. Angry tears flooded her eyes, but each one instantly sizzled away, evaporating in her teal flames.

The double doors to the captives' area came into view, and both Nathan and Thane picked up the pace, still dragging Violet between them.

"Violet, please. Stop."

At first she assumed Thane wanted her to stop struggling and run—run away from her daughter, escape without rescuing her. The request just made Violet want to rage harder. But then she realized her flames were burning both Thane and Nathan. Veniri hide was tough, but it didn't stop the sensation of pain—or the eventual wounds they'd receive if she didn't extinguish her Magneii fire soon.

Her hysteria died down just enough to withdraw her flames and her fury. She didn't want to hurt Nathan—or even Thane, for that matter.

But she really, really wanted to hurt Renard.

"Wait a second," said Nathan, "where's En'gorr?"

"Never mind him," said Autumn. "Keep running."

They'd almost reached the double doors when the view beyond forced them to slide to a halt.

About half a dozen security guards rounded the hallway corner. Ignoring the still unconscious guards, they set their sights on Violet, Nathan, and Thane and ran straight for them.

Nathan lunged, in full Veniri form. Thane followed close behind, only his elbow blades unsheathed. In a flurry of crystal shards, they hacked down the first two guards. Blood spattered across the nearest cages and pooled over the tile.

Violet froze. The sudden carnage was unlike anything she'd ever witnessed. All her training—the mental, physical, and shifter preparation—hadn't come close to preparing her for the real thing. Every trauma she'd experienced as a kid, being kidnapped, and even getting beaten up by Nika were nothing compared to what she was facing now: the need to physically fight for her life—to the death.

The fear was overpowering. Violet had spent her whole life running away from her fears, but she'd promised herself she wouldn't run anymore. In this moment, she couldn't.

For the first time in a long time, or perhaps the first time ever, she felt as if she was seeing things with perfect clarity. Not only was Solace relying on her, but all of her friends were as well.

Mere seconds had passed, yet to Violet, it was as if she'd entered a world of slow motion. Before Nathan and Thane's first two casualties even hit the floor in several gory pieces, Violet's flames ignited. All her fury and all her heartache poured into the teal fire flickering over her hands, and then she charged.

Of the remaining four guards, two aimed their electrical cannons at Nathan and Thane. Violet swiped her arm at the first one she reached, smacking her flaming hand against the barrel of the weapon. The blue electrical bolt meant for Thane was diverted to his companion, who jolted from the shock. As a result, the second blue bolt meant for Nathan ricocheted off the ceiling and into one of the massive water tanks.

A deluge of shattered glass, water, and who knew what kind of creatures rushed toward Violet and the others. The wave of knee-deep water knocked Violet's feet out from under her, and she bounced off the hard concrete, rolling two or three times across the floor. Gasping and spluttering, she stumbled back up, only to find herself face-to-face with one of the remaining guards.

With a furious scowl, the man aimed his cannon at her. A female guard still sprawled in the water screamed a warning at him, but it was too late. A flash of blue erupted in front of Violet, and a thundering crack of electricity blasted over the drenched guard with the cannon. Not even a split second later, Violet shrieked from the electrical shock that crackled through the now ankle-deep water and across every inch of her body.

After a few minutes—or was it seconds?—Thane was pulling Violet up. The aftereffects of the blue bolt were excruciating. Every muscle, every cell in her body roared with agony. Based on how both Thane and Nathan were stumbling and splashing in the water, they hadn't been immune to the shock either.

Only when the stench of burning flesh reached Violet did she realize how fortunate she was. Four charcoal-black guards and the fried bodies of the marine animals from the broken tank smoked and sizzled on the damp ground around her. If she were still human, she probably would have died instantly, just like the guards.

Shoving that horrific thought from her mind, Violet latched on to Thane's arm, and the three ran for the maze of corridors.

Nathan, still in full Veniri form, barked into his mic for directions as they hurtled through the hallway. They paused at an intersection to wait for a reply, but no one answered. Their communications with the others had been fried.

"Damn it!" bellowed Nathan, tearing out his earpiece and smashing it onto the ground. "We're flying blind."

"We've just got to try our best to backtrack," said Thane.

"Yeah, but who's going to warn us if there are guards ahead?"

"What choice do we have?" Thane rolled his shoulders back and led the way down the next hall.

With every step they took, Violet couldn't help thinking about how she was running farther and farther away from her daughter. She knew that without Autumn and Tio's guidance, there was no way of knowing which direction she needed to go to get back to Solace, but she still found herself trailing behind the others—as if the presence of her baby were physically pulling her back.

Up ahead, Thane and Nathan veered left and disappeared around the corner. Violet rounded the corner herself a few seconds later, then immediately skidded to a stop.

A solid netting had pinned both Thane and Nathan to the wall so tightly they could barely lift a finger. The net glistened a deep, familiar magenta.

"You!" Violet snarled.

Standing a few feet away from the trapped men was the blonde Magneii woman who'd fought Violet for her baby.

The woman's mouth curled into a malicious grin. "Looky what we have here." She raised an eyebrow and scanned Violet from head to toe. "You've come for round two, have you?"

Violet scowled.

The woman gave a condescending titter. "I'll make sure to finish you off this time."

Before Violet could react, a magenta whip appeared in the blonde's hand and a loud *crack* split the air, followed by a searing pain across Violet's cheek. She hissed at the sting, her hand flying to her face as she stumbled back.

Nathan and Thane shouted at Violet to run, to get out, as they struggled uselessly against their bonds. The woman simply cackled.

Violet checked her hand. No blood.

Only then did the woman's laughter stop. She stared at Violet's cheek, her brows furrowing, but the confusion on her face quickly vanished. "Oh yeah. I can't believe I forgot. *You're* a lucky one to survive a shifter bite." She tilted her head to the side, eyes glittering. "I've never turned a human before. It's almost heartbreaking to kill you."

The whip cracked again. This time, the tail swung around

Violet's neck, instantly cutting off her air supply. The woman yanked, and Violet crashed to the floor. The magenta cord tightened around her throat as Violet was dragged across the ground, clawing desperately at the binding.

Only when she came to a stop at the woman's feet did the whip slacken enough for Violet to rip it off. She dragged in deep gulps of air between coughs, still curled up on the ground.

A heavy boot collided with Violet's ribs. She howled in agony, but before she could try to push up onto her hands and knees and crawl away, another bone-cracking kick smashed into her torso.

Flashes of her previous brawl with the blonde Magneii flickered through her mind. The woman was just as strong and fast as she remembered, but this time, Violet knew what the Magneii was capable of—and this time, Violet was capable of so much more.

She caught Blondie's foot on the next incoming swing, then followed with a kick of her own, knocking Blondie's standing leg out from under her.

The Magneii crashed heavily to the tiles with an *ooph*. Before she had a chance to recover, Violet sprang onto the woman's chest and landed a punch to Blondie's jaw. The woman's head snapped to the side, but her countermoves were swift. In one bewildering instant, Violet was knocked back onto the floor, her chest pinned beneath Blondie's knee.

Violet's cry of pain came out on a wheeze as the woman's knee pressed into her sternum. Leaning in close, Blondie jabbed a finger against the bridge of Violet's nose. "All it takes is one good crack of the skull, right here, and it's bye-bye, little Magneii." A newly forged magenta hammer appeared in the woman's free hand, and she raised it high over her head, preparing to swing.

Violet rasped out three words.

The woman paused. "What did you say?"

"I said—" Violet coughed "—not a Magneii."

Flames erupted from Violet's eyes.

Blondie's jaw dropped. "Teal flames? But . . . that's impossible."

This time, it was Violet who donned a malicious grin. She threw her hands up and clamped them onto either side of Blondie's head, where they exploded into a ferocious blaze.

The Magneii shifter shrieked in agony, and the hammer fell to the ground as she writhed and yanked out of Violet's grasp. Her shrieks diminished into sobs of terror, and she staggered away, staring wide-eyed at Violet. "What are you?"

Violet pushed herself up from the ground. "Something you'll never find out."

With a flick of her wrist, a teal-and-magenta dagger hurtled through the air. The blade stabbed deep into Blondie's head, right between the eyes, destroying her Luxium with an audible *pop*.

ABSINTHE GREEN

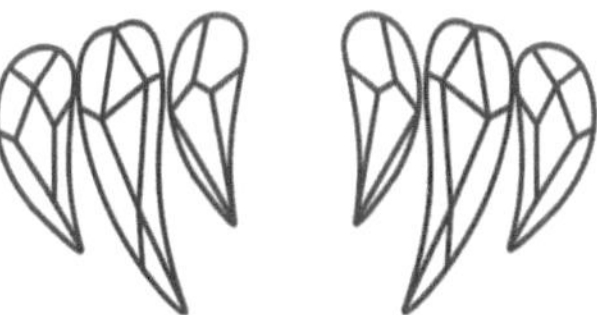

"YOU'VE BEEN PRACTICING YOUR LIGHT FORGING," WAS ALL Nathan managed to say after Violet broke him and Thane free from their magenta restraints.

The last few minutes had been hell. Watching, helpless, as Violet fought for her life was the worst kind of torment he could have ever imagined. If Violet had died in front of his eyes . . . he didn't know what he would have done.

He wanted to tell her how proud he was of her, how much she meant to him, how sorry he was for the pain he'd caused her, how devastated he would be if she got hurt. But he couldn't seem to find the words. He was about to reach out and pull her into a bear hug, but he remembered he was in Veniri form. The last thing he wanted to do was skewer her with the spikes on his torso. But when he tried to haze back, nothing happened . . . *Damn. Not again.*

"We should go," said Thane.

No sooner had he spoken than shouts and a stampede of boots echoed through the hallway. A group of security guards were dashing toward them from the other end of the corridor.

Thane grabbed hold of Violet's hand, and without another moment's hesitation, the three of them sprinted in the opposite direction and through the maze of hallways. With every anxious breath Nathan dragged into his lungs, the stomping of boots behind him drew closer and closer.

At the next turn, Nathan's heart skipped a beat. A metal gate at the end of the corridor was slowly descending. If he and the others didn't make it through before it shut, they would have to face at least four guards.

A blast of blue lightning shot past him and hit Thane square in the back. His friend bellowed in agony, convulsed, then collapsed to the ground. Luckily, Thane and Violet had released hands only seconds before, or she would be convulsing right along with him.

Violet tried to help the half-stunned Thane to his feet, but he was too heavy for her. Nathan's gaze flicked between her and Thane struggling on the ground, the almost half-closed gate, and the guards closing in on them.

Not all of them were getting out of this.

Nathan caught Thane's eye. It was clear from his expression he'd realized the same thing.

"Violet, run." Nathan pushed her toward the gate. "I'll help Thane. Run. We'll catch up."

Violet bit her lip, then nodded, but only after Nathan had slung Thane's arm around his shoulder did she actually sprint for the exit. Nathan followed as fast as he could while half carrying, half dragging Thane along with him.

"She's safe," Thane said in a low voice when Violet slid under the barrier. She was waiting for them on the other side, beckoning them to move faster, yelling at them to hurry.

Nathan glanced over his shoulder. The guards were almost on top of them.

"This is it," he warned Thane.

"I'm ready."

When Nathan turned back to Violet, it took him a split second to realize Sagan was running up behind her. The descending gate had just passed halfway down, and without even slowing, Sagan dropped to his knees and slid beneath it. Armed with a Diamantium blade in each hand, he tore past Nathan.

"Get them out of here!" the ex-hunter ordered, motioning toward the exit. Then he threw himself into the midst of the oncoming guards, allowing Nathan and Thane enough time to scramble through the rapidly narrowing gap beneath the security gate.

Once on the other side, Nathan shouted back to Sagan, "Come on!"

Sagan had made quick work of the four guards, but seven more had already rounded the corner.

"GO!" Sagan shouted. "Find En'gorr."

Nathan groaned. He'd almost forgotten about that metal idiot.

Thankfully, Thane was starting to get back some of his mobility. With both Violet and Nathan helping him along, they managed to navigate the remaining hallways at a decent pace. They'd almost made it back to the destroyed bathroom where they'd entered the facility when the unmistakable shouts and clashes of a melee echoed down the hallway.

"That must be En'gorr," said Nathan. "You two go on ahead. I'll find him."

He didn't wait for them to respond before turning around to follow the sounds of fighting. When he reached what appeared to be a lunchroom, he stopped short.

The scene before him was horrific. Torn and mangled bodies littered the floor and lay draped over broken furniture, every single one wearing a white lab coat with the Xabat Biogenetics logo on the breast pocket. Smears and splashes of crimson covered every surface, but what caught Nathan's attention even more was the other color of gore splattered among the red—absinthe green. Since when did Erathi and Sathoi shifters work together under the same roof?

The trail of bodies led Nathan into an adjoining hallway, where the clangor of a brawl only grew louder as he walked. He passed a room that looked like a surgical theater, the patient on the bed forgotten as the doctors and nurses lay on the ground in their own pools of red or absinthe-green blood.

Inside, he found En'gorr—fully shifted—surrounded by at least five security guards. Even more people in lab coats and several others in security uniforms lay motionless at the fighter's feet. With En'gorr's golden armor, his orange electricity, and the guards' blue electricity, the battle was an absolute chaos of bright light and flashing color. For several seconds, Nathan simply watched, dumbfounded. Had En'gorr done all of this carnage by himself?

Only when the final guard was struck down by a mighty clap of orange lightning did En'gorr notice Nathan's presence.

"What the hell are you doing!?" Nathan roared over the never-ending alarm.

Even behind the ferocious golden mask, En'gorr's scowl was evident. "You save baby. I kill Xabat."

Fury boiled in Nathan's veins at the stupidity of the kamikaze prince, but his rage fizzled out when En'gorr turned, clearly grief-stricken, to a huge pile of bodies in the corner. Every single corpse shone with a metallic hue, and the blood that dripped and pooled on the floor was bright orange. Only then did Nathan register that all the patients on the theater beds were splattered with orange blood. These must've been En'gorr's comrades, captured by Matthias Branstone.

En'gorr sank to one knee. "Too late. All dead."

With a heavy heart, Nathan counted at least fifteen Jiovis shifters, all cut up and discarded into a heap. In the end, the only response he could muster was "Come on, En'gorr. We've got to get out of here."

He took hold of En'gorr's arm and dragged him out of the room. The prince allowed himself to be pulled along, probably because there was no one left to kill.

But as soon as they stepped into the hallway, they were met by an army of guards sprinting directly toward them—only about a hundred feet away and rapidly closing.

"Come on!" Nathan bellowed.

But the prince stood still.

"There are too many of them!"

En'gorr ignored Nathan and pulled something out of his pocket. It wasn't until the prince flung the item into the air, straight into the oncoming army, that Nathan recognized it as a grenade. He shoved En'gorr into the hallway's intersection, and a half second later, an earth-shattering *boom* drowned out the alarm.

Where the hell had En'gorr got himself a grenade? Explosives weren't the Jiovis way of doing war.

Nathan continued to tug En'gorr all the way to the bathroom. Just as they scrambled into the tunnel, a clamoring echo behind them announced the guards' arrival.

En'gorr once again pulled out a grenade and tossed it behind him, out of the tunnel's entrance. Then he and Nathan hightailed it through the passage as fast as they could. The booming explosion that followed was a little too close for Nathan's comfort, but he and En'gorr didn't stop running until they reached the surface.

Back at the vehicles, Nathan's stomach tightened as he

scanned the faces of those who had made it out safely. All were accounted for.

Except Sagan.

He shot an alarmed glance at Autumn and Tio.

Autumn looked sick as she met his gaze. "Sagan was captured."

DON'T BE SO NAIVE

VIOLET STAGGERED OUT OF THE VAN WHEN THEY ARRIVED BACK at Maple Shire, then swayed and leaned back against the vehicle, unable to take another step. She'd replayed the mission over and over in her mind through the whole two-hour drive home—going over each step, looking at every angle, questioning every move.

How had it all gone so very, very wrong?

Overcome by another wave of grief, she slid to the ground, her whole body racked by sobs.

The others crowded around her uncertainly. Autumn crouched at her side while the guys stood in a huddle, each and every face drawn with sorrow.

"I'm sorry, guys," she choked out. "You came out tonight for me. For my baby. But after all our training and planning, Solace is still trapped. And now Sagan . . ."

Autumn pulled her into a tight hug. The others gave some words of comfort, trying to make her feel better and not blame herself. But the night's events were still too fresh, and she was still too raw. In the end, she excused herself and made to go to her room, refusing Thane's offer to walk her over. For now, she needed some space. Some time alone to mourn her lost daughter and her friend.

* * *

Violet collapsed to the ground by her bed and curled into a ball, her tears carving rivers down her cheeks.

Inches. She had been mere inches away from her daughter. Violet wanted to scream. She wanted to curse the ones to blame, but she didn't know where to start. With En'gorr, for setting off the alarm and alerting an army's worth of security when he went all Kill Bill on the Xabat staff? With Sagan, for being so stupid in sacrificing himself to ensure she and the others could escape, when they hadn't even accomplished what they'd come there to do? Or with herself, for her foolishness in thinking they had even a smidgen of hope to rescue Solace?

Violet didn't know how long she lay on the floor, crying her monsoon of misery. Her eyes were stinging; her throat was hoarse. Her hair and the carpet beneath the side of her face was damp.

With every ounce of her energy drained, she finally allowed sleep to claim her.

* * *

"Violet, wake up."

Violet groaned.

A hand gently shook her shoulder. "Violet, you need to wake up."

She slowly rubbed at her eyes and stretched her aching limbs. Her room was awash with the gray of predawn, and the twitter of early birdsong was already drifting through her open window. What was she doing on the floor?

"Are you awake?"

A shadowy form crouched beside her, and she startled, then hurried to sit up. Surely she must be still dreaming. "Sagan? Is that you?"

"Yeah," came his hushed answer.

Hesitantly, still unbelieving, she reached out to him. "Are you really here?"

He took her hand in both of his, and the unmistakably real warmth of his palms enclosed her cold fingers. "Yes, I'm here."

"But I don't understand. How did you escape?"

"I don't have time to explain it all." A heartbeat passed before he continued. "I've come to take you to Solace."

"What?" The remainder of Violet's grogginess dissipated instantly. "Are you serious?"

"Yes, but you need to come with me right now."

Not missing the urgency in his tone, she scrambled to her feet. Sagan latched on to her wrist and half dragged her outside.

Violet's adrenaline began to kick in as they weaved through the Maple Shire gardens. Sagan, half a step ahead, constantly swiveled his attention to the left and right, even glancing behind periodically.

"Is Solace here?"

"Shhh." Sagan raised a finger to his lips. "Keep it down."

Violet matched his volume. "How did you escape? Did you bring Solace with you?"

He halted at the edge of a grassy clearing and looked around before proceeding. "No. Solace isn't here. But she's safe, I promise."

Violet frowned. "Sagan, slow down. I don't understand. What's going on?"

"You need to trust me," he said over his shoulder. "We have to hurry." He yanked her around a garden bed and toward an unfamiliar vehicle parked at the edge of the forest. "Get in."

Violet yanked open the passenger door, but almost in the same instant, a nearby voice made her freeze.

"Violet, where are you going?"

She and Sagan both spun to find Thane standing a few feet away from the car. Even in the dim morning light, she could see his eyes widen when they landed on Sagan.

"You escaped? But . . . how?"

"I don't have time to explain," Sagan almost growled. "Violet, get in the car."

"Where are you guys going?" Thane asked again.

"Nowhere," said Sagan at the same time Violet said, "He's taking me to Solace."

Without another second's delay, Thane lurched forward. "I'm coming with you."

"No." Sagan shook his head. "We don't need you."

But Thane jumped into the back seat regardless.

"We don't have time for this. Get out of the car," Sagan demanded.

"Not without my daughter, hunter" came the reply.

Sagan groaned, then barked, "Violet, get in."

When all three were inside, Sagan took off, speeding through the forest, veering around each turn like a rally driver.

Violet clutched at the handle above her window. "Where are we going?"

"Not far," said Sagan.

"Care to tell us how you escaped?" Thane asked.

Sagan didn't answer. He whipped the car around another corner, and Violet was flung to the side. If she hadn't been holding on tight to the handle, she would have been thrown into Sagan's lap.

"Seriously, Sagan, I thought you said Solace was safe," said Violet.

"She is."

"How do you know for sure?"

"Because . . . I struck a deal with them."

"What kind of deal?" Thane asked.

Without responding, Sagan brought the car to a halt.

"Are we here?" Violet asked, peering out the passenger window. They were parked in a clearing a few feet from the edge of a cliff. Below was a glorious view of the valley, with Maple Shire somewhere in the distance. As the sun's first rays began to sneak past the horizon, the forest foliage was regaining its mixture of green hues.

Sagan turned the car off, plunging their world into silence.

"Where's Solace?" Thane's question held an edge of warning.

"Just wait." Sagan leaned against the steering wheel and focused on the landscape ahead.

Violet scanned the trees along with him. A second passed. And then another. She was about to press for answers when a pair of headlights pierced the silhouetted trees.

"Who is that?" Thane asked.

Violet leaned forward, squinting at the headlights. "Is Solace in there?"

The vehicle—a pickup truck—rolled in closer. Its massive bull bar ploughed through the shrubbery until it broke into the clearing, coming to a halt about thirty feet away.

Violet held up an arm to shield her eyes from the blinding headlights. Her pounding pulse quickened to a painful thrum as a man clad in typical all-black hunter attire stepped in front of the truck and blocked the beams. She drew in a sharp breath and began hurriedly removing her seatbelt when Sagan put a hand on her arm.

"Violet, wait."

"Are you kidding? That man has my baby." Before anyone could stop her, she leaped out of the car and ran toward her child.

"Violet, stop!" called a voice from behind her—either Sagan or Thane, she didn't care.

The cold morning air whipped through her hair, twigs crackled under her boots, and the rising sunlight glinted off her daughter's blonde curls. Before she'd even gone halfway to the hunter, Violet could make out a gentle cooing. Joy leaped in her chest. That was undeniably her daughter. She'd be able to pick out Solace's voice even in the middle of a rock concert. Her child was free, uncaged, and would soon be in her arms. Whatever deal Sagan had made, it was totally worth it.

Solace caught sight of her, smiled, and reached out a chubby hand. Her daughter was almost in reach.

And then Thane's roar sliced through Violet's eardrums.

"Look out!"

Several things happened at once. The face of the man holding Solace broke into a wicked grin, and four more people moved in on either side of him, each holding Diamantium weapons. Before Violet could react, something slammed into her, constraining her arms and legs. It wasn't until she plummeted to the ground that she registered the wire net wrapped around her entire body.

From somewhere out of view came Thane's raging shouts and the all-too-familiar sounds of a vicious brawl. Violet struggled against her bonds, but the more she moved, the tighter the net became. A pair of Diamantium-tipped boots moved into her field of vision, but the net had completely immobilized her, denying her the chance to look up and see who it was.

Just as panic began to set in, an agonizing wave of electricity crackled through the net and cut deep into her flesh.

Violet's shrill scream was deafening even to her own ears. When the current ended, it left her entire body numb and twitching. But even more distressing was Solace's harrowing cry ringing out over the melee. The sounds of the fight Violet assumed Thane and Sagan were in the middle of were beginning to slow down, but her daughter's screams were only increasing.

No, no, NO! This can't be happening. Every time she was given the chance to reunite with her daughter, the opportunity was snatched away.

Molten fury roiled in Violet's core—for all the endless worry, the sleepless nights, the failed missions. She couldn't take it anymore. Her body began to tremble as her inward turmoil overflowed through her extremities. In an instant, Violet's entire world turned an inflamed shade of teal. Every cell in her body vibrated. Every ounce of her torment fueled her flames.

She screamed until her throat became ragged. Then, suddenly, her body was no longer restrained. Her flames dissipated, and she scrambled to her feet. It took a couple seconds to comprehend that the black ash all over her clothes and covering the ground at her feet was all that was left of the wire net.

Other than Solace's cries, everything became quiet as all eyes turned to her, wide and disbelieving.

Harsh, angry breaths heaved in and out of Violet's lungs as she scanned her surroundings. Thane was pinned to the ground by three hunters while three more lay sprawled around him—two lying deathly still and the third writhing in agony. The blood in Violet's veins began to boil when she spotted the Xabat Biogenetics logo on their uniforms. These people had stolen her baby and caused her and her friends to run in defeat only hours ago. Her teal flames once again flared into existence, fanned to life by the all-consuming rage coursing through her chest.

A female hunter, the closest to Violet, shook off her stunned expression and charged.

Violet unleashed her full fury. She threw her arms forward, and the inferno over her body surged out like a flamethrower and roasted the hunter in an instant. The woman didn't even have a chance to scream before she collapsed in a charred heap.

The stench of burned flesh almost made Violet gag, but she pushed her disgust aside and set her sights on the men surrounding Thane. Throwing her arms out again, she released another maelstrom of teal that roasted two more men—just as Thane sliced up the third with his elbow blades. The hunters crumpled to the ground in a gory mess.

"Are you okay?" Thane asked.

Violet nodded, allowing her flames to diminish until only her eyes and hands were alight. "Are you?"

He nodded, then looked around. "Where's Sagan?"

Violet frowned but didn't dwell on the thought for long—the only thing she could concentrate on was Solace. She turned to the hunter who had her baby.

"Ouch!" Thane slapped at his arm and inspected his upper bicep.

Half a moment later, Violet shrieked as a sharp sting pierced the back of her shoulder. She reached around to feel the area, and her fingers caught hold of a small cylindrical object: a Diamantium-tipped tranquilizer dart.

"No," said Thane. "No. Not again."

The blood in Violet's veins turned to ice at the terror in his voice. She'd never seen Thane so afraid.

He collapsed to his knees, and Violet face-planted only a second later. With her mind swimming in a groggy haze, she found herself being heaved up from the ground and shoved into a crate, with Thane being thrown in right behind her.

"Where's my daughter?" Violet's words came out as a warble. She desperately fought against the impending paralysis, swiveling her head as best she could in search of Solace.

The door to the crate swung closed with a *clang*, and a face appeared on the other side.

"You!" Violet shrieked. "You . . . traitor!"

"Who, me?" Nika's head tipped back with a mocking laugh. "Oh, Violet. Don't be so naive. You're not the only one who's willing to make sacrifices for a loved one." Nika's evil grin stretched wide as she stepped to the side.

A few feet behind her, his shoulders hunched, was Sagan. Two hunters flanked him, guarding him closely with their Diamantium blades.

It was as if the world had fallen out from beneath Violet. *No. This isn't possible.*

Thane's enraged bellows were deafening. He roared at Sagan, battering himself against their metal prison. But his efforts quickly waned as the tranquilizer took over his body.

Tears filled Violet's eyes, stinging like acid within her still-raw tear ducts. With every ounce of willpower she could muster, she fought the paralysis swiftly claiming her body. "Sagan? Tell me it's not true."

He didn't meet her eyes.

"Believe it, Violet," said Nika. "Even your golden boy Sagan eventually saw reason." She thumped him in the chest. "I knew you wouldn't let us down. Grandpa is going to be so pleased you helped us snag him the hybrid."

"I don't care what he thinks," Sagan hissed through his teeth. "I didn't do this for him."

Nika rolled her eyes. "Yeah, whatever, Saggy-Aggy. You're a real hero."

He stepped up to Nika with a poisonous scowl, halting only an inch from her face. "Give me what's mine."

The two other hunters bristled at Sagan's hostile behavior. One kicked his legs out from under him, and the other angled his crystal blade down to Sagan's throat, but Nika gestured for them to back off.

Once Sagan was back on his feet, she shot him a glare of her own, then called out over her shoulder. Four hunters walked over with a second silver crate and placed it on the ground in front of Sagan. The venom in his demeanor vanished, to be replaced with . . . what? Violet had never seen that expression on Sagan's face before. Tenderness? Longing?

He slowly lowered himself to the ground and peered through the bars of the crate. There was a slight scuffling sound from inside.

"Don't be afraid," Sagan said quietly, fondly.

A soft female voice from within began to sing an odd little melody about a boy who made friends with his echo in a well.

Sagan gently laid a hand on the crate. "Mom, it's me."

PLIOKAI

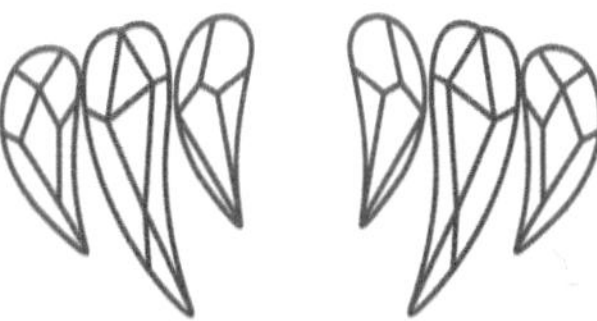

NATHAN RUBBED HIS EYES WITH THE HEELS OF HIS HANDS, THEN once again inspected himself in the mirror.

Nope, he wasn't seeing things.

A shiver of fear tingled down his spine, joining the onslaught of gut-wrenching remorse from the abysmal mission to Rivermyre. All that preparation, all that effort and sacrifice, for what? To have Sagan captured and Solace no closer to freedom than before? What had gone wrong?

Nathan scoffed. *Everything went wrong!*

They'd been outsmarted, outmanned, and outmaneuvered. Xabat Biogenetics was far more prepared and unassailable than he, or any of the others, had given them credit for. And based on the events of the previous few hours, Nathan and his companions couldn't afford to go up against Renard Branstone and his army of Xabat security again.

He'd spent most of the car ride home in Veniri form. It had taken him almost two hours to regain enough control over his body to haze back into his human form again.

Nathan's heart sank lower and lower the longer he looked

in the mirror. Would he even have the chance to face Renard and his minions again? Who knew how much time he had left?

The crystallized patch was no longer just a patch. It was an infestation of crystal flesh that now covered the side of his neck and throat, his jaw, and part of his face. The shoulder where it originally started was entirely encased, the crystallization continuing down the length of his arm almost to his wrist. It covered half his torso and nearly joined up to the section that had started on his calf, which had grown over his entire leg and foot.

The fractal surface twinkled under the bathroom lights. If the unknown prospects weren't so terrifying, he would have been mesmerized.

. . . consider putting your affairs in order.

Dawn's words held more weight than ever before, especially since he'd already decided he would do whatever it took to save Violet's baby, regardless of the consequences to himself.

Nathan hung his head. He hadn't been in the same vehicle as Violet on the way home from Rivermyre, but he could only imagine how painful that endless, somber ride must have been for her. When they'd arrived at Maple Shire, he hadn't been sure what to say or do to ease Violet's unbearable grief. There was nothing he could do.

. . . Or perhaps there was something he *alone* could do.

He rubbed at the smooth crystallized flesh as a plan started to form in his mind. If he was on the way out, he was going to make sure he left Solace in Violet's arms. The decision was made. He was going to—

An almighty *KA-BOOM* nearly ruptured his eardrums. He clapped his hands over his ears just as the ground shook him off his feet, throwing him face-first onto the ice-cold tiles. A split second later, an avalanche of splintered bathroom walls and ceiling pummeled his back. Nathan's tough Veniri hide was all that kept the shrapnel at bay, and his Diamantium skeleton ensured he wasn't crushed under the weight of the crumbled building. A human would never have survived.

The roar of the collapsing bathroom eventually died down to a pitter-patter of lighter debris. Soon, all that remained was the ringing in Nathan's ears. With each breath, he inhaled fine plasterboard dust and the overwhelming stench of something burning. There was a hiss of water gushing from broken pipes, and the spray of heavy droplets drenched every surface.

The ringing in his ears began to give way to the shrieking wails of the Maple Shire residents.

Nathan's adrenaline spiked a hundredfold. He needed to get out. He needed to find the others.

With an agonized grunt, he pushed up from the floor, heaving enough of the substantial burden off himself so he could dig free of the wreck.

An orange inferno lit up the night. Buildings were on fire or torn to shreds. People rushed from their houses wailing in hysteria. Some hustled to drag loved ones out from under piles of rubble. Mothers screamed for their children. Husbands yelled for their wives. Almost everyone was covered in dust, ash, or blood.

Nathan placed his hands on either side of his head, as if to prevent his mind from shattering along with the chaos. With as much speed as he could muster, he crawled over the wreckage, then ran through the gardens toward Gus's house. He heaved in lungful after lungful of air, breathing in the burning stench and ash as the heat of the fire washed over his bare skin.

The back door to Gus's house was still standing, but

beyond it, half the house was in shambles, and the other was covered with dust and debris. Nathan roared name after name. "Violet! Gus! Dawn! Lazareth! Autumn!" Anyone and everyone who came to mind.

"Help!" screamed a voice.

Nathan lunged toward it. Only when he began throwing beams and building chunks out of the way did he register he'd hazed into his Veniri form. His scaled hands heaved, hauled, and dug a path through what was once the hallway to the bedrooms.

"Help!" cried the voice again.

"I'm coming, Autumn!"

"Please hurry!" A hand flailed from under the wreckage.

"I'm here!" Nathan took hold of the hand. Seconds later, En'gorr appeared with his three comrades, all of them covered in ash and dust. With their help, Nathan dug out Autumn and then Gus, Dawn, and Lazareth, who were all unconscious.

"Where's Violet?" Nathan demanded.

Autumn didn't answer. She'd bundled herself up in a ball on the ground and was rocking back and forth, whimpering and crying a string of unintelligible mutterings.

Nathan knelt down and shook her shoulders. "Where's Violet? Was she with you when the explosion happened?"

Autumn looked up at him, her expression hollow. Tears had carved clean paths through the dust and ash on her cheeks. "Violet? I . . . don't know."

Fear unlike anything Nathan had ever experienced constricted his insides. He'd just turned and begun to sprint toward the rubble he guessed was once Violet's room when —*KA-BOOM!*

The second blast sent him flying backward, and his body slammed into something solid. The ringing in his ears was ruthless. When he opened his eyes, the world spun around him, bringing on a merciless wave of nausea.

Through the disorientation, a blurry face appeared in Nathan's vision—a familiar face with an unmistakable shark grin. Matthias Branstone said something Nathan's befuddled mind couldn't comprehend, then flipped a bright orange disc in the air and sauntered into the night.

The darkness swallowed the hunter's form just as Nathan plunged into the abyss of unconsciousness.

* * *

Hiccupping sobs from someone nearby dragged Nathan from his sleep. As his awareness grew, so did the sheer amount of agony in his entire body. He couldn't quite suppress a groan as he stretched his aching limbs and stiffly sat up. An instant headache throbbed through his skull, and he immediately collapsed back onto his bed to suppress a wave of nausea.

All the while, the sobbing never ceased. The stench of smoke, ash, and charred flesh laced every breath Nathan took.

He rolled his head to the side and cracked open an eyelid. The abundance of computer screens confirmed he was in Autumn's computer shack, except the desks and equipment had been shoved to one side to make way for a row of cots. Two of En'gorr's men each sat on a cot, and En'gorr himself was leaning against the wall by the doorway. All three pairs of sorrowful eyes were trained on something behind Nathan.

Hands on his still-aching head, Nathan sat up. He then registered he was still in Veniri form. How long had he been out?

Another hiccuping sob and a few sniffles stole his attention. He blinked several times to clear away the fog. Autumn,

Gus, and Lazareth were crowded around the cot beside him, and Tio sat on a desk a few feet away. All except Tio sported an array of bandages: Gus had one arm in a sling, Lazareth had an entire arm and his head bandaged, and Autumn's shoulder was marred by a nasty burn. Their expressions were riddled with grief, and all eyes glistened with tears.

"What's going on?" Nathan asked.

A hand appeared at Lazareth's hip and gently pushed him to the side.

Dawn lay in the cot, her face swollen almost beyond recognition until she smiled—a kind smile barely hovering above grief and torment. Each of her shallow breaths came with a raspy wheeze.

"Dawn?" Too many questions flooded Nathan's mind—they couldn't get past his dry lips. He jumped off his cot, the horrific memories of the Maple Shire explosions finally beginning to return to him.

Dawn's face screwed up in a wince as she pulled in a shallow breath.

"A huge beam landed on her, and it looks like it's caused a lot of damage to her internal organs." Gus gestured to their surroundings. "The infirmary was destroyed in one of the explosions. We no longer have the medical equipment or the know-how to help her. Some doctors from a few neighboring communities arrived about a half hour ago, but Mom refuses to be treated by them."

"It's all my fault." Autumn hung her head with a sob.

Dawn took hold of Autumn's hand and sucked in another short breath. "No."

"But if I hadn't been so stupid and stolen that spangle from En'gorr, none of this would have happened," said Autumn. "Matthias would never have come to Maple Shire looking for it, and you wouldn't . . ." Gus hugged Autumn as she sagged against him, her words lost under uncontrollable weeping.

"Don't you dare blame yourself for this." Lazareth shook a finger at her. There was a fierceness—a *fury* in his tone Nathan had never before seen in Lazareth's kind, understanding eyes. "That Matthias Branstone is going to pay for what he did. I swear I'm going to tear him limb from limb. When I'm done with him, he'll—"

"Peace, Laz," said Dawn's calming voice, and she enveloped his shaking hands in her own.

Lazareth's face twisted in profound misery. He jerkily nodded, then collapsed to his knees, burying his face in their entwined hands. "How am I going to go on without you?" came his muffled lament. "Please, please let me bring in a doctor."

"No." Dawn's reply was gentle but firm. She stroked her husband's hair as a single tear rolled down her cheek.

"Isn't there anything you can do?" Nathan asked Gus. "You've been Dawn's apprentice this whole time. Can't you fix her?"

Gus's shoulders hunched, and his face slackened with hopelessness. "No. Her condition is way beyond my capability."

Dawn wheezed in a garbled breath, then another. "Not . . . for long." She gave Gus a pointed look, then gently patted Lazareth's head. "I'm ready."

Lazareth wiped his eyes with his sleeves. "Dawn, you don't have to."

She touched his cheek and opened her mouth to say something, but a vicious cough stole her words.

"Mom, you should rest," said Gus.

She shook her head. "No. Much . . . to explain—" The violent cough returned with extra force, and she covered her mouth with a bandaged hand.

Nathan's sorrow grew with each of her rib-breaking

coughs. He looked around for something, *anything* that could help alleviate Dawn's discomfort. Why did he have to be so useless when it came to the medical side of things?

"Mom, are you okay? Do you need me to get you anything?" Gus asked.

Finally, the coughing subsided. Nathan's eyes grew wide at the blood that coated Dawn's mouth—the *gold* blood.

"Mom, what on earth?" Gus exclaimed.

"So much . . . to explain. No . . . time . . ." Dawn pointed to Gus and then to herself. "You are . . . I am . . . Pliokai."

Gus's brow crinkled. "I don't know what that is."

Dawn looked between Autumn and Lazareth. "Look after . . . my son."

With a heavy somberness, both nodded.

"Wait, what?" Gus gaped. "Mom, what's going on?"

Raising her hand to the side of her head, Dawn pressed her fingers against her temple. Her fingers began to glow a vibrant gold, sending a pulse of illumination under the surface of her skin that looked like the layout of an electrical circuit board.

"Mom!"

"Shh." Autumn laid a hand on Gus's shoulder. "It's okay. Aunt Dawn knows what she's doing."

After a few swivels of Dawn's fingers, a compartment in the side of her face spiraled open. She reached inside and pulled out a golden cylinder; the same illuminated circuit board pattern flickered and danced over its surface.

Nathan stared, his mouth hanging slightly open. He'd never known that the Pliokai, the Pluto shifters, could do that.

"Memories . . . everything . . ." wheezed Dawn, handing it to Autumn.

Gus began to warble out a bunch of confused questions, but Dawn cut him off by reaching for his hand. She smiled at her son and patted her chest with her free hand, then pointed to him. "So . . . proud . . ."

Nathan hung his head as Dawn closed her eyes and exhaled her final breath.

EPILOGUE

MATTHIAS CHANCED A FEW STEPS CLOSER TO THE EDGE OF THE cliff. The waves rolled and crashed below, their thunderous power rumbling through the earth beneath his feet. He was too high up for the spray to reach, but the air was thick with salt.

He checked his watch, then turned his attention to the sun setting over the watery horizon. Perfect. They'd managed to arrive a little early.

"Are we sure this is a good idea?" Axel scratched his shaggy gray beard.

"You let me worry about what is or isn't a good idea," replied Matthias.

A yelp came from a few feet behind him, followed by a thump against metal. Matthias turned to find one of his hunters banging on the Metallikite crate with his fist.

"Shut up!" demanded the hunter.

Matthias rolled his neck with a *crack-crack-crack*. The rabble he had to work with these days were becoming more impudent than the creatures he hunted and caged. But being surrounded by useless hunters was still preferable to being around his father. Renard Branstone was an incessant tyrant who had tormented Matthias for years over his fascination with the winged shifters and the possible truths behind their mythology. He'd been floored to discover Renard's dirty little secret of experimenting on humans. Who would have thought Renard was just as desperate to acquire shifter abilities as he was? But as far as Matthias was concerned, his father was going about it all wrong.

Matthias reached into his jacket pocket and pulled out his newly acquired treasure, flipping the orange spangle over and over in his hand. Even after obtaining five spangles, their beauty never ceased to amaze him.

Acquiring the opalescent pearl one had been almost disappointingly easy. As much as those peaceful Yranum shifters, affiliated with Uranus, had been a pain to track down, it had taken less effort than opening a bottle of whiskey to overpower them.

The silver spangle had been a bit of a challenge to start with, but once Matthias figured out which werewolf pack to target, his men had cleaned out and ransacked the ancient Lycan boss's den in a vicious battle worthy of a Quentin Tarantino movie.

As for the magenta spangle, hardly any bloodshed had been necessary—sadly. All Matthias had needed to do was take advantage of the Mars shifters' mercenary culture and negotiate the right deal.

The absinthe-green spangle had so far been the trickiest to procure. The Sathoi were a touchy bunch, with their creepy bulbous eyes, multiple spindly legs, and pincer mouths. It took only a wrong word or a misunderstood facial expression for one of them to attempt to trap him in their sticky webs or acidic goo. Most of his interactions with the Saturn-affiliated shifters had ended with Matthias needing a new suit and the Sathoi in pieces like a bug crushed underfoot. Then, inconveniently, Matthias would have to start all over again in setting up new contacts within the Sathoi realm. Thankfully, all his efforts had eventually paid off.

And finally, the Jiovis spangle had been a piece of cake to obtain once he tracked down the escaped Jupiter shifters to that little Erathi village. The explosions may have been a little over-the-top, but he'd wanted to make a point: those metal clangers couldn't escape from him and expect to find a safe hideout.

He could almost feel the orange spangle's power through his fingertips, even though in its current state, it was powerless.

Soon, very soon, he would have the purple spangle in his possession.

It had taken him months to even locate the Nephezai, then even longer to set up communications and build up enough trust with a Nephezai shifter to organize a meeting— a meeting with not just anyone but the Nephezai king. He'd only ever heard stories about the Nephezai king and his aquatic race. Well over a millennium ago, when the Neptune shifters were banished to the ocean by the world's Erathi leaders, the Nephezai became all but a myth, leaving behind only legendary stories of man-eating sirens and blood-lusting mermen.

Again, Axel began to shuffle his feet. The constant scuffle of gravel and dirt began to grate on Matthias's nerves.

"Please keep still," Matthias said through gritted teeth. "They'll be here soon."

"That's what I'm worried about," said Axel. "Even you have to admit we haven't had much experience with the Nephezai. You'd need to grow gills to become a worthy expert." He peered over the cliff's edge. "Why did they want us to meet them here? We're about fifty stories above the water. If they think I'm climbing down there, they're dreaming."

Another squeal, a bang, and a bellowing curse came from the group of hunters. Turning, Matthias shot a pointed look at his niece, Nika. Acknowledging his silent message, Nika punched the rowdy hunter in the arm and told him to stop provoking the animals. The hunter glared at her but backed off after a sidelong glance at Matthias.

"It's a mistake, her being here," said Axel in a low mumble.

Not bothering to reply, Matthias studied his niece for a second longer. He couldn't blame Axel and the other hunters for being skeptical of Nika. Even Matthias had been suspicious of her return. After many months of no contact, she'd appeared at the bunker sans a hunter's amulet and demanding another. Although she'd hedged around a lot of questions regarding why she left, why she returned, and what had happened to her amulet, she'd made up for it with some valuable information about the ragtag group who'd broken into his father's secret laboratory. When Matthias, Renard, Axel, and Nika reviewed the Xabat security footage, Nika had pointed out one of the intruders and claimed she was a hybrid shifter.

Matthias hadn't believed it at first, not until he himself gawped at the security footage of Violet Chambers—of all people—in all her shifter glory. Unbelievable. Never in his lifetime would he have imagined his late daughter's pathetic little friend from school would one day not only be a mother to a Veniri female but also develop dual shifter abilities.

Of course, the moment Renard heard about Violet and witnessed for himself what she was capable of, he'd demanded to get his filthy little hands on her to aid in his experiments. Perhaps she was the link in human evolution, he'd declared.

Not only had Nika been a key player in apprehending

Violet, but it had been her idea to persuade Sagan to make a trade and lure Violet into their snare.

At the thought of his son, an unwelcome churning developed in Matthias's gut. The more he dwelled on it, the more the churning grew into fury. After all he'd done for his son, after everything, Sagan had had the gall to choose his mother —that disgraceful woman—over him.

Matthias clenched his hands tighter around his precious spangle. He wasn't going to waste his time thinking about her, or about how his son had betrayed him. He would wash his hands of it all and focus on the future.

He panned his gaze over the sparkling sea, then paused and squinted his eyes, worried they might be playing tricks on him.

A shadow in the water a few hundred feet away was heading directly toward them at an alarming pace. Soon, more shadows appeared behind it. Then more and more. Matthias guessed twenty, then thirty, before he lost count. A nervous chatter began to ripple through the group of hunters.

Matthias placed the spangle back in his pocket and buttoned up his jacket.

The first shadow came to a stop about five yards away from the underwater reef lining the base of the cliff. Moments later, the other shadows halted behind their leader.

Matthias held his breath. For a few seconds, the newcomers remained still. Then the sea began to bubble and churn. The ferocious waters rolled, forming towers that gushed to the sky—up, up, up—until they were level with the clifftop, each one holding an individual figure. From this proximity, Matthias began to make out some of the silhouettes within the rippling water. Fins, tentacles, thorns, tails— the list was vast.

Matthias took an involuntary step back as the towers

began to bend toward him. Closer and closer. The rush of churning water became deafening, and ocean spray began to sprinkle over Matthias's face and suit. He allowed himself to draw in a lungful of briny air, but anticipation constricted his airways once more when the waters began to divide, revealing a deadly creature from the deep.

This would have to be none other than Qozzlotl Nagahld, the Nephezai king himself; the tangle of golden spikes on the creature's head resembled a crown. Matthias had half expected him to be carrying a trident, as was depicted in marine-related fairy tales, but instead, the Nephezai king held a weapon made of glowing neon-purple thorns.

Qozzlotl was humanoid from the waste up. His torso rippled with gills and decorative fins, and his flesh was similar to that of a shark or dolphin, mottled with grays, purples, deep indigo, and splashes of multicolored neon. A series of iridescent fins along his cheekbones and forearms matched the ones on his torso. But of all the magnificent features of the Nephezai, there were none more stunning than the numerous thorns that coated his shoulders and upper arms, most of them close to half a foot long. They glimmered with mother-of-pearl, and droplets of water sparkled at their lethal tips. Despite how ornamental the thorns appeared, Matthias knew of the Nephezai ability to shoot any one of them at will and inject their victim with a paralysis agent, similar to other venomous marine animals.

Water still engulfed the Nephezai king from the waist down, where, instead of legs, Matthias could make out the shape of a giant sea snake, or perhaps an eel with long fins that rippled down its sides.

Qozzlotl's shifted form had no need for any other adornment, yet he still wore an impressive assortment of gold, silver, and jewels. Matthias, however, only had eyes for the purple spangle that hung center-stage around the

Nephezai king's neck. He had yet to bring up the topic of spangles with Qozzlotl. Hopefully, as had been the case with most of the other shifter races, the lore of the spangles had also been watered down, so to speak, among the Nephezai.

The roaring water tower that held the king came to a standstill about a foot away from Matthias, while the rest of the towers remained over the ocean. About ten other shadows had revealed themselves behind the king—a guard.

Matthias had to crane his neck to look at the king's striking eyes, and he struggled to hold back a scowl. These creatures had been defeated and banished long ago by Matthias's kind; it should be *them* looking up at *him*.

The two Nephezai on either side of the king aimed their weapons at Matthias. "Bow, humans," one of them said. "You are in the presence of Qozzlotl Nagahld, king of the ocean."

Matthias hesitated. How he wanted to remind them who the superior ones were in this gathering! These creatures were in the presence of humans, of the Erathi, the race that currently dominated the earth and would one day surpass all the shifters and their so-called kings and queens.

But before he could open his mouth, he reminded himself why he had contacted the Nephezai in the first place. He had to keep his cool.

Gesturing to the men behind him, Matthias bowed, and the others followed suit. "Your Royal Highness, I am deeply humbled to be finally in your presence. It is such an honor." The words tasted like ash on his tongue.

The king inclined his head in reply. When he didn't make any further comment, Matthias began speaking again. "I don't want to waste any of your precious time. How about we get straight to business?"

Qozzlotl scoffed. "What is it with humans and their fascination with time and business?"

With an effort, Matthias donned a friendly smile. "So, the reason I called this meeting—"

"You called no such thing!" the king spat. "I do not answer to humans."

Matthias bit back the retort on the tip of his tongue. Was it worth reminding this so-called king it was humans who had banished his whole race to the deep depths of the ocean? "Of course, Your Highness. My apologies. But regarding the matter of—"

"I know what you want. I know what it is you truly desire."

Matthias couldn't help flicking his gaze to the purple spangle.

"Don't dare to think I am ignorant, human."

"Matthias."

The king's posture stiffened. His eyes burned with a spark of intensity.

"My name is Matthias, not human." There was only so much of this creature's pious attitude he was willing to put up with.

"I don't care. I am not here to learn names, human."

Matthias's jaw clenched so hard he risked cracking a tooth.

"I am here for, as you say, 'business,'" continued the king. "Now, show me."

Matthias frowned. After a heartbeat, he turned and snapped his fingers at his men, all the while dreaming of the day when the world would be rid of these detestable shifters. A group of hunters carried over four Metallikite crates and placed them on the ground between him and the king.

"For you, King Qozzlotl. I know how much you admire the rare and exotic land creatures. My men have scoured the globe to retrieve these very rare, almost extinct, specimens for you." He snapped his fingers again, and one of the hunters opened a crate. "This is a saola from the Annamese Mountains of Vietnam. Due to its parallel horns, it's also known as the Asian unicorn. My hunters were very lucky to come across this marvelous specimen. And this one over here is a Hispaniolan solenodon from—"

The king swiped an arm as if to shoo away a fly. "Enough. I have already stated my terms."

The back of Matthias's neck prickled with sweat, but the grin remained plastered to his face. "Of course, Your Majesty. But as I explained in my last correspondence, nullifying your banishment would take a lot of time and—"

"Time? Again with your time. We have been banished for three thousand years. Is that not long enough?!" The king's question ended on a thunderous roar. Water from the tower raged and splashed over Matthias, his men, and the caged animals, who erupted in hoots, chirps, and squeals.

Matthias wiped his face on his sleeve, allowing himself to gather words that wouldn't end in a massacre and the loss of everything he'd been working for. He set his sights on the purple spangle. "You are right to be frustrated, Your Highness, but you must understand that what you're requesting is a delicate matter. World leaders need to be approached, and there are a lot more of them now since the banishment of your ancestors. Who knows how many even know about shifters in general, let alone about you and your people? And even if they're no longer aware of your history, you can't just spew up out of the depths of the ocean and expect a warm welcome back on land. Peace treaties, alliances, border securities, all of these need to be taken into consideration before discussions to allow your return can begin."

Qozzlotl studied him with cool, calculating eyes, then burst into booming laughter. Matthias frowned and shared a glance with Axel, who shrugged.

"Forgive me, but I fail to see what's amusing." Matthias couldn't contain the derision in his tone.

When the king's laughter finally died down, he said, "Your fancy words are what amuses me. You speak of meetings and discussions, as if talking and talking and talking is what makes a great leader. No. A leader makes a decision"—he snapped his fingers—"and then it is done. It is that simple. It seems I have made the mistake of dealing with the wrong simple human. When I request a reversal of our banishment, you give me a pretty speech. And when I ask for the rarest land specimens to enhance my collection, you offer me what I already have. It is more in my interest to kill you, human, along with your men. But that is the same mistake my ancestors made long ago, so today, I will let you live. Next time, I will not be so lenient."

The king turned his back, and so did the other Nephezai.

"Wait, where are you going?" Matthias called after them.

Qozzlotl did not answer.

Matthias took a step forward. "You promised to make an exchange. I will not leave here empty-handed!"

Still, the king ignored him. His water tower withdrew to the edge of the cliff and began to make its descent

Matthias rushed to the edge so quickly he almost toppled into the water below. Without thinking, he called out, "Fine, you want a specimen you don't have. How about a hybrid shifter?"

Qozzlotl paused. The water around him rippled as he swiveled to face Matthias. "Impossible."

Matthias grinned. "I have it here with me now."

The king studied him, but Matthias recognized that glint of greed in his eye. "If this is a trick, human, I will go back on my promise not to kill you this day."

Matthias shook his head, unable to wipe the smug smirk

off his face. "On the lives of my wife and children, this is no trick, King Qozzlotl."

The king finally nodded. "Show me."

Matthias gestured for his hunters to return the animal crates to the back of the SUVs and bring out another. He whispered directions into Axel's ear, who nodded with a smirk of his own. Then, with arms spread wide like a circus showman, Matthias turned to the king. "Your Highness King Qozzlotl, may I present to you the hybrid shifter."

Axel unlocked the Metallikite crate. In a blur, two figures launched out and pounced on the closest hunters. It took a few seconds for Matthias to register that there was something familiar about the male captive.

He turned to Nika and said in a low voice, "Care to explain how one of my escaped gladiators wound up in the hybrid's crate?"

Nika shrugged. There was much more behind her innocent expression, but Matthias couldn't address that now.

Finally, after three of Matthias's men had been knocked out, Axel managed to restrain Thane on the ground with a Diamantium trident against his throat, and the struggling Violet was yanked before the king. She hissed and swore and almost broke away from the two men holding her until Nika went up and kicked her legs out from under her.

Qozzlotl looked her up and down, then with an unamused expression, he turned to Matthias. "I'm waiting."

Matthias leaned in close to Violet. "Be a lamb and shift for His Royal Highness."

"Don't do it, Violet!" yelled Thane. "Don't give them what they—*ooph*!" A fist slammed into his flesh, and he let out a low groan.

"Shift, Violet," demanded Matthias.

Violet's face screwed up into a snarl, and she spat into his face. "Bite me."

Matthias drew in a long breath before he wiped away the disgusting glob of saliva with his sleeve. Then he turned to Nika. She grinned in response, drew her arm back, and landed a power punch in Violet's face.

Violet shrieked. Once again, she tried to fight her way out of the hunters' grips, but they held tight.

"Shift," Matthias commanded again.

Nika landed another punch, but Violet took it, this time with barely a grunt.

"Shift, Violet dear, and this will all be over," said Matthias.

Thane's muffled voice began to yell again, but Violet only chuckled, the sound edged with a hint of hysteria. "You'll have to kill me first."

"With pleasure," Nika growled, then pummeled Violet with blow after blow. It wasn't until Violet began to bleed that Matthias realized Nika's glittering knuckles weren't a trick of the light.

Violet remained silent while Thane's roars reached a new level of rage.

Matthias caught Nika's wrist mid-punch and inspected the Diamantium knuckle-busters he himself had given her for Christmas many years ago. Nika's expression was wild, unapologetic. Yet Violet still hadn't shifted. Matthias gripped his niece's wrist tighter and was contemplating his next step when the Nephezai king drew closer to the almost unconscious Violet.

The aquatic shifter swiped a finger through the stream of blood oozing from Violet's lacerated cheek. "Fascinating . . ." After inspecting the viscous liquid, he turned his gaze on Matthias. "I will make a trade."

Matthias grinned. "Perfect," he said, eyeing the purple spangle.

"No." Qozzlotl covered the spangle. "This will remain with me. Only when you speak to your 'world leaders' and nullify the Nephezai's banishment will I hand it over to you."

Matthias's knuckles cracked from the pressure of his clenched hands.

"As previously discussed, these will be yours." Three of the king's subjects brought forth three tomes made of solid gold and gemstones. "But only in exchange for the Seh'vuthi pair." He gestured to both Violet and Thane.

Matthias hardly glanced at the tomes. He had acquired a fair number already since getting his first from the Veniri queen about a year ago. "Why do you want both of them? Isn't a hybrid shifter enough?"

Qozzlotl looked down at Matthias with an expression that dripped condescension. "I am a collector, and a collection holds more value when it is complete. Hybrid shifter or not, what is a single Seh'vuthi without their partner?"

Matthias frowned. That was the second time the Nephezai had used that *S* word. Perhaps it was some kind of Nephezai term Matthias hadn't come across yet. Tilting his head from side to side, he made a show of considering the terms. Renard was going to demand his pound of flesh if Matthias returned without Violet. Plus, if he didn't get what he really wanted, why should the sea king?

He'd already opened his mouth to voice his decision when Nika leaned in to whisper in his ear. His eyes grew wide at his niece's simple solution. He patted her on the shoulder and nodded once, and she turned and headed toward one of the SUVs.

"If a complete set is what you require, Your Majesty, then there is one piece missing." Matthias grinned when the Nephezai's eyes twinkled with greed. No more than half a minute later, Nika returned, and Matthias gestured to the bundle in her hands. "Here is the hybrid shifter's child."

The words had barely left his mouth before both Thane

and Violet began to beg and plead for the baby in Nika's arms. When it became clear neither would pipe down anytime soon, Matthias rolled his eyes and signaled to the men who still restrained Violet. They released her, and she sprinted to Nika and snatched the child, then collapsed in a pathetic display of crying and fussing.

"I approve of this exchange," said Qozzlotl.

"Wonderful." A pair of Nephezai guards moved in to apprehend Thane, but before anyone came near Violet, Matthias whispered gently in her ear, "Don't celebrate yet." Ignoring her venomous glare, he pointed to her child. "See this collar around your baby's neck? It contains an explosive."

Violet's eyes grew wide, and her face lost all its color. Perfect. He had her in the palm of his hand.

"Do you see that purple disc around the sea king's neck?"

She glanced to Qozzlotl and nodded.

"Obtain that disc from the king, find a way to the surface of the sea, and press this button on your child's collar. It will send out a GPS signal, and we will come and collect the disc from you. Once I have that disc in my hand, the collar will be removed, and your baby will live to see her next birthday. The countdown on the explosive is set for three weeks from today at midnight."

Before she could say anything in return, Violet, her baby, and Thane were swept away by the Nephezai guards. Qozzlotl inclined his head toward Matthias, then he and the rest of the aquatic shifters returned to the ocean and disappeared beneath the cerulean, churning waves.

ACKNOWLEDGMENTS

Wowzers! What a mission!

It's been less than a year since I published my first book, and here I am, now finished with my second. I feel like I've learned so much since Shards of Venus, and yet I have so much more to learn in this world of being an author.

Again, I owe a phenomenal thank you to my Lord and Saviour, Jesus Christ. Without His amazing sacrifice, I would have ended it all long ago. I give all credit to You, my Father in Heaven and the Holy Spirit for my life and all that is good in it. I have no doubts You've given me these stories, and it became much more apparent with this second book how much more I've relied on You to inspire me and given me the words to write. I never would have been able to finish this without You. Thank You!

To Kevin, my wonderful husband, again your support and encouragement has been stellar! And again, a massive thanks for your feedback and involvement in this journey so far. Words cannot express how grateful I am, nor how much I love you. Thanks for calling this emotional wreck your wife! xxx

Annabelle, you are such a delight and you bring me so much joy. You are so creative and imaginative, I'm always eager to see what you create next. Is it too much for me to hope that we will be writing stories together one day? I love you so much!

A big thank you Janeen Donovan, my Mum. Your support in more than just emotional and financial, has been truly grateful. It's an honour to be your daughter. Thank you for raising me, for being there whenever I need, for feeding my Enid Blyton addiction and for introducing me to authors such as Frank E. Peretti, C.S. Lewis, and J.R.R. Tolkien. I think I can safely blame you for sparking my wild imagination, haha!

A big thank you to the rest of my family! Oh, Wow! I'm so blessed to be a part of such a wonderful clan. The Hams, Donovans, Colemans, Evans', Drapers, McCuddens, Eveans', Youngs, and all the extended family. Thank you so much for your support in buying my first book and being my behind the scenes cheerleaders.

To my Alphas, the super talented Writer's Unite Group; Carleton Chinner, Julie Dickson, Tim Edwards, Suzie Eisfelder, Tarryn Mallick, and Katarina Smythe (a.k.a. Kaydence Snow). You guys are AWESOME! I'm so glad I found you guys and eventually plucked up the courage to share my budding little story. Thanks for all the feedback, the support, the great laughs and the motivation to keep writing. Gosh, I cringe to think how many tears and whinging you had to put up with from me during the writing of this book. But, you guys have been such a solid and steady support in helping me to whip my work into shape, and find the courage to "suck it up" and move on with the next step. You're all such an inspiration and I'm so excited to see what the future brings for your own amazing writing.

Treece and Dan Stubbs and your adorable little Iggy. You guys are such a blessing! Thanks for being amazing in hearing all my crazy world-building ideas, for being avid beta readers, and for being available to help me brainstorm and fix several of my plot holes. You guys rock!

To my Hervey Bay bible study group and to the St George Sisterhood, thank you for remembering my writing journey in your prayers. Whether I'm facing the successes and the struggles, your prayers and spiritual support has been priceless. Thank you so much!

A big shout out to all my beta readers who volunteered their precious time to read through my manuscript and to provide me with honest feedback. You all kept me on my toes and picked up several inconsistencies compared with the first book. Taking on a beta reader role is an epic job and I'm truly grateful. Thanks Heaps!

And to my editor, Kirstin Andrews, what words can I possibly use to describe how grateful I am for your hard work in polishing Flames of Mars? Getting this manuscript done was a messy and mammoth task this time around. But you helped me to see it through to the end. I know I mentioned it to you before, but I feel so "uplifted" when I go through your edits. I can clearly see how you've helped to improve my work. Thank you so much for all the work you put into editing my story. It's been such an honour to have you as my editor. Please don't ever leave me!!

For the amazing cover, thanks so much to the amazing team at Deranged Doctor Design. I was mesmerised by the cover you made for the Shards of Venus book, and just when I thought you would have a hard time topping it, you totally outdid yourselves with this Flames of Mars cover! Thank you so much for your fantastic work in bringing my world visually to life. Wow! I can't stop looking at it.

A huge thanks to AViVA for taking a chance on little ol' me and allowing me to use your "Blame it on the Kids" song for my book trailer. I'm stoked I've discovered your music and I'm so excited to for your SELF/LESS book!!

I hope I haven't forgotten anyone. If I have, I'm so sorry! xoxo

ABOUT THE AUTHOR

Tjalara Draper began her writing career at the start of 2016 when the stories in her crazy imagination kept growing. After a short online course in Creative Writing, she was thoroughly convinced she needed to pursue her all-time dream of becoming an author.

She's wife to an amazing man who is currently training to become a doctor, and mother to a spitfire of a daughter, who becomes more creative and outgoing with each day that goes by.

When Tjalara isn't writing her next book or tackling laundry monsters and wrestling dishwashing shenanigans, she's bound to be somewhere flying on wishing chairs, swimming with the mermaids, marking her skin with shadow hunter runes, raising dragons, or being a poison taster for the commander.

GET IN TOUCH:
Website: www.tjalaradraper.com
Facebook: Tjalara Draper Author
Facebook Group: Tjalara Draper's Reader Lounge
Instagram: @tjalaradraper_author
Amazon: Tjalara Draper Author Page